T0284285

LUNAR COURT

AILEEN ERIN

INK MONSTER
LOS ANGELES, CA

INK MONSTER

First Published by Ink Monster, LLC in 2019
Ink Monster, LLC
4470 W Sunset Blvd
Suite 145
Los Angeles, CA 90027
www.inkmonster.net

ISBN 9781943858392

Copyright © 2019 by Ink Monster LLC
All rights reserved. This book or any portion thereof
may not be reproduced or used in any manner whatsoever
without the express written permission of the publisher
except for the use of brief quotations in a book review.

Cover by Ana Cruz Arts

For my Facebook Ink Monster Superfans group.

Y'all are the bee's knees. Just FYI. ;)

A drop of sweat trickled down my face, carving a path through the sand stuck to my cheek. No matter where I looked, I saw mirages of lakes and seas and oceans. But there wasn't any water and I was so damned thirsty. If I ever found my way out of here, I'd spend forever washing the sand out of every crevice of my body. After I murdered Eli.

An answering growl rose up inside of me. My wolf and I were in agreement for once, but there was nothing I could do about Eli's stupid games. Right now, I had bigger problems, like hunger and dehydration. I bit off one of the buttons on my shirt to suck on. It helped stimulate saliva, but that wasn't going to be enough. Not long-term. I needed water. I needed it now. And more than that, I needed to go home.

I started down a dune, keeping my eye on the next one. The first hour here I'd been in awe. I'd never been anywhere like this, and the heat had been a shock coming from the Texas winter. I'd pulled off my hoodie and tied the sleeves around my forehead to keep my eyes clear and my head covered. But then the heat had risen, and the exhaustion of climbing up the dunes, gaining an inch for every three steps, had stolen the last of my patience. I wanted the fuck out of here.

"Damn it, Eli. What the hell am I doing here?" I blew out a harsh breath. I didn't know who I was more pissed off at—Eli for dropping me in the middle of the desert or myself for being stupid enough to willingly go with him. If there was one thing I knew now, it was to not trust the archon.

More than an angel, Eli had the power and ability to do whatever he wanted. His only quest was to keep the world going. To keep the balance between good and evil. And he had free rein to do that however he saw fit. Over the last week, that meant helping me and my friends. Today, who knew what side Eli was on?

I didn't think he wanted me to die, but I wasn't certain that he really cared either.

Christ. Why did I agree to come with him? Nothing good came from a desperate move. But I had been stupidly desperate for an escape.

The last few months had been utter chaos. I'd fought caves full of vampires, slayed a horde of demons spilling out of a portal from hell, and sealed off the mortal realm from Satan's second-in-command with my friends. In the process, I'd bound myself to twelve other supernaturals—some I didn't even know —and I wasn't sure what that meant.

I should've stayed at St. Ailbe's to find out, but Cosette had been there, sitting next to me, so freaking tempting. The high from the magic we'd used the night before made me jittery. I could feel my wolf making a demand to grab her—to hold her and fix what was between us—to make her mine—and I...I couldn't let myself do that.

Wanting what I couldn't have was nothing new for me—I'd had long, hard years of that growing up—but wanting Cosette as anything more than a friend? That was a whole other level of torture. There was no way I could be with a fey from the Lunar Court, especially not a princess. The fey in her court controlled the moon, and I was a werewolf, tied to the moon. I'd be a slave, unable to even know if the things I did and felt and thought were my own. But I still couldn't stop myself from wanting her, even if having her was suicide.

But then—as I was about to start saying the words that would tie us together—Eli had popped in out of nowhere. He offered me a distraction, and it felt like an answered prayer, or fate, or maybe just an easy out. One I probably didn't deserve. But I'd jumped at the chance before I could think about it. Before I could claim Cosette in front of all our friends. Before I could destroy both of us in one dumbass move.

Damn it. "What the hell am I doing here?" I screamed up at the sky again. I wasn't sure where Eli had gone, but I was sure he was laughing at me. "Get back here, you asshole!"

I sat in the sand, unable to keep going without some explanation and a gallon or two of water. "You wanted help, so here I am. But I'm not playing your game."

The desert was definitely not my thing. I liked cold. I liked the woods and the hill country around St. Ailbe's. I liked green, and life seeping from the ground under my feet. All I could smell here was sand and heat and my own sweat. Everything in this desert was dead, and if I didn't get somewhere soon, it wouldn't be long before I would be dead, too.

Eli appeared in front of me, wearing his usual faded jeans and white shirt, looking perfectly refreshed. His long blond hair was tied back. When standing, I was easily a few inches taller than him and more muscular, but looks often lied in the supernatural world. Subtle clues were the only way to guess at someone's power. His ponytail was perfectly still as the wind moved around him, keeping the sand away from his face.

I clenched my jaw, and the fine grit in my teeth crunched. A subtle but effective reminder of who was more powerful.

The girls seemed to think Eli was handsome, but all I saw when I looked at him was a whole bunch of danger I didn't need.

"You smell," Eli said.

"Walking through the desert all day will do that." I used part of my shirt to wipe the gritty, sand-soaked sweat from my face as I stood.

With a snap of his fingers, a water bottle appeared in Eli's hands, and he tossed it to me. I wanted to bash in his face with it—but water, perfectly ice-cold water. I drank it down in three gulps.

"You could say thank you."

Eli's reprimand felt like sandpaper against sunburned skin. It was enough to have my wolf howling for me to rip the archon's face off, but then I'd go back to being stuck in the Sahara with no water, no food, and no way home.

I crumbled the bottle and tossed it to the sand. "Another one." And I wasn't saying please.

He rolled his eyes and snapped his fingers again. The bottle popped and expanded as it rose from the sand then filled with water and flew toward me.

"Nice trick." I caught the bottle before it could smack into my chest. I drank it down and tapped the side of the bottle for Eli to refill it.

"You're immortal. Dehydration wouldn't kill you." But he snapped his fingers anyway.

Once the bottle was full, I carefully set the bottle in the sand and then yanked the hoodie from my head. The archon was full of shit. "I can die from all sorts of things. Including dehydration." I grabbed the bottle and dumped it over myself, cooling my body instantly. The water dripping down my skin felt like heaven.

"Nah. You'd be painfully uncomfortable and might go a little crazy, but you'd survive. You weren't easy to kill before, and now that's even harder. Thanks to me." He pointed at himself like I should be thanking him, but I wasn't going to thank him. He could read my mind, so he should stop expecting it.

Using his magic to power our spell last night was probably one of the stupider things my friends and I had done. We'd opened ourselves to all kinds of shenanigans, courtesy of Eli, and I wasn't sure I'd live to see this through.

The empty water bottle crumpled in my hands and I threw it down along with my hoodie.

5

Eli gave me the same look my father had given me so many times. One that said I was pathetic and worthless.

"You're being dramatic. That's the look on my face. Not the pathetic and worthless crap."

I didn't like that he could read my mind.

"But I can. So, get over it. A day in the desert is nothing more than a little discomfort."

I could take discomfort, but only when it had a purpose. "You bamfed me here and then left. I'm trying to be cool, but if you don't tell me what's going on, we're going to have a problem."

"A problem?"

He was baiting me. I knew it and wasn't about to give him the satisfaction, but my wolf had always been a dangerous hothead. "No." I was telling him as much as I was telling my wolf. "You're more powerful than me. Starting a fight with you would end painfully—possibly deadly—for me." I broke eye contact to give my wolf a second to believe what I'd said. "You needed my help, so I'm here. But I'm done with your bullshit. I want food and a bed, and as far as I can see, I'm not anywhere closer to that than I was hours ago. There's literally *nothing* here. So why am I?"

"Well, at least you're not stupid."

"Not stupid? That's a real compliment coming from you." My voice turned gruff and thick, the effects of my old injury were worse when my wolf was close to the surface.

"Don't worry so much. You'll get food soon and your wolf will stay as hampered as ever under your tight rein, lest you show any hint of being alpha. And since you've been so *outwardly* patient—"

I growled. The guy could read my mind, and I knew it. That didn't mean I was going to like it or get used to it. And he sure as shit didn't have to bring it up when he—

"Calm down. I'm happy to report that you are nearly to the Court of Gales."

His words were a million tiny daggers, stabbing fear through my soul and twisting as I realized how completely screwed I was. He'd said Court of Gales like it was a good thing, but I knew that if I continued east, the only thing I'd find was my own death.

The fey hated me and my friends. For a very solid reason. We were caught on video and it went viral. We'd been fighting a demon. Some of us shifted. Cosette pulled a flaming sword out of nowhere. And in one three-minute clip, the existence of the supernatural world was outed to humans.

Except the fey didn't want to be outed, so they retreated to their underhills—the magical realm where their courts resided— and closed themselves off to the mortal world. From what Cosette said, they were more than a little pissed off about the whole thing. And they blamed us.

Court of Gales? Eli was an asshole and he was going to get me killed. I opened my mouth to tell him to take me back to Texas, but he spoke first.

"Do you or do you not want to save Cosette's life?"

I inhaled. The sand felt like embers in my lungs, but I barely felt it. All I could think was that Cosette was in danger, and I had to get to her. But I was in the Sahara, thousands of miles away.

The shift started deep in my soul. Fur rippled along my skin as I battled for control. The human side of me wanted to ask Eli questions, but the wolf didn't give a shit. He wanted to fight and he was more than happy to have a go with Eli.

Pain drove me to the ground and it felt like every muscle in my body was ripping and tearing and reforming into its new shape. The wolf was clawing its way free, driven by his need to find her—to get to her—to be with her no matter the cost, no matter how impossible it was—and it hit me in that moment as I screamed in pain what an idiot I was.

Only one thing could make my wolf this powerful. And with that realization, I was able to take control again. My body slid back to its fully human state, and I lay flat on the ground, trying to catch my breath.

"You done?" Eli sounded bored, but he could be bored. I was in the middle of a fucking revelation.

I'd thought I could get over Cosette with a little distance, a little distraction, but nothing was going to change what I felt for her. It was way too late for that.

Cosette was my mate. My *mate*.

The bond between us was tiny and weak and unacknowledged, but I could feel it now. So fragile. So, so faint. I hadn't noticed it, but my wolf knew. He fucking *knew*. That's why he was going to claim her this morning.

Shit. I slammed my fist into the sand next to me, sending the grains flying through the air. I needed to track her down, and that meant going back to where I'd seen her last. I stood from where I'd fallen, sand raining down from my clothes. "Take me back to campus *now*."

"I will if that's what you want, but she's not there. She left as soon as you did."

I willed myself to hold on to my shit while I figured out what the hell Eli was saying. "She's not there?"

"No."

"Then take me to wherever she is."

"No. She's at the Lunar Court. There's no way I'm taking you there."

Fur rippled along my skin as I closed the distance between us, ready to tear his throat out if he didn't tell me what I needed to hear. "Is she okay?"

"So dramatic."

I growled and he rolled his eyes, effectively taunting my wolf even more.

"She's alive, for now. But she won't be for long if you don't keep heading east."

I paced away from him for a few steps so that I could think. I knew she didn't like being at court, but she never told me why. It never occurred to me that it was dangerous. Her mother is the *queen* and she had Van and a ton of other guards to protect her. She should've been fine. Something had to have gone wrong.

"Something *has* gone wrong." Eli was reading my mind again, but this time I didn't care. I wanted the answer. "The Lunar Court is destabilizing, and there's been a hefty reward for Cosette's head. One that's too tempting for them to ignore."

Motherfucker. "Then you should've grabbed Tessa or Dastien or someone *Alpha*." I hated that I had to say it, but it was the truth. Even if it burned in my gut hotter than the fires of Hell. I was alpha—little a. *Little* power. "I won't survive there. I'll be a slave. Worse than a slave. I'd be no help to her and she can't—"

"Not if you go to the Court of Gales *first* and gain more power. Or—more accurately—alter your tie to the moon."

Everything stopped—the wind, the heat, the feeling of exhaustion that had been beating through every muscle in my body —and all I could hear were his words echoing in my mind.

Someone in the Court of Gales could change my lunar tie?

This was huge. Mind-blowing. Seemingly impossible.

But if it were true, then Eli wasn't just going to help me save Cosette's life. He was offering me a chance to have a future with my mate. I would be able to survive in the Lunar Court without fear of being controlled.

No. There had to be a catch. Power always came with a cost, and that level of magic—untying my werewolf from its link to the moon? That was a sell-your-soul kind of bargain.

"If it gives you a shot at being with Cosette, what price wouldn't you pay?"

My annoyance at Eli and his shitty, patronizing tone hit me first, but was quickly obliterated by complete and all-consuming fear. Fear that made my vision speckle and gray and narrow until my knees grew weak, and I knew if I didn't get air into my lungs soon, I wasn't going to stay upright for much longer. But I couldn't. I couldn't breathe. I couldn't think. I couldn't fucking believe I was considering entering the Court of Gales alone.

But that's exactly what I was going to do. I would give up everything I was for her, and that scared the shit out of me.

Eli was right. Even if I was tricked into exchanging my soul for the releasing of my lunar tie, it would be worth it. If Cosette was in trouble, then there wasn't a price I wouldn't pay. "How much farther?"

Eli disappeared before answering, and I was alone again in the sweltering desert.

I reached down for my hoodie and saw a full bottle of ice-cold water next to it. And a note.

So you don't get too uncomfortable while getting everything you've ever wanted.

I crumpled the note and threw it on the ground. "You could've left food, too."

I waited for a second to see if something would appear, but nothing did. So, I tied the hoodie around my head, grabbed the bottle, and headed east again. I felt better than I did, and now, I had a purpose. That made all the difference.

I was going to beg, borrow, or steal enough power to save Cosette, even if I had to paint the floor in blood.

CHAPTER TWO

COSETTE

I STRAIGHTENED my back as I approached my mother's golden throne. Even seated, she was elevated above everyone else. The focal point of the room. And not just because of the moonlit glow of her skin or her elegant white suit and golden heels. No, it was the power she commanded that kept everyone's eyes on her. Always. She was the Queen of the Lunar Court, the most powerful fey court, for a reason.

My mother's advisors and the court's first circle stood around the stage. I hated them all. So did she. But they'd been playing the fey's deadly power game of who could kill me since I was twelve and I couldn't show weakness now, even when I wanted to fall to my knees and beg my mother for help. And yet, what I was going to say would equate to the same thing in their minds. But I couldn't let that stop me.

Van, my head guard, brushed a hand across my back. It was something that no one would notice, but it was a cue we used. I turned back to him. He tilted his head down, just a little bit. It was his tread-lightly-Cosette look. And I knew it—damn him, I was planning on being careful with my words—but I was also desperate.

I closed my eyes for a brief second, just long enough to settle my nerves, and then stepped through the ring of advisors to stand directly in front of my mother. All of their chattering stopped at once.

"What is it that you need, Cosette?" My mother's voice echoed through the enormous room. She didn't need to speak so loudly. The thousand-chandeliered room behind me was completely empty, but magic and power were my mother's game. And with that one question, she'd thrown so much magic into the room that my mouth went dry, my heart sped, and I considered if Van wasn't right after all. Maybe this was a bad idea.

Too late now. "I've come to ask a favor."

One of my mother's advisors beside me scoffed, and I could almost feel the disgust and pity filling the throne room with every breath. Their looks held a tinge of green-eyed bitterness.

"Another favor? Do you think that's wise?" The way she drew out her words slowly made it perfectly clear what answer she wanted, but she was going to be disappointed.

"Maybe not wise, but necessary." I didn't want to do this—not with an audience—but I didn't have a choice. Chris was missing. "I need your help."

"Again?" There was an edge to the look that she gave me. The way she tilted her chin ever so slightly told me that she was already annoyed with me.

I swallowed, bracing for her reaction to my next statement. My palms were sweating and I itched to wipe them, but didn't dare show my nerves in front of this group. "I need to speak to my father, and I need you to help me reach him."

There were gasps in the room, but I kept my eyes on my

mother. No one ever spoke of my father, and I'd obeyed that request. Until now.

"You will not want to pay the price I'd ask for such a thing."

My mother's eyes were cold, but I didn't dare let myself shiver. "We would bargain, as is our custom, but it's been weeks —*weeks*—since Eli took Christopher, and I can't find anyone who has seen or heard anything about where they are. He isn't in Texas. He isn't with any coven—and I've contacted *all* of them. He isn't at any of the courts. I haven't checked Heaven or Hell yet, but they're next on my list." The room grew brighter with my mother's anger, and I felt her power press against me, urging me to stay silent. But that wasn't happening. Not until I'd gotten what I'd needed. "My father can check both Heaven and Hell for me, but I've no way to reach him. I need use of your mirror to—"

"You dare still speak of him?" My mother's anger made the walls pulse with moonlight.

Everyone in the room took a knee, except for me.

It took everything in me not to back down. She was my queen, my ruler, my mother, and she was pushing more magic at me than I'd ever felt before. I fought it, and I managed to step closer.

This wasn't going well, as expected, and I needed to change the venue. That would give her enough time to calm down a bit, give her the freedom to say yes, and give me the ability to bargain properly. "I request a council in private."

"Cosette. You—"

"Your office," I said the word sharply, making it sound like a demand.

My mother stood from her throne—slowly, like a viper about to attack—and I knew that Van was right. I was on dangerous ground. If I couldn't get her to understand why I was asking this, my queen would never forgive me. Because from the way she held herself—coldness in her gaze—the power filling my head, it was my queen, not my mother, that stepped down the three steps from her throne, coming for me.

"Please, *Mother*. I need your help." I used "mother" because it would remind everyone in this room—including her—that I was the queen's daughter.

I was taking risks, ones I couldn't afford. I knew it, but I didn't care. I'd already cashed in more favors than I wanted in order to find out anything about where Chris was right now. I would've given up if I'd heard one whisper that he was unharmed, but I hadn't. Just silence.

"All right, Cosette. If you've a private matter, as your mother, I will give you council."

I let out a long slow breath. "I won't take much of your time."

I followed her to the hidden door behind her throne. Van started forward, but I shook my head. I didn't want him around for this. He was my personal guard, but he didn't need to hear me beg.

The walls of my mother's office brightened as we stepped inside. Gold and white marble filled the room. We walked across a rich deep blue carpet, flecked with gold and silver—like the early night sky—covering the floor. An ornate gold-framed mirror hung behind her desk—one she took calls on, for those who knew how to reach it and dared to try. A sitting area was off to one side, with a large black velvet couch. It was piled with pillows in rich purples, teals, and magentas. A galaxy of pillows fit for the queen of a celestial court.

My mother strode to her desk, leaned back against it, and waited for me to talk.

"Are we truly unheard?"

My mother gave me a soft smile, as if proud of me even

though I ceased being a child long ago. She lifted her hand in the air. "Ears may not hear. Eyes may not see." The magic took root and she tilted her head. "Satisfied?"

"I've never asked you to reach my father before, and trust me—I'm not taking this request lightly. But I must talk to him, and you have to help me get—"

"I don't have to do any such thing." The soft smile disappeared along with any sign of approval. She straightened from the desk, and there was anger on her face like I hadn't seen since she first saw the video that destroyed our whole way of life.

I usually would've backed down—I didn't like to piss off my mother—but not today. "It's been weeks and—"

"Do you trust Eli?"

"I did once, before he'd left me—*alone*—in the Court of Gales, surrounded by enemies, badly injured, bleeding, barely hanging on with no way to get home. But I think it's safe to say that no, I don't trust him. Not anymore. Do you blame me?"

My mother's anger cracked a little, and she gave me a sly grin. "Eli's not *all* bad, and—"

"He has his own view of the world and we're all expendable to him." I crossed my arms, daring my mother to say otherwise.

"Now that's not fair." She went back to leaning against the desk. The soft smile was back and I relaxed just a little bit. I was winning her back, one piece at a time.

"Eli favors you because of your father. I don't think he'd call you expendable at all."

I wasn't sure that was true, but I'd give her the benefit of the doubt. "Maybe so, but Christopher?"

My mother's nod had a finality that terrified me. "Expendable."

"You agree with me, but won't help? Christopher matters to *me*. He's my *friend*."

"That feels perilously close to a lie. Don't test me, daughter.

Telling a lie is treason. It's the only law that keeps our court from being a total political cesspool, and the law would lose its meaning if I didn't universally enforce it." Her voice grew colder with every word. "Don't force my hand on something so trivial, Cosette."

I'd seen her kill before, but executing me would break something in her. And a broken queen was dangerous. But at least I wouldn't be alive to watch the burning and blood and death that she would wreak on the court after her heart blackened.

"No. I won't lie to you. Not ever." So, I didn't dare say anything about my feelings for Chris. "I've done everything you required for nearly two *centuries*. I have been and will continue to be your spy. I will go wherever you send me. I know the last few months have not gone according to plan, but—"

My mother straightened again and I knew I was losing her. "According to plan?" Her tone was a sharp, honed tool. One she used to get her way. "Try again, daughter of mine." There was no humor left in her, and I knew I had to tread lightly.

"Fine." I clenched my fists. Mother was in a *mood* today. "They've been a disaster for the fey, but I'm not alone in the blame." I couldn't be held solely responsible for everything. She knew that.

"No one is saying that you are." Her softer tone allowed me to take a breath, but then she stepped toward me. "However, the situation has changed. I know you've made this new pact with the other supernaturals, and I'll allow you out as you are needed for that and that alone, but not for *this*. Not for some werewolf. You need to start acting the part while you're here. No more blowing off suitors. No more dodging dinners. You show up and you play the part or you will *die*."

I met her gaze. "And which part am I supposed to play now?"

"Stop that disrespectful tone before you truly anger me."

I bowed my head. It was the only apology she'd get from me right now. She'd kept me safe and alive and protected my whole life. It hadn't come without a cost for either of us, but I needed help and she was refusing me.

"You were my spy, and you've done a fine job of it. Now, that job has passed. Your brother will pick it up well enough."

That was a truly terrible idea. "Him? He can't even think one step ahead, and you think he can do three or four? You want to talk about perilously close to a lie?"

"Right." My mother laughed softly, and her look grew soft. The queen became my mother with one laugh. For a second, she was the woman I loved, not feared. "Well, he'll either make it or he'll die."

That was a truth. A brutally harsh truth.

Humans liked to talk about survival of the fittest. The fey lived survival of the fittest.

The assassins started coming after me on my twelfth birthday and my mother did nothing. If she had, I would've seemed weak and the attempts would've doubled. Instead, I was given guards—Van and a few others. It was up to me to keep up my fighting skills and maintain my relationship with my guards so that they couldn't be bought. It was up to me to prove that I was worthy of keeping my own life. That was the fey way.

For a time, the assassination attempts were terrifying, but they made me stronger. They became my normal.

Eventually, I got tired of fighting for my right to live. I got sloppy, and I nearly died. And so my mother sent me away.

I was her spy. After a good long while, I found a home in the Denver coven. I'd liked my life there.

But then I'd been sent to Texas. And damn it all. I loved it there. Even through the blood and demons and danger, I'd found friends. I'd found *Chris*.

That day we went to wipe the minds of the police officers...

He saw through me somehow. He saw *me*. The me that only my mother and Van got to see.

Nothing was the same after that night. For a lot of reasons.

Where are you, Chris? If only you'd answer my messages...

"Cosette?"

I blinked once. Twice. Bringing myself back to the moment. "I've asked everyone and no one has seen Christopher. I need my father to check where no one else can. I'm begging. *Begging*. If—"

"Don't lower yourself to beg."

She got quiet for too long. I knew better than to speak when she was quiet like that, so I waited for her to speak again.

"And don't you dare lower yourself to make bargains. You are more than fey. You're a princess. You *will* act as such. If you keep after this young werewolf, one of two things will happen. One, he would have to come to court. You know that he cannot survive in our world."

She was crushing me, and I struggled to keep my face calm. To keep my eyes from welling. To keep my heart from shattering with the weight of her words. "No. He can't survive it." It was why we'd never become anything more than friends. Nothing more than a hug. No kiss. Nothing that could feed my poor, starving heart.

"Two, he refuses to come to court, and the assassins would find him and kill him."

She was silent, waiting for me to say something, but there wasn't anything for me to say. Nothing for me to feel but the crushing knowledge that I would ruin the one person I longed to save.

"Either way, your *friend* is dead."

She put her hands in her pockets. I wondered if it was to keep from reaching out to me. But it didn't matter. No comfort would help me. Not from this.

18

"What good does it do to keep reminding my council about the werewolf? To keep beating it into their heads you're *weak*?"

I stayed quiet. We both knew the answer. It was dangerous to say his name ever again.

"Why do you keep *harping* on going after him?"

"Because—" My voice quivered, my heart raced, and I felt like the world might end if I answered her honestly. But I had no choice. I had to confess the truth to her, even if it broke something inside of me.

I looked at her then, so that she would know the brutal, honest truth, and maybe—*maybe*—that would convince her to help me. It was my last desperate act to save him. "Because I love Christopher."

My mother winced. "Oh, Cosette."

I hadn't said it aloud before. Not ever. And if I didn't see him again, it would be my greatest regret.

He knew how I felt. Even if I never said the words. I tried to tell myself that he knew, but it wasn't the same as actually saying the words to him. I was fey. Words were everything to us. And I'd kept them from him.

The pity and disgust that filled my mother's face was almost enough for me to choke on. She took one single step toward me and I braced for her words.

"Oh, Cosette. A *weak* werewolf of all things." Her pitying tone was like little knives slicing my back.

I wanted to shout at her, but she wasn't wrong. He was a weak werewolf, and maybe he wasn't even *my* weak werewolf. But he was more than that, too. "He sees me and I don't have to be anything else in front of him. I don't have to pretend or worry that he might one day stab me in the back. I don't have to be afraid of who I am or what I say or how I feel when he's with me. I can just be me, and I am enough for him. Just me. Just *me*."

Suddenly, she was holding me against her, and for a moment, it felt right.

"I understand the attraction." She spoke softly. "I had my own werewolf, but these things never work out. Not with one of them in *our* court. Not with someone like you, who can influence without meaning to."

"I know." I hated it, but I knew. Truly I did. But if I could just get my heart to go along with that...

She ran her fingers through my curls, giving me as much comfort as she could. "Donovan was *strong*, and it still couldn't last."

I knew that, too. Donovan was the strongest, and if he couldn't keep up with our court when he dated my mother, then no werewolf alive had business trying.

She pulled away from me, but kept a grip on my shoulders, and stared me in the eyes. "I need you to hear me on this. The attempts on your life are about to get a whole lot worse."

I stepped back from her, breaking her hold on me. "Let them try. I'm far from the child I was." And if they were going to keep the one thing from me that I wanted, then I had a lot of anger that needed releasing. I'd be happy to focus my wrath on them.

She nodded slowly, as if willing me to be rational on this. "Yes, but you've been gone from court for years now."

"And I've maintained my abilities. I'm faster, stronger, and my magic isn't a small thing anymore. It's grown over the years." I had a little gift of foresight. Not as much or as visual as Tessa, but it was enough to give me an edge. That, with the extra speed and strength and my father's arsenal of enchanted weapons meant I was tough to beat.

"True. True." She gave me a small shrug. "But you'll get tired eventually. Sending you away won't work again. I'm sure you gained even more power from this spell you've done, and your enemies want to harvest it."

There had been a magical high for a few days, but it had faded. I wasn't sure what that meant. "If I have gained anything, I'm as of yet unaware."

"Hmm." She was quiet for a moment, and I wasn't sure she believed me. I wasn't sure I believed me either. That kind of magic always came with power. And a cost.

"Even so, it's time for you to accept your place at court and solidify your power base so that the madness ends once and for all."

No. Accepting my place here wasn't something I ever wanted. Having to fight for my right to breathe every day was exhausting. I could do it in small doses, but permanently? Not a chance in hell.

"Look at it this way..." Her grin was back, but I wasn't sure I was going to agree with whatever she said next. "It's not as if you have to worry about ruling this bunch."

I snorted in surprise. "No. Thank the heavens for that."

"And I thank the heavens I have one child who doesn't want to compete with me for the throne."

"True." I'd rather die than take control. Court was too fraught with drama. Deadly drama. And politics. I couldn't stand the politics. It was revolting the way the fey acted toward each other. Always with a knife at their friends' backs. Ready to stab should the need or desire arise.

I think that's why Chris and I got along so well. His pack had been one of the worst run in history. We both lived our childhood surrounded by violence, and now yearned for a quieter life. I wasn't sure either of us would ever get it, but we're both from long-lived races. There was always a chance. I hadn't managed it yet, but—

I took a breath, and forced myself to think the next thought. Even if it hurt.

But Chris would never have the quiet life he wanted and deserved. Not if I kept pursuing him.

Letting Chris go was like turning my heart to ice and heaving it onto the marble floor. It would shatter into a million tiny pieces. I'd never find all of them before they melted away into oblivion. I'd be broken forever.

A single tear escaped.

"You have to forget him." Mother wiped away the tear. "If you truly love this werewolf, it's the only way."

"And how well did that work out for you?" My tone was too sharp. I was snapping at her, and she didn't deserve it. But damn it, letting go of Chris hurt something so vital, so deep inside of me, I wasn't sure I'd ever get over it.

My mother laughed, not caring about the sharp tone I'd used. "I've had a lot of different loves in my life. I've managed to get over nearly all of them."

"I know. You have children from three different sires."

"Yet only one from your father. You're special to me."

I was the youngest of my siblings, so it made sense that she still talked about him the most. "You still miss him." It didn't take a genius to know that. My father was special. He was an Archon. Their whirlwind romance hadn't lasted more than a fortnight, but he left his mark on her. He gave her me.

"I will always miss your father, but he was not meant for this realm." She let out a long breath. "Love can come and go, but this court is enduring. You're past the marrying age, and with everything that's happened these past few months—especially with your new magical ties—I can no longer shove you in a corner and help the court forget about you. You've become way too visible. You'll be allowed to leave when you're needed for this new council pact you made, but other than that—you need to focus on your power base at court. Marry. Not next month. Now. Find someone strong with good ties and for the sake of the heavens, get it done fast."

No. I couldn't stay here indefinitely. The court would suffocate me, emotionally if not literally. I couldn't marry someone else when my heart belonged to another. The mere idea of it was revolting. "There has to be another way."

"I'm afraid not. Perhaps someone from the Solar Court would suit?"

My laugh was equal parts annoyance, exasperation, and desperation. "Now, I'm questioning your sanity. A Solar fey? *Really*, Mother? They're too hyped up on their own importance. We'd have to line the walls with mirrors to keep him occupied."

"Fine." She sighed and relaxed back against her desk again. "Then Leaves? I've always found them quite fun."

"Leaves? You want me to marry someone from Leaves?" They were nice enough, but all they wanted to do was party and see where the days and nights took them. They were amazing archers, but I wasn't sure that any of them would be much better off here than a werewolf. Lunar Court was the definition of deadly.

"Well, then, my dear. Is there someone from our court?" She crossed her arms. "Perhaps Van—"

"No." I left no room for negotiation in my tone. Van had been my guard for a long time. He'd watched me grow up, and while that kind of thing was common among the fey, for a relationship to change as a person grew, I couldn't with Van. He was too much like my father or even an older brother to me. It just could never, ever happen.

"Well, I've a list of suitors. A whole binder full." She walked around her desk, pulling out an actual binder. "The letters started arriving a few weeks ago. I took liberties as your queen and mother and burned the ridiculous ones."

My eyes widened as I took in the three-inch thick tome. "I'm grateful for that at least." But the binder was still too large.

"You should be. Some quite strange ones in the mix. Even for the fey." She handed me the binder and it weighed as much as the moon in my hands. "Pick someone kind and *strong*. Someone who can survive this madness. Someone who can be a true partner. Or pick someone you could kill if you can't stand them in a year. But be quick about it."

"I can't." My throat was dry and my hands were sweaty and I couldn't even begin to process what she was saying. The thought that I had to pick a husband when Christopher was in danger... "Not now. Maybe later when—"

"Put him out of your mind." She tapped the binder in my hands. "You may read through the binder here or take it with you. Cry, if you must. But do that here and now in this space where no one will know. And when you leave this room, the facade goes back up and thicker than ever. Strong. Colder than moonlight over ice. And with no more mentioning of this were-wolf of yours. Ever. Do you understand me?"

"Yes, Mother."

"Ugh. I hate it when you call me that. So formal."

I blinked and another traitorous tear slipped free. "And what would you prefer?"

"From you, when it's just us, Mama." She rubbed her thumb across my cheek, taking the tear with it. "Always Mama."

"I'm sorry, Mama." Saying it felt as if the long years of torment were gone and I was a child again. But they weren't gone, and I was about to go through another wave of it.

"I love you. Be safe." She cupped my cheek for a moment before striding though the door, slamming it behind her. She'd pretend that I'd annoyed her again with the werewolf business, but leave Chris out of it. She wouldn't hurt my standing at court, even if it cost her something.

My legs were unsteady as I walked to her couch. I sat heavily, and when the tears threatened to drown me, I welcomed them.

CHAPTER THREE

CHRIS

TODAY NEEDED TO END. I'd been okay for a while. I had a plan and a purpose, but after a few more hours walking in the desert, I wondered if Eli was fucking with me. It wasn't a crazy thought. He seemed to enjoy stringing Tessa along, so it wasn't much of a stretch that he would do the same to me. But why?

I took the last swig of spit-warm water and cursed him for not leaving me food. I'd forced myself not to drink it all at once, but it'd been hard. And now I was out of water and hunger was making my wolf edgy. If Cosette was in danger, then I wanted to be with her—my wolf wanted it even more. But I was done with this farting around in the desert bullshit. Court of Gales be damned.

My wolf howled at me to stay the course, but I ignored him and turned west. Still, I couldn't make myself move, even knowing that there was nothing to the east. Nothing for miles in that direction and if I kept going that way, I would just walk until I fell down dead.

The sun was falling behind the dune in front of me, and there was nothing that way either.

I wanted to trust Eli that I was headed somewhere that would help Cosette, but there was literally nothing here. Nothing as far as I could see in any direction. Unease settled heavy in my empty stomach and I knew this entire day had been a waste. I was a waste. What was I even doing here?

Cosette.

I turned east, but then I looked west again. I had to go west. The urge to head that way hit me hard.

So, I had to go west. I had to start that way before I died. I needed—

Son of a bitch.

I spun back to the east.

Those sneaky bastards and their sneaky fucking magic. I knew what this was.

I took another two steps east.

This—*this*—was finally something familiar. These wards didn't hit as hard as the ones at the coven's compound—it was way more subtle and insidious than that—but they were wards all the same.

The magic that kept anyone from walking on the coven's land was like hitting a wall of anxiety and dread and terror. There was no subtlety. Their wards smacked me in the face and it was like a switch flipped in my brain. All I wanted to do was run to get away from the slimy magic that coated my skin. Crossing them was nearly impossible, but I knew when I hit them because I could see the houses in the distance—just beyond the magical barrier—and I could tell myself to ignore it and keep walking.

But the fey were sly. Their wards must've wormed their way into my mind hours ago. Slowly filling my head with doubts and worries. I'd started to move slower and slower. I'd wanted to rule that out as exhaustion, but picturing Cosette in danger was enough to fuel me for days. I knew the only way to save her was to keep moving forward, and I'd still turned around.

I didn't feel any greasy magic along my skin. My wolf wasn't scenting anything other than my own BO and sand and heat, but Eli said that the Court of Gales was to the east. I couldn't see anything ahead of me, but the fey's underhills were hidden on a different plane of existence than the mortal realm. So, it made perfect sense that I couldn't see anything. But that didn't mean it wasn't there.

Nice try, assholes. But your wards aren't enough to keep me away.

I took another step, and then another. My wolf was on edge, sensing a fight to come, and he wasn't wrong. I might need him soon. The hair on my arms grew thicker and my nails became a little too long, a little too sharp to be considered human.

I took another step, and the magic grew. I could almost hear the voice worming its way into my head, urging me to turn back.

I took one more step and my teeth tingled with magical pressure. I was getting closer.

One more step.

Then another.

And one more. An internal battle waged inside of me with every foot I gained. My gut was telling me to turn around. To run. To get the fuck away from here before I got myself killed, but that was the magic.

I pushed it away. I could do this. For Cosette, I would do it.

One more step.

The wind rose, violently whipping the sand into the air, blocking out the harsh sunlight. A dozen fey bamfed in, surrounding me, dressed in all white—white shirt and white loose pants. Their faces were guarded behind intricately carved golden masks that covered their eyes, leaving only a small slit to see through. Each mask had a different design, and I wasn't sure which one was the leader of the bunch. But it didn't matter. They were fey. Every single one of them was dangerous.

I raised a hand to protect my eyes as the wind moved faster. Something told me that if I shifted this would get a whole lot worse, but that left me at a disadvantage. I could fight as a human, but without claws and teeth, I was minus the weapons that came with being a wolf.

Hold strong. That's all I could do while I waited for them to stop their display of power. They were going to make a decision about me soon. Either kill me or see what I wanted. From what Eli said, I was assuming that I was going to pique their interest.

The wind was gone from one breath to the next. The sand fell to the ground and the sun glared brighter than before.

I lowered my hand. One of the fey had come forward to stand in front of the rest. The person lifted their mask, revealing a beautiful woman with skin the same color as the sand. The whites of her eyes swirled with black and gray smoke, and at times, I couldn't tell where her irises started or if they were even there. And the way she looked at me—like I would make a pleasant snack—made me take a step back from her.

My move made her grin widen, and I noticed that her canine teeth looked a little more defined, not like mine when in my wolf form, but somewhere in between that and normal human. But combined with the way she licked her lips and narrowed her gaze as she stepped toward me was enough to give me the distinct impression that she could literally eat my flesh and enjoy it. She leaned toward me and breathed in deep, scenting me. Why do that unless she was going to hunt me?

I knew that werewolves were playthings for the Lunar Court, but I'd thought that was exclusive to them. Now I wasn't so sure. But it didn't matter. I didn't matter. Cosette was in danger. I had to be nice, even if I wanted to run in the other direction.

She finally looked away from me to scan the horizon, and I was thankful for the break.

"Why are you here?" she asked.

"I need help, and I heard you could help me."

The woman turned back to me with a feral grin. "Oh. Help? And what would you be giving us in return?"

I stepped back again before I could stop myself, and she laughed.

She fucking laughed at me.

Damn it. What was Eli getting me into? I couldn't make a bargain with a fey. I'd never think of all the loopholes. And from the looks of this fey woman, she could tie me up with millions of them.

"Elilaios—"

She hissed and I stopped speaking.

"What would the archon have us do with you?" She glanced behind her. One of the others nodded, and she turned back to me. "Fine. You may come in, but if you break any of our rules, you'll be ours."

I swallowed the fear until it was only a small leaden stone in my stomach. "What are your rules?"

Her grin came back slowly and filled with the kind of evil that forced goose bumps to skitter across my skin. "It wouldn't be any fun if we told you, now would it?"

I wasn't sure I could respond to her with anything other than sarcasm, but I also wasn't sure if that would break a rule. I didn't know anything about the Court of Gales or what they might consider off limits. How was I supposed to not a break a rule if I didn't know it existed?

She spun and waved the other guards to start forward.

When I stood rooted to my spot, she looked back at me. "Don't be shy. You have everything to gain by coming inside."

"And nothing to lose?"

She laughed. "Oh, no. You could lose everything." She shrugged. "But what's life without a little gamble."

I wanted to tell her that life wasn't all about taking risks. That it was about love and respect and giving, but she didn't give a shit what I thought life was about.

The fey guards lined up two-by-two as they moved toward the closest dune. The fey woman waved me to follow them, and I obeyed, now sandwiched between the rest of the guards and her.

I didn't trust this woman enough to have my back to her, but I wasn't going to show weakness. Not right now. I stepped forward, following as instructed—unable to see where we were going—but when the guard in front of me walked straight into the wall of light reddish-gold sand and disappeared, I stumbled.

Damned fey magic.

I'd never been inside a fey court. Never intended to. Everything I'd heard about the fey and their underhills was that they were to be avoided at all costs. But I figured if I ever did have to enter one, Cosette would be by my side.

She'd told me a couple of things. That if I ever ended up in a court, run. And if I couldn't run, then I was to never show weakness. Ever. Yet I'd already done that twice by stepping away from the fey woman. And the masked soldiers herding me were warning that there would be no running. Not today.

So, I put on the calm, cool facade. One like I'd seen Cosette wear so many times. I'd be stupid not to be afraid of the fey. I'd be a real idiot not to be terrified to enter their land. Yet I was going to ignore that feeling.

I was here to help Cosette, and I would never, ever let her down.

I stepped into the wall of sand like it wasn't a completely insane thing to do.

My breath was taken from me as I entered what looked like

a tunnel into an underground cave. I hadn't had much luck with anything underground. My ex-pack's favorite form of punishment was beating the shit out of me and trapping me underground without any food or water. And after the more recent ones filled with vampires or an open pit to hell, I wasn't much for being underground. At all.

Being under the dirt made my lungs and heart tighten until I thought I'd never breathe again because the walls were closing, crushing—

But they weren't. They weren't moving. I was fine. I was *fine.*

I took a long slow breath in, and it was enough to take the edge off of my panic. The scent wasn't right. It didn't smell of dirt or dampness, but there was a fresh breeze that smelled clean and calming. It took me a second to identify the various smells, but—lavender—that was the calming part. And there was some sage, too.

I liked sage. Sage meant cleansing, and I didn't mind that, especially when I was willingly walking into a fey court.

Once I gave myself a second to actually take in my surroundings, I knew my first assessment of the court wasn't right at all. This wasn't a cave. It was so much more than that. The floor was smooth and even, like someone had taken a blowtorch to the sand, turning the top layer into glass. Underneath, the sand pressed up against the glossy surface. It had a beautiful perfection to it, and I knew that no matter how hard I tried, I wouldn't be able to re-create it in my art.

Whatever the material was, it was magic.

The floors curved up to meet the walls, and the ceiling arced high overhead. Torches along the walls were lit every three feet, flaring to life as we stepped down the wide hall. The breeze flickered the flames, and I glanced to the sides. There weren't any doors along the hall, but it was leading somewhere. But where?

The hallway was just wide enough for the fey guards to keep walking two-by-two. I couldn't see what was beyond them, and unless something changed, there was going to be no way for me to escape.

A bitter smoke with sweet overtones, like stale apples, rolled up the hallway, burning my nose and eliminating the lingering sage from the air. With each step we took, the scent grew stronger.

I sneezed and one of the fey in front looked over her shoulder and laughed. They knew what they were doing. Scent was one of the main advantages I had. It was almost like another form of sight, and that smoke was blinding me. It made me uncomfortable and uncertain. Although I was uncertain for a lot of reasons.

The line of fey in front of me parted, revealing a room. It was filled with low round tables, surrounded by rings of multicolored pillows. Silk-covered lamps hung from the ceilings, casting a dull, multicolored glow over everything. There were no sounds coming from the crowded room, but I could see two small groups of musicians performing between the tables, dancers moving around the room, along with people playing some sort of betting game that involved a lot of animated yelling and glittering, glowing golden coins. Yet, the only thing I could hear was the faint rustling of the guards' clothes. I couldn't even smell the food from the platters that covered every table, and I didn't think that was only because of the smoke.

This was it. I was about to be severely outnumbered by a room full of fey. I gave myself a few seconds to be scared.

One.

Two.

Three.

And then I shoved it away because being afraid of the fey when I needed their help would do me no good. It was a useless emotion right now.

The fey woman slid past me, giving me a grin over her shoulder as she moved closer to the busy room. "It'd be best if you did not discuss what you see here." She shrugged. "Although if you did, you'd make my job so much more fun."

"And what's your job?"

She spun to face me. "Killing you."

I wasn't sure what to say to that. She'd made no move against me yet, but if she did, I'd defend myself.

She was quiet for a little longer than I was comfortable with. "If you get out of line."

"I'll do my best to stay in line. Especially if you tell me where the line is."

"We've been over this. I don't like to make things easy. Especially when power is up for grabs." She spun back to face the room. "Come and be welcome."

As soon as the words were out of her mouth, the other sounds came. Clanking of plates. The yelling and betting. Laughing and music and dancers' steps. More scents came, too, but all dulled by the too-sweet smoke.

The rest of the guards dispersed into the room, but the fey woman motioned for me to follow her.

She walked to one of the few empty low tables, and sat on one of the surrounding pillows. Yanking down her hood, she tossed her mask on the table. The others had faded into the crowd, masks gone and I could only spot them by their loose white pants and shirts. They were the only things in room not brightly colored.

The fey woman motioned to a servant in a corner, who rushed over. She said a few quick words in what sounded similar to the language I'd heard Cosette use with Van some-

35

times, but I could've been wrong. Did the fey have different dialects?

A second later a bowl of rose-scented water and a towel appeared in the servant's hands.

The fey woman nodded, and then turned to me. "Wash your hands. It's not polite to be dirty while dining."

I raised an eyebrow. It'd been a while since I'd been considered a child, but even when I was younger, my parents didn't care much about that kind of thing. My father was too busy beating the shit out of me to care about a little dirt. But still, I took the bowl, happy to rid myself of some of the sand. I dipped the small towel into the copper bowl, and hoped it wouldn't offend anyone if I wiped off my face first.

The fey woman grinned. "Much better. You're quite handsome, although I didn't mind the dirt exactly."

I wasn't sure what to say to that, so I kept my mouth shut, even if the wolf was urging me to ask for help now. To hurry. But I couldn't do either. Not yet. The fey took words very seriously, and I didn't want to say anything or ask for anything that I didn't have to. At least not yet.

I dunked the towel back into the bowl and was surprised to see the water just as clear as it'd been before. Where did the dirt go?

I glanced up at the fey woman. She was just watching me. I was sure this little bit of magic wasn't anything to her, but it was impressive to me. I quickly finished washing my hands, and as soon as I was done, the fey woman clapped her hands.

Platters of food appeared, covering every inch of the table. My stomach rumbled, and yet I didn't grab for the food. There were bowls of creamy things, yellow things with chunks of white and green. Roasted yams and carrots and other vegetables. Some other pickled cold vegetables. Cheeses and nuts and dried fruits filled one great copper platter. And then a pile of breads—sweet and those that I thought smelled faintly of garlic and cheese and spinach—were piled high in a large bowl. But no meat. Not anywhere.

"You may eat," she said.

I considered her for a second. It would be rude to ask for meat when all of this was offered to me and I was a guest, but I was also a werewolf. We needed more calories and more protein than any other species in the mortal realm. But if I was going to ask a favor, I was going to need more information.

"What do I call you?"

"Rayvien."

"Ray-v-ehn?" I asked to make sure I was saying it correctly.

She titled her chin down one time. "That's right." And the smile was back. The evil one.

"You're intimidating me on purpose?"

"Not exactly, but it is a fun side effect." She leaned forward and grabbed a piece of bread, swiping it through a creamy sauce. "Go ahead. The food at this table is okay for you."

I looked at the rest of the tables, almost all of them had at least one or two platters on them. Most of it meat. "But the food at the rest of the tables?"

She put down the bread. "I'll give you one free piece of advice because I find you amusing."

"And what will that cost me?"

She leaned back in her chair. "Ah. So, Cosette *has* been teaching you."

I didn't say anything. I didn't dare. I wasn't sure where I stood with her, but I knew this was all very tentative, and I needed to save my favors for the big ask—more power.

"You don't have to answer," Rayvien said. "I know her, and even if she did cause quite a stir here a few years ago and I wouldn't exactly call her a friend, I still would like to avoid her wrath. So, I'll do my best not to kill you unless ordered otherwise."

"Funny. I thought you said otherwise."

She gave me the tiniest of shrugs. "It was fun, but I still can't say much, except that not everything here is as it looks. You'd do best to pay attention to all of your senses." She tapped her nose, and I would've understood her even without the completely obvious hint.

The smoke was intentional like I'd thought. It wasn't as strong here, but I still couldn't scent things fully. Everything in here smelled faint and dull and I had trouble telling one note from another. Was it yogurt or milk? Garlic or cheese? Safe or poisoned?

She glanced around the room and waved a hand. I twisted to see a server coming forward with a platter of meat.

Finally. This. This is what I've needed all damned day. The wolf had me reaching out before I could think twice, snatching a drumstick as soon as it was within reach, but just before my teeth ripped into the tender, juicy, perfectly spiced morsel, a scent hit me. It was barely there, but it was enough to make me pause. Enough to make my wolf pause.

I lowered the meat and looked to Rayvien.

Disappointment warred with laughter on her face—a unique combination I'd never seen before—but she finally tipped into laughter.

I smelled it again. It was almost sour, but meat didn't sour like dairy. "Poisoned?"

"No. Not exactly."

I didn't know what not-exactly-poisoned meant, but I didn't need to know. I dropped it on the table and reached for the water bowl and towel again.

"Wise choice." Rayvien stood from the table. "Enjoy the food. I'll be back. Do not move from here until I say."

"Fine, but I'd like to speak to someone about why I'm here."

"Sit. Stay. If Cosette trained her pet dog well...then we'll see."

Pet dog?

It took everything in me to remember that I wasn't supposed to kill Rayvien. I was surrounded by fey, and acting out now would be beyond dumb. So, I swallowed the insult, even if it burned all the way down.

"I'll be waiting." At least I wasn't out on the dunes without water anymore. Even if I didn't have any meat, if I ate everything on the table, I might have enough calories to keep my muscle mass stable.

Rayvien moved around the tables, stopping to talk to someone here and there, until she made it to an especially rowdy group of gamblers. I thought she was getting someone for me, but then she slid onto one man's lap and I knew I'd better settle in.

I grabbed a hunk of bread, and debated which bowl to try first. I took a bite and it was surprisingly delicious and rich. I paused for a few minutes, drinking sips of water while I waited to see if it truly wasn't poisoned. But when nothing happened, I remembered that the fey didn't lie. So, I could safely assume that the food on this table was okay to eat. I lost track of time as I shoveled bite after bite after bite into my mouth. Hoping that with each calorie I ate, the wolf would quiet just a little more.

Because he was getting loud about wanting me to hurry up and find Cosette. But I couldn't do that until I figured out how to break my tie to the Lunar Court. This was going to take some time, but my wolf was an impatient bastard. If he didn't shut up, I was going to end up losing control and shifting. And if my wolf tried to fight the fey, I knew—without any doubt at all—I would die, and then where would that leave Cosette?

CHAPTER FOUR

COSETTE

I WAS thankful that only Van was waiting in the throne room when I left my mother's office. He knew me well enough not to say a word. Just a nod before turning toward the exit. The facade I usually kept effortlessly, firmly in place felt as broken as my heart. I tried to hold myself together as we walked in silence to my suite, but it was impossible.

I would get it together. I just needed…I just needed something. But I didn't know what.

I hadn't even stepped through the carved wooden doors of my suite before Van ripped into me.

"Are you out of your bloody mind?"

Him shouting at me was the last thing needed. "I don't think so. At least I wasn't, but now, I'm quite sure."

I pushed the door closed behind me and leaned against it. My eyes felt swollen and tender from the tears, but my heart felt worse. Without Chris, without love, without the hope for happiness in marriage, I felt I had nothing left. What was the point?

"Oh, Cosette. I'm sorry."

"Don't be." I couldn't stand his pity. It wasn't like I was supposed to enjoy my life here.

I'd never hated my suite more. Never hated court more. Never hated being fey more. I wanted to burn the whole place to the ground, but mother would never let me.

I stared at the enormous flower arrangement placed on top of the tall, oak table in front of me. It served to block the view of the room beyond it—a living room with two doors leading off on either side. One led to my bedroom and bathroom. The other to the dining room and kitchen.

The suite wasn't large—given my station at court—but I didn't need anything big. I usually wasn't here long enough to put a second bedroom to use. My suite didn't have any magical furniture or glowing walls because I didn't care about this place enough to invest in or make those kinds of pieces.

But the rooms were decorated nicely. The living room was filled with a beautiful marble-topped coffee table, a comfortable-enough navy couch, and some deep-brown leather armchairs that almost swallowed me whole when I sat in them. A colorful woven rug tied the area together, but it was void of any knick-knacks or pictures or anything that would show even an ounce of my personality.

The rest of my suite had all the elements needed for a home, but this wasn't my home. It was a place I visited when forced. A place where assassins came to kill me. A place that I had absolutely no love for. My true home was in Denver. Where assassins didn't exist and where loved ones cared about me for who I was, not what I was. But just thinking about Denver made me feel homesick, heartsick, and empty. And this place? This place was my prison.

I rested my head back against the door, staring at the ceiling as I thought. My mother was right. It was for the best that Chris would never come here. Never have to see me in this place.

Never have to deal with the court. And from here on out, I had to focus on not thinking about him. At least for a while.

I stepped away from the door and around the ridiculous flower arrangement, fully entering my suite.

Van stood in front of the couch. I liked to circle around the room like a mad person whenever I was the least bit upset, but Van was the opposite. When he was mad, he got very, very still. He'd been my guard for long enough that I knew just by looking at him how mad he was. I was mad, too, but I was also defeated.

Van had given me a moment to catch my breath, but I knew that was going to end soon, just like everything always ended.

Cradled in my arms, the binder felt so impossibly heavy that carrying it for a second longer might shatter what was left of me. And yet, here I was. Holding the damned thing.

"You're right."

Van finally unfroze, stepping toward me. "Of course I am. About what?"

"That I'm out of my mind, but that doesn't change what I've done or what I've been ordered to do."

"What's happened?" All the anger was gone from Van's tone, and replaced with soft concern. "You look like... What did she say to you?"

"Nothing she hasn't said before, but this time it felt different. Worse. More final." I made my way to the sitting area and threw the binder on the coffee table. It hit the white marble top with a resounding *thwack*.

"What. Is. That?" Van drew the words out as he approached the binder, staring down at it as if it held the plague inside.

I shared the sentiment. "Suitors for my consideration." I sat down in one of the armchairs, hoping that feeling of the soft leather surrounding me would be comforting, but it wasn't. At least not enough to outweigh the heaviness inside me.

Van moved to sit on the dark blue velvet couch. "Please tell me you're joking. I thought you had an agreement with her."

"Afraid not." I kicked my feet up onto the coffee table, trying to hide the stupid thing from view with my boots. "I've always managed to put it off—to put her off—but not this time. Apparently, the way things have unfolded the last few months have put me in the spotlight again, and we're about to get busy. We'll be neck-deep in assassins until I solidify my power base. So, marriage."

"We can hold them off. We've done it before, but you can't... I mean, who—"

"If you're about to insult me, please know I don't have the energy for it." I wasn't sure who in their right mind would take me on, but I didn't need anyone else pointing that out. I grinned at Van. "My mother offered me your hand."

His face went pale. "You're joking."

"No. And I like my life—even if I don't enjoy it at this moment—so I'm not lying either." I was probably hateful for taking some joy in his reaction, but I couldn't help it. He was in as much misery as I was at the thought of us marrying.

He rubbed a hand down his face as he took it in. "I wouldn't accuse you of being so stupid as to lie, but really, Cosette." He looked me in the eyes. "Me? She honestly still doesn't understand?"

"I don't think my mother will ever understand us." It seemed like my mother put us together all those years ago with the hopes that we'd fall in love, but that didn't happen. Van said he felt as if he were my father, and that's how I felt, too.

I spun in the chair, throwing my legs over the arm so that I could watch Van. I relaxed as I watched him think, resting my head back against the other arm of the chair.

Van sighed and I felt it as if it were my own. He leaned

forward, resting his elbows on his knees as he looked up at me. "It *has* come up before."

I gave him a small smile. "I know." And we'd thankfully stopped it from happening.

"So, it's not a surprise to either of us." He dropped his gaze to the floor. "It's not a bad idea when you set aside our feelings on the matter."

I snorted. Now he was the one that had to be joking.

"I can see why she suggested it."

Wait. He was joking. Wasn't he?

Van blew out another long breath, and then rolled his shoulders back as he sat tall. It was something that he did right before he went into battle. That one move had me worried. It was Van's version of freaking out.

"When do we marry?"

Oh, wow. He honestly thought I'd agreed to it?

I wanted to drag it out—torture him a bit for yelling at me—but his posture looked like he was ready to take a hit, and I couldn't do that. Not to him. "I refused, of course."

"Oh, thank the heavens." His shoulders relaxed and he started laughing, his cheeks pinking ever so slightly. "You had me worried that you agreed to it."

"I thought it'd be obvious. I can't... With you." I stuck my tongue out. "And if I'd agreed to it, why would I have a binder of suitors to choose from?"

He laughed. "Right. I just can't think straight when your mother is being...how she is." Van's face grew serious again as he met my gaze. "I would've done it. For you, I would still do it." He sounded like he'd enjoy that as much as he'd enjoy facing down an execution squad.

"That's *so kind* of you." He was lucky I was somehow in a teasing mood. Otherwise, I might've picked a fight with him.

He gave me his cut-the-crap look. "You know what I mean.

45

I've watched over you since the day after your twelfth birthday. I care for you, *deeply*. You're my only family, and I'd do anything for you. But marriage? I—"

"Save it, Van. I know all this, and though I do love how well you've looked after me, I have no desire to...bed you." To say the word *sex* with him... It felt icky even thinking it. I didn't know what my mother was thinking even bringing up marriage with him again.

"Will you look through the binder?" I motioned toward it without actually looking at it. "You know more about the other courts than I do."

Van was once considered a god among mortals and feared among all the fey, high and low, court or exiled. He was more powerful than I was, and I wasn't sure why he'd ever agreed to be my guard. But my mother brought me to see him all those years ago, and he'd said yes without a second thought.

I later learned that he'd grown bored of life. He saw the scared child I was, and guarding my life gave him a purpose again. It seemed like we were exactly what each other needed at the time. I trusted him with my life, and that meant I could trust him to find someone in this awful binder that I wouldn't hate.

"It would be my pleasure." He grabbed the binder and started flipping through it. "I'll show the other guards, too. They might have some insight into the other courts, and depending on who is in here, might have some knowledge of the specific suitors. How are you handling it?" He asked without looking at me.

"What?"

He closed the binder and set it back on the table. He reached forward, wrapping his hand around my ankle and looking straight in my eyes. "How are you handling letting Christopher go?"

Van might as well have punched my heart with that question. I pulled my ankle free and turned to sit correctly in the

46

chair. My hair hid my face as I stared at the carpet. "I'm not handling it. My heart—"

I felt the magic before I saw the blade swinging toward me and jerked back. The sword split the air in front of my face.

An assassin. In my suite?

I dropped from my chair and kicked it back hard. The impact broke something in the chair and from the shout, broke something in the intruder, too.

Too close. Too close.

"Van!" But I didn't really need to call out to him. He was already there. Sword out.

Van slashed at nothing, but whatever magic hid the assassin from view faded as he died. Blood splattered the floor, my clothes, my face, but I didn't care.

My mind raced to catch up with how fast my heart was pounding, but all I could hear was my harsh breaths. All I could see was the severed head rolling toward me.

I put my foot out to stop it. His long blond hair obscured his face, and I moved onto my knees—needing to know who had almost killed me—and brushed the bloody strands away.

The blue eyes had lost their life, but were frozen wide. The mouth hung open. The fey's nose had been broken a time or two, but he still had all his teeth. A few days scruff covered his face, but worse than the scent of his blood was the scent of his sweat.

But who was he? No recognition came as I stared at the face. I stood and stepped back from the body. I wished I felt something more, but this was so normal for me that all I felt was glad that I had lived and he had died. Now there was one less fey for me to worry about.

Except there was a bigger issue. More than just one single assassin. "How did he get in here? This is supposed to be my only safe space at court."

Van muttered a spell, and magic ringed out around us, filling the room. "It's only us now. Bronio was supposed to have cleared the room moments before we arrived. I apologize for not double—"

"Don't. I don't want your apology." Being at court brought out a coldness in me that I didn't like. The sooner I found a way out of here, the better. But first, I needed to know who was behind this particular attack and how he'd made it into my suite. "Who?"

"His name was Godrian. One of Tiarnan's men."

For a moment, the swish-swish of Van running his cleaning cloth along his sword was the only sound in the room.

One of Tiarnan's men? My oldest half-brother? He was behind this attempt on my life?

I strode away from the body, unable to look at that face for one second longer.

This was worse than I'd thought. This wasn't just power-hungry fey trying to reach for a higher rung. Killing me wouldn't do anything for Tiarnan. He was older than me. Higher in rank. Closer to winning the throne, should something ever happen to my mother. This didn't make sense. My brother had to know I wasn't a threat to him.

I turned to Van, who was standing with his arms crossed as he watched me. "Please tell me this is about the news report. That he's just mad at me for everything and wanted to get under my skin."

"You know I can't do that." Van's voice was tinged with an apology. He was going to say something I wasn't going to like. "If this was about being forced into hiding, he'd have acted when it happened."

I moved to sit in the farthest chair from the body. "Then what my mother said is true."

Van inspected his sword for any lingering blood before sheathing it. "She wouldn't lie."

I swatted that comment away. "I know that, but that didn't mean I wanted to believe her."

Van moved to stand between me and the offending body, and I hoped he had an answer for why this happened. "You gained more power, and Tiarnan doesn't want you getting ideas about usurping his claim to the throne."

"I don't want the throne." I leaned back in the chair and wished things were different. That this court would somehow change, but it never did. "I thought after all this time—after everything I've done—that would be clear enough to everyone at court."

"You could've changed your mind."

"I haven't."

He crossed his arms. "But they don't know that." Van's tone was patient and logical and annoying the shit out of me.

I stood from my chair. I couldn't sit still or else I'd do something I'd regret. "He's my brother. He should know how I feel about this, and if he didn't, he should be man enough to come talk to me." It shouldn't hurt, but it did. I was disappointed in him, and if he'd acted out—that meant that the rest of the court wouldn't be far behind.

"That's not the way of the fey."

I wasn't sure if I wanted to laugh or scream or cry or punch Van in the face. But it wasn't Van's fault our people were so twisted. And nothing I could do would fix this. My new power was going to be a problem.

A thought hit me. I spun to face Van. "Are Elowen and Kyra at their courts?" Solar and Leaves courts were different than Lunar in some key ways, but not in this. They gained power, and that meant they'd be in the same boat as me.

"I'm not sure where they are. I haven't had a ton of contact with the other realms since we got here."

The way time behaved in the fey courts always caused communication problems. Unless I used a mirror like my mother's—which was extremely rare and not worth the favor—tech behaved terribly. "I'll send word to them. Either way, they should be on alert." I sighed. Although they wouldn't thank me for the warning. By telling them, it showed concern, which meant that I thought they were weak.

Court politics was tiresome.

"How long has he been here?" I pointed to the headless assassin on the floor.

Van glanced down at the body beside his feet. "From the look of him, days." Van nudged the body with his foot, and then looked at me. The anger on his face had me taking a step back. "He's been here for *days*, watching us, waiting for you to be distracted enough to make a move, and I had no idea...."

"No." That he'd been here for so long made all the hairs on my arms stand on end. He'd been watching me. For *days*. There was a reason this would never feel like my home no matter how many knickknacks I put up.

"Why didn't he act sooner?"

"I don't know."

Days? "Why didn't we sense him? Are the wards failing?" We had some around my room to keep me safe while I slept. No one without approval of three guards should've gotten past the door.

"No. The wards are fine. I tested them when I reinforced them a moment ago."

This was so much worse than I'd thought. "That means we have a traitor."

A traitor. How was that possible? I'd trusted my guards with my life for years, and for them to betray me now? After everything we've been through? "Are you sure?"

"If anyone clears the room other than me, it takes *three* guards to reset the wards. The guards always check when your staff come in and out of here. Which means at least three of my men knew there was an assassin inside your suite and covered his tracks, repeatedly. I'm not sure we can trust anyone right now." There was ice in his voice now. I'd only heard it a few times before, but whoever betrayed us was already dead. They just didn't know it yet.

He was right. My guards had been with me for so long that I treated them more like family than I did my own blood relations. If they'd turned on me, then I wasn't sure who I could trust besides Van.

I strode to him, resting my head against his shoulder. "I hate it here." The whine in my voice hurt my pride a bit, but I couldn't help it. I really, truly *hated* court.

Van wrapped his arm around me and squeezed my shoulder. "I know you do. Marrying the right one should help this."

I pulled just far enough away from him to see his eyes. "Are you sure?" Because I wasn't so sure. If my own brother had turned against me, then what good would marrying do?

"The right match will be a show of power and with the blessing of your mother, you'll be reconfirmed at court. It will prove that you're playing along. Even the gods have to play by the rules to keep peace in the realms."

He was quiet for a second, but the firm press of his lips told me that he was holding something back.

I wasn't sure I wanted to hear it, but I wasn't one to shy away from any challenge. "Tell me."

Van looked at me with such pity that I was drowning in it, and I wasn't sure how much more bad news or hard truths I could take.

"Even marrying won't solve this."

Apparently, I had to swallow down one more hard truth today. "Why not?" I rested my head against him again, needing some comfort before he told me the rest.

"You have an archon for a father, and you've hidden the extent of your abilities from court. We don't love mysteries. They're too close to untruths. Any power-hungry fey will be hard pressed to stop themselves from trying to kill you. If not for the power they'd gain by doing it, then for the recognition they'd receive by finally uncovering what and who you truly are." He grew quiet, but the quiet was filled with the pressure of the words he was holding back. His body had stopped moving with his breaths, and I knew he was doing his best not to say whatever else was on his mind.

"Just say it." I wasn't sure it could get much worse, but whatever it was, I needed to hear it.

"Eli is another factor in this whole mess."

In my mind, Eli could be blamed for a number of things. I'd run into him exactly three times in my life, and I'd barely survived the second time. But I wasn't so sure that I could put all of this on Eli. "Why exactly?"

"It's been over a century and a half since this court has gotten wind of an archon, let alone had one visit. That much time was enough for the fey to forget or put aside the mystery of who Cosette Argent is exactly. You're the queen's daughter and spy and that was good enough for them for a while. You got to come and go as you pleased, and no one knows Eli was involved with what happened with you at Gales thirty years ago. No one from Gales would talk about it, and you wouldn't either. Only you and I and your mother know the truth. And the time before that—"

"Was a secret, too." I hated what Van was saying, but he was right. I stepped away from him.

"But the power Eli gave off when he entered your mother's throne room a month ago was felt across *all* the fey realms. Anyone who chose to forget who sired you remembered in that one single moment. And then shortly after, you gained even more power through him."

"If I gained power, then so did you. Why aren't assassins after you?"

"I was already a god among the fey." The confident smirk on his face was annoying. "They'll never forget who I am or what I can do."

Of course. Maybe if I pretended to be a god, they'd leave me alone, too.

I moved over to the couch and sank down into the cushions. I'd never met my father, but if he was anything like Eli, I was glad of it. It'd taken me so many years to get the court to forget about me, and now I wasn't sure I had the patience to play the political games while I waited for them to forget once again. If they ever did. Fey didn't like to make the same mistake twice.

"Why do they have to constantly test me? I want no part of this. I've made that perfectly clear."

Van sat on the couch, resting his feet on the coffee table as he stretched out beside me. "Because we're fey. It's what we do."

"That doesn't make it right."

"And the fact that you think that proves to everyone you're not entirely fey."

A while ago, that truth would've burned me. My mother was the queen of the strongest court and yet I still wasn't fey enough. But I'd learned not to care about what anyone thought of me a long time ago. It'd been a hard lesson to learn. The only ones I really cared about were Van, my mother, my friends...and Chris.

The pain of even thinking his name burned the breath from my lungs, but I ignored it. This was going to be my new normal.

I tilted my head to look at Van. "So, what do we do?"

"This is so very tricky." He glanced over at the body. "We've done too much that has angered all of the fey recently—not just our court. *All* of the fey. If word gets out that the assassination attempts have already started, if we show any weakness at all, then the rest will start circling."

Suddenly the fact that Eli had Chris was the least of my worries. There were some nasty fey out there that I wanted nothing to do with. The stuff of nightmares. The kind of fey that would make the one that held Meredith captive seem like a pleasant day at the beach.

"If this man hid here with my own guards' help, at the order of my own brother, then it's already too late for a cover-up. They're already after me. That's what my mother was warning me about. The fey want me dead." I had a terrible idea. "It might be better to throw the body into the hallway. Screw them and their games. Let them come."

Van's slanted smile was pure evil. If he wasn't on my side, I'd have been afraid. "Are you sure that's how you want to play it?"

"No, but let's do it anyway."

Van waved his hand, and the body disappeared. "And now?"

I stared at the binder again. "Shit, Van. Just shit. I've waited this long, and I can't stomach it." I'd rather face down all the fey than marry someone I didn't love. I looked at Van, hoping that he'd have something else to tell me. Something to make this easier.

He nudged me with his shoulder to get my attention. "It wouldn't have to be forever. Just long enough to let things settle," he said, trying to ease my burden, but I wasn't sure that made this any easier to stomach.

Van eyed the binder again. "I bet you there's not a single Lunar Court suitor in there."

I closed my eyes for a moment. "I'd be an idiot to take that bet. They hate me here. It's why I've been a spy for so long." I blew out a breath as I considered. "And that means we start visiting other courts."

"Yes."

I looked at Van. "What's more dangerous—a princess visiting another court filled with enemies or a princess staying at her own court, also filled with enemies?"

"I'm not sure. Because that body outside your door means that all traditional court protections against you will be removed."

I laughed, but it wasn't because I thought this was funny. It just kept getting worse. "That should make it even more fun. Good thing you used to be a god."

"Good thing." Van winked at me. "But I did find out one little tidbit while you were arguing with your mother that might improve your mood."

"What's that?" I'd take anything at this point.

"Your mother's been playing with time again."

My heart nearly stopped. Depending on which way she'd twisted time, that either meant Chris had been with Eli months or days, instead of weeks like I'd thought.

"How long has it been in the mortal realm? How long have we been down here to them?"

"Eighteen or so hours in the mortal realm to our three weeks at court."

I let out a whoosh of breath. Nothing would've shocked me more. The power it took to make that much of an impact was immense. She was opening herself to attack wasting so much of it for so long. "Why? She's never played willy-nilly with the underhill's time like that before. That's a massive lag."

"My best guess? She been giving you time to come to terms with letting Chris go, and now that you know, you'll be able to relax, fortify your power base with marriage, and then go find him and in time help with whatever Eli's doing."

"That's..." I took another breath. "Okay." That meant Chris was fine. I could cry from relief. But my relief didn't last long.

"Oh, no." If mother was going through that much—expending that much energy on time games—then she wasn't joking around. I *had* to marry and quickly. "There's no getting out of it this time, is there?"

"I'm afraid not. If it's any consolation, you've lasted longer than any of your siblings. They married for power by their eighteenth year. Not that any of those marriages lasted, but..."

"I know." And I was old. Much older than any of my friends in Texas knew. Only Chris knew the truth about me.

But I'd never needed to marry for power. I had enough on my own, just as my mother had enough. I could choose to marry for love, and so I'd waited. My siblings called me a hopeless romantic, but I didn't care. I let them laugh at me behind my back—and to my face—for years.

Marrying for power now was a blow I hadn't expected. "So, what do I do?"

Van stood and gave me a pointed look. "You shower before you get blood all over the rest of your furniture."

I glanced down at myself. He was right. Blood had sprayed my shirt and pants, and now that he'd told me, my face felt a little itchy. I hated when blood got on my face. "I hadn't realized any had gotten on me."

"It did."

"Yes. I see that now." I snapped and then instantly regretted it. "My apologies."

"Not needed. I'll shower as well. We'll meet back here in one hour. And just like before, I'll be staying on your couch until it's safe. I'll move some of my things. I'd ask that you don't dismiss the rest of your guards yet."

"Why not?"

"I want to weed out who exactly has turned against us, but we'll need to be on alert at all times until then. I'd be more worried if you still had more than fifty, but the good news is that you only have the required twelve guards for a nonheir princess on staff right now."

I closed my eyes, letting myself wallow for a moment. "I can't believe this is happening."

"We'll get through. We did before, and you're stronger now. Older and—dare I say—wiser?"

He wanted me to laugh, but I couldn't. I hoped he was right. I couldn't thank him, so I did the next best thing. I gave him a hard hug. "I appreciate you."

"And I, you." He rubbed a hand down my back. "We'll be quick. If there's someone that could fortify you at court, we need to find him. Fast."

"We'll find someone." I had no other choice. Not anymore.

CHAPTER FIVE

CHRIS

AFTER WHAT HAD to be at least an hour, I was still alone at my round table. There were exactly eighteen of them in the room, all raised about a foot and half or so above the pillow-seats. There were a few tables that only had three or four people sitting at them, a couple were empty, but the rest had at least six each. Nearly one hundred and twenty people in the room and not one single person had come to talk to me.

It was hot as hell in there and the scent of the sweet smoke wasn't helping me at all. Gone was the feeling of air moving, and I didn't like being underground. Not even a little bit. It was funny how I'd hated being out on the dunes with the hot wind, and now I was desperate to have even a few seconds of that wind back. I picked up a piece of bread and hoped that food would fix how I was feeling, but after inhaling the rich food, I was left only with a churning brick in my stomach. And yet I was still hungry.

My wolf needed meat, but there was none here. Rayvien had warned me, and I was taking that warning seriously. I'd

AILEEN ERIN

heard stories about nonfey entering the underhills, never to be seen again. Some of them warned not to eat anything or else risk getting trapped here. I wasn't sure that eating tainted, rotting meat would trap me, but it could make me sick or worse...

A voice rose above the others. One of the fey men stood from his spot, throwing a tray of food across the room. In a flash of fire and smoke, the man disappeared. The room was silent for a second before the whispers started.

I'd given up on trying to eavesdrop hours ago. I spoke English, French, and a touch of Spanish. Anything else was a bust. Whatever fey dialect they were speaking, I didn't know it, and I had yet to hear the few fey words Cosette had taught me. If I'd had paper and some charcoal, I would've been happy to spend the time there sketching all the faces and commotion of the room, but I had nothing else to do but wait.

A few minutes later, the room was back to normal. The fey alternated between talking—or more accurately, yelling—with each other while they traded their little sparkling coins. I wasn't sure if they were placing bets or if it was a weird game or if the coins signified something else. I couldn't figure it out, and Rayvien hadn't come back so that I could ask her. She was still at the same table, sitting on the same man's lap, and hadn't spared me a glance since she left me with the order to wait.

She showed the man sitting across from her a large, glittery disk, bigger than the quarter-size ones that seemed the most popular. He reached for it, trying to snatch it from her. Rayvien laughed and the coin disappeared.

This was getting stupid. What the hell was going on? I felt like a waste of space just sitting here, but she'd told me to sit and wait. Maybe it was a test, but of what? Patience? Or a test to see if I was willing—and daring enough—to disobey the only request made of me so far?

I needed help from the Court of Gales, so I was hesitant to go against Rayvien, but I couldn't get over the fact that Cosette was in danger and I was stuck here doing nothing. My thumb might as well have been up my ass for all the good I was doing her. And what was the *point*?

I glanced at my phone for the hundredth time. I'd tried to send a million messages to Tessa, Dastien, and Cosette, but none of them were going through. Cosette said that tech was a little unreliable at court, but I'd never believed it was this bad. I'd spent the last six weeks alternating between being annoyed that Cosette wasn't answering my messages fast enough and desperately missing her, but as I watched another message fail to send, I was no longer annoyed. Now I was impressed she'd managed to get any messages through at all.

My hand started to tighten around the phone and I heard the barely there groan of metal and glass. I let go. It wasn't the phone's fault it wasn't working. I wiped a bead of sweat off my face. It sure as shit was hot enough to be hell in here, but it didn't resemble what I'd seen in the chapel.

"It won't go through," a voice said behind me.

My wolf rose up. Fur rippling along my skin and I instantly shut down the change. I won the tug-of-war I played with my wolf, but it cost me precious calories.

Damn it. I hadn't heard him coming. The loud, smoky room was blocking my senses, and I hated that. But my wolf hated it more. I turned to watch the man move from behind me to sit at my right.

The man's skin was a dark tan. His beard was long and had a few strands of gray running through it. His long hair was pulled back away from his face. He was smaller than me, and if I didn't know he was fey, I might've assumed I could take him in a fight. But assuming something with supernaturals was stupid.

We sat quietly assessing each other. Staring him down wasn't the same as staring down another Were. I didn't feel the pressure of his power pushing at me, urging me to back down. But still, we were two predators figuring out a possible threat.

My cell buzzed in my hand. I didn't want to look away first, but something told me that this man would hold my gaze for days before he looked away. Being fey meant he was a host and since he was talking to me, a potential ally. So, I gave in and looked at my phone.

Another goddamned failed message. "Is there a network I'm not seeing?" I finally asked.

He tilted his head. "You could say that."

Cosette was usually more straightforward, at least with me, but I'd noticed how she talked in circles sometimes with everyone else. Usually that meant that there was something there, whoever was talking to her just wasn't asking the right question.

I had to change my approach. "What would *you* say?"

"I'd say that you are a stranger here, and we're not about to let you into our court and let you call in all your wolfy friends with a simple location finder."

Except I wasn't sure my friends could get here that fast. Not without help. "So this is specific to me."

"Yes."

"That's some trick." The way witches worked, to do something specific to me, yet covert, they'd have to take some of my hair or something personal from me. But I'd been purposefully ignored all evening, and no matter how much my senses were dulled by the environment, I was pretty sure I'd notice if someone had taken my hair.

"We have our own ways of doing things."

"I'm sure." Aside from Rayvien, this guy was the only one to engage with me since entering the Court of Gales' underhill. I wasn't sure what to make of him yet, but if he was talking to me, then there had to be a reason.

I held out my hand. "Christopher Matthews."

The man looked at my hand without taking it and grinned. "Ziriel."

I lowered my hand, not offended at all. "And what do you do here at court?"

"I rule it."

I opened my mouth to say something but nothing came. I wasn't sure why he was even talking to me, and yet I couldn't waste this conversation. I came for help, and he—whoever he was—might be the one that could give it to me.

"You think I'd put one of my fey next to you and risk their life? A werewolf I don't know, don't trust?" The grin on the man's face disappeared, his eyes went hot and dark, and as I kept my gaze locked on his, it was as if I was back in the chapel in Santa Fe. Back where the open pit to hell spewed demons into our realm. His gaze held the same heat and depth of that open pit.

I held my breath as I realized three things: I didn't know anything about the Court of Gales, the fey here seemed to be aligned with something dark and sinister, and if I wasn't extremely fucking careful, agreeing to come here would be the last mistake I'd ever make.

"I would say it's a pleasure to meet you, Christopher Matthews, but you're the reason we're in hiding and I haven't decided if I'll forgive you for it yet."

I pushed away the fear that was rising up before it could take hold of my thoughts. It wouldn't do me any good right now. I wasn't in Santa Fe, and as far as I knew, this underhill wasn't anywhere near hell. And even if I was out of my depth, Eli had sent me here for help. He wouldn't have done that if it would put me in imminent danger.

"You don't want to be in hiding?" It was my understanding that the majority of the fey actually asked for this. So, I was surprised to hear otherwise.

"No. No, we don't want to be." He leaned to the side a bit, placing his elbow on the table as he looked at me.

Okay. Maybe I understood what he wanted. "And you want *me* to do something about it." It wasn't a question because I was pretty damned sure of the answer.

His smile came back, bigger than before, and he twisted to the side. "See! Marsta!" Ziriel yelled across the room. "I told you he wasn't going to be as blond as he looked."

A woman sitting at the same table as Rayvien yelled something back at him and Ziriel laughed. A few others started yelling and a quick exchange of coins rippled through the room. Rayvien gave me a long look before turning back to the man whose lap she was still sitting on and whispered something in his ear.

I was too baffled by the exchange and whatever was happening with the coins to be insulted. "Thankfully, no, I'm not an idiot, but I don't think that I can do anything to help you."

The man leaned toward me. "I can smell Eli in your blood and feel Cosette Argent in your Were magic. If you don't help us, it won't be because you *can't*."

That creeped me out. I wasn't aware that either were true, even if both made sense. "You're giving me too much power. I might be connected to both, but I don't control Cosette and I sure as shit don't have any influence over Eli." That was the absolute truth. "The archon does what he wants."

"But Cosette is your mate?"

I didn't want to lie to him, but I wasn't sure what the truth was. The bond barely existed. Neither of us had said the words to cement it, so technically she wasn't my mate. Not yet. She was well within her rights to refuse the bond, but saying that she wasn't my mate would be very close to a lie. And lying to the King of the Court of Gales seemed like a very stupid thing to do.

"It's complicated."

"Fine. Keep your secrets, but convince Cosette's mother to stop this madness. We can't live like this much longer. The courts will implode."

It was funny that he thought I could change anything to do with the fey courts. "Honestly, I'm not sure I can help. I thought the fey majority ruled. Didn't you vote on this?"

"Only two of the courts *mostly* wanted to go into hiding—including Lunar. And even their court had some reservations about it, but what Helen wants, Helen gets. The Lunar, Solar, and Midnight Courts are among the strongest. The elemental courts…we're powerful, but not like *them*. Our power is made of a different breed." Ziriel gave me a small smile, as if he were goading me into guessing.

I didn't know what kind of power the Court of Gales had, but I knew that I was here because they could do what no one else could. "I can't help without going to the visit the Lunar Court, and I can't do that until I break my lunar tie. Can you do that?"

"Maybe. With the right incentive. You see, Gales like living in the mortal realm. We're made of smoke and wind." He motioned with his hand and he faded, turning to smoke for a split second before reforming. "Neither can flourish when confined."

He was trying to intimidate me, and if I were anyone else, that would've worked, but I'd been subject to a lot of power plays growing up. I'd learned that the best way to survive them was not to engage. No matter what I said to him, he wasn't going to be happy. I barely had control over my own life, so there was really no way I could help him overrule the fey.

After a long moment, he let out a frustrated huff. "Are you sure you want to get rid of your tie to the moon?"

It took my mind a second to process the abrupt subject change. "Yes."

"Eli and I had a nice chat. You see, the archons and my court are good friends. Both of us thrive in the gray area and enjoy collecting information."

"Can you get rid of my tie?"

"Yes, of course. I can do that for you, but I'll need something in exchange. Nothing comes without cost."

"I'm willing to bargain, but I can't guarantee to get your court out of hiding." I couldn't promise something that wasn't in my power.

"We'll see what you're willing to part with when given the correct incentive. And what kind of guarantee you're willing to give as a result."

I didn't like the sound of that. Not even a little bit. When the incentive was saving Cosette's life, I knew I would part with a lot. I had a feeling that we would've sat there staring at each other for a while, but something smacked into my face. I glanced at the floor to see a piece of bread, and then looked up to see Rayvien staring at me from across the room. Her gaze was colder than ice as she watched us.

What was her deal?

"Don't mind her. She's just angry."

"At what?"

"Me." He grinned. "She's my wife, and she was once friendly with Cosette. Although that has been strained for the last few decades."

I wanted to say something about how Rayvien was currently sitting on another man's lap, or that he'd said he didn't trust me with anyone yet he let Rayvien bring me inside and sit with me. Either she was extremely powerful or he didn't give a shit about his wife. Either way, it wasn't my business, but I was really hoping it was the former.

Ziriel snapped his fingers, and a platter of sour meat appeared on the table between us. When he bit into it, the scent grew stronger, and my stomach rolled.

"Rayvien! Come!" He yelled with his mouth still full.

The room grew quiet, and Rayvien slowly rose from her spot. She gave a not-too-gentle pat to the man's face and stalked over. Her gaze narrowed at Ziriel. "What is it?"

"Show our guest to his quarters."

An order? From her husband?

I really didn't understand them at all.

Ziriel stood from the table. "Rest and be welcome." He pulled a glittering coin from his pocket, throwing it high in the air.

The coin dropped down to hover in front of my face. I looked to Rayvien, but her face gave me no clue as to what the coin was or what would happen if I accepted it.

The room was still quiet, as if everyone inside was holding their breath. The small, dime-size coin emitted a high-pitched ring as it started spinning in front of my face.

I thought again about what Eli had said—what would I sacrifice for Cosette?

Everything. I would sacrifice everything for her.

I snatched the coin from the air.

"Good choice." Ziriel's smile sent a shiver through my soul.

And with that, Ziriel turned to smoke, disappearing from the room with a small breeze.

There was quiet for another couple seconds, and then

everyone in the room jumped to life. Trading coins. Even if I couldn't understand the fey words, I knew the yelling was trash talking. And a lot of pointing at me.

"Come," Rayvien said before starting toward one of the room's many exits.

She led me through a series of hallways. The glass floor seemed like it should've been slippery under my feet, but it wasn't. It made me wonder how much of this place was illusion and how much of it was real.

The coin felt cold in my hand when it should've warmed to my body temperature by now, reminding me that nothing from here on would be as I expected it to be. I wasn't sure if that was comforting to know or scary as fuck. Probably both.

As we moved away from the main room, a slow, steady breeze filled the underground passageways, pushing away the sweet smoke. But we'd been on a downward slope for our entire walk. My chest constricted more and more with every step we took, and even though the air started to smell of sage again, the soothing scented breeze couldn't dry the sweat beading on my forehead.

I hated being underground. My Alpha—my grandfather—used to lock me up in a deep, dark dirt pit. It was ten-feet square and seventy-five-feet deep and I'd scream for him to please let me out as he closed the trapdoor. But then, he'd order me quiet. Not even a kid could disobey their Alpha.

I used to sit in there—unable to utter a sound—and try to figure out what I had done to upset him. When my wolf finally matured, I realized that my grandfather's behavior had nothing to do with me. My pack was filled with bitten, broken, and rejected wolves. The Seven—who were supposed to protect and rule all the werewolves—should've killed all of them long before I'd been born.

It'd been a while since I was set free from my pack. A long time since they threw me, beaten and barely breathing, into the punishment pit for the last time. But no matter how many years passed since my pack was sent to hell or how far away I was from that seventy-five-foot hole in the earth, I still hated being underground. Hated the still air that strangled my lungs. Hated being held at the whims of something far more powerful than me.

Another bead of sweat ran down my face, but my hands were shaking too bad to swipe it away. I didn't even try. Every muscle in my body was tightened to the point of pain, and my heart felt hard and heavy as ring after ring of barbed-wire panic wrapped around it.

Fighting a cave filled with vampires and seeing the depths of hell open before me only intensified my hatred of being underground, but here I was, descending into the unknown depths one more time.

I had to tell myself that I was doing this for Cosette as we stopped in front of a stone door. Cosette was worth everything. My easygoing nature was a defense, and one that I'd use here. I worked on easing my tight muscles, telling myself that this was something that would pass, as all things did eventually. I just had to get through it.

Rayvien put her hand on the door and it turned into scentless smoke. "In."

The room was nice. A door inside was open to a bathroom. A mattress lay on the floor surrounded by colorful pillows. Books in various languages took up one wall. Even without a TV it was nicer than my room at home, but I was left with one big question. "How do I get out?"

I'd never seen a non-Were give me such a wolfy grin before, but that was what I was looking at.

Before I could say anything else, Rayvien shoved me

through the doorway. I hit the floor in the room and turned just in time to see the stone re-form.

My heart sped and my lungs tightened and the room seemed to get smaller and smaller and smaller until I stumbled back, falling onto the mattress behind me.

Trapped. I was trapped in a glorified cave with no way out.

CHAPTER SIX

COSETTE

I SHOWERED to scrub all of the blood from my skin. It took longer than I wanted, but the assassin's blood had trickled deep into my hair, behind my ears, and somehow—even though I didn't physically fight him—it was under my nails.

When I was satisfied that every speck was gone, I changed into something I could fight in—pants, boots, a pull-over that had plenty of room. I had weapons I could call in on command —including some given to me by my father. I didn't like using them. They made my heart race with power in a way that terrified me, but I had used them before. I would again if I needed them.

I hated that my life revolved around this. Around a battle of powers and assassination attempts. It's why I left court.

I checked my phone. No messages from Chris.

Damn it, Chris. Answer me.

I sent one more before I could stop myself. My feelings about Chris were bordering on obsession. I wasn't sure why I was so terrified. I didn't trust Eli, but he wouldn't have shown up to seal the spell if he was going to let Christopher die on some stupid mission of his.

But there was always a chance that something could go wrong. Even if I couldn't be there to help, I wanted to at least know what was going on. And yet I had my own drama to deal with.

I was questioning everything. Every interaction with any fey I'd had for the last three weeks. The murmured whispers behind my back that I'd brushed off. All the deals I'd cashed in —*years'* worth of favors—that got me nowhere. Had I been sealing my own fate? Was I still alive by dumb luck?

But no one had tried to kill me until today, and if anyone tried to poison me, then it hadn't worked. I think I would've noticed both, but clearly I hadn't noticed an assassin that was in my suite for days. *Days.*

Mother of God. My focus was terrible if I let someone in here for that long. If I knew then what I knew now and everything that it was going to cost me and how miserable I was going to be, maybe I wouldn't have agreed to spy on the coven—

No. That wasn't true. Even with everything, the end result was happy. I'd made true friends in Texas and didn't regret a moment I spent with them. They would never plot against me or use me, and they certainly didn't fault me for not being honest about what and who I was. Instead, they always seemed happy to see me and grateful for my help, even if my gut turned into a bottomless, bubbling pool of green envy when I saw how happy Dastien and Tessa were together.

I didn't want Dastien—he wasn't my type—but their love seemed so easy. No limits or bounds. They had a true partnership in less than two decades, when I'd dreamed of it for nearly two centuries and had nothing to show for it.

And with that horribly depressing thought, I left my bedroom and plopped onto the couch in my living room. The cleaning staff must've been here because there wasn't a speck of blood anywhere in the room, the chair had either been fixed or replaced with an identical one, and the air smelled like fresh roses.

But they'd left behind that awful binder. The cover gleamed a little, and I wondered if they'd cleaned it, too.

I wanted to burn the thing, but that wouldn't solve any of my problems, no matter how much I wanted it to.

I knew what I was: fey.

I knew what my station was: the youngest princess in the Lunar Court.

And I knew what my fate would be: someone who would never find love in marriage.

But I had to stop thinking that this marriage was the end of everything, because it wouldn't last forever. This was for right now. And when my future husband inevitably tried to kill me, I would kill him. And maybe after that I'd have enough power to free myself from the traditions of court and marry for love.

That was my new plan.

Ending the pity party, I flipped open the book and started reading. With each letter, I got angrier and angrier. I couldn't believe the things these men had written to me, and more than that—I couldn't believe these were the top picks. There had to be some sort of mistake.

But my mother couldn't lie and—

I startled when someone sat next to me. I stood, dropped the binder, and pulled a flaming sword from nowhere.

Van sat back slowly. "I didn't mean to scare you." One of his hands was out, but the other was on the hilt of his sword. I knew he'd pull his sword and let me go a few rounds with him if that's what I needed, but it wasn't.

I vanished the flaming sword in my hands—thanking it for coming when I needed it—and tried to slow my pounding heart.

"I've been..." I kicked the binder. "...reading that stupid thing. You just caught me by surprise."

Van looked like he was ready for a fight in his boots, loose pants, and fitted shirt. His hair was braided along the sides and tied back in a knot, instead of his usual low ponytail. I couldn't see any weapons, but I knew when he looked like that, he was lethal.

Van picked up the binder from where I'd kicked it, and I was glad I didn't have to read it anymore. It was Van's binder now, and I wasn't taking it back.

"Anyone good in here?" he asked as he sat on the couch and flipped it open.

"No! It's horrible. Absolutely horrible. Some of them are love letters, but they're from people who don't know me. It's... creepy." I sat on the couch again, slouching against the back. "The rest read like job applications. Which seems soulless. I'm supposed to marry someone who's a good fit for the job?"

"And what were you expecting?"

"I don't know. Chemistry. Attraction. Respect—"

"All of those things could come once you meet the men."

"Love?"

Van shrugged. "Maybe, given time."

I gave him a look that I hoped told him that I thought he was full of shit.

Van tapped a hand on the binder. "How about I choose some for you to look at?"

"Please." I would give anything not to have to make a decision. If there was anyone worthwhile in there, I trusted Van to find them. Maybe that would save me some of the pain.

After a moment, Van looked up. "Now this guy isn't all bad."

I leaned over him to read. "Which court?"

I caught Van's wince from the corner of my eye, and I knew I wasn't going to like which court this supposed match was from.

"Gales."

I reclined against the back of the couch and grabbed one of the pillows beside me, hugging it to my stomach. "You can't be serious. That's the best you've got? The last time I went there, I almost died. They hate me so much that I'm not sure they won't kill me on sight. And you know that they've bred with—"

"I know, but—"

"No!" It was evil what Gales had done. "I can't! What if I got pregnant?" I hit Van with the pillow.

He grabbed it from me. "If we do this right, you might only have to bed him a couple of times. Use protection and—"

I wasn't sure what look was on my face, but I felt appalled at the garbage that Van was spewing. Use protection? Use *protection?* There was no protection from what they were.

Van shook his head and handed me back my pillow. "You're right. We'll avoid Gales." He flipped a few more pages. "Although they could provide a unique advantage."

Oh, come on. He couldn't really be serious.

I stood, no longer able to sit still, and threw the pillow on the couch. "They eat rotted flesh—sometimes rotted *human* flesh—to gain their powers! It's evil, Van. *Evil.*"

He just looked up at me, waiting for me to calm down enough to state his case. I'd seen the look so many times over the years, but I really, really didn't want to hear it this time.

And that was me being a child. I was old. I couldn't afford to be childish about anything.

I paced to the wall to give myself time to calm down. I needed to think strategically, and to do that, I needed to let go of my own feelings about the Court of Gales. Van wouldn't have brought it up if it didn't make some sort of sense.

By the time I was in front of the couch again, I'd convinced myself to at least hear him out. "All right. What kind of advantage?"

"They're powerful. They have the ability to foresee things—"

I snorted. "Turning into smoke to eavesdrop in Heaven and Hell. Not from their own abilities." I crossed my arms and waited for him to give me something better than that.

"Cosette. Listen to me on this. You can't discount their knowledge, and because of their influences, they have bargains and chits with all kinds of fey and demons and angels and supernaturals, high and low. So many people go to them for their advice. They're the only ones that can tell the future so accurately. Your mother might like to discount them and call them flighty since they literally turn to smoke and disappear, but don't be so discriminating. Having a match in the Court of Gales could make a lot of sense."

My instinct was to say no, but that was going to be the same with everyone else. The court didn't really matter. He had a point, as much as I hated it. "But Gales skirts the lines of good."

Van put the binder on the table and stood in front of me. "Don't we all from time to time?"

"I don't know if I could live with myself if I had to bed a demon's cousin, let alone marry one." I pressed my hands against my eyes, as if I could unsee—unthink—all of this. "Oh, God! I can almost hear what you're thinking now. We're going to get into a moral debate over this, aren't we?"

"No, Cosette."

Van laughed and I dropped my hands so that I could see his face.

He pulled me in for a hug. "I wouldn't do that to you, but the more I think of it, the more I think Gales is where you should go. For the lying alone. That could come in handy while we solidify your power. They can do what we wouldn't be able to."

Damn it all. Van had a point.

"Put aside the morality for a moment. If matched with the right person in Gales, you could have access to any number of bargains. Think about how you could use their assets to your advantage. You could change the way of the fey just as you've always wanted."

I rested my forehead against his shoulder. "I want things to change, you know I do, but that feels dirty. I don't know that I'd be able to live with myself if we did it this way. Not after all the fighting and sacrificing we've done to keep the mortal realm safe."

"I know, but everything in this world comes with a price."

But was it one I wanted to pay?

Van pulled away from me, keeping a light grip on my shoulders until I looked up at him. His blue eyes were the kind of bright that only happened when he really believed he was fighting for the right thing.

"You don't have to marry one of them, but I suggest at least meeting the someone from Gales first. Their power might be dismissed by the rest of the fey, but it shouldn't be. Go in with an open mind, and let's see."

This sounded so hopeless. I wasn't sure I was going to like anyone at Gales. "And if I can't stomach marrying any of them?"

"Then don't!" He gave my shoulders a little shake. "We'll go to one of the other courts and find one you can stomach until it gets quieter here. And when that happens, I'll kill him for you."

I almost laughed, but the laughter died a quick death, even before the breath could begin to leave my body. I stepped away from him. "That's insane. You can't kill my future husband for me."

"If I'm remembering correctly, I killed for you not two hours ago in this very room, just as I have done many, many times before, and I've no regrets about it. I don't see how this would be any different." There was ice in his voice, the kind that used to scare me as a child, but now it made me thankful. Thankful that he cared so much for me. Thankful that even if I didn't have a father, I had him. But mostly, I was thankful that if I was forced to marry someone, I wouldn't have to kill him myself.

"I know, but this would be different."

He shrugged, and the cool exterior vanished. "Or *we* could get married." He sounded like he'd enjoy it as much as I would. Meaning not at all. "It would be a marriage in title only. We could make them believe we were together. We wouldn't lie, but we could go around the truth of it."

But we'd still have to cement the union at least once. "I..." I couldn't do that. Van was like a father to me. "I want what I can't have. Anything else sounds horrible to me. I'm not sure I trust myself to make a rational decision about any of this when my heart is on the line." It didn't matter if it was Gales or Leaves or Midnight. Anyone that wasn't Chris would finish breaking my heart.

"You have to let him go." Van's voice softened further. "Your Chris can't survive at court. His very nature won't allow it."

"I know." But every time I heard that, a little flake of my iced-over heart fell to the ground, lost forever. "We've done impossible things. We saved the world. Twice. We defeated Satan's second in command. Why can't I find a way to help Chris survive here? An amulet. A spell. Something that can save my heart from this."

Van sat again and leaned back against the couch. He rubbed a hand over his forehead as he thought quietly. "You know, you make a good point."

Hope, all fire and precious and bright, lit in my soul. "If I could find a way to give Chris enough power, then he could survive here. Right? So, what would I need to do to make that happen? Because I can do it. I have power and favors still owed to me. I haven't given all of them away over the last few weeks. Almost. But not *all*. Just— There has to be a way."

"I..." Van considered for a moment, and then put his elbows on his knees, back bowed as he thought some more. Eventually, he let out a breath.

I knelt in front of him, grabbing his hands. "You've thought of something?"

"Nothing that I think could really work. He'd have to somehow not be a werewolf. With that side of him, I just don't see how he could live here. Donovan couldn't and he's arguably the strongest wolf alive right now. Do you think Chris would give his wolf up for you? That he would let us kill the other half of his soul? If his wolf were gone, then maybe it would be possible."

I swallowed. All the hope burned to ash. "No. I don't know how I could even ask that of him. It wouldn't be fair, and he'd hate me for it. Resent me. Killing his wolf would be a wound that would never heal. It'd fester until it destroyed both of us."

"But he doesn't trust his wolf. That's what you told me."

"He doesn't trust it."

"Then maybe he wouldn't mind it as much as you think?"

"No. It'd be like chopping off one of his healthy, working limbs, just because he didn't like the scar on it. You saw where he came from. How we found him. In that pit? Of course he doesn't trust his wolf, but he will. I know he will. He's around a healthy pack now. Eventually, he'll have a healthy relationship with his wolf. I can't take that away from him. I'd never ask him to."

Van nodded slowly. "Then you have your answer."

Yes. I guess I did. "Court of Gales, then?"

I rose, and Van stood, too.

He grabbed the binder from the table. "I'm meeting with the guards in an hour. The court is abuzz with the dead body found outside your quarters."

I laughed at that, even if it was a hollow sound. "I bet they were."

"We'll find the traitors. I already have a few ideas about who they are among the twelve of them."

I did, too. "I think we're probably on the same page."

"Always. We can weed them out while at Gales. We'll take the usual seven—three loyal, four traitors—and we'll see who makes it back alive. Just like the good old times." He was trying to sound cheery, but it just came off as fake.

"If you say so, then I guess it must be true."

"It is, and I'll talk to your mother for you. Inform her of our destination and have her tell the king that we shall be there by the evening. Sound okay?"

No. It sounded awful. "I'll pack a few things."

"Best to make sure you can fight in everything."

Fight. Now that was something I could enjoy. "Is it insane that for the first time, I'm actually looking forward to more assassins?"

"If you're insane, then I'm right there with you." He pulled me in for another hug. "For the record, I hate all of this for you."

I leaned into his strength. "Me, too. But it doesn't change anything."

"I know." When he pulled back, there was a sadness in his eyes that took my breath away. "Believe me, I know. I'll make this as short-lived and bearable for you as I can."

"I'm so glad that you took me on all those years ago. You make this better. I don't tell you often enough."

"You don't have to say it because I feel the same. I would've faded into the beyond without you. And I will endeavor to keep making it better every day as much as I'm able." He stepped away from me. "I'll be back."

"I'll be ready."

When the door closed behind him, I gave myself exactly thirty seconds to wallow before packing.

Court of Gales? This was going to be a disaster. One that would end in bloodshed, but hopefully not too much of my own. Which should provide a hearty distraction from my heartbreak.

CHAPTER SEVEN

CHRIS

I BEAT ON THE DOORS, begging someone to let me out, for a good ten, twenty, who knew how many minutes before realizing that no one was coming and I was making myself look like an idiot. So I paced. Even though my legs were tired from walking the dunes all day, I paced back and forth across the room, around the bed, into the bathroom and then circled back around. I kept moving until I wasn't sure I could walk anymore. And then I did push-ups until my arms shook and my face hit the floor. I had to make myself tired enough that I could sit still, and I wouldn't stop until I crashed.

Being a werewolf meant that it took a while to find the end of my strength, but I finally found the end after countless burpees. I was officially tired. The kind of tired that made my muscles throb and ache and would only be cured by a big juicy steak and sleep. But apparently the steak wasn't going to happen. Not here. And sleeping in the glorified cave/prison cell was proving to be harder than I'd thought even given the exhaustion.

I rolled onto my stomach and pushed my head under the

pillows, hoping to block out the feeling that I was trapped, but my wolf was quietly, insistently urging me to run, run, run. Fight, fight, fight. But there was nowhere to run. Nothing to fight. What I needed was sleep.

Sleep.

The wolf growled at me, and I could feel him rising up.

Shut up.

I rolled onto my back and kicked off the covers. The mattress was soft, the sheets were made from fine-spun silk, the pillows cradled my head, but my wolf and I were in agreement about one thing: We'd rather sleep among the dunes.

I wouldn't even complain about the sand whipping into my face all night long. At least there I would've been able to see the stars and moon. Hear something other than my own too-quick heartbeat slamming in my ears. And I wouldn't feel like the walls were closing in on me until my body felt wound tight, tight, so tight that the hot, heavy air threatened to suffocate me.

I closed my eyes, trying to feel for any breeze, but the room was tomb still. My wolf wanted me to shift. Wanted to beat down the door. Wanted to find Cosette. But this room was made of fey magic, and no amount of brute strength would get me out of here. And I wouldn't give my wolf control. Not here. Not now.

But we'd spent too many nights locked underground. Too many nights held captive. Until the last time almost killed us.

Being here brought too many long-buried feelings to the surface. So many that I felt like I was hanging from a cliff while trying to keep my wolf from going feral. Both of us were struggling to separate this room from the pit in the ground, and I wasn't sure how much longer I could hold on.

My fingers lengthened as I fought his panicked demand to slam into the door until either it broke or I did. But I never, ever gave him control, and I wasn't about to start today.

I rolled again, this time into a ball with my forehead pressed against the mattress. This had to stop. I needed to sleep. But there was no one to joke with here. No one to flirt with. The room had books, but no blank paper. No pencils. No charcoal. No dirt to draw in.

But there was one thing I did have.

I closed my eyes and pictured Cosette. The way the light glittered just a little around her. The sweetness of her moonlit scent. The softness of her dark-blonde curls.

This wasn't like all the other times I'd been locked up. This was different. This was for Cosette. If I focused on it—if I focused on *her*—then everything else wouldn't matter. Because it was *different*.

I wanted to save Cosette, and if being trapped under the earth one more time was all it took to help her, then I was getting off easy.

My mind started to focus on memories. The tinkling sound of her laughter. The way we saw through each other's facade like it was made of mist. The way I could lie next to her, drawing for hours under the sunlight in the woods while she read a book, and feel totally at peace...

Slowly my body started to relax—muscle by muscle—until the tide of dreams rose high enough, sucking me down into a past I never wanted to relive.

I was trapped. Trapped again. I'd betrayed my pack and was being punished, but if I saved even one life, then it would be worth it.

Please, God. Let it be worth it. Or don't let me live to see what comes next.

I hadn't been able to send word to another Alpha—I had orders I couldn't break—but my grandfather—my Alpha—hadn't said anything about letting another supernatural know. I'd tracked down a pixie and made an impossible bargain with him.

I would give him one favor—one IOU—and he would bring someone powerful enough to kill my entire pack. But would the fey come in time to save the innocents in town?

I didn't know. God, please. Let the favor be worth it. Someone had to come...

Stupid. This was so stupid. I slammed my arm into the wall beside me. It didn't hurt anymore, but it'd healed crooked. If the pack ever let me out of here, they'd have to break it again. Which was probably the point. They enjoyed breaking me.

I'd been sitting here for two days, but there was nothing else for me to do but wait. I leaned my head back against the dirt wall, wishing I'd left. I mean, I really should've left, but my mother was weak. Leaving her with the pack would've broken something in me, but staying here, sitting in my own shit for days, and having only my mother's betrayal for company? That had broken me more than the beating did. More than the boiling black oil they'd poured down my throat for telling their secrets.

Even though she hated my father as much as I did, she ran straight to him and told him exactly what I'd done. Fucking mates. They were dysfunctional. It was completely and totally insane to let yourself be tied with a mate bond.

My wolf growled his agreement.

Two days ago, when I felt myself falling, falling, falling seventy-five feet into the pit, all I wanted was to finally have some peace. I was ready to die.

But I didn't die. I was in the ground, but not dead. My wolf was pacing inside me, itching to get out, but changing with my arm like this would be painful and only make the injury harder to fix. Not that I could shift when I didn't even have the strength to stand.

Sometimes sunlight filtered through the grating above me. Sometimes it was moonlight. But I couldn't see the sky. Never the sky. Couldn't see through the grate. Couldn't reach it. And there was no way for me to get out of here.

This wasn't my first trip to the pit, and yet I'd still tried to get out. I tried every time. I had to make sure because maybe this time would be different, but it wasn't ever different.

The faraway ceiling was a ten-by-ten slab of concrete with a grated trapdoor dead center. It was too far for me to reach and too hard for me to punch through if I did reach it. The walls were made of packed dirt. The bottom was a mess of mud and other things I didn't want to think about.

The sour and musty smell of decay was starting to grow, and I was pretty sure it was coming from inside my throat. From the oil they'd poured down it. My bones had healed, yet my throat still felt raw. I tried to swallow, but the little bit of saliva I had felt like shards of glass going down.

So, tonight, right now, I realized that I was finally getting close to my wish coming true. I was going to die. Soon. In this pit.

The only thing that was keeping my sanity was knowing I'd done my best to get help, and that this would all be over soon.

But for now, I was alive. More than hunger or the pain in my throat, it was the thirst that was getting to me. I'd given up on yelling for someone to come help me. My voice didn't even sound like my own. Not anymore. It was so raspy and hoarse and so impossibly foreign that sometimes, when I talked through my fears in the dark, I could almost convince myself that this wasn't me. That I wasn't here. That this was a nightmare that I was seeing through someone else's eyes.

But tonight that was done. This was me. And I was thirsty. So fucking thirsty. All I wanted was some ice-cold water. Or some ice. My throat... My mouth was drier than the desert after a century-long drought, and if there were a devil here, I would sell my soul for a thimbleful of water. But I was alone. Alone with only the scent of blood and sweat and shit filling the tiny room. I wished that my sense of smell was gone, but it hadn't dulled. I wanted—

My thoughts quieted as the earth throbbed. Then again. And again.

Footsteps vibrating down to me.

Someone was coming.

And then someone opened the trapdoor. Pure, unfiltered moonlight hit me and I blinked quickly before protecting my face.

I waited for grandfather or one of his bitten, broken, reject wolves to yell at me. Taunt me. Throw something sharp down to me so that I could hurry up and end it.

"Are you alive down there?" The voice was soft and melodic and filled me with the first sliver of hope I'd had in years.

Air. Clean air breezed through the open trap door. I breathed in deep, not even caring about the smell around me. When I pushed past all those scents I could smell moonlight on the grass, jasmine, dew, and something sweet and fair. Like sugary moonlight.

Sugary moonlight?

The fey. It was a fey that opened the door. They were here.

I was too scared to say anything. I didn't know what kind of fey had come, but I had hope... Hope of salvation. They'd either help me or kill me, and either was fine. As long as something changed.

I tried to speak but nothing came out. I tried to stand, to get even a little closer to the top to see who it was, but my legs were shaking and I fell back to the ground.

I couldn't make out the face. Just the shape of a head blocking out the moonlight. My vision must've been blurry because I could've sworn the moonlight almost wrapped around whoever was up there.

"Can you speak?" Female. A female fey had come to hunt

my pack? We were almost all bitten Weres. A few had mates, like my father, or were born Were like me, but the rest... Men. Insane, feral, deadly werewolves who loved the taste of warm blood.

I hoped she hadn't come alone.

"Van! Come quick."

Not alone, then. That was good.

Within a second, a man stood in front of me. Fey—because he didn't drop down from the trap door. He just appeared.

The fey man was tall and looked strong. His hair was long and whiter than starlight. "You're the one who called?"

I tried to swallow a bit, but the pain... "Yes." My word was more croak than anything else, and I dropped my gaze to the floor.

Other than the pixie, I'd never met any fey. I wasn't sure if they played the same dominance games that we did, but pissing him off now would be stupid. And yet I had to ask. "Wa-ter?"

He pulled a bottle from nowhere and handed it to me. The water was cold and felt like salvation. I drank in little sips, savoring the feel of each drop as it rolled down my tortured throat.

"Most of your pack is gone." He paused. "We're waiting for them to come back, but now that I see you, maybe I should hunt them."

He definitely needed to hunt them. "Kill. People." I fought for each word. "Eat them. You kill them. Before..." I realized a second too late that I ordered him to do something. I bowed my head. "I-I'm—"

"Don't. I was getting bored at court. Seems like a good night for a deadly game of chase. What did they do to your voice?"

"Burn. Oil."

He crouched beside me, careful not to touch too much of anything on the ground. "Open."

I opened my mouth wide and tried not to flinch at the wince on Van's face.

"Not oil. Vampire blood. It was boiling?"

I nodded. I wanted to cry at how stupid I was. Of course it was a supernatural hurt. That was why it was going to kill me.

"They're giving you a slow, painful death. Vampire blood doesn't act as quickly as the venom in their saliva, but just as bad." He touched my throat for a second, glowing brighter, and his magic felt like moonlight on a warm night. For a moment, the pain in my throat lessened, and then he stood.

"I'll need help to heal this, but that should ease the pain temporarily."

I nodded. It didn't hurt quite as much, but still hurt pretty fucking bad.

He stood, but before he could leave, I knelt, hoping he'd take mercy on me. "Don't leave me. Don't leave me down here. I—" My voice cracked and it wasn't just the sound of my voice, but my soul. It was cracked—broken—and I wasn't sure who I was anymore. But it didn't matter as long as I wasn't in the pit anymore.

He grabbed my hand and the world spun. If I'd eaten anything, I probably would've lost it then, but there were so many sounds that I didn't care that my stomach was rolling. I managed to keep the little bit of water down because the air was so shockingly clean and pure. And there were so many stars.

I started to cry and fell hard. My face slammed into the ground and I didn't care because I wasn't in the pit anymore. My tears fell into the grass and dirt, making their scent richer. I wasn't sure why I was crying exactly because there were too many reasons and feelings to be able to put them into words, but the strongest one of all was freedom. After all these years, I was really and truly free.

My grandfather had cut all my pack ties before he beat me.

He hadn't wanted me to be able to draw strength from them while I died in the pit. He wanted me dead as much as I wanted it. But I hadn't died. These two fey had saved me.

Which meant I was free. For the first time since I was born, I didn't have ties to my twisted, evil pack.

I was truly free.

"Van." The girl's voice said again. "Help him. He's crying in pain."

"That's not about pain, Coco."

"I know, but some of it is. Heal him."

"You know I can't heal what's really hurting him, just as I am unable to heal what has broken you."

It was that sentence that stopped my tears. I rolled my head to the side to see the most beautiful person in the world. She stood there with a flaming sword in her hand, covered head to toe in black leather, with boots that laced up to her knees. The woman looked like an avenging angel, here to collect the evil souls and ready for the fight. Her blonde hair had to be incredibly long and thick for all the braids and twists that covered her head, and I wanted to take out all the pins to see if it was as silky as it looked. But it was her soft skin that really had me in awe. It was glowing like moonlight, and I felt drawn to her. If she asked me for something, I wasn't sure I'd ever be able to say no.

She was fierce and frightening, but as she stared down at me, I saw something fragile in her, too.

"He'll be fine until we can get him to a better healer, but the innocents in town won't survive," the man she called Van said. "The stupid pixie said nothing about an injured wolf or innocents. We have to hurry. That's where your pack went? To the town?"

I nodded. "They've been coming and going. Sometimes I hear them. Hear screaming. But they're not here right now."

"You go. I'll stay with him," she said.

Van gave her a silent nod, and then was gone.

"Does it hurt?"

"I don't care about the arm." My voice was so garbled with my raw throat that I could barely make out the words, but somehow she must've understood me. "It's my throat that's infected. They poured boiling vampire blood down it."

The sword disappeared as she knelt beside me. "Van's a healer, but he's right. You'll need someone better, and the innocent humans come first. You're lucky it wasn't venom."

"I'm not sure I'd call myself lucky."

She pressed her lips tight, like she was stopping herself from saying something, before she spoke again. "Do you need anything else?"

Food, but if the healer wanted to straighten my arm, they were going to have to rebreak it. I didn't want to eat only to throw it up. But the thirst was something that could be fixed. "Water?"

"You need to sit up a little to drink."

I tried to sit, but couldn't. She took pity on me and sat beside me, brushing her hand across my forehead before gently lowering my head and upper body onto her lap. The water was just as cold as before, and felt like sweet relief on my throat.

Oh, God. I was so tired that I wasn't sure if the arm was worth the effort. I wasn't sure I was worth the effort. "I'm sorry."

"Why are you sorry?"

"I stink and I'm getting you dirty and—"

"And you're alive. That's the only thing that matters." She drew a breath and let it out slowly, as if she were preparing me for a blow that was about to come. "I've witnessed a lot of evil in the more than one hundred and fifty years that I've been alive, and too many people victimized by that evil. You'll be upset for a while, and that's understandable. But soon, very soon you'll have to decide what you want the rest of your days to look like. You'll wither as if you never left that pit. The abuse you've suffered will weigh on your soul until it kills you." She paused. "Or you'll learn to let go of the past—all the abuse, all the time in the pit, all the horrors you've seen—and truly be free of it."

I wanted that. The truly free part.

"From here on out, no one has control over how you feel but you. No one has control over what you do but you. No one can hurt you but you. I hope you learn to see the beauty in life and find some peace. Because calling us here? That was brave. If you don't remember much from this day or tomorrow—because you will be in a fog for a few days—I want you to remember this one thing. Live. Let the desire to live burn like a fire in your gut until you can do nothing else but thrive."

"Is that what worked for you?"

"Yes and no." She smiled, and it radiated the beauty of her soul. I knew in that moment that I would draw her face—that smile—every day for the rest of my life.

She was salvation. She was my—

There was a crash in the room.

I woke up with my wolf screaming for me to let him out. To find the enemy that had entered my room. To fight the pack that came back to the land in the next second. I wanted to relive that moment when I first got to see Cosette fight. I'd been worried at first—I hadn't been in any shape to help her and Van was still gone—but she'd been so fierce and beautiful and deadly. That was when she officially started to own my soul. My wolf wanted me to attack the enemy that had woken me up. Kill. Kill. Kill him for interrupting my little bit of peace.

But my wolf was going to get me into trouble. I kept my eyes closed for a second, huddled under the covers, holding onto the feeling of seeing Cosette smile for the first time, savoring it so that the feeling would get me through whatever came next...

I wasn't sure if it was being confined that brought up that particular memory or if it was because that was the first time I met Cosette—when she saved me—but I didn't care. I was alive because of her. I thrived because of her. And now, I would do whatever it took to help her.

Time to get to work.

I rolled to sit, resting my legs over the edge of the low mattress. "Hello?" My rasp was always worse in the morning, and worse still with the wolf close.

"Oh. You're awake." The squeaky voice came from a few feet in front of me, but I couldn't see anything there. "Time to get up! Time to get out!"

I was very, very relieved to hear that, but I had questions. "I can't see you."

"Oh!" In a flash of smoke, a creature appeared. Two feet tall and nearly just as wide in the middle. It wore what might have been a skirt wrapped around its waist, and dragged on the floor, hiding its feet from view. Its head was bald and its teeth were pointed out over its bottom lip, but it was the eyes that had me standing. Red, glowing demon eyes.

I'd seen those eyes before, but I had to know for certain. "What are you?"

"Ooh!" It clapped its hands, the fingers—too long and slender for its body—ended in sharp points. "A game! A game! You have three guesses. If you don't guess right, I get a bite! A bite!"

A bite? With the pointy teeth, I didn't doubt it was meant literally. But I only needed one answer. "Are you a demon?"

The thing doubled over in what I thought must've been laughter, but sounded more like a rustling, rasping hiss. "Demon? Do I look like one? Oh, that's so funny! Ziriel will get such a kick out of that." And the thing disappeared in a puff of smoke.

I was left standing there with my mouth open but hadn't missed the fact that it hadn't said it wasn't a demon.

Goddammit. What kind of fey court was this if it allowed demons inside?

The thing popped back in, still laughing. "Ziriel found it so, so funny-funny!"

Perfect. I was clearly making a great impression on the king. "But are you a demon?"

"Oh, well. Not exactly a demon. Not exactly not a demon either. It depends on who you ask, but you haven't found what I am by name. Not yet. That's one guess wrong! Two more! Only two more! Then I *get my bite*." Its voice grew deeper at the end, and everything in me screamed to kick-stomp-kill the creature, but that wasn't my way. There could be something good inside this being, even if I wasn't sure what that was.

"Guess more! Guess more! Need my bite! Haven't had werewolf in so long!"

"How big of a bite?" Because now I wanted to know what I was dealing with more than I did five minutes ago. That answer of not-exactly-demon, not-exactly-not-demon was bullshit.

"Oh, I'm just a little thing. You wouldn't think I'd take too much, would you? And you're a powerful wolf. You would heal."

Supernatural hurts healed human-fast for us, and his look-at-me, I'm-so-little routine didn't convince me at all. The fey could be tricky with their size. I bet this little one could will himself bigger than the room if he wanted. One bite could swallow me whole.

I'd heal? What a crock of shit.

"What are you doing in my room?"

"Time for a bath for you. It's all ready."

"I thought you said it was time to go."

"Yes! Yes! It *is* time to go, but first a bath."

"Okay." I wanted a bath, so fighting him on that seemed like a waste of energy.

"And then Ziriel wants to see you. King has plans." The little thing rubbed his hands together, pointy nails click-clacking as they moved.

"Great." Plans. Maybe now I'd get to talk to him about what he wanted to trade for more power. The sooner I figured that out, the sooner I could find Cosette and help her.

CHAPTER EIGHT

COSETTE

FAVORITE KNIFE?

Check.

Favorite sword?

Check.

Leather pants? Spare boots? Make-up? Short shift dress, suitable for fighting or dancing?

Check. Check. Check. Check.

Everything else magical I could call in with a thought—like my father's weapons—which meant my packing was done. I closed my duffle with a zip and sat for a second on the bed. I started to give myself one minute to wallow in my own misery but was interrupted by a soft double knock on the door.

Van peeked in, took one look at me, and stepped inside, shutting the door behind him with a click.

He closed the distance between us in three quick strides. "You're having second thoughts?" He placed his hands on my knees as he squatted in front of me.

I glanced down at him, hoping to use some of his constant, steady strength to silence all the doubts in my mind, but it didn't work. Not like it usually did. "When am I ever not having second thoughts?"

"This is the smart move."

I gave his hands a squeeze. "But is it the right one?" I wanted to say that something about how wrong this felt, but it was more than that. Everything about finding a husband like this was going to feel terrible.

He stood and stepped back from me. "Coco—"

"Oh, stop. You only call me that when you think I need babying." I didn't need babying. Not now. I didn't know what I needed, but it wasn't that.

He crossed his arms as he glanced down at me. The look on his face was enough to tell me that he didn't agree. "So you're fine then?"

I couldn't say that without lying—we both knew it—so I needed to change the subject. "The guards you picked are ready?"

"Yeeeeeesss." He drew the word out for a while, as if deciding whether or not he was going to accept my change of subject. "Want me to tell you who's coming with us?"

At least we'd dropped the whole am-I-okay thing, but I didn't love this subject either. "Not particularly. I'd rather bring none, but since you won't reconsider it?"

"Not on your life."

"Then save your words. I'll find out soon enough." I stood and grabbed my bag.

"No. I'll go get them. When you hear us come into your living room, make them wait before coming out."

I laughed as I sat on the bed again. "Always making me out to play the princess."

"Because you are one, even if you like to pretend you're not. It always does them good to remember who and what you are.

It's been a long time since you really showed yourself at court. A long time since you've needed the guards."

And now we were on another topic we didn't agree on. "Who cares if having twelve on hand is what's expected of a princess. I told you to let them go when I moved to Colorado."

Van crossed his arms as he glared at me. "And I told you we might need them again."

I stopped just short of rolling my eyes at him. I didn't need the guards. Not even a little bit. "If some stupid assassin kills me, then that means I was lazy and I deserve to die."

"Don't say that again." His words were deep, cold, stabbing, and they made me feel like the worst kind of person.

I took a moment to breathe, letting my frustrations go. I hadn't meant to upset him. "I apologize. I—"

He vanished from one second to the next, without letting me finish my apology.

"Damn it." There was no point in pissing off Van. He was sometimes my best friend, sometimes my stand-in father, and all-the-time a pain in my ass, but I loved him. I was taking out my own situation on him, and he didn't deserve that. Not even a little bit.

My attitude needed an adjustment.

I unzipped my bag, pulled out one of my small daggers, and went to my dresser. There was one more thing I needed to take with me.

The entry door to my suite slammed, and I knew that Van and the guards were in my living room now, but I had plenty of time since Van wanted me to make them wait.

In the top molding of the dresser was a hidden drawer. Very, very gently, I stuck the tip of the blade in and wiggled. After a second, the drawer opened just enough for me to stick my finger in and tug. Most fey would hide things with magic. They were arrogant and their arrogance made them stupid. They tested for hidden pockets of magic, and when nothing turned up, they left. No one thought to actually take the time to search a room. Hiding something physically from sight was much more effective than hiding it magically.

When the tiny drawer was open, I pulled out the chain. Dangling from the tiny chain was a locket. The locket was a tiny round moon made of opal. The hinge was hidden by the loop that attached the chain, and even more disguised by the glittering, diamond star charms that hung around and dangled at different lengths on either side of the locket. At a causal glance, it looked like a fitting accessory for a princess in the Lunar Court, but then...

I slid my fingernail in the hidden crack along the bottom of the moon and it popped open.

Chris.

I rubbed my thumb over the image. His face was slightly tilted away from my phone when I took the picture. Great beams of light cut through the trees behind him, as if God himself was gracing us with the most perfect light. Chris was smiling the way he only did when he was drawing. We'd spent the day together in the woods. I read a book while Chris drew for hours. The soft scratch of his charcoal against the page blended with the quiet chirping of the birds. It was the best day I'd had in over a century, and I knew enough to cherish it.

He didn't know I took the picture or that I printed it or that I stuck it in a locket that I kept hidden from everyone. I was too scared of what it meant to wear it, and maybe it was crazy to pull it out now. But if I was surrendering my life to this court, my body to a husband, at least I could keep Chris close to my heart in this one tiny way.

I gently snapped the locket shut and held it in my hand for a second. I could do this. I would do this.

I fastened the chain behind my neck and tucked the locket under my shirt.

There. I was keeping him—and myself—safe by finding a fey husband, but that didn't mean I had to love Chris any less.

I shut the secret drawer, making sure the molding lined up perfectly, hiding it from view, and quickly grabbed my bag. I stowed the blade inside and strode to the door, but paused for a moment with my hand on the doorknob. Beyond it was my living room where a team of my guards were waiting for me to take the next big step.

I was doing this. Making this big change. And when I left my room, my life as I knew it was going to be over.

I didn't want to go to Gales. I didn't want to be with my guards who were possibly traitors. I didn't want any part of any of this. But I'd learned that sometimes life was doing things you didn't want to do. I just wished I didn't have to do them so often.

I pulled the locket out and gripped it in my hand. *I hope you're okay, Chris. I'm so sorry I couldn't do more to help you, wherever you are.*

I let the locket drop back under my shirt and threw open the door. In the second it took for the door to crash into the wall, my facade was in place. Confident. Proud. Sassy. Takes no shit. Loves to shop and read magazines. Cares for no one but myself.

I stepped into the seating room. "Hello, my ever-loyal guards." They were standing around, chatting, in their full battle gear—leather head to toe, swords hanging at their hips, other weapons strapped here and there. "Everyone seems dressed for a fun day at the park."

"Ready?" Van asked. Any sign that I'd pissed him off was gone—hidden, forgotten, or buried, I wasn't sure. But it was gone, and I was grateful for it.

"I'm ready for battles, blood, or dancing. If we have any

luck, we'll get all three and find me a suitable husband." I gave Van my best I-can't-wait smile and threw him my bag.

He vanished it mid-air with a wave of his fingers, and we turned as one to give our full attention to the guards.

I knew that Van had selected three that he was pretty certain were loyal, and four that he was reasonably sure were not. I'd rather just take the pretty-certain-loyal ones, especially since Gales was our first stop and I already had enough enemies there, but Van wanted to weed out who was against us as quickly as possible. He'd call in other guards as we killed off the traitors.

And if we found the replacements to be traitors? Well, we'd kill them, too.

It all seemed a bit bloody to me—especially when some of these men had been guarding me for nearly two centuries—but Van wasn't concerned. Which meant I shouldn't be concerned. Which meant that I could focus solely on finding a husband.

Maybe Van could just kill me too while he was at it?

A throat cleared to my right.

"Yes, Bronio?" I asked.

For someone of the Lunar Court, Bronio was annoyingly typical. His straight black hair just nearly brushed his shoulders. His skin was the color of warm moonlight, giving off a hint of a glow in the dark. His eyes were dark as the night sky. And his heart was darker still.

In the past, he'd been an asset, enjoying hunting down assassins before they could find their way to me, but now that I really looked at him, I was pretty sure Van had labeled him a possible traitor. He would've been one of my guesses, too. I wondered if I should've set him free years ago. He was a little too bloodthirsty, even for us. And that was saying something.

"If this trip to Gales is anything like it was last time, then I think we're all ready to get on with it." His hand rested on his sword, his fingertips absently tapping the hilt as he spoke. Like he was just itching to pull it free. "The rumors after that were legendary."

"It's been a long time. If you're still upset about missing out, you should get over it," I said it with false sweetness and gave him a saucy tilt of the head, when I really wanted to smash his face into the ground until he was covered in blood. Then he could really get a feel for how fun my legendary trip was.

Missing out? What a joke.

Bronio's grin was cold and dead, and if I had any doubts about where his loyalties were before, they were gone now. "No matter. I've always had a certain fondness for Gales."

Gurhan snorted. "That's because there's plenty to kill in Gales."

He also was my pick for a traitor, since he was all buddy-buddy with Bronio.

"I didn't realize you were all so bored. Maybe I should've brought you to the chapel in New Mexico with me," I said.

"Of course you should've. No reason Van should get all the fun," Bronio said.

Fun? He really thought that had been fun?

"We can't do our job if we're not with you," Wilken said with such soft seriousness in his voice that I almost laughed. He was even leaning forward, slightly bowed, as if asking for forgiveness. His golden blond hair fell into his face, hiding his dark brown eyes.

"It's a wonder I can't smell the shit from here with how thick you're laying it on." Van's tone was as sharp as his blade. "Please, tell me how you'd rather have been in the chapel swarming with demons, open gate to Hell, instead of here, eating your fill, drinking your weight in wine, and sleeping with anything that would bed you?"

I nearly choked trying to stop the laugh that was rising up. I wanted to cheer on Van for his brutal assessment of Wilken. The man was my brother Tiarnan's best friend. The same brother who'd sent the assassin Van killed in this room today.

I'd been surprised when Wilken asked to leave Tiarnan's guard to join my own, but after three weeks of interrogation and investigation, Van decided Wilken would be an asset to my guard. But now Tiarnan's assassin somehow got into my personal rooms?

Wilken was quiet. He couldn't lie, so he was stuck. But he was probably another traitor.

"Right," I said. "Anyone else have a grievance they'd like to air?"

The rest of them were quiet. Nex, Taslin, Cyros. All with black hair, tied back in a long, low ponytail. Each with crystal blue eyes. I'd thought they were triplets growing up, especially since they were always together, but they weren't. They weren't as old as Van, but close. Pretty damned close. And I was pretty certain they were loyal. Out of any of my guards—aside from Van—I'd spent the most holidays with them.

Which left Pratis. He was quiet—not just now, but always—and even if Van thought he was a suspect, I wasn't sure. He had white hair and even whiter skin, but he somehow always managed to fade into the shadows. I'd known the man for over a hundred years, and I still felt like I knew nothing about him. And yet, I trusted him.

But Van said he was bringing four traitors and three loyals with us. If Nex, Taslin, and Cyros were Van's choice for loyal guards, then that meant that he didn't trust Pratis. Which said a lot to me.

The men had all gotten very still. They knew they were being tested, but none of us would acknowledge it. That was part of the fey game. As a princess of the Lunar Court, if I couldn't survive my own corrupt guards, then I wasn't worthy of living.

I hated court for so many reasons, but I really truly hated the way that it had turned my guards—who I'd treated as family for so long—into possible enemies for no good reason.

"What did my mother say?" I asked Van. I didn't want anything too personal said in front of guards we didn't trust, but if we didn't discuss what we were doing, then they'd get suspicious.

"She said not to come back until you've found your match."

Huh. That was giving me a little too much freedom. With that single sentence, I could leave the courts entirely for years—centuries—and as long as I didn't marry anyone, I didn't have to come back.

No. That was way too good. There had to be a catch. "Did she say anything else?"

"You officially have a fortnight before she'll pick someone for you." Van's apology flickered across his face before his cold facade snapped back into place.

Damn it. This was worse than I'd thought. So much worse.

I knew deep down that my mother loved me, but she'd pick someone who was a powerful, smart match. Whether or not I could stomach sleeping with him wouldn't even cross her mind.

Power. She'd want someone with power and she must already have someone in mind. But who did she—

"Oh, God. Again?" I met Van's gaze. "She'll make me marry you. She won't care that we—" I snapped my mouth shut before I said too much.

"Yes. She didn't say it, but it was implied. Thoroughly. So let's go and be decisive. You don't like a man, you say so. We move on to the next. Immediately."

I swallowed down any fear or hesitation. I couldn't trust

these guards with my true feelings, and I'd already said too much. "Then I guess we'd better go."

Pratis and Wilken stepped out of the room in front of me, then me and Van, with the rest following after. Their footsteps were silent on the floor, barely noticeable if not for the way the floor lit with every step. The magical floors helped the court guards to keep track of who was walking around in our under-hill. For some it looked like the night sky or a shooting star following their path or a planet depending on station, court, and status. It was a beautiful bit of spellwork. I watched the floor under my feet brighten with a crescent moon surrounded by stars as we moved through the hallways, and with every step, I wanted to tell Van to take me away from this path.

It should've only been a five-minute walk to the gateway room, but the halls of the Lunar Court were always filled with fey wanting some sort of acknowledgment. They moved around our group—maids and guards stopping along the walls to bow as I passed—and I gave them a nod. I hated the bowing, but it was part of life here. One of my guards intervened when any nobles we passed motioned for me to wait or gossip, with a polite, "She's needed at another court presently," and a small bow.

Even though we kept the exchanges quick, the short walk seemed to stretch on endlessly. I wished Van could just grab my hand and pop us into Gales. That we could be there already and get on with it, but that wasn't allowed. Van could move in and out of our court whenever, wherever, however he wanted, but using his abilities to get into another court was different.

If Van popped into any other court or traveled within one that wasn't ours, they would see it as an attack. And while starting a war would be a wonderful distraction from husband-hunting, it would also be a terrible pain. So, we would enter Gales using the proper gateway protocol. Boring but safe.

The gateways served as the official entrance for those

visiting another court's underhill. They were in a specific, guarded location that could be blocked—magically and physically—if a court was being attacked. Usually, I preferred to travel through the mortal realm to get from court to court. It gave me a break from all the political plotting and a chance to catch my breath, but using them today meant that going from our court in Ireland to Gales in the North African desert would take no time at all. Since I only had a fortnight—fourteen miserable days—to find someone to marry, today I would force myself to use them.

Van walked beside me, his hand on the hilt of his sword. I thought about calling in some weapons but dismissed it. If we passed someone in the hall and I had a weapon out, it would send a message that my guards weren't trustworthy and that I was vulnerable to attack.

Everything I did, everything I said was scrutinized. It was one of the many reasons I hated living here.

I glanced down the corridor that we were passing and stopped.

Tiarnan.

I assumed he was waiting for me. The guards must have told him we were walking the halls. But why he was there, I didn't know.

Of all my siblings, Tiarnan looked the most like me. Same dark-blond curly hair. Same brown eyes. Same small nose—although his was a tiny bit bigger than mine which suited his more masculine face. But despite our similar looks, we'd never gotten along.

He didn't approach and I didn't either.

Finally, after a long moment, he bowed his head ever so slightly.

I gave him a little finger wave. I'd won the first round, but there would be others.

Van nudged my shoulder with his to get me moving.

"If he comes after me again, I'm going to have to do something about it," I whispered quietly to Van.

"Unfortunately, yes."

"Doesn't he know that he'll lose?"

Bronio's laugh came from behind me. "I think that's why he keeps trying. He doesn't think he'll lose."

I spun to walk backward so that I could see Bronio's face. "And if it came down to me and him? Who do you think would win?"

Bronio's smile fell. "I don't know."

Wilken was walking beside Bronio, and I couldn't stop myself from asking him the same question. "Between me and Tiarnan, who do you think would win?"

"I honestly don't know, which is why I joined your guard."

I held his gaze for another moment, two, three, but his face—his eyes—were giving me nothing. He could've joined my guard to help me win or—far more likely—he could've joined my guard to make sure Tiarnan won.

Van grabbed my hand and spun me so that I was walking forward. "Enough of this. Focus on where we're going." He gave me a sly smile. "Plus, interrogating your personal guards while in a public place is a little too flashy."

"And throwing the beheaded man into the hallway wasn't flashy?"

He laughed. "Fair enough, your highness. Fair enough."

Ugh. Why was he being so formal? "I hate it when you call me that."

"We're going to have to be formal for a while."

There was nothing I could say to that, so I didn't. I'd wanted to leave court—desperately—but not to head to Gales to see if Ziriel's son was serious about his offer of marriage.

Too soon, I saw the great doors to the gateway. For some

reason I expected my mother to be waiting to say good-bye or wish me luck or something, but the three visible gate guards pushed open the massive door—the room was as empty and hollow as my aching heart.

When I was younger, I used to like coming here. No one ever bothered me and it made me feel like I was outside and far away. The ceiling had been magicked to look like the night sky. The moon hung low and full, providing enough light to see the room. The stars glittered, and every so often, if you stayed in here long enough, a shooting star would cross the sky.

The walls were meant to look like the Irish forest outside the underhill. When I stepped inside the room and the doors closed, it would almost feel as if I'd left the court. It would smell like grass and dirt and the dewy night air, and as far as I could see, it would look like I was outside, but the illusion was broken by the ring of six hexagonal floor tiles, each leading to a different court.

When I was younger maybe the fact that I could jump on one of the tiles and actually leave helped me feel that way, too. To feel free. But today was different. I wasn't young anymore.

I didn't want to step inside the room. There was no freedom there. No matter how hard I tried to tell myself that this was the best thing—the only thing—for me to do, I wasn't ready.

It seemed silly to hesitate now. Silly and stupid because I was showing weakness, and just as I thought about turning around to leave, Van gripped my hand in his.

"It could be worse." He pulled me to his side.

I let my head rest on his shoulder. "How?"

"We could be going to Leaves."

A startled laugh slipped free from me. "Wrong. Leaves would be an improvement. They might be a little too focused on lazing about for us, but at least they're not evil."

"Gales isn't evil."

I gave him a look that said he was full of it, but he'd given me enough of a push. His strength would get me through this.

I let go of his hand and pulled my locket out of my shirt, gripping the warmed opal moon in my hand as I finally stepped inside to walk the inner circle of tiles.

The four-foot wide hexagon for Leaves was painted with a beautiful forest. The boughs on the evergreen trees were covered with a light dusting of snow.

I walked to the next tile—Gales. The painted tile was the color of sand. The night sky glittered above the dunes. To the northwest, a sandstorm was brewing, heading toward Gales.

"They've got trouble coming," I said to Van.

He came to stand near me. "Not necessarily. There could just be an actual sandstorm in the area."

I shook my head. "A sandstorm brewing in the northwest. As in where we are? Just as we're about to enter their court?" I sighed. "I have a bad feeling about this."

I didn't have the Sight, not like Tessa, but I had some variation of it. It was more like very strong intuition combined with being able to see all the different paths a life could take. The red string of fate tried to pull each person along their path, but if they were strong and kept their eyes open, then a lot of heartache could be avoided.

Except I couldn't see my own path. I couldn't see my string of fate. All I had was my intuition, and I knew that something very, very bad was coming if I went to Gales.

"It could be nothing." Van said it as though he knew it was something. He gave the signal to the guards to move ahead, and at that one simple gesture, icy dread ran through my limbs until it hit my heart, and its beating slowed.

Slowed.

Slooooowed.

Until the *thump-thump* became a *thump...thump...* And in between the beats, my guards were moving. Fast. Too fast.

Cyros and Taslin stepped around me and onto Gales' tile.

Thump...

Cyros and Taslin disappeared.

Thump...

Too quickly. They were moving too quickly. And I was too slow to realize that the ice slowing my heart, my mind, my body was dread.

I couldn't do this. I hadn't stepped foot in Africa, let alone into Gales, for more than thirty years. The last time nearly killed me. This time, I might live, but my heart and my soul wouldn't survive.

I couldn't do this. I really couldn't do this.

Thump...

Two more guards stepped onto the tile. Pratis and Gurhan were gone.

Thump...

Oh, God. But I was going to do this. I was going to Gales again.

Splinters of ice seeped into my heart, making it painful and heavy in my chest, and with each beat, it was telling me to back away. To run. That nothing good would come of me stepping onto that tile.

But the rest of my guards—Bronio, Wilken, and Nex—were already there. Their feet touched the tile, I knew there was no turning back now. I was moving too slow to stop it.

They disappeared.

Too late. It was too late.

Taslin came back. "It's safe. Ziriel has been alerted of our arrival. Time to come, princess."

And then it was as if the slow, hard, icy grip of fear pounding into my heart was suddenly gone and I couldn't feel anything. I was floating somewhere above my body and all I could hear was my breath in my ears. The only thing keeping me grounded was the feeling of Van's hand gripping mine.

I glanced at him. We'd been through a lot together. Good and bad. Things that made me feel invincible and things that made me feel like I'd never be able to pick myself up off the floor. But he was the one thing that had been constant in my life since I was twelve.

He gave me a we-can-do-this nod.

I gripped Van's hand hard and prayed he was right.

We stepped onto the tile as one.

I closed my eyes and tried to block out the dropping sensation—as if I was falling—and then it was over. Traveling through the gateway wasn't nearly as disorienting as when I traveled with Van, but still unsettling. I took a moment to catch my breath before opening my eyes.

Everything sped back up. The dread was still there, but I had to let it go. I couldn't let it control me. The fact that the facade had slipped at all was bad, but the second I saw Ziriel standing in front of me, it slammed into place firm and fast. His smile was there, but the hint of the red ring around his pupils was enough to tell me he wasn't happy. Not at all.

At least that made two of us.

The walls of the room looked like they were made from swirling sand, pushed back by an invisible dome around us. The only thing that broke the illusion were the torches hovering an inch from the wall spaced evenly around the circular room. The flames weren't flickering or sputtering out like they should've been if the wind were that violent. Only the smallest breeze floated through the middle of the room, smelling of sage and lavender—a signature of Gales, meant to soothe and cleanse anyone who entered their realm. I wished it worked on me, but I'd seen too much here to be soothed by something so simple, and I wasn't sure there was enough sage to cleanse me after all my years of spying and bargaining, not to mention the killing.

A great boulder of a door blocked the exit, and I knew it wasn't going to move until Ziriel decided I could be trusted.

"I didn't expect to ever see you again," he said after a long moment.

I laughed as if I didn't hate being here. "I didn't expect your son to bid for my hand in marriage."

"The boy always has had an eye on you. Especially after he saw you take down three of our court in under ten seconds."

"I learned from the best." I gave Van a smile. He stood there, calmly watching us talk. He wasn't one to really speak up, and he wasn't flashy with his power. Usually that worked out well, but today I needed to lean on his strength. "He was a god, you know." It was always good to remind people what they were up against, and I knew it wouldn't bother Van at all.

"Yes, well..." Ziriel trailed off.

There wasn't much he could say to top that, which was fun. Point to me.

"I hope you know the rule stands. I didn't want to let you or Van come back. Not after last time." He stepped toward me. "But my son begged me, and I am nothing if not a doting father."

The image of Ziriel as doting? Now that was funny. I gave him a haughty grin. "Didn't you almost kill him the last time I was here?"

He scoffed and waved his hand through the air. "Water under the bridge."

I raised my chin slightly, a small challenge to him. "And is our water also under that bridge?"

"No." His voice grew deep and dark. If he was anyone else, I would've pushed him farther, but Ziriel was dangerous and not a man to threaten. Especially in his own court.

Bronio moved to get between us, but I shook my head,

telling him to back down.

Ziriel was mad. That was fine. Eli had put me on the mission to find out what was twisting the Court of Gales toward evil, and after a few days, I'd found the source.

I'd killed more than a few Gales that day—although not nearly as many as Van did when he came to rescue me—but I caused a problem for him across all the courts. Everyone wanted to know what happened and why, but in the end, when Ziriel held an enchanted knife to my throat, Van had given Ziriel a vow of silence in return for me. I'd taken that same vow before Ziriel would let me go.

Van and I wouldn't ever tell what was twisting this court, but that didn't mean the rest of the fey weren't asking Ziriel a million questions he didn't want to answer. My time here was too violent to be covered up completely, which meant I'd put Ziriel in a very bad spot.

But as I stood there watching Ziriel closely, I knew that Van was right. Even if the entire Court of Gales was a darker shade of gray than I liked, the benefit of having a match here was huge. For their knowledge, their horde of bargains, and their ability to lie, it was worth it.

So, I'd face Ziriel now, and hope that we could make peace with the past. I kept my back straight and my chin raised as if I were balancing a crown on my head. I preferred not to wear one —the fey knew who I was on sight—but the posture conveyed power. I'd need that to make another deal with Ziriel.

"I'm coming to meet your son. I won't raise a hand to one of your people, as long as you don't attempt to hurt me or one of mine. The second you cross the line, the nice Cosette will be gone and the Cosette that slaughtered a large chunk of your court will be back. And this time, I have Van with me. You won't get close enough to put a knife to my throat again. So, go ahead. Say what you need to say, and then let's move on."

Ziriel's growl wasn't like one of the Weres. It was much deeper, and filled with a magic that skittered along my skin.

He stepped close to me, so close that our noses nearly touched. The ring of red around his pupil grew brighter with the demon side of him rising.

He stood there, staring at me for a second, but I didn't flinch. I wasn't afraid. You had to have something to lose to be afraid. Just by being here, I'd already lost everything that mattered to me. I only had a locket as a memory of my few fleeting days of happiness—the ones I longed for that I'd never get back.

So, he could stare at me all he wanted with his demon cousin's eyes, and I would feel nothing.

He finally stepped back a few inches. "You don't speak of our secrets to anyone or put your nose in my court where it doesn't belong. You will not question my people about our ways or make anyone here feel less than. And if you hurt someone—"

I swiped my hand through the air. That was way too open for interpretation. "I'll not take the blame for soft feelings."

"Fine." Ziriel stepped closer again. "If you hurt someone *physically*, your life will be mine."

I wanted space, but there was no way I was stepping away from him. I wouldn't back down. "That's a hefty price you're asking for."

"I'll not have you causing trouble a second time. I'll not lose another of my people to any Argent. Especially you."

"Now that makes more sense. You're angry not just at me, but at my kin, too."

He tilted his head, just slightly. "I've not had good luck when your family comes to visit."

That was understandable since I shared similar feelings. "Then let me put your mind at ease. I'm not here as my mother's spy or on Eli's behalf. I'm here to find a husband. I'll meet with your son, and if things go well, share a meal or two before making my decision. If it's not a match for either of us, then I'll be on my way. As long as yours don't hurt me or mine, I'll not hurt you or yours. Fair enough?"

He nodded "Fair."

There was one more thing I had to add. "I should also mention that there was an assassination attempt today."

Ziriel laughed and all the seriousness of the last few minutes melted away. "It's a wonder no one's killed you yet." He tapped his fist on my shoulder, but not hard enough to hurt.

I grinned, not needing to say anything to that. He knew exactly who and what I was. "If assassins come, if someone attacks me, I will aim to kill no matter what court they call theirs. I will not make the first move, but I will make the last one. I will not be held accountable for loss of life when I didn't start the fight."

"Fair." Ziriel crossed his arms as he considered, his gaze never leaving mine. "Someone attacks, you may do as you will."

Good. That was a deal-breaker for me. "Terms are done?"

He nodded. "Yes. Come and be welcome." He opened his arms wide, waving toward the doorway. The stone that was blocking the exit disappeared.

Three of Ziriel's white-clad guards walked out first, behind them four of mine. Then Ziriel and me. Van and the last of my guards went next, with three more Gales guards behind them.

I walked next to Ziriel down the arced hallways in tense silence. Every bit of wall, floor, and ceiling were glossy smooth. It looked like glass with sand pressing against it, but it wasn't glass. It was magic.

At any given point, if enemies found a way inside, Ziriel could collapse a section of his underhill without a thought, suffocating the enemy under countless tons of sand.

It was a much more brutal way to keep control of who was

moving through the underhill than ours with the spelled floors, but maybe more effective in terms of protecting the court. But knowing that the whole place could collapse had always made me feel a little claustrophobic during my visits. And more so this time. The halls were noticeably empty aside from us, which meant he was prepared to do whatever he needed to defend his court.

I needed to focus on something else before I started feeling like the magic was failing.

Van brushed his hand across the small of my back and I looked at him.

"I'm here." He mouthed the words, and I took a breath.

He was here this time. Let Ziriel collapse the place. Van would get us out of here before we were crushed.

Which meant I could breathe enough to make small talk with Ziriel.

I gave a Van a nod, and focused on Asheral. "Where is Asheral?"

"Waiting to dine with you. I have your favorite tea waiting."

I brushed a hand against Ziriel's arm. "You remembered?"

"Oh, Cosette. There's not a thing about you I don't remember. You nearly killed half my court before you collapsed. Anything I didn't know about you, I made a point of learning. I even gave up one of my favorite chips for a good bit of gossip on you."

"You didn't have to do that." I pressed my hand to my chest. "If you had a question, you could've just asked me."

He gave me a sly look. "And you would've answered?"

"No. Probably not." I grinned, and this time it was a real grin. Ziriel was fun to banter with. "But a girl does like to be asked."

"Lunar fey and their riddles." Ziriel pulled me to a stop. This time he laughed and gave me a big hug. His arms squeezed tight before letting me go. "I did miss you. It's been so boring since you left."

I squeezed him back. "Didn't you just finish threatening my life? Again?"

"Oh, Cosette. The Lunar Court has ruined you!" He pulled back, but squeezed my shoulders. "Do you know nothing of love? There is such a fine line between it and hate. What's a little blood when the woman doing the killing does it with such grace? All without getting a drop on her. How did you manage that bit of magic? No matter who I ask, they don't know."

I didn't have a good answer for him because it didn't always work. Otherwise, I wouldn't have been washing blood off myself today. "A gift from my father."

He dropped my shoulders and stepped away from me. "Ah. So not something you can show me?" The man sounded like I'd kicked his puppy.

"No." I didn't want to talk about it. The truth was that I didn't know much about my father at all. I'd never met the man. Never spoken to him. The only archon I'd ever met was Eli, and he was more trouble than he was worth.

And just like that, Eli was there in front of me. Only Van's hand kept me from stumbling backward into him.

This was just like Eli. Popping in like he'd been reading my mind for days. Invasive piece of—

"I take exception to that thought." He was in his usual light jeans, a white button-down with sleeves rolled up, and wings out, spread wide for everyone to see.

"Get out of my head, Eli!" I gave him a hard shove, but he held onto my hand and pressed it over where his heart should've been, but I wasn't sure the archon had a heart.

"Oh, come now, Cosette. I have a heart, and you love me."

My mouth dropped open and I yanked my hand free. "You've got to be joking. You know I don't trust you."

His wings seemed to spread out and surround me as he leaned down. "Do trust and love always go together?" he whispered to me.

I wanted to say yes, always, but that was a generalization and I couldn't be sure how every single person—supernatural or not—alive felt.

"See? Love. And if you don't know that you love me, you will soon." He grinned as he stood tall, wings spread wide again. "Before the Lunar Court's fortnight is over," he said, louder, for everyone to hear.

"Why are you meddling? What are you up to?"

"Wouldn't you like to know?"

I wanted to smash that coy look off his face. "Yes. Yes, I would. Before you get me killed." I stepped toward him. "What do you know?"

"Everything." And he popped out.

Fury burned bright as he disappeared without helping. It was typical behavior for Eli, but it seriously pissed me off like nothing else. Maybe if he hadn't almost gotten me killed before...but I didn't trust him anymore. If Eli was here, then something was about to go terribly wrong.

I spun to Ziriel. "What was Eli doing here?"

"Well, it seems whenever he comes to visit, you're not far behind."

I gave him a seething look, and Ziriel held up his hands.

"Eli's been coming in and out the last couple of weeks."

"Why?" Eli didn't show up unless there was trouble brewing, and I really, really didn't need anything else on my plate. Wasn't it enough that I had to find a husband? "What's going on?"

"*Uh-uh-uh.*" Ziriel wagged a finger in front of my face, and I wanted to break it off. "You weren't sent to spy. Remember? You weren't going to ask questions. Remember?"

I inhaled and let out a breath. "Fine. But if people—from any court—start dying while I'm here, I get to ask you questions."

"One question."

"Ten."

"Two."

"Nine."

"Two."

"Eight."

"Three."

"Five. Final offer."

"Five is acceptable."

I shook my head. Fey negotiations were always tricky, and Ziriel loved his deals. They were the currency of the Court of Gales.

"Now, let's go find your son."

Ziriel clasped my shoulder again. "I think I would enjoy having you as a daughter-in-law. You're so fun to bargain with."

I rolled my eyes. "You're exhausting."

"But as lovable as Eli?"

I laughed. "Sure. You're as lovable as Eli." Although that wasn't saying much at all. Still, the man made me laugh. I hadn't really met his son the last time I was here, but I wondered what kind of man he'd be. Ziriel was handsome enough. Maybe his son would be, too.

I just really hoped this worked out. I gave Van a quick glance. He was there, behind me, guarding my back as always. I trusted him—loved him—but not the way that mattered. Not for marriage.

As much as I loved Van, he wasn't an acceptable plan b. There was no way I could go through with marrying him. Not in a million years.

CHAPTER NINE

CHRIS

I WAS SITTING neck-deep in warm water in the fancy claw-foot tub, surrounded by floral scented bubbles, and I'd never felt more uncomfortable in my life. I wasn't sure I'd actually ever soaked in a tub before—maybe when I was a kid—but I didn't like the idea of sitting in my own dirt. I preferred a shower, where the dirt would just wash away.

But it wasn't just being in the tub that was making me uncomfortable. I couldn't stop thinking about how the little fey beast could go invisible. Was it watching me now? Was the room actually packed with fey just staring at me, while I sat here in the dirty water like a chump?

I had zero shame about my body, but the thought of someone secretly watching me while I bathed creeped me the fuck out.

I grabbed a washcloth and scrubbed it along my skin as quickly as I could, and then I got the hell out.

A large, bright red towel hung on a bar next to the tub. I snatched it as I stood and wrapped the towel around my waist, not caring that I was getting water everywhere and soaking the towel. I walked over to the sink, resting my hands along the edge.

It wasn't just me that was creeped out—my wolf was, too. He was pushing me to let him out, which was bad. At this point, taking a break from being human and letting him free for a bit sounded amazing, but I couldn't. I'd never let him have free rein before, and I wouldn't start now.

I closed my eyes and took a breath. The little beast said that Ziriel wanted to talk, and I needed to be human to do that. I wasn't going to be trapped here forever. Once I had what I needed, I'd leave and never come back. And when I was gone, we'd go for a nice long run in the woods.

That made my wolf quiet for a bit, but the mirror revealed that my eyes were still glowing light blue. My wolf was still there peeking out at me, but I was in control. I was always in control, and it would stay that way.

Rubbing my hand down my cheek, I thought about shaving, but I wanted out of the room more. Plus, even if I could stand the few minutes it'd take, I'd need to figure out how to burn the hair. I couldn't trust that putting it down the drain was enough to get rid of it when even the tiniest hair was enough to make a spell.

There were a ton of elastics in a little container by the sink. I took my mess of wet, wavy blond hair and pulled the top portion back. I needed a cut, but that wasn't happening today. For now, I just needed it out of my eyes. I couldn't fight as a human if it was in the way.

There was a pile of neatly folded clothes next to the sink. A gray T-shirt. A pair of black jeans. Pretty nondescript, which was good. I pulled on the clothes quickly, and then grabbed the socks.

The little beast was waiting for me just beyond the door into the bedroom. He'd made the bed and was fluffing the pillows.

The little beast disappeared for a second, before popping right back up in front of me. "You're ready!"

I took a step back to keep from touching it and held out the socks like a barrier. "Just need my shoes."

"Oh, you don't need those." Its voice trailed off a bit.

I looked where I'd left my shoes, but they were gone. What was the little beast up to? "I'd rather have them." I didn't leave any room for negotiation in my voice.

The little beast hadn't told me his name, and I hadn't figured out a way to ask without having to talk to him more. That wasn't fucking happening. I had to fight the urge to kick him every time he came near me, but I know I shouldn't. Kicking someone smaller than me was stupid. Especially when there was a massive possibility that he was actually dangerous and I had zero clue what his abilities could be.

But I really wanted to know why was he hanging around my room.

The little beast pulled the nightstand away from the wall, grabbing my shoes from behind it.

It hid my shoes? Weird. I wanted to be creeped out all over again—and I was to a degree—but I was confused more than anything.

I took my shoes from its outstretched hand and shook out a pile of sand from each before pulling them on. I still couldn't believe I was in the desert, but then I also knew I shouldn't be surprised. I knew very little about the fey. After Cosette and Van pulled me out of the pit and killed my pack, it took me a while to get my shit together. Years. I'd been lost and scared and not sure of what to do with my life. Figuring out about the pixie and the fey and the bargain I'd made... That hadn't been on my radar. Not until after I'd run into Adrian.

"Come. Come. Stop sitting! There is food. Food! We are late! Late!" The little beast bounced with each repeated word.

I shook my head at the little beast's antics. Most of the time it reminded me of an anxious toddler, but then sometimes, it was terrifying. The deep voice it used before I took my bath made me think there was much more to the little beast than I thought. "Lead the way."

It ran through the stone door like it wasn't there, but when I put my hand on the stone, it was still as hard and impermeable as ever.

The little beast reappeared. "I forgot. I forgot! Hold hands."

I looked down at the offered hand. It looked more like a tangle of pointy, spiny fingers. Did I really need food?

Damn it.

I eased my hand around its fingers, trying to keep the wince from my face, but I was fucking failing. They were thinner than they looked and a little slimy and no part of me wanted to touch the little beast unless I was killing it.

But killing it would be bad.

Cosette. This was for Cosette.

The little beast tightened its grip on my hand and I couldn't help the shudder that ran through me.

"Come!" He pulled me through the stone, and it burned like I was being quickly dragged across sandpaper that touched every single inch of my body.

"Shiiiiit!" My voice was high-pitched with the shock of pain and I tore my hand free of the little beast's spiny, slimy grip. I bent over, waiting for my body to heal. Pain always felt so much worse when you weren't expecting it. If I'd known...

"Oh no! Your face is burned."

"I'm aware." But even as I said it, the sting eased and I could breathe through the pain until it faded away.

"Oh! It's all healed."

"Yep." Thankfully. A hurt like that wouldn't last long. It

wasn't truly magical. I just wasn't meant to rub against stone so intimately.

My nerves eased a little when I realized we were going back to the big room I'd been in yesterday. The dining hall might have seemed confining when I first entered Gales, but after being in that tiny, cave-like room all night, I was ready for the big, breezy room—annoying smoke and all. And now I might have a chance at making a bargain and actually be able to help Cosette.

There was so much that could go wrong, and I couldn't afford to fuck it up. I already had one bargain out there with a pixie. Most of the time, I didn't think about the bargain I'd made or what happened with my pack. It was firmly in the past, but the dream from last night brought it back to the front of my mind. I'd bargained for a good reason and, at the time, I wasn't really thinking about the consequences. Then, after I was free from the pit, I was too busy trying to survive. I'd shoved the bargain in some faraway corner of my memory, and I'd hoped that it would just disappear forever. But it wouldn't.

The more I learned about the fey, the more I realized that at some point—probably when I least expected it—the bargain was going to bite me in the ass. I'd been stupid and not put any restrictions on it. At the time, it made sense. A favor for a favor. But I knew better now.

Yet here I was. Desperate again. Bound to make another stupid bargain if I wasn't very, very careful. I wasn't sure how much time I had, but I wanted to get to Cosette now. Today. So, I had to figure this out fast.

The little beast slowed its pace as we entered the dining hall. The room was filled with sunlight so bright that it almost gave the impression that we were outside, but when I looked up, there was nothing but ceiling. The light was just another fey illusion.

The room was packed full. People talking and laughing. There were platters of boiled eggs, fruits, breads, and cheeses. But no meat. The betting game was still going on, as was the yelling, but the smoke wasn't as thick as it had been last night—which I appreciated. I could breathe a little better without it, and I definitely felt more confident as I caught some of the subtler scents in the room.

Ziriel had given me one little gold coin, but he hadn't explained what it was or how to play the game. "Is that some form of poker or—"

The little beast let out a coughing laugh. "For some. *Would you like to play?*" His voice turned menacing with the question, and everything in the room darkened and dimmed—the sounds, the light, the smells. I heard its words echoing in my mind.

Would you like to play?

Would you like to play?

Would you play?

I closed my eyes, trying to shut out everything. But the echoing words were making it impossible to think.

I wanted to say yes, just to shut up the damned noise, but play what?

No. Cosette had been pretty clear. When dealing with the fey, every tiny detail had to be thought of before agreeing to anything.

I opened my eyes. It's red stare the only visible thing in the darkened room. "What are the rules? What are those chips?"

"You'd find out *if you played.*" I didn't think it was possible for its voice to grow any deeper, but it did.

The echoing started again and I shook my head slowly, trying to stop it. "No." The word sounded drawn out, but I hadn't intended it to. "IthinkI'dbetternoooooot." Each word slurred into the next.

And just like that, the light brightened, the sounds got

louder, the smells stronger. I blinked, and the fog lifted from my mind.

"Ah. You're not any fun."

No. I wasn't fun. Actually, I was pretty pissed.

My wolf rose up and the growl slipped free. The shift started and I fought with everything I had to keep him down. My sharp nails dug into my palms and I tried to shove the wolf down, down, down, because I was terrified that if I let him out, there would be blood and it would be mine. I was pretty sure if the little beast could take over my mind like that, then he was much more powerful than I'd thought.

I'd never felt anyone trying to control my head before. Sure, Alphas issued orders, but I could feel them like a blow—I had to submit or fight to disobey. But this was sneaky and made me feel dirty. I didn't like it one bit.

From the start of the little beast asking me if I wanted to play couldn't have been a long exchange, but that was enough to change my perception of the little beast as it waved me forward. It might still be two feet tall and chubby around the middle, but I knew my gut had been right. There was something dangerous lurking under its skin.

"Come! Come! Food! Food!" The little beast led me through the tables to one that was completely empty.

Great. No chance to get any help or answers.

The little beast shoved me onto the pillowed seat. "You stay here. Here! Better if you don't leave. Dangerous fey live in Gales. Stay."

I nodded. "Okay." That wasn't a problem. Especially if the little beast was leaving.

It clapped its hands and food appeared. "Safe food for werewolf." Without another word, the little beast disappeared, and I was glad. It would be a while before the memory of its voice in my head would fade.

I leaned forward to check out the platters of food it had left. Eggs—thankfully—but still no meat.

Damn it. My wolf was going to starve here. I needed meat. Clean meat that didn't smell sour.

But food—any food—meant calories. I piled my plate high with eggs, bread, and cheese hoping to get enough calories in to limit how much muscle I lost while I was here. My thighs and arms were already noticeably smaller.

I was on my second plate when Rayvien sat down beside me. "How are you?"

"Good." I was exhausted and still hungry despite the food I'd already eaten, but I wouldn't admit any of that to her. "How are you?"

"Fine." She'd swapped the white fitted shirt and loose pants for patterned leggings and a rich green flowing top. I wasn't sure if that meant that she wasn't on guard today, but it didn't matter what she was wearing. The way she was staring me down told me that she was still lethal.

"You look well rested," she said after a minute.

"I slept." I couldn't say I slept well, but I did sleep. "But I've got a ton of questions. Do you think you could answer them?" She was Ziriel's wife after all. She had to have some answers.

"Maybe. Maybe not." She put her elbow on the table and leaned toward me. "But you should ask them anyway."

She'd given me a flirty smile—and I was about to say something flirty back—but all my thoughts fled from my mind when smoke filled the whites of her eyes. It swirled around, getting darker in some spots.

She blinked and the smoke was gone, but it had been enough to remind me exactly what I was dealing with.

I was about to ask a fey queen questions, and I had to use my words carefully. Yet still sound casual.

So, I faked it. Faking wasn't anything new to me. I'd used it plenty in my ex-pack.

I gave her a smile. "All right." I leaned toward her. "What's that little beast's name? The one who brought me from my room."

She doubled over with laughter and slapped a hand on the table. The table clanged from the sparkling rings that covered each of her fingers. "Oh, shit. Little beast." She laughed for a while longer and I couldn't help but join in.

I was winning her over. This was good. "What's wrong with calling it a little beast?"

She wiped under her eyes. "Nothing. Nothing at all. It's honestly the most accurate name, but it's also insulting and to insult—"

The little beast popped in. "No! No! We have a game! No cheating! No telling!" And just like that, he was gone.

Rayvien's face lost all signs of laughter or humor. "You didn't enter into any kind of bargain with him, did you?"

I wasn't loving how quickly Rayvien had gone from flirty to serious. I blew out a breath as I tried to think back to its exact wording. "No. I don't think so."

"Then what was that about?"

I gave her the rundown of the exchange.

"You're fine. Just don't guess any more." She wrinkled her nose a little. "Better to live in ignorance on this one."

"That's my plan."

"Good." She leaned toward me again with the flirty grin back in place.

Good. This was better.

I leaned toward her, hoping she'd give me some more answers. "So, what's the deal with the coins? The game?" I motioned all around me.

"It's not really a game per se. The coins are different things

—but mostly representations of bargains. Different sizes show values. Small chips for people who put too many restrictions on their bargains or their standing in court is shit. Bigger for fewer restrictions, or if they're powerful." She leaned closer to me. "Ziriel and I keep an official tally of all bargains made across all the courts." The words were little more than a hushed whisper.

That was interesting. Really interesting.

Did she know about my bargain with the pixie? The bargain was made on my land, not at any court, and she'd said *court* bargains. But maybe I was reading too much into her exact words.

Even if she really meant that she knew about *all* bargains, it would be stupid to bring up my bargain. If she somehow didn't know about it, then my asking her might make her go find it. A few trades and Rayvien—or worse, Ziriel—could own my chip. I didn't want that. It was going to be hard enough to get Ziriel to cut my lunar tie. If he had my chip, I'd already owe him something. I'd be doubly screwed.

No. It was much better if that stayed quiet. I needed to start fresh with Ziriel, but I had one other question. "The chip that Ziriel gave me yesterday? What was that?"

"Don't worry. It was a courtesy chip. No bargain made by taking it, other than to know you were willing to play the game. But it's not worth anything either." She turned to look at the table next to us. "Look at them." She motioned without pointing to the table, and I saw them watching us. Whispering and passing coins back and forth, and then they stopped.

I think I liked that even worse. "Why did they stop?"

Her eyes smoked up again for a second before they cleared. I wanted to ask what it meant, but it seemed rude.

She nudged me with her elbow. "They're waiting to see what you're going to do. If you'll turn into a wolf? If you'll yell at me. If I'll yell at you. That kind of thing."

Me? This was all about me? "Seems kind of silly that your conversation with a low-ranking werewolf would cause all of that."

"Oh, you know that's bull as well as I do. How could an ordinary wolf ever snag the impossible Cosette Argent?"

My mouth dropped open, but no words came out. Our friends didn't even know about our relationship. How could Rayvien know anything about it? "I haven't snagged her."

"Isn't that why you're here? To save her? So that you can be her mate?" The I-know-everything smile on her face made me like her a little less. "Or have I gotten bad information?"

There was no point to denying it, not when admitting the truth might gain me an ally. "No. It seems like somehow you know everything. From Eli?"

She shrugged one shoulder. "He didn't talk to me, but I have other sources."

"Then you know what I need?"

She leaned closer. "Yes."

I didn't even care that her eyes had filled with smoke again. We were getting somewhere good. "And can you help with what I need?"

"Only Ziriel can, but he'll only do it for a price." She looked away, twirling one of her rings around her fingers as she thought. "It will be a very hefty bargain. Trust me on this. You don't want him getting anything from you."

I wasn't sure I trusted her yet, but I wanted to hear everything she'd tell me. "Then how do I get what I want?"

"You have to find a way."

Find a way? How? It was like she was giving me pieces of a puzzle, but none of them fit together.

This was some fey bullshit. If she would just tell me what I needed to do, I'd do it. All I needed was a plan of attack and I'd make it happen. But her vague advice wasn't doing me any actual good. "I don't understand what you're trying to tell me."

"Don't worry. You and Cosette will figure it out together."

What was she talking about? "Cosette's not here."

"Is she not?"

A familiar laugh hit me.

Cosette. Cosette was here? No. It was another fey trick. There was no way—

And there she was.

She was fine. Laughing. Walking into the room with Ziriel. She touched his shoulder and he laughed at something she said.

There she was. Five tables away. Her skin looked pale and she looked a little thinner than before, and there were the tiniest shadows under her eyes that hadn't been there two days ago, and I wondered what she had been doing...

My wolf rose up, demanding a shift, demanding I take what was mine, but I closed my eyes and pushed him away. I wasn't like Dastien. I wasn't going to go around biting my mate, forcing the issue. He was lucky Tessa didn't die in the transition. And he was doubly lucky that her sanity didn't crack either. I knew too well what happens when someone is bitten to ever bite Cosette, even I was pretty sure biting her wouldn't do anything. She was fey. She couldn't be changed.

The human side of me wanted to go talk to her right then. The night before I'd left, we'd had a fight, and...

But I was a rational werewolf. I had to do the right thing. Which meant I would wait here and assess how she was doing. Figure out why she was here. Why I was here. What Eli was really up to.

I'd deal with everything else later. Privately.

"Do you know what's going on?" I asked Rayvien. "Does she know I'm here?"

"And this is where things really get interesting." Rayvien pulled a coin out of thin air and tossed.

It flipped through the air, and then she caught it. Studying the coin in her hand as if it would tell her something.

"I know why you're here," she said finally. "I know why she's here. As does everyone else in the room. But neither of you have a clue about the path that you're on. That's why so many have gathered to bet. It's never this busy here. Should be an interesting few days. If it all goes well, maybe you and Cosette won't be the only ones to get what you want. Maybe I'll get it, too."

"Is there something that you need? Something that by helping you, I could help Cosette?" Because I could get behind that.

"No. You can't help me. Not directly."

I didn't understand Rayvien at all. If my getting what I wanted could help her get what she wanted, then why wasn't she helping me? Why wouldn't she give me some clear steps to follow to break my lunar tie?

Cosette laughed again, and I wanted to go over there. But I couldn't. Not yet. Not with so many people around. Cosette was her mother's spy, and I was in way over my head with all of the fey politics. If she was playing some game for her mother or something else was in play, then I couldn't fuck that up for her.

So, I'd sit and I'd wait and I'd protect her if anything started to go to shit.

"Asheral," Ziriel yelled across the room.

A tall, dark-haired man stood from one of the tables in the center of the room, turning to smoke for a moment before reappearing in front of Cosette. He was dressed in a dark shirt and loose black pants, but the way he stood next to Ziriel—confident and proud—made me think he was more dangerous than the guards in all white.

I started to stand before I could stop myself, but then she laughed and smiled, holding out her hand. I sat again, watching them, wanting to rip off the guy's face, but it wasn't her real smile. She wasn't showing her teeth and her chin wasn't tilted down the way it does when she's really, really happy about something.

So, I let out a breath and waited.

I wasn't sure what Eli was up to, but I was definitely here for a reason. Here for her. I just didn't expect her to be here.

"Who is that?" I was done with flirting with Rayvien. Now I needed whatever information she'd give me.

"Asheral. Ziriel's son."

Cosette was meeting with a prince? Why? I knew she was a spy for her mother, so maybe it was nothing, but... "Wait. Asheral's your son?"

"No. Not mine. I'm about three centuries younger than Asheral." She paused. "I'm forty-one. Ziriel was married before me. Many times."

For a second, I looked away from Cosette to give Rayvien my attention. "He was?"

She nodded. "No one lives long when married to him."

"Then why did you marry him?" It seemed like a dumb thing to do when everyone who married him died.

"Why indeed?"

That didn't sound good, but my attention went back to Cosette as she wove through the tables with Asheral to sit at an empty one.

I'd been watching the room for a while yesterday and today. I'd studied all the faces, and Ziriel's son was never at a table alone.

I didn't know what they were talking about—it could've been anything—but something about the way he looked at her, like he owned her, made me want to give my wolf control. Just this one time, I wanted to let him free.

Cosette took a cup of tea that Asheral offered to her. Her fingers brushed his as he passed the cup, and I started to growl.

Rayvien patted my hand. "Down boy. If you start acting out now, you'll ruin all the fun."

"What fun? What's going on?"

Rayvien flicked her dark hair over her shoulder as she leaned closer. "Can't tell you."

Fur rippled on my skin and I was seconds away from letting go. "Won't. You won't tell me." The rasp in my voice got thicker, more pronounced.

"No. I won't." She looked away from me, busying herself with the plate in front of her. "I have too much riding on this." She'd muttered that so softly, that my Were hearing barely heard it, but I definitely heard.

At that, both the wolf and I settled down. It was the sincerity in her voice that shocked me the most. "Why did you come sit with me today?"

She smiled, but it was a sad one and had zero flirting in it. "To try and get you to trust me. I've been eavesdropping across all the realms."

"All the realms?"

"Mortal. Fey. Heaven. Hell."

"You've been to Hell?"

She smiled, but didn't give me an answer. That was probably enough answer for me.

"If you get what you want, it will set off a ripple through the fey. I want that for us. So, if you need help with anything, anything at all, please come find me. What I can do right now is limited because of my husband, but I can do *some* things." She gave me a small smile—one that was totally different than the flirty ones she'd tossed my way a few minutes ago. "See you soon." She disappeared in a puff of smoke.

Fuck.

I wasn't sure I'd ever get used to the fey popping in and out, but the way she turned to smoke before going... It was creepy.

There was a lot creeping me out in this court. Something wasn't right here, and it wasn't just that Cosette was still talking with Asheral. Sipping her tea. Looking beautiful. Radiant. A few of her guards—including Van—stood behind her, while the rest were standing along the walls. It seemed like they were too far away to do any good, but what did I know.

I leaned forward on the table, trying to tune in and hear what she was saying, but the room was so damned loud.

And then it happened.

A puff of smoke and someone was there. Behind her. Knife raised. Then three more. Another.

This. This was why I was here.

I rose from my seat. My wolf wanted control, but I didn't trust him. Not around Cosette. Not in a room full of dangerous fey. I grabbed one of the carving knives out of a hunk of sour meat on the table next to mine.

But from one heartbeat to the next, Cosette was out of her chair. Blade in hand. Killing one. Her men had killed the rest. It was over before I'd even moved ten feet.

I stopped, feeling a little unneeded.

My wolf still urged me to fight and kill. To protect our mate.

But she wasn't our mate. Not really. Not yet. And she was fine. No one to kill.

This couldn't be why I was here. She was protected, but she didn't need protecting. She didn't need my help. So why did Eli drag me here with some nonsense about breaking my lunar tie?

A servant with a tray full of dirty dishes tried to get past me, and I realized I was standing in the way like an idiot. I should just sit back down, and then I could figure out a way to go talk to her without making a huge scene. I just needed to wait.

But as I watched, one of the guards who was crouching next to one of the bodies stood. I watched him as he stared at Cosette. The hunch of his shoulders, the grimace on his face, his scowl all added up to one thing. Hatred. He hated the person he had to protect.

His long black hair was pulled into a low ponytail, and he looked almost like an exact copy of two of her other guards. But they weren't acting shifty.

The guard put his hand behind his back, reaching for something. The other guards all had blades—each one with a different size or style—but they all had them strapped to their hips, but this guard was obviously reaching for a blade that wasn't exposed.

He was close to Cosette. Too close. I could be wrong, but I didn't think I was. The way he was moving—slowly, carefully. His hand was moving to something he had tucked against his back. And that look on his face?

No. I couldn't risk letting him live. If I was wrong and he hurt her...

The knife I'd pulled from the sour meat was weighted wrong. I flipped it a couple of times—quickly—just enough to get a feel for it—before I hurled it with everything I had across the room.

The knife turned—flipping over and over and over—as it flew across the room and *thwack!*

It hit the guard in the right eye. For a second, he stayed upright, and then the life went out of him and he fell to the floor.

Shit. Shit. Just shit.

I hoped it was the right call, but for a second, I had the worst kind of crushing regret.

Everyone in the room was silent, like the room took a breath before turning to me. And that made what I was feeling so much worse.

"Nex?" Cosette's gaze sifted from her dead fey guard to me, and her mouth dropped open.

She was always so cool, calm, and calculating when she was in public, but for a second, I saw pure fear on her face before the facade snapped into place.

Fear of what? She couldn't be afraid of me now. Could she?

She sent a quick look to her other guards. The other two that looked like Nex both shook their heads. She gave one last look to Van, before she spun to the man she'd been sitting with and gave him an exaggerated eye roll with a shoulder shrug.

I wanted to know what the deal was with her guards, but that would have to wait. I couldn't ask here in front of all these fey.

"Ziriel!" Cosette yelled his name. "Really? Assassins from your own court? This is poor hospitality."

I wanted to cheer her on for her faked outrage when I knew it was fear that she was feeling. The woman was an amazing actress.

Ziriel appeared in front of Cosette in a puff of smoke. "Don't go killing anyone else!" Ziriel held up both hands in surrender. "That one wasn't my fault." He pointed to the guard I'd killed.

The room was still so quiet, listening in, but there was a soft clinking of coins as they passed hands.

She nodded. "No. That one is all on us."

Ziriel looked at me from across the room. "Do you want to speak to the wolf?"

"No. He did me a favor." Cosette bent to the body and picked up something. "This is a royal killer."

Royal killer? What did that even mean? But it was definitely a weapon. I knew at least that much, which meant that I was justified in killing her guard. It was a huge relief to know at least I'd been justified.

Ziriel stepped back. "Watch where you point that."

Van stepped forward, grabbing the three-inch blade. The handle was made of glowing crystal and the blade glittered with magic. With one wave of his hand, Van vanished it from sight.

Good. At least it was gone.

Cosette looked at me for a second before glancing at Ziriel and I knew I couldn't stand there anymore. I sat at the nearest table with an opening, while I waited for things to settle down. I didn't feel like I could leave Cosette quite yet, and I wanted to hear what they were saying. From my very limited time at Gales, I knew they were nothing if not noisy.

"How about a drink, Ziriel?"

"Are you sure that's all you want? Something to drink?" Ziriel's condescending tone made me wish I could forget he was the king here. If anyone else talked to Cosette like that, I'd destroy them.

"I came here for Asheral."

What did she mean she was here for Asheral? I scanned the room to find Rayvien but I didn't see her anywhere. I had more questions and this time I'd ask them. I might have even asked the people who were sitting at my table, but they were quietly leaving, one by one.

Were they afraid of me? It was probably good if they were.

"All right. And what of your guard?"

"Van is already sending a replacement. Tell me if you need funds to clean your carpets of his blood, but I'll not pay for the blood of yours."

Was that even a thing? Paying to clean the rug when you killed someone? The fey were messed up if that's all they could talk about in that moment.

"No. I wouldn't dream of making you pay to clean rugs." He looked her up and down with a hungry grin, and I wanted to smash his face in. "And yet, no blood on you. Just as I remember."

She shrugged and lifted her chin in the air. A classic sign that she wasn't going to tell him anything.

"If you figure it out, you'll tell me?"

"Not on your life." She smiled. "I think I'd like something harder than tea. Wine?"

"As you wish." Ziriel bowed a little.

"But no blood in mine. Of any kind."

Blood? In the drinks? That made me glad that I'd stuck to water.

But blood combined with soured meat seemed really off to me. Was this normal for the fey or just exclusive to Gales? I was going to have to ask Cosette once we got out of here.

"Of course. I wouldn't dream of giving you anything not vegetarian. I think I learned from my mistake last time." He clapped his hands and a man came running.

I sat there, waiting for my nerves to calm, but I didn't think that would happen. Especially now that she was here and even the people guarding her couldn't be trusted.

For a second, I thought Eli was wrong about her needing saving, but now as I saw them scrambling to clean up the blood, saw her ignoring me, and saw ownership in Asheral's eyes as he stared at her—as he reached for her and held her hand—I was left wondering one thing: What type of saving did Cosette really need? And who did I need to save her from?

CHAPTER TEN

COSETTE

I WAS SITTING, smiling, nodding appropriately, but my mind was seventy-two feet away. Halfway across the room. Wishing I was sitting, smiling, nodding appropriately next to Chris.

He'd definitely heard how I skirted the truth about wanting to talk to him, and I'd seen the flash of hurt. But didn't he know that it was because I more than wanted to talk to him—I *needed* to talk to him. I had so many questions.

Like what in God's name was he doing at the Court of Gales? And how much had Eli told him about my situation? Because it was very clear that Chris knew something was going on. He hadn't seemed fazed at all, and that led me to one more question:

How did he learn to throw a knife that well?

But I couldn't ask any of those things. We were at court and in public. I was sure the rumors about how I'd given away so many bargains to find out where Chris was had made its way to Gales. I was sure everyone in this room was laughing at me, but I wasn't sure I cared.

I was supposed to be deciding if I could marry the man sitting next to me, but how could I even think about Asheral when Chris was right there. Seventy-two feet away, maybe less.

It was too much. Too much for me to—

"Are you sure you're all right?" Asheral asked.

"I'll be fine. My mind's a bit scattered though." I took a sip of the wine, and my hand didn't shake, despite the fact that I was on the brink of a meltdown.

Chris was here. How was I going to do this with him here? Eli was such an asshole.

I drank some more to calm my nerves, but it wasn't helping. The wine wasn't half bad, but wasn't great either. If I was anywhere else, if I could do what I wanted without worrying about what people would say or how they'd interpret it, I'd drink the whole bottle and ask for another, but I was at court. I had to follow my rules of survival, especially since there'd already been two attempts to murder me within minutes of getting here. And the man who had my heart was approximately seventy-two feet away while I was bartering my body for power.

If there ever was a time when I deserved to drink the bottle down, it was now.

But instead, I took one more sip and forced myself to place the cup carefully on the table. My hand wasn't shaking, but inside, my nerves were shot. "I pretty much expect attacks from assassins wherever I go at court. That's why I'm finally looking for a husband." The words didn't have even a hint of the bitterness that I felt, but I could almost sense Chris straightening at them.

Damned werewolves and their good hearing.

Asheral nodded, but it felt like he was waiting for something. Or maybe he was just as distracted as I was. A strand of his long dark-brown hair fell in front of his face as he leaned toward me. "Apologies for being pushy, but the attack from your guard? That didn't upset you? I'm trying to get a feel for what life with you would be like."

"Are you afraid?" I teased him with a small smile and then grabbed the cup again, holding it to my lips.

He leaned away from me and I knew I hadn't given him what he wanted, but I wasn't about to tell him that I was terrified. Not because Nex almost killed me, but because Chris being here changed everything.

"No, I'm not afraid of assassins—even from the Lunar Court's top guards—but isn't that an exhausting way to live?"

He had to be joking. I put the cup down without drinking. Of course being under constant attack was exhausting, but that's how the fey lived.

I took a measured breath, forcing myself to stay calm. He wasn't trying to frustrate me. I had my own issues. "Again, this is my normal. Isn't it the same for you here?"

"No." A little half-grin teased one side of his mouth as he looked around the room. "We like our betting, but we don't test each other the way your court does."

Wow. That was an incredible lie. My opinion of him was plummeting fast. Maybe the Lunar Court had an extreme aversion to lying, but I didn't think Gales were that bold-faced. "And that's why you have a new stepmother every year or so?" I reached for my wine again and took another sip.

The whites of his eyes showed hints of smoke flowing through as he turned back to me, and his shoulders seemed to loosen. "Okay. I guess I see your point."

There. I was winning him back. But I wasn't sure I wanted to. If there was smoke in his eyes, then he was one of *them*. "Anyway, I'd thought if any of my guards tried to assassinate me, it would've been Wilken." I glanced behind me. "He's the blond there. My brother's best friend."

He leaned toward me, and I knew I had him with that.

Asheral was as much of a gossip whore as his father. "The brother who just sent an assassin after you?"

"That's the one." I tossed a wave to Wilken, but Wilken's bored expression didn't change.

Asheral rested back, placing his elbows on the pillows behind him again. "They're not quite guards if you don't trust them, are they?"

"You're right." I leaned forward, touched my hand to his, and gave him a demure smile.

I caught Van watching me out of the corner of my eye.

See, I told him with a single shrug. I was playing the game. One I'd played so many times before. But it felt different this time. Worse.

I pulled my hand away from Asheral a little too fast, and tried to cover it up by taking another sip of wine. This time a bigger swallow, hoping it'd drown out the guilt.

I set down the wineglass, not loving the bitter acidity in it, and pulled out the locket, holding it in my hand. As if it would make me stronger and able to hold a conversation with this cocky, lying—

I took a breath. *Calm. Must keep the facade in place.* But the facade was slipping. "As I'm sure you've heard, I have some traitors among my guard, but I'm working to weed them out. The wolf did me a favor."

He crossed his arms, and I wondered if he'd noticed that I'd pulled back. "How many guards do you have?"

It was strange that he asked, but I didn't have anything to hide. There wasn't anything he could do to me by knowing how many guards I had. "Currently, twelve." But I didn't really think I needed any. It might be easier to just let them go now rather than wait for one of them to stab me in the back.

"You've had more than twelve?" He tilted his head to the side, as if he were confused.

Why was he confused? There wasn't anything off about having a number of guards at court, especially for young royals. "When I was a child, I had thirty. Sometimes nearly twice that. Sometimes less. But I'm not at court much anymore. And even if I was, I don't need them."

"No. You don't. But then you didn't even bring them the last time you came and you seemed to be doing just fine."

"Hmm." I had been, until Ziriel sneaked up behind me. It still burned that Van had to rescue me that night.

I couldn't read anything from Asheral's face. I wasn't sure if he was mad about what had happened, impressed that I'd killed so many before Ziriel put a knife to my throat, or out for revenge. Nothing showed.

"Don't worry about my father. You were outnumbered. Two against all of us." His eyes were filled with smoke, which told me that even if his words were a little flat, something was brewing under the surface.

I smiled as I was supposed to, but I couldn't really talk about what happened. "You were here?" I remembered him from before, but I didn't remember him being in the room when Eli and I started the fight. To be honest, that day was a blur.

"Yes. And it's not something I'll forget." He pressed his lips together, and I knew this probably was a lost cause. There was no way he'd be able to look past what I had done, to marry me, and I wasn't sure I could either.

Coming to Gales was exhausting me. I felt like a thick fog was settling over me, and I wasn't sure if I was crashing after the adrenaline rush from back-to-back attempts on my life, or if it was just normal disappointment at how badly this was going. "As you know, I can't speak about it, but I hope that what plagued your court is gone."

"That's the problem, isn't it?" His smile this time was filled with bitterness. "We have different ideas where the shades of gray fall."

I suddenly felt cold, scanning the room. "All that and they're still here?"

"In some form or another. You were too many centuries too late to change that. You see, there is no separating us from them anymore. We are one."

"Wow." That was it then. It was official. I couldn't marry into the Gales. Knowing what I knew. It just... It wasn't possible.

My gaze found Chris, who was leaning forward, elbows perched on the table, watching me. I had to warn him. Did he know about the meat?

Oh, God. If he didn't know...

I turned to Van, and he nodded. Not needing me to say any words. He crossed the room and sat down next to Chris.

"Are you okay?" Asheral was looking at Van, and then turned to me. "You've gone pale. Something I should know about?"

"No. Everything is fine." I took a big sip of wine to buy myself some time. I was gripping the cup a little too tightly, and made myself relax. I had to calm down, but Chris being here was throwing me massively off my game.

I flashed Asheral my biggest smile, but I was tired. Utterly exhausted. That wasn't surprising since I hadn't gotten much sleep lately, but my eyelids shouldn't be so heavy. "So, I don't know much about you. I know about your father, but I don't think we spoke last time I was here." One more sip of wine, and I would be able to do this. I could do this.

I lifted the cup but it slipped from my hand, and I couldn't bring myself to care or do anything about it. All I could think was that the wine looked like blood splashed across the table.

The room started to spin and I felt myself bottoming out.

"Cosette?" Asheral reached out, touching my arm, and I wondered if he'd said my name before, but I couldn't think. "Are you okay?"

I looked at the cup of wine. The bitter taste. The way I couldn't control my nerves.

"Van!" I yelled, but it came out much softer. Barely a whisper.

I felt myself falling...

Falling...

Falling...

Strong, familiar arms caught me and I left out a soft sigh.

"Chris." My voice was soft and airy but the arms tightened around me.

"I've got you." The rasp was thick in his voice, but I knew I was safe, so I let my dreams take me to another place. A safer place. A place where he held me before...

A soft brush of fingers pushed through my hair, and I looked up to see Chris' face hovering over mine. He let out a slow breath. "Glad you're awake again."

He had me cradled in his lap, resting with his back against a brick wall.

"Where are we?"

"Couple buildings over from the police station. I didn't want to carry you very far. Michael is coming with a car in a few."

I'd wiped the minds of everyone who knew that those two officers were coming to the compound—a simple bargain mixed with some forget-me magic—and as usual, it left me drained. "I passed out, didn't I?"

Chris smiled, and there was mischief in it. "Don't worry. You still looked elegant when you fainted, and I didn't let you hit the floor."

I wanted to laugh, but I couldn't. Not while I was immobile, splayed across him.

I tried to sit up, but couldn't. "This is embarrassing."

He tightened his grip on me. "Nothing embarrassing about you falling into my arms, princess."

I laughed, and nudged his stomach with my elbow. "Shut up."

"Never." He gave me a wink.

"The tables have turned."

A little crease formed between his eyes and I wondered if he'd know what I was talking about.

"Are you really, right now, referring back to the night we first met?"

How did he always know what I meant? Even when I was talking in circles. He always saw through my fey bullshit. "A little. Yes. But I've got questions—"

"Don't. Don't ruin this with something so serious. And don't compare how you are right now with how you found me." His whole body had tensed and his easy smile was gone.

"I'm not. I was... That was rude. I just thought if I joked about it, maybe you'd finally talk to me about what happened. Can we please finally talk about how you ended up at St. Ailbe's?" He started to say something, but I didn't let him get it all the way out. "Don't joke or flirt. For once."

"I..." He took a breath. "I learned pretty quickly that you have to just let go in life if you want to survive. To ride the ups and downs as they come, because they will. Good and bad. Even as a kid, I had to laugh every chance I could. If I let the bad stuff bother me, if that was the stuff I held on to, then I wasn't going to survive. Although I wasn't feeling funny the night you found me." He said the last with a laugh, but it wasn't funny.

I poked his side. "Nothing about that was funny."

"I don't mean to upset you. I'm actually very appreciative of what you did for me. You could've killed me with the rest of the pack."

"No. I couldn't have." I struggled to sit up, and he helped me, moving me off his lap to set me on the pavement. It was cold and hard and I missed the warmth of being in Chris' arms, but I couldn't have a normal, rational conversation with him like that. Not when all I wanted to do was pull his head down and finally know what his lips would feel like against mine. To know what he'd taste like. To finally give in to everything I wanted from him.

"You okay?" There was something about the sound of his voice that I found comforting and sexy and everything I knew I shouldn't feel.

I did what I always did, and pushed away any romantic feelings, but it was getting harder and harder to do. "I'll be fine. I wasn't expecting twelve people to be inside the police station. I usually top out at five or six."

Chris nudged my shoulder with his. "Why didn't you say anything?"

I leaned my head back against the brick wall. "And what would that have changed? Did we have another choice?" Because if any fey—even Van—heard about this, they'd lose their mind.

"No. I guess not."

"Exactly." I'd done what I had to do, and that was that. "At least I protected our secrecy. If it ever got out that the fey existed and it was my fault, my mother would..."

He reached for my hand, and I knew I shouldn't take it, but I couldn't stop myself.

I turned my head to look at him, and saw his eyes flash bright. "What would she do?" He was ready for a fight, but there was nothing he could do.

"I don't know. But I don't want to find out." And I didn't

want to talk about that. Not when I had questions and Chris was finally open to answering them. "So, no one knows your true age?"

He let go of my hand to run his fingers through his hair. "Adrian knows. I sometimes think Dastien suspects, just because I'm a better fighter than I should be for my station in the pack, but I have a lot more experience than anyone there."

"That's probably a safe bet."

"Yep. What else have you got for me?" He turned his head to look at me. "I can see all those questions brewing under the surface."

He was right. I always had one or two or ten brewing in my mind. But which one first? "What happened to you? After..."

"After your fey friends healed me and took me back home?"

"Yes. Start from there." I gave his hand a quick squeeze and let go.

He shook his head. "Only for you." He stared up at the night sky quietly for a while, and I looked up, too.

The moon was waning, but still beautiful. I wanted to watch Chris, but if he needed space to answer my question, I would give that to him.

"I was lost," he said after a while. His words were soft and quiet. "For a long while. I didn't have a pack and I didn't want one. Except for some visits to the nearby town, I'd never left my pack's land before then. All I knew was what you saw. So, I kept to myself. Partly out of fear of other people, but also fear that I'd hurt anyone I got close to. I didn't know if there was something bad in me that—"

"There's not." I was ending that question immediately. "I wouldn't have saved you if I'd seen anything bad in you."

He looked at me. "I know that now, but it took me a while to really believe it. You know?"

I nodded. I did know.

"So, I wandered." His gaze went back to the night sky. "Most of the time I stuck to the woods."

I should've checked on him more or done something more. He shouldn't have had to live like that, but I knew he'd stop talking if I showed even the tiniest hint of pity. "And how did that go?"

"About how you'd expect." He laughed. "I was a mess. I hunted in my wolf form. Found shelter when I needed it. Eventually, I was in my wolf form and I ran into another Were."

"Who?"

"Adrian."

"Ah." So that was why Adrian knew. "He's a nice one."

"The best, but I ran away. He came back with more Weres. I was terrified, but his Alpha shifted and talked to me. It was the first time..."

"The first time what?"

"The first time I realized what I'd missed."

He looked at me then, and he had a soft smile on his face that didn't quite cover up his sadness. I wasn't sure what he was going to say next. "What? What did you miss?" I finally asked.

"Family. Not people who want to kill you all the time, but real, true family. You know?"

"God. I know how you feel." That hadn't been what I'd expected, but I understood. "I've felt that way for nearly two hundred years. When I see Tessa and her family—"

"Jealous doesn't even begin to cut it."

Exactly. He knew exactly how I felt. I don't know why that surprised me, but it did.

I scooted away from the wall so that I could see him easier. This time, I wasn't looking away.

He looked at me, too. "The first Sunday I went to their house, I was like—is this what normal is?"

"No." I reached over and squeezed his hand, and this time, I didn't let go. "There is no normal. It's a myth. Everyone is just trying to do their best with the circumstances that they have. Some have it better than others. Some get it easier. It's not about what's fair or what you deserve. You get what you get, and sometimes that really sucks. But you can't let it get you down because you are good." I paused. "Can I ask you a question?"

He threaded his fingers with mine. "Anything, princess."

I laughed. "God. I hate it when people call me that, but you make it funny. How do you do that?"

He grinned and the flirt I knew and loved was back. "Just my charm."

"How old are you?"

"Twenty-eight."

I'd thought he was even older than that, but living through that kind of torture aged a person. "A little old for St. Ailbe's, don't you think?"

"Aren't you, too?"

"Yes, but I'm not actually going there. I've been spying on the coven."

"Okay. Sure." He scooted away from the wall just a little bit, so that we were almost sitting face to face. "After Adrian found me in the woods, we became close. His Alpha was actually really great. He got me on my feet, and didn't make me join the pack—which is really unusual, but I think he knew I would've run if he'd pressed it."

He was quiet for a second, and I was scared that he wasn't going to finish. But if I rushed him, I knew he'd shut down with some joke.

"When Adrian was heading to school that fall, he told me to come with him. He said that I was kept ignorant of what being part of a pack meant and it was time that I learned. I hadn't joined his pack—still haven't—but he said that I'd get better if I was at St. Ailbe's and if I could see a regular therapist that they'd bring in... Honestly, I don't know why I agreed, but I was so lost, I think I would've done anything he told me to. I trusted him, and you know what—he was right. Being at this school, I feel like I'm finally learning about what I am. Sometimes it makes me sad about how I was raised, but mostly, thankful that I survived."

Honestly, it was a miracle that he'd survived and not just survived but managed to be healthy—physically and mentally. And then to be able to fight against evil like he was...

Chris was amazingly strong. In that moment, I was so proud of him and his courage that it was almost bursting from me. But I knew if I showed it, then he'd tell me he wasn't courageous or anything to be proud of, so I covered up all those feelings.

Instead of giving him any compliments, I nudged his leg with my foot. "Didn't I hear that you kissed Tessa?"

His cheeks turned a pretty shade of pink. "I know. Stupid."

"You're ten years older than her." I tried to jerk my hand from his, but he held on.

"Yeah, but you're a hundred and twenty-something years older than me and I'd still make out with you." He ran his thumb over the back of my hand.

A surprised laugh slipped free. He always managed to make me laugh when I wasn't expecting it.

"And I...I don't feel my age. I spent most of my childhood locked up or fighting for my life or healing from the latest beating. I'm still a teenager in a lot of ways. At least that's what my therapist says. Sometimes I feel like a kid, but some days I feel old and tired. You know?"

"Yes." Oh, God, I knew. I'd never had a childhood—not when politics and assassins and power plays were a part of my daily life. Most days of my life I felt like a physical weight was dragging me into the ground.

I'd left court over fifty years ago to spy, but there was a sinking in my stomach that told me I was about to be sucked back into that house of horrors any day now. I hoped that wiping the policemen's minds would make it go away, but the feeling was still there. All I wanted was the freedom to live

"Anyhow. I probably shouldn't have kissed her, but you know what's crazy?"

"What?"

He leaned closer to me. "When I heard that Michael let a bitten werewolf live—and stay—at St. Ailbe's, I kept a close watch on her. My pack was all bitten wolves and they were twisted. Sick. Really fucking evil."

Oh no. He didn't really think that Tessa would end up like them, did he? "I remember, but she's not like them."

"No. But I didn't know that at first. I didn't understand Michael's decision to let her live." He shook his head. "And then she tried to run away, and I was like...here we go again."

Chris ran his free hand down his face. Usually he tried to laugh off or flirt away his anxiety, but I saw it.

He took a shaky breath. "Anyway, I caught her before she could get away. Never moved so fast in my life. I made some stupid joke, but I couldn't let her leave. Not until I knew if she needed to be killed. Those first few days she would forget to eat, and I'd make her a sandwich, but what I really wanted to do was make sure that she had the tools to survive and the people around her that would help her learn to deal with her wolf. I kissed her because I saw that strength in her, and I thought she was going to be okay and that maybe because of who I was and what I'd grown up with...maybe she was the reason I'd lived through all that. So that I could be with her and help her not turn into one of them. Everyone at St. Ailbe's is so hyperfocused on finding a mate, and for the first time I saw the logic in it. Tessa and I somehow made sense in my mind."

He was so sweet. I understood why he'd done it, and it did

make sense, but that's not how things worked. If he was looking for a reason behind his childhood, I wasn't sure he'd ever find it.

Children are innocent, and sometimes born into the worst situations, but as we grow up, it's up to each and every one of us to face every day with courage, put our painful past behind us, and work hard to grow better, every day in every way.

Chris was doing that, even if he couldn't see it in himself.

"It sounds so stupid now... But when Tessa ripped open Imogen's throat, I was worried that she was going downhill. And when she refused to shift... That was scary. That's what will break someone's mind. But Dastien was who she needed. I'm just really thankful it all turned out okay."

"Me, too." They were true mates, and that was special. I was happy for them on days I wasn't jealous of what they had. "I have a question, but I don't want to upset you."

"Ask." He tugged my hand gently. "I don't mind, even if it upsets me. I owe you my life."

"You don't owe me anything." But I still had more questions. "Do you know what happened to the town? To the humans? Do you ever go back to your pack's land?"

He was quiet for a long time. His face got this haunted look, his eyes were glowing with the wolf, and I knew it was probably because he felt threatened even just thinking about the place.

"I don't know what happened to them. I haven't been there since you and Van brought me back after healing me. I scrounged all the money from the houses and some supplies—a tent, clothes, and all the food I could fit into my pack—and I took off. I figured the people didn't want to see me, and..."

I wanted to say something, but he kept talking and I wasn't about to interrupt.

"But a couple of years ago, a lawyer found me. He'd been trying to track me down for a while. I didn't realize that you covered up their deaths so well, making it official in the human records."

A little line formed between his eyes as he waited for confirmation, and I gave him a nod. "Yes, we always try to cover our tracks. Having so many go missing at once would cause a lot of questions, and it seemed better to get death certificates."

He stared down at the pavement. "I wasn't thinking about any of that."

I nudged him a couple times until he looked at me. "Why would you? You had enough on your plate just trying to recover from all of it."

He huffed one loud breath and pulled his hand from mine. I instantly missed the warmth of it.

"As the only surviving member of the pack, everything in the pack's accounts—land, money, stock portfolio, the businesses in the neighboring town—is mine. It's how I can afford to go to St. Ailbe's. But other than that, I don't touch the money. I've thought about going back and burning the whole place—houses, barns, everything—to the ground, but I don't know what good that would do. It's not going to solve anything and it won't fix what happened there."

"If you ever change your mind about going back, I'll go back with you. All you have to do is say the word, and I'll have Van take us. We can burn it or tear it down or sell it."

"Selling it..." He looked at the stars again. "I wouldn't be able to use the money. I can't—"

"You can't right now, but maybe in ten years. Twenty." The look he gave me was full of doubt and denial, but I was right. "A little time and distance solves so many of life's problems. And I'll go with you whenever. It doesn't have to be today or tomorrow. You saved me from hitting that dirty police station floor. So now I owe you."

He laughed, and it was a strained sound, but it relaxed him a little. "Let's call it even."

"Even." I liked the sound of that.

"I never thought I'd see you again, but I'm glad we're friends."

Headlights pulled up and a window rolled down. "Get in!" Michael's voice called out to us.

Chris stood and stuck out his hand to pull me from the ground. I took it.

"I'm Christopher Matthews," he said as he pulled me up. "It's good to finally get to know you, and to have a friend who really knows who I am."

"Cosette Argent." I grinned at him. "It's truly lovely to see how good you're doing. I have to say that I'm pretty proud of you. And it's nice to have someone who knows who and what I am, too." I gave his hand a squeeze before letting go. "Friends."

It was the last moment before everything went to shit for me, but I went to bed that night with a smile on my face for the first time in a long time. I had a friend who knew what I was—who I was—and still wanted to be my friend. Not to use me or anything like that. We both had secrets from our group, and I would keep his. Just like I knew he would keep mine. And the past we shared would be another secret.

I didn't know how far that friendship would grow, but over the next few weeks, as my world went sideways, Chris was always there. Making me laugh. Keeping me sane. Being the light in the dark.

I was pretty sure he loved me back, and I wasn't sure if that made things better, but it definitely made them harder.

There were voices talking, pulling me from my dreams—from my memories—but I wanted to go back to sleep. I wanted to be back there and stay in that moment. Relive it over and over. It had been so simple. No politics or games or strings. Just honesty and respect and friendship.

But my head was pounding, and I couldn't.

A moan slipped free as I sat up. I blinked. Even the dim candlelight was too bright. I closed my eyes tight. My head felt like someone had slammed it into the floor over and over and over. I rubbed my hands on my scalp but there was no blood.

If I was feeling this bad, Van had to be close by. "What happened?" My voice was strained with pain, and even just the sound of my harsh whisper made the throbbing in my head worse.

"You were drugged," Van said softly from beside me. "Poisoned."

That made sense, given the headache. If it wasn't so painful, I'd have laughed. I cradled my head, hands against my temples, as I hunched over. "Three attempts on my life in less than what?"

"Twenty-three minutes." His voice was soft, but I could hear his anger sizzling underneath.

I blinked my eyes open again to find Van crouched next to my low bed. My vision was still blurry and I couldn't make much out beyond his face in the low candlelight.

"That's a new record." I was making a joke, but it was actually terrifying that someone—probably multiple someones—wanted me dead so badly.

"Indeed." He didn't have a hint of a smile, even after my lame joke.

"How long was I out?" If it was a few minutes, the poison wasn't that bad. If longer, then...

"Two hours and six minutes. I healed you relatively quickly, but you were sleeping soundly and I didn't want to wake you. Better to let you come to naturally."

I reached out and grabbed his hand. That tiny movement

made the room spin and my head pound louder. I could hardly think it was so bad.

Two hours was a long time, which meant I must've been pretty close to dead. No wonder Van was being serious. He'd saved my life again. "I appreciate you so much."

Van squeezed my hand back. "And I you. Gave me a scare. Let's not do that again."

"No." I massaged my temples. "God, Van. Why does it still hurt?"

"I don't like that at all. It shouldn't be, after...but I think I can fix that." Van reached out, placing his hand on my forehead.

Within a second of his hand touching me, the pain started to recede, and I could finally think about something other than how bad my head hurt.

And then all at once my heart dropped to my feet, my body felt cold, and I knew that something was very, very wrong. Because he couldn't be here. It was too dangerous and I already had so much on the line...I couldn't do what I had to do if he was here.

I squeezed my eyes shut. *Please don't let him be here. Please don't let him be here. God can't be this cruel.* "Chris?"

"I'm here." His raspy voice came from behind me.

Damn it. Why couldn't just one thing be easy for me?

I finally looked up at the room. It was typical Gales. Mattress on the floor, surrounded by pillows. Bookcases filled with books—because they were seriously antitech here. No TV. No Wi-Fi. Not for guests. Only candles lit the room, but even in the dim, flickering light, I could now make out the riot of colors.

And there was Chris, leaning against the wall by the stone slab door. Arms crossed. All signs of joking gone. But he was still beautiful. Even more beautiful than the picture inside my locket.

No. Damn it all. "But why? Why are you here?"

He stepped away from the wall. "Eli—"

"Screw, Eli. Leave. Go back to Texas. I can't..." I looked at Van, and the tears came. "I can't do this with him here. I can't do it. Having him here is going to get me killed."

"What's going on? Why are you here? What were you talking to that man about?" His voice was insistent and determined, but I knew that when I answered his questions, it was going to break something inside him just like it'd broken me.

After everything he'd been through, I didn't want to do it. I didn't want to tell him. I didn't think I could get the words out. But I had to tell him.

This was the one time I couldn't talk in circles. Not to him. Not about this. I had to say the plain words, even if it would hurt me just as much to say them as I knew it would hurt him to hear them.

"I'm here to find a husband."

His face grew pale. "What?"

"After everything we did...after the spell Eli did...my people..." I turned to Van.

This had nothing to do with Ziriel or his court so I was free to tell him what I wanted. My mother hadn't restricted me on this subject like she loved to do. Finally, I could actually tell Chris what was going on in my life, but I still couldn't say the words. "God. Where do I even start? How can I explain this shit position that I'm in?"

The pity on Van's face made bile rise, burning the back of my throat, but I swallowed it down. I just wanted him to say the words so I didn't have to. Maybe that made me weak or a coward, but I knew Van could do this for me.

"Our people like to test each other." Van stood, facing Chris. "See who is weak. If they're easily killed then they aren't worthy of their spot in the court. Cosette is a bit of a mystery because she's so high up—a princess in the strongest fey court—but also because of who her father is."

I hated that I was a mystery. After all these years, my court still didn't respect me. They couldn't stop testing me, even though I'd proven myself worthy countless times. But it was all because of my father. I lay back on the bed and closed my eyes, letting Van do all the hard work this time.

"Who's her father?" Chris asked.

"An archon."

"Eli?" There was a thread of horror in his voice and I didn't blame him. I definitely didn't want Eli to be my father.

"No. Another. It doesn't matter." Van was quiet, but I waited in the bed for him to finish.

"For the last little while, Cosette has been a spy, as you know, and living away from our court. But with things changing recently, the fey have been reminded of her power and are testing her. The only way to stop it, is for her to partner with someone powerful enough and steeped in the courts with lots of alliances so that it would seem stupid for someone to speak ill of her, let alone try to assassinate her."

"Got it." Chris' voice was snappy.

"See, Coco. He understands."

"Ugh." Our groans echoed each other.

"Don't call her that," Chris said. "Just because I understand doesn't mean I like it."

I sat up now, and they turned to me. Van still had pity on his face, but Chris—the muscle along his jaw was tic-tic-ticcing and I knew he was more than mad.

"I always wanted to marry someone who made me feel...like you make me feel, but... Oh, God! What is wrong with me?" I swiped away a tear. "I still can't say the stupid words. I—" My voice broke on the most pathetic sob.

Van moved away from me to make way for Chris.

Within a second, Chris closed the distance, sat on the bed, and swept me onto his lap. I wrapped myself around him, burying my head in his neck as I cried.

"I promised myself I would say it if you were here, and I can't—"

"Hey. Hey." He rubbed a hand down my back. "Don't cry. I know you're madly in love with me."

My sobs turned into a laugh. "How do you know that?"

"Because I'm really hot."

The laughter turned to giggles and I pulled away from him.

Chris rubbed his thumbs under my eyes, wiping away the tears.

"How do you always do that?"

"Do what?"

"Make me laugh."

"It's just my special talent." He gave me a small, sad smile. "It's either laugh through the pain or let it consume you. So I choose laughter."

The tears started again, because that was just so Chris. I knew what he'd come from—what he had to overcome—and that he was still so lighthearted and kind after everything...

"Don't cry over me." He wiped my tears again. "I was wrong before. I'm sorry for what I said last night, but I have a plan."

The dread that I'd been feeling since I'd arrived here rose again, and my tiny fraction of Sight that I had was screaming that whatever Chris said, I wasn't going to like it. "What kind of plan?"

"Eli brought me to Gales because he said someone here had enough power to cut my lunar tie."

I scrambled backward, off his lap. "What? No. You can't be serious. Breaking your lunar tie might mean you'd lose your wolf. Forever."

"I figured that might be the case."

How could he say that like it was nothing? "You can't cut your tie. You'd end up resenting me—hating me—and I—"

"You can say a lot of things, Cosette. But you can't tell me how I feel about this. I wouldn't hate or resent you. I could never."

No. I had to convince him how bad this would be. There was a reason why I hadn't left the Lunar Court entirely. Severing a magical tie had big consequences. "You don't know that."

"Neither do you."

Fine. I needed a new tactic. There was so much wrong with this "plan" that I had plenty to argue. "Do you know what kind of deal you'd have to make? Do you even know what you're dealing with here? You—"

Van cleared his throat, cutting me off. I looked at Van and he gave me a small shake of the head that reminded me to keep my mouth shut.

Damn it. Damn Ziriel and his stupid, stupid deal. And telling Chris? That was amateur hour. I was better than this. Smarter. Yet having him here, it was making me weak and stupid.

So stupid and so, so weak. Which I couldn't afford. Not right now.

Oh, no. I turned to Van, but he gave me a slow nod. He was thinking the same thing that I was.

I must've done something horrible in another life, if this is what it all came down to. If this was what I had to do.

Because it was going to kill me.

But it was the only option I had left. Maybe that's why I had the dream I did. Not because of being held in Chris' arms, but because I'd done this kind of thing before in front of him. Now I just had to do it *to* him.

I was already broken, my heart in icy tatters, but that didn't mean that Christopher had to be this way, too. He deserved more than I could give him. He deserved the quiet life that he wanted. He'd worked too hard to be pulled into my mess. I'd never, ever be able to give him what we both wanted.

Maybe if I could help him find his peace—a life with family and children and a quiet home in the woods—then that could be enough for me, too.

So, I'd do it. I'd hammer the ice pick into the frozen remains of my heart, shattering what was left of it. I could do this for him. If I let him go, then I would be left empty and alone, but he would be free to find happiness. That would have to be enough.

I opened my eyes and filled my essence with the power of the Lunar Court. Moonlight pulsed through my veins, making my body hum with its power. Not everyone in the Lunar Court had control over the lunar tie. To have that, the fey had to be born into our court, descended from the original Lunar fey.

Being a princess of my court, I had more than that. I had too much power over the lunar tie, and over any werewolf, even the most Alpha of them all. I could change their minds, memories, decisions, and control their actions.

I always swore I would never, ever use it on my friends. It was a line that once crossed, I'd never come back from. But it was too late for me. I might as well take that final step and help protect the one thing that mattered to me.

"After I am done talking, you will leave this room and you will forget that you love me." The light went out of Chris' eyes and they glazed over as the magic hit him, and I knew it was working.

"Once you're home, you will forget that you were ever here." My voice was shaky with the power at first, but then grew steady. "You will forget seeing me alone. You will delete our messages to each other and get rid of any and all evidence of our friendship. And when you're done, you'll forget all about our relationship."

Chris stumbled back a step, and his wolf rose to the surface trying to fight, but there was nothing he could do but surrender to the magic.

"We will be casual acquaintances at best. You will find me annoying and only barely tolerate me. I was someone who saved you a long time ago, someone who fought with you in the chapel and helps out when she can. Nothing more. When someone asks about me, you'll change the subject. If they ask about our relationship, you will say there isn't one. There never was. And you will never, ever return to any fey court ever again."

The last of the magic washed through him.

The wolf settled down and his eyes turned to their normal blue. He dropped his head for a moment and let out a gasp, as if he felt the memories physically rip away from him.

There was a ringing in my ears as the magic I'd called in started to settle, leaving me a shaking, empty, heartless husk.

"I'm sorry." He pressed his hand to his forehead as he looked around. "I must be lost. Can someone help me find my way home?"

Van nodded. "It'd be my pleasure. This way." Van gripped Chris' elbow, leading him out of the room.

Chris stumbled a few steps and looked back at me.

It was like he still saw me.

Maybe it hadn't worked. I held my breath, not wanting to give in to the hope that he'd remember everything. That he was secretly powerful enough to stand up against the power of the Lunar Court. Because that would be impossible. And yet, I had this tiny, flickering flame of a hope left.

He opened his mouth to say something, then stopped. "I'm sorry for interrupting. I'll see you around campus," he said, and then he was gone. Van tugged him quickly to the door. He held his hand to the stone, and it slid soundlessly away.

Van gave me one last look before he pulled Chris into the hallway beyond.

As soon as the stone slid back into place, I gasped as if there wasn't enough air in the room to breathe. The pain in my chest grew until I crumpled on the bed, sobbing.

I'd thought I'd cried everything out in my mother's chambers, but I hadn't.

I thought I'd felt all the heartbreak I could, but that wasn't true at all.

I knew for a fact that the other half of my soul was now gone —forever. And maybe in a hundred years, the pain would dim enough for me to be thankful that he was safe and happy, but all I felt was dead. All I felt was empty. All I felt was the last bit of love and hope in my life melt away.

The magic I'd used to control Chris' mind had wiped out the little bit of energy I had in me. After not sleeping or eating for three weeks while trying to find out what Eli had done with Chris, and the aftereffects of being poisoned, and now all of the layers of emotional turmoil and heartbreak...I was done. I had nothing left.

Nothing left.

I wanted to go back to Colorado. I didn't have it in me to pretend that Asheral was husband-worthy. I didn't want to visit any other courts to find someone that didn't exist anywhere, or with anyone but Chris. I didn't want to do anything but cry and eat cake for the rest of the fortnight.

And when my mother dragged me to the altar, I would say the hollow words, because I had no fight left in me. Doing this— controlling Chris and wiping all evidence of the love we shared from his mind—killed what little fight I had left.

And now I was done.

So beyond done.

When Van came back, I'd tell him to take me to Colorado. He could meet with my mother separately and decide on a man strong enough to satisfy the court. They could tell me when to show up, and that would be that.

I didn't care. Not anymore.

Until then, I was done and I wanted to be left alone. I deserved at least that much. That one tiny thing.

CHAPTER ELEVEN

CHRIS

I FELT wooden as I moved through the hallways, following Van. We were underground somewhere, but it didn't look like any place I'd been before. Something about it made me worry, but my wolf was sound asleep like he'd never been before.

A bead of sweat rolled down my cheek and I brushed it away.

It was hot here. Why was it so hot? Wasn't it winter?

Jesus. Where was I? What was wrong with me? Why couldn't I remember what I was doing here or how I got here? Why did my head feel like it was filled with smoke?

Shit. I was finally losing it.

Fear, strong enough to take my breath away, coursed through me—someone needed to put me down. I'd lost time and that was the first sign that my wolf was winning control. I didn't trust him. He... He was too angry, and that could twist easily into something dark. But it was too late. I'd already been infected by the evil insanity that ruled my pack. If I couldn't remember where I was or how I got here, and I couldn't reason any answers to the questions racing through my head, then it was way too late for me.

I knew I was doomed. I'd been stupid to follow Adrian to St. Ailbe's. Stupid to try to have friends. But maybe if I asked Donovan to do it, he would. Yes. I knew he would. Dawson was too soft. He'd spent too many years watching over temperamental werewolves to do it, and he'd work too hard to try to save me.

I didn't have any fight left in me. I was done.

So that was my plan. Get back. Call Donovan. And end it before I did any real harm. If I tried to do it myself, I'd just end up losing to the wolf. No. I needed Donovan's help.

God. The way Cosette looked at me. Maybe I'd done something bad already. Maybe that was why I was here.

I looked at Van for a second. There was something stiff about the way he was moving. He wasn't an overly friendly guy, but he didn't usually walk around looking like he'd just tasted something gross.

I had to ask. "Van?"

He stared at the ground for a second before sparing me a look. "Yes?"

"Where am I? Did I do something wrong? Something bad?"

He kept a steady, even pace moving forward down the sloping hallway.

This place didn't feel right. I was sure at any second, the whole place was going to cave in, but Van didn't seem to have the same concern. He wasn't watching the ceiling or the walls like I was.

"Why would you think that you did something bad?"

I must really be losing it if I was creeped out by this place—with no clue how I got here—and Van was fine. "The Weres in my pack would lose time or forget what they did as a wolf, and I don't remember what—"

Van stepped in front of me, gripping my shoulders. "Don't worry. You're not like them. You'll never be like them. You've done nothing wrong. All of that is in the past. Let it stay there."

I took a breath and let it out slowly. I didn't know much about the fey, but they didn't lie.

Okay. Okay. So, maybe it wasn't as bad as I thought. "I don't understand. I'm really confused. Why am I here? Where are we? How did I get here? I can't seem to remember—"

"Don't worry about any of that. You'll be home soon."

"Okay." Home. That sounded good. Except St. Ailbe's wasn't safe anymore. It'd been good for me for a while and I didn't want to give up on it, but Dawson had shut down the school. Everything had changed, and not for the better.

I was going to have to leave. Maybe find a quiet spot in the woods again. Be alone for a while because there was a hollowness in my soul that was threatening to swallow me whole, and I wasn't sure if I was safe to be around anymore.

Van couldn't lie, but maybe he didn't know that I was losing it.

Donovan. I would call Donovan. He'd help me.

But there was something else I didn't understand. Something off. Where was my wolf?

If there was any kind of danger, my wolf would've risen up, but he was sleeping soundly. Peacefully quiet. Maybe quieter than I'd ever felt before.

Wait.

No.

There was something wrong.

I stopped walking.

Something was missing. But what?

I rubbed my hand across my forehead as I tried to remember. There was too much smoke filling all the empty spaces in my head. All the spots where memories should have been. And all I had now were a bunch of questions.

Why was I here? Where was I? It didn't look like any place in Texas, that was for sure. Torches on the walls. Golden sand pressed against glossy surfaces. The scent of sour apple smoke filling the hallway.

No. This was wrong.

I stumbled as Van grabbed my arm, tugging me to keep up the pace. "This way. You'll feel much better once you get to your own bed. I promise."

Shit. Had I been drugged?

A little beast popped in before me with red eyes and long, pointy fingers.

I stumbled again. "Holy shit. What the fuck is that?"

The little beast's eyes glowed brighter and it was like the whole hallway dimmed to give it that light.

"Where are you *taking him*?" His voice had been playful, almost childlike at first, but the last words deepened until I could almost hear echoing screams it taunted from its victims in the night.

"Home." Van tugged me forward again. "I'm taking him back home via the gateway. As is allowed."

"No!" The hallway darkened even more until all I could see were its glowing red eyes. *"Our game's not done."* The little beast's voice grew darker than the hallway.

Game? What is it talking about? I'd never play any game with that thing. If anything, I should fucking kill it. Just being around the little beast made me want to stomp on it.

"I don't care about whatever game you have going. Whatever it was, it's over now. Go away!"

"No. *You don't talk to me that way.* And he's mine here! Ziriel said so!" He disappeared in a puff of smoke.

What? How did it just vanish? "Was that a demon? Are we in Hell? Am I dead?"

Van let out a long sigh and gripped my arm again, tugging me forward. "No. You're not dead and Hell is much hotter than this, but let's hurry before we get into trouble."

"Okay."

Wait. Why did I keep agreeing? I searched my memories for whatever I was forgetting—

A stabbing pain hit my head and I hissed. "What's wrong with me?"

"You'll be fine." Van dragged me a few more steps. "You just need some food and sleep. It's been a long day. Come on. We have to hurry now."

"Okay."

What the fuck? The word just kept slipping out of my mouth, but nothing about losing memories and being confused was okay. I needed answers, and I was beginning to wonder if I could trust Van at all.

I jerked my arm free from Van's grip, and a section of the ceiling two feet in front of us fell to the floor, sand spilled down until we were fully blocked.

Van started back the way we came, but the little beastie popped back in—this time with company.

The man wasn't as tall as me, but he looked like he'd have fun roasting me on a spit. His long black beard was flecked with gray, and his long hair was pulled back from his face. "What do you think you're doing, Van?"

Van moved to stand between me and the man. "It's time for young Christopher to go home. He's gotten in over his head."

"No." The man's voice grew threatening and smoke swirled through the whites of his eyes as he stepped toward Van. "You'll not be taking him anywhere." A few men dressed in all white and with carved golden masks popped in a puff of smoke behind the man.

Van gripped the hilt of his sword. "Yes. I will. He's not of your court. He's under our protection, and I'm going to take him home. Now."

I didn't understand what was going on. I wished I could dunk my head in a bucket of ice water to clear the fog from it. Why didn't I understand what was happening?

Because someone had messed with my head. It was the only answer my muddled brain could come up with.

I didn't want anyone getting into a fight over me. It wasn't necessary—I wasn't worth any kind of bloodshed—but maybe this new guy could help me. "Who are you?"

The man looked at me for a long second, and then turned his head—as if he were listening to something far off.

And then he laughed. "Oh, she's good. But Eli doesn't want him to leave yet. So, I think I'll keep him."

His fist slammed into my face before I could move. Blood gushed down my face, and I reached for my wolf, but he was still asleep.

What. The. Fuck.

"That should've worked." The man ran his other hand down his beard.

I grabbed onto my nose with both hands. Broken. Damn it. Only one way to fix this.

One.

Two.

Three.

I let out all my air and straightened my nose before it could heal crooked. Pain spread from my nose through my body for a second, but then it was over. I'd learned the hard way to always set my nose if there wasn't any more fighting happening. I'd moved too slowly before and it always hurt so much worse to reset it when it was broken and healed.

I wiped the blood from my face with my T-shirt. "What the hell is wrong with you?"

The man crossed his arms. "I'm trying to fix your head." He stared at me as if I were a puzzle he was trying to solve. "You should be grateful."

Maybe I should be. There was something about the guy that I didn't like, but I couldn't deny the fact that my head was in a fog.

"Leave him," Van said. "I don't want trouble again, Ziriel. This time I will show you the full force of who I am."

"Hold your threats. I've been told to help him remember, so I'm helping him remember." Ziriel gave Van a look. "Even I won't go against Eli's wishes."

Ziriel turned back to me and his eyes started to glow bright red.

I stumbled back. "A demon."

"Not a demon."

Then what the fuck was he?

He studied me for a minute, his hand stroking his beard. "Ah. Something more subtle then. I think I get it now."

He placed his hand on my head before I could move.

The searing pain was back again—quick and fierce—but then it was gone. And when it left, the fog in my brain was gone. My wolf growled. The haze over my memories lifted. I could think again.

And I had answers again.

Everything I'd forgotten—that Cosette had made me forget —came rushing back.

It wasn't some faceless fey that had pulled me from the pit. Cosette sat with me. Cared for me. And from the moment we became friends behind that police station. To the picnics and

175

hikes. The stolen moments and texts and messages where we shared our biggest fears, dreams, everything.

The moment when I knew I loved her as more than a friend. That I wanted her more than anything. And the second right after it when I realized I couldn't ever have her. That I was too weak. Even after everything I survived, I wasn't strong enough to be with her.

To Eli coming. And realizing that she was my mate. To Van sitting at my table, telling me not to trust Gales and not to touch the meat. But I already knew all that. He didn't have to tell me. I wasn't a fucking idiot. I knew the meat smelled wrong.

Damn it, Cosette.

I wanted to feel betrayed, but I understood why she did it. I understood what drove her to cross that line.

But damn it, Cosette.

She should've trusted me to know what I felt and how I felt.

I realized I was in the hallway with Van, Ziriel, and the little beast, when I should've been back in that room with Cosette. Telling her how badly she'd just fucked up.

"Excuse me. I need to speak to someone." The guards made way as I ran down the hallway.

"You owe me." Ziriel yelled at my back, but his voice had a hint of threat in it.

I didn't like that. Not at all.

I spun to him, not slowing my pace much as I ran backward. "Do I? Or did Eli tell you to do it?" I didn't ask him to fix me, and I wasn't going to make a bargain with him over something he'd already done. Not unless I had to.

He shrugged. "This one's on the house. Next time, you'll pay like anyone else."

"Fine." Because it wasn't going to happen again. Cosette was going to stay out of my head until I broke the lunar tie. Like I told her I was going to do.

Goddammit, Cosette.

I started moving faster and faster and faster until I was sprinting down the halls, following Van's scent through the twists and turns until I was standing in front of the stone door. Her sobs echoed out into the hallway and I wanted to shake her for doing this. Not just to me, but to herself.

I stood there quietly for a second. Not to catch my breath, but to get my emotions steady. I'd been low then high and I needed to find center so that I could convince her that everything was going to be okay. I was still pissed, but it'd dulled a lot. She was hurting worse over this than I could ever hurt her.

Now, I just had to get inside the room. I wasn't sure how these doors worked exactly. They seemed to disappear and reappear at will, but not for me.

Van stepped up behind me, placed his hand on the stone, and it slid clear of the doorway.

I gave him a nod, and then stepped into the room. Van closed the door behind me, leaving me alone with Cosette. Finally.

"Honey, I'm home!" I sang.

She sat up not even caring to wipe her face. "What... How are you here? What's going on? Is that *your* blood?"

"Eli told Ziriel to reverse it." I sat next to her on the bed and grabbed her face in my hands. I wasn't going to let her look away. Not when I needed her to really listen to me. "Please. Don't ever take away my memories again. It left me feeling empty, like I was ready to die."

"Oh, God." She sobbed harder.

"But it's worse than what you did to me. Taking away my memories means that you've given up, and I won't let you. Ten years ago, you told me that I had to let the desire to live burn like a fire in my gut, and I was lost for a while, but those words... They kept me going. I found that fire eventually, and I fed it.

But you're not? By doing this—by following your mother's orders—you're letting it die. Please, don't give up. Not yet. Not now. So, don't do that again. Ever."

Tears fell from her eyes and I brushed them away with my thumbs. I hate that she hurt herself so much while trying to protect me, but she had to understand that she couldn't ever, ever mess with my head again.

"I won't do it again." Her voice was shaky and broken. "It hurt so much worse than I thought it would, and I'm sorry. But I'm so tired and I..."

She didn't need to tell me she was exhausted. I could see it in the dark circles under her eyes and paler-than-normal skin.

I needed her to understand something and I wanted to make a joke to ease her into it, but there was no easing into this. "You can't make me forget you without killing half of my soul. You're my mate, Cosette."

"I can't be!" She slapped a hand over her mouth as she jerked away from me. I could almost see the thoughts running through her head as her eyes widened. "Oh, no. I think you're right. How did I not know?" Her words were muffled behind her hand, and silent tears slipped down her cheeks. "Oh, God. This is a disaster."

I laughed, because that was the only thing I could do. "Tell me how you really feel about it."

She slapped my shoulder. "Shut up," she said while failing to hold back a laugh that was half-sob. "This is bad."

I knew she didn't mean to be insulting, and I didn't take it that way. She was scared. That's why she'd tried to take my memories away. She didn't want me to get hurt. If I went home with her today, I would be eaten alive. But I wasn't going there like this. Not until I broke my tie.

"You're just going to have to get used to me. You're stuck." I gave her a wink and hoped a little joke would help her stop crying. She was already too tired and didn't need to exhaust herself any more. "Shouldn't have agreed to be my friend. Crucial error on your part."

"No. I feel drawn to you—I always have—but I thought it was just because I'm from the Lunar Court and you're a were-wolf. And then I thought we were friends that were attracted to each other. It...it can't be more than that. I would've known..." She fell onto her back, covering her face with her hands. "Are you sure I'm your mate?"

I scooted to lay beside her on my side. "I'm pretty fucking sure."

"Shit. This is a *disaster*." She spoke through her fingers.

I pulled her hands away from her face. I needed to see her face when we talked.

"What are we going to do?" Her voice had a bit of whine to it, and that was definitely not the Cosette I knew.

"We're going to be okay, and I'm pretty sure it's not a disaster."

She rolled onto her side to face me. Her eyes were so swollen and red. "How?"

I brushed a piece of tear-stained hair away from her face. "Where you go, I go. Simple as that."

"No. You can't. The thought of you meeting my mother terrifies me. The things she'd do to you... The things my brother would do. What kind of monster would I be if I allowed that to happen? I just... You can't—"

Her fear grew stronger, stinking up the room with its sickly sweet smell.

"Take a breath." I cupped her cheek. "It'll be okay."

"You don't know that. You can't possibly know that. I know I seem strong, but it's something that I've worked hard on. I'm not invincible. I wouldn't agree to marry someone on a whim... I need to marry for power. I have to do this or—"

I rubbed my thumb across her cheek. "Do you trust me?"

"Yes. Of course I do. But I have a very, very bad feeling about this. I don't have Sight, not like Tessa, but I have something. And it's screaming at me that this... It will go badly." Her words were nearly whispers as we spoke, face-to-face, lying on the bed.

"Yeah, but didn't you have a bad feeling about the chapel? And that turned out okay." I grabbed her hand.

"Fair, but it was actually bad." She absently stroked her fingers across my wrist. The movement made my wolf settle in a way that I'd never felt before.

He wasn't in a deep sleep like he had been. For the first time, he was alert and awake, yet calm and content.

"You've had a bad feeling about a lot of things, and we've survived so far."

A little crease formed between her brows and I wanted to kiss it away.

"Maybe, but it's usually horrible getting there."

"Well, focus on the end, not the hellish second act." I grabbed her hand, stopping the movement of her fingers. I wanted her to really hear me. "I'm going to cut my lunar tie, and then I'll do just fine in your court."

She shot up from the bed, standing on it. "You can't do that." Her voice was more shout than anything else.

I knelt on the bed, reaching for her hand to pull her back down. "To save you, I'd do anything."

She held her hands clasped at her chest, moving as far away from me as she could. "You shouldn't. You can't."

I waited with my hand out until she took it. I pulled her down to kneel in front of me.

Another tear rolled down her cheek. "You don't understand what losing the lunar tie would be like."

She was so desperate, and I wasn't sure she could think

through her fear. I had to know why she was so against it. "Then tell me."

"I..." She was quiet. "I don't know what it would be like because no one has ever done it before." She looked over at the door. "Van!" She yelled. "I have need!" She sat on the bed, and I sat next to her, waiting for Van to enter the room.

The door slid open, revealing Van. "What is it?"

"Close the door."

Van stepped inside and put his hand against the empty doorway. The stone slid back into place.

It must've been a handy fey trick, because the doors certainly didn't do that for me.

"What do you know about breaking the lunar tie?" I asked.

"I don't know anything about it. No Were has ever tried. I don't know if you'd lose your wolf or if you'd die or maybe nothing would happen."

I turned back to her, with a grin. I was going to win this. "See? No need to flip out, then."

"Flip out? Flip out! You could die!" She gave me a shove, but it was a half-hearted one at best.

I caught one of her hands and tugged her until she settled against me with a sigh. "Van," I said.

"Yes?" he answered. He'd been quiet and out of the way in the corner, which I appreciated, but now that he'd answered her question, I wanted privacy.

"Get out," I said.

"I'll be outside, keeping guard."

When the door closed behind him, I tugged Cosette tight against me. "I'm not like other Weres. I don't love being a wolf unless I'm in a secluded area. Even when I shift, even when we're fighting vampires and demons, I don't trust him. It's something I've been working on, but..."

Therapy had done a lot, but it hadn't fixed everything.

"I don't think I'll ever be as okay with my wolf as most Weres. My past makes me hate what I am. The constant battle I feel with him is exhausting. I won't miss it. So, don't worry there. So, if I lose my wolf, I'm okay with that. If nothing happens when I lose the tie, then no big deal either. It's a risk worth taking."

She sat up, pulling away from me just a little bit. "Are you sure?" The way her voice rose a bit higher showed just how unsure she was, but I could be confident enough for the both of us.

"Of course I'm sure." I smiled at her, hoping to tell her with that look that everything was going to be okay. "And the other possibility? We're not going to think about because it won't happen. You can't get rid of me that easily."

"But—"

I squeezed her hand to cut her off. She had to stop thinking the worst would happen. "There's at least a two out of three chance that everything will be fine."

"That's still a one out of three chance that it won't."

I could feel the argument rising up in her and I had to shut that down. Fast. "You can't think that way. I won't die. You have to trust me."

"No. This isn't about trust. You're in a court that you know nothing about. You're ignorant here, and that could cost you something more than I am willing for you to pay." She looked away from me, waiting for me to counter what she said but we both knew I couldn't.

She was right. I didn't know much about the fey, so I needed another argument. Something that she couldn't disagree with. "Eli wouldn't have sent me here if it was going to kill me."

She scoffed at that. "Eli doesn't give a shit about any of us."

Oh, man. She was being so stubborn. "I don't think that's true, but let's at least agree that he cares about the new council.

If either of us dies, Tessa, Dastien, and everyone else would have to get together and redo the spell. If we're really mates, it's very possible that if I die, you might follow me. Who could fill our spots? And would he really want to spill more of his own blood for the spell?"

She was quiet. Her eyes were darting around the room as she thought, as if she'd find some answer written on one of the walls.

I was getting through to her. Finally. I just needed to keep going. "It's in his best interest that we both stay alive, and he was the one who brought me here, insisting that I find a way to get someone here to agree to break my lunar tie. He said that the only way to help you—to save you from your assassins—was to break it. I have to assume that it's not going to kill me. That he wouldn't bring me here just to let me die."

She looked down, and tried to pull her hand from mine, but I wasn't going to let her.

"I...I just don't trust him."

I tapped on her forehead until she met my gaze again. "Why?" I needed to know if I was going to understand what was going on.

"I'm not allowed to talk about it."

Another law or rule or bargain. "Damn it. Your fey ways are really messed up."

"I know. This one is on Ziriel, though. Not my mother. I can't reveal anything about the last time I was here or anything else that I know about Gales." She was quiet again, and I knew she was trying to think around the oath she made.

"I overheard you talking with that guy about the last time you were here—Asheral. You killed a lot of their court?"

She looked away again. "Are you sure you still want to be with me? Knowing that I have that killer in me?"

Was she honestly worried about that? In all the times we'd

talked on the phone, texted, messaged, she never brought up anything like that before. "I've seen you kill. That night, after you saved me. Van left to check on the humans, but my pack came back. You killed most of them before Van came back to help you. I saw you do it. You killed in the chapel. And I know you're a lot older than me. You must've been in countless battles."

She slowly nodded.

"Did it bother me when you killed my pack?"

"I don't know. I didn't ask."

Damn it, Cosette. She was always thinking of the worst thing. "No. It didn't bother me. I was grateful that someone could do what I couldn't."

She finally met my gaze again, and I took a steadying breath. "I love you, Cosette. I see you. I see exactly who you are, and I'm willing to risk everything to be with you. You matter to me."

"Oh, shit." Her chin dropped to her chest.

I laughed, because it was kind of funny. "Not exactly what I wanted to hear, but okay."

"Damn it! Don't make me laugh. Especially when I'm about to make an idiot of myself." She pulled a necklace from under her shirt and lifted the chain over her head. "Look at it."

I glanced down at the necklace she was handing me. This was going to make her look stupid? I sometimes thought I knew her, but other times... "I don't know—"

"It opens, you moron."

"Moron?" I gave her my most fake-stern look I could manage. "It's no wonder why I love you when you treat me so well." I found the tiny crack. I opened it and saw a picture of me. God. I didn't even know she took it. But knowing that she was wearing this made me feel like I could do anything—defeat anything—to make this work.

I snapped the locket shut, and put it down on the bed. "Oh, man. You have it bad. Stalker-level bad."

Her cheeks turned the prettiest shade of pink. "Shut up."

I crawled up her body, forcing her to lie back on the bed, until my nose was touching hers. "You're carrying a picture of me around. You're in love with me. Like, kind of obsessed with me."

She laughed. "You're such an asshole. I wish I could hate you."

I shook my head as I hovered over her, our lips barely a breath apart. "But you don't. You love me."

She closed her eyes. "I do. I really do."

"Good." I pressed my lips to hers, and when she gave out a breathy moan, I lost myself in the feel of her.

We'd slept in a bed together, but we'd never crossed any lines. Never. Not once. No matter how much we both wanted to. But now, today, I was going to cross all of them. And I wasn't going to let her out of that room until we'd both had our fill.

CHAPTER TWELVE

COSETTE

MY BREATH CAME in quick gasps as I lay over Chris. His heart was frustratingly steady. He ran his hands through every curl in my hair, and I wanted to stay like that—tangled with each other—forever. If I squeezed my eyes tight enough, I could almost make myself believe that we could have a simple life. Something happy and bright and full of love. I could almost, almost believe it if I tried. But not quite.

It'd been nice to lose myself in Chris for a moment, but his plan was insane at best. Deadly at worst. The stakes were impossibly high. And I was terrified to leave the quiet, momentary safety of this room. I didn't know what would happen next or what was going on beyond these walls, but I'd waited so long to find this—to find love. I knew how impossibly fragile life was, even for us. One wrong move and it was all going to crumble. I couldn't afford to make a mistake. I wasn't sure I could take it if the worst happened.

I ran my fingertips down his arm, finding his hand. He brushed a soft kiss on my forehead, and my heart felt healed and complete. This thing I'd been searching for my whole life had finally been found. I was Christopher Matthews' mate.

I was fey and could never be turned into a werewolf. I didn't know what that meant for the bond or what it would become, but I could feel the magic that tied us together now. We'd crossed the line, and there was no turning back. For either of us.

But there were so many things to deal with. Nex was dead, and that meant that I had to question Cyros, Taslin, and the rest of my guards. I needed to yell at Ziriel—even if my heart wasn't fully in it—for two attempts when I was supposed to be under his protection. But I guess he'd never quite said that he would stop anyone from trying...

Ziriel probably wasn't worth the effort. My guards weren't either. It wasn't worth the breath I'd use to speak the words, but I had to say something. If only to remind everyone else that I was paying attention, not easily killed, and that the weight of the Lunar Court would be on them if they kept on this path.

My mother was going to be very angry that I was with Chris. She'd warned me not to do it and told me that I'd be at risk if I allowed my relationship with Chris to continue. Although sometimes I wondered if she would mourn me at all if I died. Maybe. Or maybe she would think my death showed a weakness in me.

I used to think I understood our relationship, but not anymore. Not for a while.

"What are you thinking so hard about?"

I didn't want to be the one to bring him down to reality. I didn't want to be the bad guy. Not right now. "I thought mates were supposed to read each other's minds."

He tugged my hair for a second, before running his fingers gently through it again. "We didn't say the words. We didn't exchange blood. It's not official."

"It feels pretty official." I could smell him on my skin, feel his skin on mine, hear his heart beating. I wasn't sure how much more official we could get, but I was honestly a little relieved. There was still hope for him, even if there was none for me.

"I want to say something dirty, but I'm not sure if you'd find it funny or not."

I sat up just enough to rest my chin on his chest. "Try me."

"Okay." He opened his mouth, but then his eyes flashed electric blue, and he slid out from under me. In one second he transformed into a big, blond wolf.

What in the—

And then I sensed them. The magic tingling on my skin, urging me to stay calm. Stay still. Stay easy to kill.

I jumped up from the bed, and twin flaming blades appeared, one in each of my hands. Three men were there but Chris was already fighting. I moved to stab one, but he disappeared in a puff of smoke.

Damn it. A third attempt from Gales? We had to leave.

But first, they were going to remember how I'd killed so many of them before. Gales' fey could disappear in a puff of smoke, and that touch of invisibility made so many of them think they were invisible. But they were all predictable.

I waited for a count of three, and raised the blades high. I quickly swiped down, crossing my hands in front of my body. I felt the thickness of flesh as I moved, and then a *thump*.

A man fell at my feet.

"Cosette?" Van's voice called through the door. "I don't want to ask, but was that just…"

When I turned, Chris had already taken care of the other two.

Oh, God. He thought the fight sounds were… "No! Assassins. One second. We need to get dressed, and then we'll need three bodies cleaned up."

The door started to slide open, and I grabbed a sheet from the bed.

"Gales," he said as he stepped through the door.

I guessed the assassins could've been from any court, but couldn't he have given me a minute?

He checked the bodies quickly, and then rose. "Okay. I'll need to grab Ziriel. We need to talk to him about all of this, and we should probably leave soon."

As always, Van and I were on the same page. "Just give me a few minutes before you grab him. I'd like to be dressed before I have any more visitors."

Van nodded. "I'll wait until you're ready, but I'll move the bodies outside."

"Good."

Van waved his hand through the air, and the bodies clunked into a pile in the hallway.

He slid the door closed as he left.

Chris' wolf prowled around the room, checking for intruders, but they would be invisible. I closed my eyes and sent my magic out, testing the room.

I felt nothing, but I'd felt nothing before the attack, too.

Chris shifted back. "You okay?"

I nodded. "That was quick."

"These fey seem lazy, but I have a feeling we should get dressed. That was a little too easy."

I let the blades go back to wherever they went, thanking them for their swift help, before stepping off the bed. "Well, that was something."

"I thought it was more than something." Chris ogled me in the stupidest way.

I couldn't help but laugh. "Put some clothes on." I told him because if I wasn't careful, I was going to ogle him back.

"Okay, but I'm kind of hoping you won't." Chris waggled his eyebrows.

"Ziriel will come. Probably with his son." I glanced at Chris. "You sure you want me to stay naked?"

"I changed my mind. You should definitely get dressed. I don't want any more fights today." He disappeared into the bathroom, and I heard the water splashing as he washed off any blood that stuck after his shift.

I quickly grabbed my bag, pulled on a pair of leggings and a loose sweater. My hair was a mess, so I tugged it into a messy bun and put a spike through it—a hair accessory that was also a weapon. The more things in my life that served a dual purpose, the better.

"You held your own against these guys." I'd seen Chris fight before, but not against the fey. I never expected he'd move that fast and effectively.

"I've been paying attention." Chris was sitting on the bed to put on his boots. He left the top half of the laces undone, tying a loose knot around the ankle before calling it done. "They like to puff in and out, but the scent of the sweet smoke gives them away. I don't see them actually smoking anything, but that scent is everywhere. Especially when they come and go."

"That's right." It'd been annoying the first time I came here, but I didn't have the nose that a werewolf did. I sat beside him to pull on my boots. They were soft, supple leather with no heel and enough arch support that I could run or fight in them. The red stitching standing out against the black leather gave them beauty that I loved. "Does the smoke bother you?"

"Oh, yeah. I feel like part of me is missing without my sense of smell, but I'm getting better at filtering out the sweet smoke and focusing on the other layers in the air. Takes more focus, but saved our ass this time." He squeezed my leg. "Really big tell, don't you think?"

I shook my head. "You always manage to surprise me."

"Good." He kissed me.

It was soft and ended too quickly, leaving me reaching for him as he rose from the bed.

"How do you want to handle this?"

"What? Us?" I asked as I finished tying the laces on my boots, sad that he hadn't deepened the kiss.

He pulled his blond hair away from his face, tying it with a band. His cocky grin was back. "I meant how do you want to handle the dead guys and a possibly upset Ziriel, but I'm really glad to know you have your priorities straight. Let's talk about us instead. That's way better."

"Damn you." My cheeks heated and I couldn't believe myself. This was stupid. I was stupid. Chris was such a massive distraction, and I had to learn to focus better than this. "We can't stay here. This court clearly has an issue with me, and—" I pressed my lips tight.

"They definitely hate you here, but you can't tell me why."

"No." I shook my head. "I can't tell you anything. The deal I made with Ziriel was very clear. But I don't think they're going to give up. So, we'll leave." But where were we going? "What's your plan exactly?" Did he even have one?

I stood from the bed. He hooked a finger in my belt loop and tugged me toward him.

"Rayvien told me that Ziriel will cut my lunar tie, for a price of course. She also said that you and I would figure it out together. I like that. The together part."

I couldn't believe that Chris had convinced me to go along with finding a way to get his lunar tie cut—especially one that involved Ziriel—but I was too weak to make him forget again. If there was a way to be together, then I had to try.

This was very tricky. If we didn't do it right—?

"What do you think he'll need to make the bargain with me?"

I pressed my forehead against his chest. "I think he wants the original bargain you made with the pixie. It's worth more than when you first made it. And even more after today." I looked up at him. "I was going to go track it down myself—I hate that it's out there—but I haven't had time to—"

"Cosette. It's fine." He gripped my hips, giving them a little shake to stop my rambling apology. "You don't have to explain. I made that bargain and I stand by it, and if it'll help now, then great."

"No." He didn't understand. He couldn't possibly understand.

I stepped away from him to pace. I needed to think, to make him understand. "You didn't place any restrictions on it. The things that stupid pixie could do to you or make you do? Some of the fey are way more twisted than your old pack. And if that pixie sold it to someone—someone really bad—then who knows..." And it just got worse from there.

I faced him, but he didn't look worried enough. He was listening, but I couldn't tell if I was getting through to him.

"But if you give that bargain to Ziriel in exchange for him breaking your lunar tie? This could get ugly fast. He might seem a little easygoing, but he's the King of Gales for a reason. The things he could ask you to do are..." *Damn it.* "I'm not allowed to tell you the secrets of this court, but please believe me when I say that it's bad. I don't want Ziriel to ever hold your bargain."

"Okay. Then we need some other chips." He moved toward me again, hands out like he was trying to not to scare me away. "Maybe I can use one that's not mine. You were a spy. You must have a ton."

I wanted to laugh or cry or scream in frustration, but he

didn't know what I'd done to try and find him. "Not as many as I used to, but I have some."

"Then give me one of yours. That's all I need."

He made it sound so simple, and I would do that if I could. I'd give him every single one, but my hands were tied. "I can't just hand them over, no matter how much I want to. It's our law. We'd have to strike a deal in order for me to give you one."

"So, we strike a deal." He took another step toward me. "I'm sure I'd be okay doing whatever you want in exchange."

He was joking, but this wasn't funny. I couldn't help him. Not with this. "No." My voice was firm and cold. I wasn't going to budge on this, and he had to know that.

"Why not?" He sounded hurt.

I was explaining this badly. "Because my—"

Van entered the room. "I sent Pratis to stall Ziriel, but he knows some of his guards are dead. We have a little bit of time, but not much."

"Why not?" Chris asked, ignoring Van's warning. "Why can't you give me some of your bargains?"

Shit. No one knew this but me and my mother. Not even Van. And if Ziriel found out, it'd be spread across all the courts, and no one would ever trust me again. "Because my mother owns first rights to all my bargains. If I make a deal with you, she has to decide if she wants it or not, and only if she doesn't, then I can have it."

"No." Van stepped toward me, his look of outrage almost comical. "Even Helen wouldn't do something like that to her own daughter."

"Yes, she did." I'd kept this from Van for so long because I knew it would make him hate my mother even more than he already did.

"I don't understand," Chris said. "Why are you so upset?"

"I'm more than upset..." Van's tone was nothing less than

fuming mad. "Because every bargain takes a little slice of the soul from each side who makes it. The slice doesn't hurt you—fine—but as the bargain maker—you have that bit of your soul missing while you wait for it to be completed. But she doesn't own the bargain?" He turned to Cosette. "Do you?"

"No." This was going about as terrible as I thought it would.

"And she's also not fulfilling what I guess would be your half of the contract?"

"No. That's up to me."

"So, your soul is tied up in it, *and* you risk your life doing whatever task you had to do *and your mother gets the favor owed!*" His face was turning red as he yelled.

This was not good. "Van. Calm down."

"You were never allowed to keep them? Not any of them? All those years?"

"Some." I shrugged, trying to play it off as not a big deal, but it was. I knew Van was right. "I got to keep the ones she didn't want."

"So, Helen gains everything—bargains from all over the fey courts and mortal realms—while losing nothing. Risking *nothing*. While you risked your soul and your life." He clenched his mouth shut so tight, it was a wonder he didn't crack his teeth.

"You were wrong not to tell me," he said after a moment. "I would've put a stop to it. It's...It's...I have no words for what that is."

"Evil comes to mind." Chris reached out to me.

I stepped back. I really, really didn't want to get into this right now.

"Is your mother evil?" Chris asked.

"I don't know. My mother would do a lot of things that I would never consider doing, and many of them aren't nice." It would make things so much easier if I could just hand a few chips over to Chris, but that wasn't how it worked. Not for me.

"Mother made the bargains the price of my freedom years ago. I understood what it meant—so don't get too bent out of shape—but I was desperate." I laughed and it was a sad, frustrated noise, because I felt even more desperate right now than I did all those years ago. Nothing good would ever come from that particular emotion.

I started pacing again, running my hand down my face, hoping to somehow find patience to explain this to the two most important men in my life. "The deal was that I'd spy for her, but any favors I gained and any information I learned, she would own first. It seemed like a fair price for my freedom." I kept pace, adding in waving my hands around, and I was sure I looked half-crazed, but the pieces were coming together. I couldn't stop moving until I had a clearer picture.

"Yes, I have bargains in my possession. I keep them until I've fulfilled my half of each, then she collects. But I can't *use* any of them unless I want to face her wrath. Which I don't. And the few that she rejected... I've used nearly all of them the last few weeks."

"Why?" Chris glanced between me and Van, waiting for the answer.

He wasn't going to like this, but it didn't change what I'd done. I stopped pacing to face him then. "To try to find you." The pool of dread I was sinking into grew deeper and deeper with every word I spoke. "It felt like a day for you, but my mother monkeyed with the time in our underhill. It's been weeks for me."

"So, the one thing that could've helped us..."

I swallowed, pressing my hand against my stomach, hoping to ease the churning inside. "I didn't know what Eli had done with you, but I knew no matter where he'd taken you—it'd be dangerous. I wanted information, so I bartered for it with the reject bargains that my mother didn't want, but no one had any good information. Nothing useful anyway. But even if I could give those to you, I'd have to make a bargain with you, which then my mother would own. And believe me—she wants me married to—" *Shit*.

Oh, just shit.

It was like a stone had been slowly dropping to the bottom of a pool and I was just now seeing how deep and far those ripples in the water went.

I'd been screwed over. By my own mother.

She'd been playing me for years. *Decades. Half a century.*

I'd never forgive her.

I spun to Van. "She slowed down time."

"Yes. We've been over—" Van stopped and pressed his lips together, his classic I'm-thinking-this-through look. And then he went very, very still. The kind of stillness that meant he was planning a very elaborate death for my mother. "If she did that—"

"She did. I never saw it. We're idiots, Van."

"I'm not following." Chris didn't know what he was up against. I'd tried to tell him what my court was like, and why he should avoid it, but I didn't really explain much. Or maybe just didn't explain the right things.

There was a ringing in my ears and I moved to sit down on the edge of the bed before I passed out. "My mother screwed us over." The Queen of the Lunar Court had been playing me for so long, and now she'd really, truly tried to destroy my happiness.

For what?

"How? I'm not following."

Now, now I wanted to cry. My mother was the queen for a reason. She planned and connived and schemed better than any other fey. She saw moves from so far out, so far ahead, and I wasn't sure anyone would ever be able to go around her, let alone me.

Chris knelt in front of me and ran his hand down my cheek. "Tell me. I can't help if you don't tell me."

"She slowed down time in my court." The words were slow at first, but as I spoke, as the realization hit me of how hard I'd been played, the words came faster. "I thought it'd been three weeks—three weeks that Eli had you doing God only knew what dangerous thing and you were nowhere to be found... I wasn't eating or sleeping, and I definitely wasn't thinking straight. But now that you're here, I...I think this was all a setup."

I turned back to Van. "You were wrong. I don't think she was giving me time to realize that I had to give up Chris. She was waiting until I had nothing left, and she was going to force us to marry. And once we were both miserable, she'd hone us. Use us as her weapon. She's losing control of the courts. They want out of hiding. They want her gone. We're the only thing that could keep her from fully losing control."

"You're right." Van's hand found the hilt of his sword. "You're absolutely right."

I wondered if my mother had forgotten who she was playing this game with and what he'd do if he was pushed too hard.

"She gave us a fortnight."

Van laughed. "She's truly evil, but she forgot something."

"What's that?"

"That we don't like to play by the rules. If she forced us to marry, there's not a chance in all of the four realms that we'd fight to help her keep control."

"That's something, but..."

Chris' hand tightened on mine. He was still kneeling in front of me, but I couldn't look at him. Not yet. Not when I was still processing this.

"She meant in Lunar Court time," I said to Van. "Didn't she? Not an actual fortnight for the rest of the realms. How long is that really?"

Van ran a hand over his brow, but his hand shook. I'd never seen him shake before. He was always still when he was angry. My mother was truly stupid if she was pushing Van to feel something for her beyond anger and hatred.

"We have a couple of days everywhere non-Lunar Court. Maybe less. Maybe more if she stops wasting all that magic and Lunar Court moved to match the mortal realm more evenly."

I didn't know why I was so surprised by all of this, but I was. "Not my mother. She's got power to spare. Even with that. She might mess with it to give us less time than we think. Just to make sure she really screws us."

Van let out a series of fey curses that I wouldn't translate, even to Chris. "I didn't realize. The way she said it, like she was doing us this big favor—a fortnight to find someone or marry— yet the threat was there. Marriage. The timing. All of it. But I heard what I wanted. She played both of us." His hand tightened around his sword hilt. "She'll pay." His words had a finality that sent a chill right through me.

I'd seen Van angry and hurt. I'd seen him on a battlefield, slaughtering hundreds in a breath. I'd seen him do things that both terrified me and made me so thankful that he was on my side. That he was my surrogate father. When I didn't have strength, he'd given it to me and taught me to be who I was today, but this...

I'd never seen his cheeks show any sign of color, but his were blood red. I'd never seen his eyes brighten and glow.

This was an angry god, and I was sure whatever was going on in his head—my mother was going to regret her actions.

Chris moved to sit next to me. "We both have horrible mothers. Another thing we have in common." He brushed a kiss on my temple, and wrapped a hand around my shoulder. "It'll be okay."

"I don't know if I'll ever be okay." I was seeing my mother in a whole new light, and a part of me hoped—desperately—that I was wrong.

"So, what's immediately important is that I can't use any of your bargains. What about yours? Do you have any bargains that I could use?" Chris asked Van.

Well, that was certainly a question. One I wondered how Van would answer, especially since he was already so on edge.

I waited for Van to do something—anything—holding my breath, but then he just laughed. A soft huff of a laugh, but still it was there. And I took a breath.

Thank God for Chris. Even when he didn't know what was going on, he had impeccable timing.

Van rolled his shoulders and the red in his cheeks started lessening. "I don't do bargains."

The haughtiness in Van's voice made me smile.

"What does that even mean?" Chris stage-whispered to me.

"It means that Van doesn't need to ask for any favors, and no one has ever been brave enough to ask a favor of him." I rested my head against Chris' shoulder.

Trying to find a way around this one was impossible, and it was Chris. If we were going to really be together, he had to know what Van was. "Most fey are scared of Van."

"Really?" Chris asked.

"Yes. Really." Van's dead-eyed stare—daring Chris to ask him again and see what happened—made me laugh.

"Don't make the former god mad, Chris."

"Former god?" Instead of Chris looking scared, like I thought he would, the little tilt of his head told me he was intrigued.

"Yes," I said. "So, our plan is to..."

"We find the chip. Come back here. Give Ziriel the chip in return for cutting my lunar tie." Chris stated it with such confidence and ease that I almost believed him.

"Van?" I asked.

"It's as good of a plan as any. I guess we can meet with an oracle to track it down. There's one—"

"No. I know who can find it."

Chris sounded certain, but how? There wasn't a chance he knew this world better than me. "Who?"

The door slid open and Ziriel walked into the room, flanked by three guards and Asheral. "I told you not to kill any of my men."

The man should've at least knocked. He was being incredibly rude, especially since I was a guest and his people had tried to murder me. Again. "I said that I wouldn't act first, but if attacked, I wouldn't just take it. Their deaths are on you." I stepped toward him. "You've lost control of your court."

"I haven't lost control—"

I gestured to the bodies beyond the door. "Then you've never had control. Just as I said before."

"Careful." Ziriel's tone carried the promise of violence soon if I said anything more than that.

I hated that he had me cornered on this one. "Three attempts. How long have we been here Van?"

"Four hours," Van said. "Two of which you were sleeping."

It seemed quick, but when I really thought about it, I wasn't sure I expected anything different from Gales. "Four hours, Ziriel. Which means it's time for me to go."

"So that's it?" Asheral frowned at me, as if he were disappointed. "You're leaving?"

For a second, I thought he seemed sad to see me go, but that wasn't quite right. He'd been as distracted as I was when we were having tea. "You didn't really want me, did you?"

"I wouldn't say I wasn't intrigued by the idea, but I'm not necessarily looking to marry either. I think there might have been more than curiosity for me if it hadn't been for your wolf." He looked at Chris. "Good luck. You'll have your hands full if even her own guards aren't trustworthy."

"I don't think she needs my help." Chris moved a little closer to me.

"No," Ziriel said. "No, she certainly doesn't."

"I, Christopher, and my guards will be gone within the hour. I need to make plans to our next destination."

"Good." The breath Ziriel took told me he was relieved we were leaving. I'd cost him more than these three lives since I showed up.

I guessed in Ziriel's eyes I was a terrible guest.

"I'll leave these guards outside the door." He motioned to the three he brought with him. "For all the good they'll do."

"Maybe they can fight with my guards. Do me the favor of weeding out some traitors?"

"I have a feeling you'll be back." The gleam in Ziriel's eyes was full of mischief. But then he hadn't been relieved we were leaving. It was something else. But what?

Before I could think too hard about it, Ziriel puffed out—his son went with him—and I was left with a feeling of unease. "He knows too much. We're being played. Again."

"I know," Van said. "But to what end?"

"I don't know." I thought this was all about finding me a husband or about breaking Chris' tie, but something wasn't adding up.

I started pacing around the room. Van and Chris waited patiently, standing next to each other, tracking my movements.

There was one big question that I couldn't figure out. Why would Eli care about me and Chris? Breaking Chris' lunar tie would help our relationship, but it didn't do anything but allow us to be together. I didn't need Chris' help to stay alive, because not only was I strong, but I had Van—a former god—to watch my back. So, this had to be just a romance play, but archons weren't in the business of matchmaking. Eli was no cupid. He had an ulterior motive.

But what? I couldn't figure it out.

"What's wrong?" Chris stepped forward, grabbing my hand before I could pace away from him. "What has you so frantic?"

I blew out a long breath. "I just... Something's wrong, but I can't figure it out. I sense something on the horizon and it's bad, but what?" It was black and dark and made me feel like the world was about to end.

"What is it Cosette?" Van asked. "You know better than to ignore what your Sight gives you."

"God, I'm exhausted." I stepped into Chris, leaning my head on his chest. "It's not Sight. It's not specific enough for that, but... I have a terrible feeling that this is going to go very badly."

"What's the worst that could happen?" Chris asked.

There were plenty of awful things that could happen. I pulled away from him enough to see his face. "Off the top of my head? We could die. My mother could force me to marry someone horrible. Or you could become a captive of the Lunar Court and be a slave for an eternity before they—"

"Okay. Stop." Chris wrapped me tighter in his arms. He ran a hand slowly up and down my back until my breathing calmed. "I'm not letting anything stop me from being with you. Not any premonition. Not your mother. Not my lunar tie. So, let's go see a girl about a bargain. Okay?"

"Who do we need to see?" I wasn't sure I wanted to see anyone but the pixie about the bargain.

"Rayvien. She said they keep a record of all the bargains, and that she would help me if I needed anything. Apparently, if we get what we want, then there will be a ripple through all of the courts, and will lead to whatever it is that Rayvien wants."

A ripple? Just like what my mother was doing? Maybe it was a coincidence, but...

That just figured. There was absolutely no way that Rayvien would want to help me. Not in a million years. But if it got her something she wanted, then maybe it was a possibility.

This was about to get very, very tricky. If I could trust an oracle, then I would rather go to one of them rather than talk to Rayvien. But oracles liked to speak in riddles and give out half-truths.

Even knowing that, it might be better to ask one of them where the bargain was. At least the oracles didn't hate me.

CHAPTER THIRTEEN

CHRIS

THERE WERE WAY TOO many people waiting for us outside Cosette's guest room. Not just the three guards. Ten. Maybe more. I wasn't counting, but it was enough to set me on edge.

It'd taken me a while to get used to all the people at St. Ailbe's, but once I had a routine, I was fine. During the last few months, that routine had gone to shit. I tried to go with the flow as much as possible, but fighting demons for the last month and a half had been exhausting. And now these fey were staring at me with glowing red rings around their pupils· and smoke flowing across the whites of their eyes?

No. Fuck that.

I was really starting to wonder what was going on with this court. Were these really fey? Because they looked nothing like Cosette or Van or her other guards. I'd never, ever seen rings of red in her eyes and I doubted I ever would. There was something evil brewing under the surface of Gales, and maybe Cosette couldn't tell me anything about it, but I wasn't a complete idiot.

Everything in me said it was time to fight, but these guards hadn't made a move yet. So, I'd wait, but my wolf rose to the surface and I let him. He hovered there, just beneath my skin, ready to jump in if I needed. I knew my eyes were glowing and my beard was probably thicker than it had been a second before, but I didn't really care if the fey noticed. I didn't care if they saw it as a threat or even just impolite. I had a feeling showing them a little of my wolf was okay since they were doing the same thing with their creepy demon eyes.

Van motioned with one hand through the air, and I stopped. "What?"

"I'm going to talk to the guards. I'll catch up."

"Of course." Cosette gave him a regal nod. Not a hint of how much affection she felt for him on her face. The facade was there, and even if it was a necessary evil, I hated it.

Soon. We'd be away from here soon.

Cosette and I continued down the hallway with Ziriel's guards trailing behind us. Their footsteps were so silent that I wondered if they were hovering above the floor in their smoky way, but when I glanced behind me, their feet were touching the floor, and their hands held short, curving swords.

They'd armed themselves? My wolf started to growl as he broke free, but Cosette grabbed my arm, gave it a tight squeeze, and instantly shut off the shift before it could grab hold.

Christ. I needed to hold on, but my wolf had a taste of a good fight and that gave him some release. He wanted more. More bloodshed. More fighting. More killing to defend Cosette. As much as I wanted to ignore him, I was starting to wonder if maybe he was right. Fighting might be the only thing the fey truly understood.

Cosette's hand drifted down my arm to hold my hand. She gave it a squeeze—telling me that she was here for me, just like I was here for her—before dropping it.

I was still pissed, though. Not at her—at every other fey here.

Three times. They'd tried to kill Cosette *three* times. I knew that her life was difficult, but I didn't expect it to be so fucking violent. Even when she'd told me. Even though I'd seen her kill before. Even when she said that our childhoods weren't that different, I was still expecting it to not be that bad. I'd assumed she'd exaggerated to make me feel better about the pack I grew up in, but now I knew—more than ever before—that she needed me. She had saved me from my pack, but she'd never been able to free herself from hers.

She needed to laugh, and I could help with that. I could ease the weight she carried. Even if she didn't truly believe me, getting rid of my wolf—if it even came to that—was a small price to pay for her safety and happiness.

We went back into the main dining room that seemed to serve as an all-around gathering place. I wondered if they had private places to eat or if this was just a Gales thing, or maybe even just a fey thing. But it was just as packed and noisy and full of way too many scents as it had been every other time I'd come here.

A few shouts seemed to be about us, and I grabbed Cosette. "What are they saying?"

She shook her head. "They speak another form of fey here, and I speak very little of it. But I caught something about us being back." She motioned with her chin to a nearby table. "I think they're betting about us."

"Seems accurate, especially with what Rayvien told me."

"What did she tell you?" she asked as we stepped around the tables. The betting seemed to hit a fever pitch and they were getting louder and louder with every table we passed.

I spotted Rayvien seated at a table across the room and headed toward her. "Not a lot." I glanced quickly at Cosette, and there was something about the squinting look in her eyes that made me smile. "Wait. Are you jealous?"

"No. That would be ridiculous."

But she was, just a little. I leaned over to whisper in her ear. "That's good, because I was ridiculously jealous when you were flirting with Asheral."

She turned and our noses brushed. "You were?"

"Big time."

She gave me a grin so big that it felt like the room had gone quiet and made me forget about all the people that were watching us. I wanted to close the distance between us—to brush a kiss against her lips, but Cosette pulled away.

"Rayvien's over there."

"After you, princess."

"Shut it." Her words were quiet, but the smile told me everything I needed.

She was obsessed with me.

Rayvien didn't seem to be paying attention to anything else in the room except for the person she was laughing with, but when she stood from her spot on the pillows before we got to her, I knew that was all for show. She waved us over to her table without ever taking her eyes off the woman talking to her.

She tossed her long black hair over her shoulder, finally turning to us as we stopped beside her. "I take it you're coming to say good-bye," she said to Cosette. "Don't want to marry into Gales after all?"

"I'm not saying no, but I'm not saying yes either."

Cosette was so full of it. She didn't want to marry into anything, but I guessed she didn't want anyone to know that. I could still smell her on my skin, so I wasn't sure how much being coy about it mattered now.

A quick scan of the room told me that everyone watched us, but more than us—Cosette. They were tracking her every moment with a healthy dose of fear and envy in their gaze, some with a little violence in there, too. I saw how she stood tall, head held high, a haughty look so thick in her gaze that it annoyed even me.

But when I looked deeper, the fear and anxiety and worry that this could all go impossibly wrong hovered over her. She didn't have any tells. No clenching of her fists. No mannerisms. Nothing that I could visibly see. But something in her brilliantly fake smile told me exactly what she was thinking.

Enough of the posturing bullshit. We didn't have time for it. "Can we talk?" I asked. "In private."

"Of course." Rayvien motioned us to follow. "I have a spot where we can speak in confidence."

She led us down a hallway, through some twists and turns, to another room. It was small, with a reading nook that was surrounded by bookshelves. The room didn't smell like sweet smoke, instead it was sage and lavender. Large crystals of all colors were sprinkled on the bookshelves, and there were a few salt rock lamps around the room that gave the room a dull orange cast. Little colorful containers—some with spouts, some without—were sprinkled on the shelves, too. I wondered if they held herbs like the ones Claudia and Tessa used, but it didn't really matter. Not right now.

Rayvien motioned toward the doorway, and a slab of rock slid down and hid the room from view. "We'll not be heard in here." She smiled at me. "So, what can I do for you?"

"I need to know where the pixie with my bargain is."

Her grin turned into something hungry, and I knew that I was about to get into trouble. "Do you?"

With the way she was looking at me, I knew she knew where it was. "Yes." I met her gaze, and I didn't dare look away.

"All right." She drew out the words and I knew I'd said the wrong words.

Shit. What had I asked? I replayed the last second, but before I could think it through, Cosette was there, saving my ass.

She stepped closer to me. "No." Cosette's voice was strong and confident. "We want to know where his bargain is. We don't care about the pixie if it no longer has it."

"See, Christopher." Rayvien touched my arm, and it took way too much effort not to jerk it away from her.

"This is the difference between asking the right question and asking the wrong one. The pixie is of no consequence, since the pixie doesn't have it anymore."

Rayvien was being a total asshole. She knew what I meant, but I was going to have to be careful with my word choice. Even with someone I thought was an ally.

Damn it. I couldn't believe I'd almost messed this up.

"Who has it?" Cosette asked. "Someone in Gales?"

Rayvien sat on one of the pillowed chairs. "No, but for me to tell you anything more than that, we'll need to come to terms."

"Ask." Cosette's word was brittle and hostile, and I could swear she almost stomped her foot.

"I want freedom from Ziriel."

Cosette shook her head. "Then you shouldn't have married him."

Rayvien looked away for the first time since we started bargaining. "You know why I did."

I didn't know, but I knew staying silent sometimes worked better than speaking.

"Do I understand it? Yes." Cosette sat next to her. "Was it wise in the long term? Clearly not. But you were thinking so shortsightedly, Ray. That's how you've always been."

"You say that to me now, but then I look at you with the wolf and I think that maybe we're both not exactly long-term thinkers."

They both looked up at me, and neither of them seemed happy.

Okay. This was getting ugly, and we didn't have time for that. "Stop. Whatever you're talking about, I don't give a shit. We don't have a lot of time before Cosette has to be back to her court." We had maybe a day to figure this all out or else Cosette was going to have to get married to someone else. That couldn't happen. I wouldn't let it.

I knelt beside Rayvien. "I need that chip to get Ziriel to cut my lunar tie. Unless you can think of another way."

"There are a lot of ways you could do this."

I officially hated—*hated*—the fey and their bullshit word games. "Any that don't end with me dead?"

"When dealing with cutting ties, death is always a possibility."

Circles. That's all the fey did. They talked in circles and now I wondered if they were working out all their frustrations by being vindictive. "You said you kept track of all the bargains. You know where mine is." It wasn't a question. If she didn't want me to know that, she shouldn't have told me.

"I do."

"That's why you married him." Cosette reached out to her before stopping herself. "Someone has a bargain from you?"

Rayvien scoffed. "There are a lot of bargains—"

"Not like that. Not one to him." Cosette was quiet for a second, and I knew she was holding so much back because I was here. Because of the deal she'd made with Ziriel.

"If I'd known, I could've helped you."

"How? You were kicked out. There wasn't a chance you were coming back, and..." Rayvien shook her head. "I don't regret my decision—not even now—but you may live to regret this."

"How can you ever be free of Ziriel?" I wasn't opposed to

helping her, but I couldn't help anyone else until my lunar tie was gone and Cosette was safe.

"By killing him...and by helping you, I'm going to get that honor."

"What do you know?" I asked. I was pretty sure she wouldn't tell me, but I didn't think it'd hurt to ask.

"I've been eavesdropping across the realms, and I saw a path. One where my fate was linked to what you two will do. It's in my best interest to help you, so I will."

"Then help us," I said. "Tell me what to do. As soon as my lunar tie is cut, I'll help you get away from Ziriel."

"Absolutely not!" Cosette shoved me. "Don't commit to something you—"

"Don't worry so much, Cosette," Rayvien said. "He won't have to do anything. I will. But honor for what we were—what Gales used to be—means that I have to warn you that there will be a very, very steep price to be paid by Christopher. Are you sure you want to do this? Running away from your mother might be a better idea."

Cosette stood and started pacing around the room, like she did when she was nervous, but I knew that I wasn't going to hide—not from her mother or anyone else. I wouldn't cheapen our relationship by running from the hard things. "Whatever the price is, I'll pay it."

Rayvien nodded toward Cosette. "But this will be hardest for her."

"And for me?" I asked.

"It will be most painful for you." She looked at me then, the smoke in her eyes darkened and swirled. "And that's all I'll say."

"Okay." I wasn't afraid of a little pain. I'd experienced a lot, and I was still alive. "Tell us where the bargain is."

"I'll tell you. But if everything comes up roses for all of us, then I want something in return."

"No." Cosette's voice was sharp and she stopped her pacing to stand in front of us. "If it all goes well, then your freedom will be your reward. You'll get nothing else from either of us."

I stood and put a hand on Cosette's shoulder to stop her from ruining this. I had no idea what had happened between her and Rayvien, but it didn't matter. My wolf couldn't strike out in anger here and neither could Cosette. This was our only viable option.

"What do you want?" I asked Rayvien.

"A favor."

"I can't promise you anything." Cosette's voice grew high with outrage. "My queen—"

"Not from you, Cosette. From Van."

"He doesn't make bargains." We'd literally just been over this, but Rayvien hadn't been there for it.

"Ask him. Call him here."

"Fine." Cosette sighed and crossed her arms. "Van. I have need." She whispered the words, and I didn't understand how Van was supposed to hear her.

A minute later, there was a soft knock on the door before it opened, revealing Van. "Yes?"

"She will tell us what we want, but only if she has a favor from you."

Van looked at her, and even not really knowing much about the fey, I knew enough to be afraid. "Oh. Is that right?" The words had a rumbling undertone that stank with the spice of dark magic.

I rose to stand next to Cosette, watching her head guard closely.

I was seeing Van in a whole new way. A god and now this? I couldn't guess what his powers were or what he'd been worshiped for, but seeing him like this made me glad that he was on my mate's team. I hoped that meant I'd never have to fight him, because I was pretty sure I'd lose.

"I want..." Rayvien swallowed, and I was pretty sure I wasn't the only one affected by his magic. "I want to see my brother. Will you take me to him?"

The anger was gone from Van's eyes, and all that was left was pity. "He's gone, Rayvien."

Van sat next to her, and both Cosette and I stepped away to give them a little bit of privacy.

"You cannot follow him there as you are now. Unless you'd like me to change that for you, too?"

Her lightly tanned face paled a few shades and then some. "No. Not that. I just..." She swallowed again. "I need to know that he's okay."

"He's not. Not where he went."

Hell. I could read between the lines enough to understand that much.

And now I had even more questions about this court and what had happened here.

Rayvien's bottom lip trembled once, twice, and then she bit it hard enough that I could smell copper in the air. "Are you...sure?"

Van nodded. "I am very sure. I wish I could tell you that everyone we loved went to a good place, but after what he did here... There is only one place for him to go."

"Then it was pointless. Marrying Ziriel. Everything I did?"

"No. His actions don't diminish yours, especially the sacrifices that you made out of love." Van was quiet. "I could ease your memories of him. Make them not so sharp that they stab you when you think of him."

He could do that? I knew Cosette could—I'd seen her do it—but I'd hoped that it was just a Cosette-thing. Who else did I need to guard my mind around? Was there some kind of magic to protect me from it? I was going to have to ask Cosette. And if she didn't have something, I was going to ask some of the witches.

Rayvien shook her head. "I appreciate the offer, but I don't mind the pain if it means that I'm remembering him." Rayvien was still for a moment, but then her eyes flashed red and a single tear slipped free, running down her face. She didn't swipe it away or try to hide it. She didn't even acknowledge it at all.

"Your bargain is with the second Princess of Leaves," she said, still staring off at nothing.

"Elowen?" Cosette stepped toward them.

Wait. Elowen of Leaves. I knew a fey named Elowen. Not well. I'd only just met her before we did the spell to seal the mortal realm from Hell. I didn't get to talk to her before I left with Eli, but how many Elowens in Leaves could there be? "The one in the alliance with us? That we just did a spell with? Our Elowen?"

Cosette smiled at me. "I don't know that I would call her ours, but yes." She turned back to Rayvien. "Are you sure?"

"Yes."

"Why wouldn't she tell us she had his bargain?" Cosette asked.

"Why would she?" Rayvien sounded like she'd argue anything with Cosette just for the joy of it.

But I didn't have the patience for any of that. "No. That's fucked up. I know her and she didn't say anything? Why not?"

"Well, it's not like she had a lot of time," Van said. "You vanished pretty quickly."

"Always the voice of reason." Cosette teased him.

"Someone has to play the adult here," Van said. "In all honesty, how much time did you spend talking to her?"

I thought for a second. "I think we maybe traded a couple

sentences." He was right, but I was still annoyed. Why did she have it? And would she give it back? "Okay. We go to Leaves."

"She's not there," Rayvien said.

"Where is she?" I asked.

"She's at the Lunar Court." Rayvien reclined back against the pillows. When she looked up at Cosette, the ring of red seemed brighter than it was a second ago. "With your mother."

The one place I couldn't go. We were so screwed.

CHAPTER FOURTEEN

COSETTE

THIS WAS BAD. Worse than bad. I couldn't take Chris to the Lunar Court to get his bargain. What on earth was Elowen doing there? She had literally no reason to be there, but I guess we had to go get her.

The second that thought crossed my mind, my Sight went crazy. The unease slithered up my spine, like a black snake of death and sadness, and I knew that something truly terrible would happen if we went to the Lunar Court. "No. We're not going after her. Any other ideas?"

I wanted to pace around the small library, but I forced myself to stay still.

"I'll get Elowen." Van rose from his spot on the pillows. "But I won't leave you here. I don't trust our guards and I don't trust Gales. I'm going to drop you in the mortal realm. I'll grab Elowen and bring her to you."

"And if she won't come?" I asked.

Van didn't roll his eyes at me but with the way he huffed and crossed his arms, he may as well have. "I know you might not believe it, but I can be convincing."

"Okay. But be careful. I don't trust my mother. Not anymore."

"You shouldn't." Rayvien stood from her spot on the pillows.

Rayvien didn't have Sight, not like Tessa or even like me, but she had information. Lots of it. Like most in the Court of Gales, she was able to travel with a thought to the mortal realm, to the gates of Heaven, and the doorway to Hell. The fey courts were guarded to their invasions, but everywhere else was fair game. She couldn't visit there physically, but her smoke form could stay there for days, listening in on the chatter.

The way she said that—like she knew more—made me turn to her. "What do you know?"

"I won't tell you anything else than I already have without a price. And from you, it'll be a steep one."

I stepped toward her, ready to beat it out of her if I had to, but Christopher grabbed my arm.

"It's fine. We don't need to know anything else. We know your mother is bad news, so we're not going to trust her." He tugged me to his side. "Let's get out of here before something else happens."

He was right. I knew it, but I was too emotional about all of this. The betrayal I felt from my mother was too bright and new to feel rational when it came to her. But we needed to leave.

There were always things to consider when a fey queen was doing everything she could to manipulate us, and a fey king was waiting to take advantage of our desperation. I wasn't taking anything for granted. "Where do we go? What can we call safe?" I was fine leaving Gales, but we needed a secure destination. Somewhere no one would find us.

"Near the entrance to our court seems logical," Van said.

Ireland. "So, with Donovan." I'd lived so close to his pack's stronghold, but I'd never actually gotten to explore the castle. That could be fun. Plus, I'd get to see Meredith.

"No. Donovan has enough issues with his pack right now." Chris squeezed my hand, and I looked into his crystal blue eyes. The wolf was on edge—I could feel it pacing just below the surface—but not close enough to make his eyes glow. "Does it matter where Van leaves us?" He turned to Van. "I mean—you can get to anywhere in a flash, right?"

"I can go anywhere." Van gave him a little shrug, as if that great power was no big thing at all. "It doesn't really matter as long as it's nowhere crowded. It should also be somewhere no one would know to find you or somewhere with allies. Aside from that, I can go anywhere. Even places I've never been before."

Chris gave me a look that I didn't understand. It was guarded yet something about it made me feel nervous and scared. I couldn't feel the bond the way that Tessa and Dastien seemed to—I couldn't read his thoughts or feel his emotions—but I wondered if maybe I was starting to sense it. "What?"

"It's probably a terrible idea... I wasn't ever planning on going there, but no one would look for us there. Other than you and Van, no one really knows enough to find it, and there's definitely no one around."

"Where?" I didn't care if it was a terrible idea. If it was something he wanted...

"I wonder if we could go back to the place where we met."

I was glad he didn't say where aloud for Rayvien to hear, but that was the last place I thought he wanted to go. From what he'd told me, he hadn't been back there in years and didn't want to. I wasn't sure what had changed, but something must've. "Are you sure?"

"Yeah. It's time. We're going to get rid of my lunar tie, and the idea just kind of hit me. No one knows where it is, right?"

"That's right," Van said. "We didn't tell the healers. Only the three of us and the pixie you bargained with know."

"I can't worry about who the pixie might've told. If it's just us then...I think going back before my life changes again? It's fitting."

It made sense, but still, I didn't have a good feeling about it. Not as bad as I did about going to the Lunar Court. Just a stark unease that slithered around my heart and tightened until even my limbs felt heavy with dread.

I yawned suddenly, and Chris rubbed a hand down my back. "You okay?"

"I'll be fine." Not that it mattered, but I was exhausted. It'd been a long few weeks, and I hadn't slept much. The last day had been especially emotional, and it was finally all catching up to me. "Let's go back to where we met."

"Then it's settled," Van said. "I'll take you there, and then I'll find Elowen and bring her to you."

"Okay." At least we had a plan. I wasn't sure if it was a good one, but it was better than nothing.

I turned to Rayvien. We'd been friends once, and maybe we were allies now, but I still didn't trust her. She'd given us a little bit of help, but I wasn't sure it would be enough to repair the relationship. Too much had happened.

Still, she'd been a close friend for a little while, and I hoped that she got what she wanted, as long as it didn't cost me what I wanted. "We'll be back."

She bowed her head just a little bit. "I'll look forward to your return."

I reached for Chris, grabbing his hand right as Van grabbed my other arm. Everything went dark for a second. Wherever we were—between space and time—was dark and scentless and had no air. The pressure in my head built as we tossed and turned, and then it stopped so suddenly, like I'd slammed into a wall.

I'd gotten used to the sensation over the years, but Christopher fell, his face landing in the tall grass. His was breathing hard as he cursed.

"What the hell was that?" Chris' voice was as rough and jagged as his breathing.

"Nothing comes without a price." Van had a little grin on his face.

"Don't be a jerk, Van." I squatted next to Chris. His forehead was pressed to the ground, and I realized I'd probably forgotten how bad it felt. "You okay?"

"I'll live." It was a statement, but it almost sounded like a question.

"You're going to need a jacket," Van said, and he was right. The cold wouldn't kill me, but it was uncomfortable.

He called in my bag, and I dug through it until I found my leather jacket. "I'm going to need one for Chris, too," I said as I pulled it on.

Van gave me a little nod, and a second later, a coat was in his hand. A black leather with thick cozy lining.

I spread it over Chris' back like a blanket. He could put the coat on when he recovered.

I looked up at Van. "Go. Find Elowen."

He raised an eyebrow at me, as if to say that Chris needed to toughen up, but traveling was Van's power. He was in control. He'd never be able to understand how truly terrifying and disorienting it felt to be dragged along with him.

"Until I return." Van gave me a wave, and then disappeared.

I ran a hand down Chris' back, and then stood. He needed a second, and I wasn't about to judge him for it. I kept watch while I waited for him to recover. Traveling with Van was way worse than traveling with Eli. I didn't know what it was about Van's powers that made it so unpleasant. I'd asked him once, and it hadn't gone well. At all.

Five years ago, when the pixie requested my help, I'd

researched the pack. All the pixie said was that there were werewolves that needed killing, and nothing about the town needing saving, and nothing at all about Chris. So, I'd taken the time to do my homework. The more I dug into the pack's history, the worse it got, and I spent too much time wondering why the Seven had let the pack exist. When I finally realized that the why didn't really matter, that they needed to die, it was almost too late for Chris, and already too late for some of the humans living in the town. There weren't a lot of things in my life that I regret, but not getting here sooner was one of them.

When we'd rescued Chris, the whole compound looked rundown at best. The people who raised Chris didn't really care about anything but violence. The pack was insane, full of sociopaths, and it made me wonder how someone like Chris had survived. It should've broken him. And in a way, it did. He kept his wolf so chained up that he didn't care about losing it forever. He talked about breaking the lunar tie like it was giving up his favorite paintbrush, but it would be worse than losing a limb—he'd be losing half of his soul. I was sure he was more alpha than he realized, but it didn't matter if he was the most alpha wolf alive. He'd never survive in my court.

Which brought me back to why we were here. To say good-bye to Chris' wolf.

I shoved my hands into my pockets to keep them warm. "Be right back." I walked away from Chris, taking in the land and the buildings. Being here now brought back a lot of feelings for me, and none of them were good.

The tall grass of the plains was broken by sections of trees and brush here and there. The large farmhouse that Chris had called home looked like it needed to be condemned. A massive spray painted red dick on the wall of the main farmhouse and the "stay away evil freaks" on one of the trailers told me it probably wasn't a werewolf that came back here to do the damage to the buildings.

The trailers that made up most of the pack's compound weren't looking any better than the farmhouse. There were a couple of houses in the distance with some broken windows and graffiti on them. If I was going to bet on anything, I'd put my money on the town taking out some of their anger and grief on the compound. It made sense after what had been done to them.

The afternoon sun was high in the sky. I'd left my cellphone in my bag, which I was sure Van had vanished to God only knew where, otherwise, I'd check for messages. Instead, I walked a little closer to the fenced-in barn. They used to have cattle in there, but they were long gone. The thick, yellowing grass crunched under my feet. The air was chilly, and I wished I had a warming spell, but I'd live. Walking the land would warm me up, and Chris' old pack had plenty of it. Thousands and thousands of acres amounting to nearly twenty square miles. Aside from the eyesore houses, it was a beautiful piece of land.

The pack was started by Chris' grandfather—a very wealthy man who had been bitten as a young boy. He managed to hide it from his parents for years, but eventually, something in him twisted.

He probably would've been a terrible person if he'd been human. Maybe not a murderer, but probably an abuser of some kind.

A *clang* sounded underneath my foot and I found what I'd been looking for. The pit. The metal grate covering it was overgrown now, but still there. Chris had thought about burning this place to the ground, but I wanted to come back and fill in this pit. It was evil.

Chris groaned and I started back to him. I hadn't gone far—fifty feet or so—but I wanted to check on him.

He'd rolled onto his back, lying with his forearm across his eyes, blocking the sun. He hadn't shaved in a while, hadn't cut his hair, usually his clothes had holes from too much wear, and I knew he didn't give a shit about how he looked or designer brands—not like I did—but watching him made my heart race with wanting and need. He just had to smile at me and I was done. Done. I'd never felt like I would give up everything for someone before, and even if I couldn't let him go, this was terrifying.

"You just watching me?"

He was hot, and he knew it. He liked to use it as a way to hide his emotions. I couldn't help but wonder what they were.

"Are you okay?"

"Yeah. Just need a sec. Is anyone here? It smells...like people are here."

It was probably the new paint job, but that didn't mean that anyone had stuck around. I was pretty sure that was the scent Chris was smelling, but I sent my power out, searching for any hidden enemies. I closed my eyes as my magic swept over the land. It felt like opening a door inside myself as it searched for things I couldn't see. I knew Van would've done it before leaving me, but it didn't hurt to double-check.

After I was sure there was nothing around, I closed the door on my magic. The exhaustion I was feeling was getting worse. I was going to need a nap, but we didn't have time for that. I'd sleep when Chris was safe.

"What did your magic find?"

I looked down at him, but he was still lying there, with his arm over his eyes. "You could feel it?"

"Yep."

I wasn't sure what a werewolf could sense, and I always found it interesting, but now wasn't the time for questions. "I don't see anyone, and neither does my magic, but there defi-nitely have been visitors." I looked out at the houses and trailers. "There's graffiti everywhere, and I'm pretty sure every single house and trailer on the compound has been broken into and ripped apart. And one of the far ones might have been burned."

A hand grabbed my ankle, and I looked down at Chris.

"Sorry I'm taking so long. I don't know why this hit me so hard." His voice was deep and raspy, and his eyes were electric blue.

"Because traveling with Van blows, but I've been doing it for a very long time. I'd forgotten it used to take me the better part of an hour to adjust. Knowing you, you'll be fine in a second."

He laughed like I meant him to. The grass and leaves and sticks crunched under him as he sat up and put on the jacket, leaving it unbuttoned.

"You sure you're okay?" I didn't like that his skin was pale and he looked thinner than usual. Not enough to make me really scared, but enough to have me worried.

"I'm fine. I need meat though. I think that's why it hit me so hard."

"You didn't have any while you were there, did you?" I held my breath, waiting for his answer. He hadn't been there long, so the signs might not show yet, but even one taste…

"Almost."

I swallowed down my relief.

"I had a leg in my hand, nearly bit into it, but I caught this barely there whiff of something that I didn't like. I'm not sure if it was poisoned or what, but…" He trailed off. "What is it? Why did it smell like that?"

Damned Ziriel. "I'm not allowed to say right now, but there could be a way around it." I just wasn't sure how exactly. He'd have to figure that out.

"Okay. Can you answer yes or no?"

"No. That's too close to telling you." And I wouldn't risk being caught a liar.

"Okay. I'm just going to say some options of what I think it could be, and then I'll know when I hit it."

"How?"

He grinned at me, all full of smugness that should've annoyed me, but didn't. "I just will."

"Okay. Give it a try."

He leaned back on his elbows and looked up at me. He watched my face so closely it made me uncomfortable. "Poisoned?" He studied me.

"Rotten?" He was quiet again.

"Not quite that. Okay. Okay."

He turned his head, looking toward the large farmhouse he'd grown up in. When he glanced back at me, his eyes were glowing blue. "Human?"

I stayed painfully still. I couldn't go back on my bargain. I couldn't show anything.

"No. Closer, but no. Rotten human?"

I didn't say anything. Made no movement. Kept my steady, even breathing.

"Wow. That's fucked up." He stood slowly from the ground.

I opened my mouth to ask how he knew, but I couldn't say anything that would confirm it. The point was, he knew. And he hadn't eaten any of it.

"They're demons or something close. Unless that's a fey thing."

Maybe I should've been insulted, but I wasn't. "A fey thing?"

He stepped close enough to thread his fingers through my belt loops and yank. "But I know you don't even eat meat."

I let my hands rest on his shoulders. "No. I've had enough bad meat to turn me off of it entirely. How are you doing?"

"Better. I don't think it would've hit me this hard if I wasn't so hungry. No amount of cheeses and bread will fill me up the way a nice big steak will. My wolf is off balance."

"If I remember correctly, the town's a couple miles down the road. Want to head there first then come back?"

"In a second, I..." He stepped away from me to stand there—really taking in the land for the first time—and it was as if his eyes shut down all emotion. "This place looks worse." His rasp was deeper than it had been a second ago. It was the only clue I had that this was affecting him at all.

"It does. I didn't think that was possible—"

Chris huffed out a low laugh. "What should I do with the land?" He turned in a circle.

"I don't know." I shrugged because it didn't really matter to me. This was just land. He could sell it or burn it or he could bulldoze everything and start fresh. But the thing was, he didn't have to do anything at all. He could leave it for the next fifty years. That he was asking me what I thought about it made me think that he was—maybe for the first time—thinking of what he might want to do with it.

"What's going through your head right now? What do you think about this land?" He'd gone quiet and it was making me anxious. I was worried about him being back here

"I don't know. I definitely don't want to live in any of these buildings. I'm not even sure I want to go inside any of them. Now that I'm feeling better and looking... I think the scents are probably old." He pointed to something fifty feet away.

"What is that?" I tried to squint to make it out, but there wasn't anything there.

"Beer can. You can see the glint from the can in the sun. I bet the townies party here."

"Right. Well, we could tear them all down. Get rid of them."

"Yeah..."

He didn't want to tear them down and he didn't want to live here. I wasn't sure what was left. When he looked at me, his beard was thicker. Something was wrong.

"What is it? What has you warring with your wolf?"

He closed his eyes and I could feel his pissed off wolf and saw the way his fingers were lengthening...but I needed him human to talk to me. I put my hand on his arm, and sent my magic into him—a little line of cool moonlight to soothe the wolf.

When Chris opened his eyes, they were back to their normal blue. "If I break my tie and we marry, what then? Will you be able to leave the court?"

Marry? God. I hadn't even really gotten that far, and he had? "Maybe. After a while." I blew out a breath. "I don't know. I hope so, but I... It feels like such a stretch that I don't know if I even want the possibility entering my head. I'm in so much shit for everything that's happened."

"None of it was your fault. Your mother has to know that."

"They don't care." I shook my head. "And clearly my mother doesn't either." Especially now that I pretty much knew that the last few weeks had been a total manipulation game from her.

He held my hand, and I was glad he was here. My magic might soothe his wolf, but his touch soothed my soul.

"It's funny. I think I've had it easier than you."

"What? No." He was so wrong. "I've never been beaten, broken, and locked up for days on end with no food or water. I might have assassins coming after me, but I also had Van. My mother gave me guards, and they used to be loyal. I'll never—" I shut my mouth, hoping to shut down my anger with it, but I'd never forget the way he looked—he smelled—when Van pulled him out of that pit. And now that I knew him—how amazing he was—I just wanted to kill his pack all over again.

But slowly this time. So slowly that they'd feel every hurt I'd give them.

I could feel my hands growing hot with the urge to call in my father's weapons. This kind of anger wasn't helpful. Not right now. I closed my eyes for a second—feeling the hot rage and letting it go—before I opened them again. "There's no way that I've had it worse."

"No. The pity can go." His tone was sharp, and I opened my mouth to apologize, but he stopped me. "Don't. It's okay. I'm—"

"Don't you say that what they did was okay!" He was really starting to piss me off.

"Hey. Calm down." He pulled me into a hug, running his hand down the back of my head, holding me close. "I'm not saying that, and I'm also not saying what I went through for the first twenty-three years of my life was anything other than absolute shit, but you've been alive for longer. With no one except Van to care about you. At least my mother was horrible and is now dead. Everyone who hurt me is dead. But you're still stuck living in a dangerous place you hate, and you'll always be under her rule."

I got what he was saying, but it wasn't the same. "Maybe." I rested my forehead on his chest.

"So, let's dream for a little bit." He pulled away from me, leaving one arm around my shoulders to keep me close, and he looked around the land. "I want to do something with this land. Something good should come from all of this and from the money that I can't touch for myself. I wouldn't..." He was quiet while he thought.

I stayed there, resting my head on his shoulder, waiting and ready to hear what he said next. But if he needed time to think, I was okay enough to give him that. I wanted him to have the freedom to dream, especially if he was turning this nightmare of a place into something good.

"Hmm." His voice rumbled into me.

"What?"

"I want to tear this place down—every building and structure and fill the pit with cement."

I laughed and he stopped talking. "I had that same thought about ten minutes ago."

"It's a good one." He squeezed my shoulder. "And then I think I want to do something nice. Something the opposite of what my pack did. I want to build a sanctuary."

Wow. I really liked that idea. "A sanctuary for who?"

"For anyone that doesn't fit in. For bitten and lone wolves. For fey who want to be gone from the court. For witches that want protection from their coven. It seems like it could undo, just a little, the evil that was done on this land."

I looked around, trying to envision this place as something other than it was. "You'd have to get the land cleansed."

"Oh, no shit." He laughed and stepped away from me, turning in a circle as he looked at the land. "Claudia and Tessa and maybe Samantha, if she'll agree to come out here. I want them to come here and clear it. Get rid of all the evil. And then I want to take the pack money I inherited and build something good here. Teach art to people that are struggling. Maybe grow some food here. Raise some cattle? I don't know. But it's a lot of land and a lot of money. I spent years running from this place and swearing I'd never touch even a cent, but what good does that do? Being homeless didn't fix me, and ignoring it didn't fix me either. You know?" Chris was staring off in the distance at the buildings, but all I could do was stare at him.

I was blown away. I hadn't expected him to ever want to come back here. But to come back and rebuild? It was amazing.

"What?" Chris said, and his cheeks pinked, just a tiny bit, but it was there and adorable.

"Is it dumb?" He shoved his hands into his pockets and

stared at the ground. "I mean, I can't use that money for me, but for this... Seems like that would... It's dumb."

"No." I grabbed his belt loops just like he'd done to me, pulling him against me. "It's not dumb. Not even a little bit."

Chris' breath was shaky. "And depending on what the town is like, maybe we can grow it. Build some businesses there. I think—"

I pressed my lips to his. I wanted this dream—his dream. It was a good one. Turning something bad into something good? God, if that wasn't just so Christopher Matthews, I didn't know what was.

I wasn't sure if we could make it happen soon or not, but if we survived all of this, if we got through it, having a quiet life here, building a safe haven, that was something I could really get behind. Neither of us had ever had a home, and this dream of building a home not just for us, but for any supernatural that had been rejected? It was a huge, beautiful dream and I wanted to help make that happen for him.

I pulled away from him. "Have you always thought of this?"

He shook his head. "No. After you pulled me from the pit, for the longest time, I was searching. For a hot second, I thought the reason I'd gone through all of that was so that I could help Tessa."

I punched his stomach, and he laughed.

"The hot second passed, and I wasn't sure what the point of all of it was. But then I was fighting demons and everything and it didn't matter. I was back to surviving and making sure that innocent people lived." He blew out a breath. "But I was looking out here, and the idea... I could turn this land to something good. A sanctuary. I like that. It feels right."

"Do you want to go look inside the buildings? See if there's something salvageable?"

He shook his head. "No. Even if there was, I don't want

what was here tainting what could be. We don't need to do anything now, but long term, I think this could be good."

"It could be amazing. We could teach people to fight so that they can defend themselves. There are so many fey that would love this—not just me—and..." I smiled at him. "Sometimes you surprise me. Under all the flirting is an amazing heart." He opened his mouth and I knew—I *knew*—he was about to ruin it with a joke. It would be something funny and I'd laugh, and he'd successfully diminish how good he was. So I put my hand over his mouth, stopping him. "Let's go see if there's anything open in town. Get that wolf his steak."

"I'd be happy with chicken nuggets at this point."

"I know I'm a vegetarian and a little biased, but I saw a video of how those are made." I couldn't help but make a face. "I hope we can do better than that for you. Which way?"

He pointed to a little path beside the farmhouse that led into the woods. "It's about an hour walk down that path. Less than that if we ran." He grinned at me. "But I'm not in a rush. I just like hanging out with you."

"Me, too." I took his hand and started toward the path. Because if there was one thing I knew, it was to enjoy the quiet moments when they came.

Once Elowen got here, everything was going to change. I had this sinking feeling in my stomach that I couldn't ignore anymore. A heaviness, and I knew it was about to get worse before it got better. I couldn't *see* anything exactly. Not like Tessa. I didn't have that kind of power. But I knew something bad was going to happen.

But for now, I'd watch the way the sun shone through Chris' hair, making it glow. The way his lips moved as he talked. His soft Texas drawl cut with the rasp from the scars. His easy smile and laugh, because this man knew how to fight, but he also knew how to love and laugh. He knew how badly everything could go—just like I did—and still he managed to stay calm despite the storm I felt brewing inside me.

But if something happened to him, I was scared about what I would do.

I would chase him from this life to the next, but not before this world burned for destroying him.

Just as I thought it, I could almost smell the smoke. The fire. The blood. And it was like everything just hit me at once. The last three weeks. Trading all my bargains. Skipping meals. The assassins. The poison. The constant worry and fitful sleeping. The feeling that I was on the verge of the end and I was wrung dry of everything I had left.

I started to stumble over my feet, and Chris caught me.

"Are you okay?"

I grinned at him, because if I didn't, I would start crying. "I hope I will be." Because I couldn't lie. I hoped I would be okay eventually, but probably not any time soon.

His smile faded. "What is it? What do you know that I—"

I jumped up on him, wrapping my legs around his waist. "I love you." I stopped him with my words and with my body because I couldn't stomach finding a way around the truth. I couldn't lie. And telling him my fears and why they were scaring me would kill his hope.

I couldn't do that. Not when he'd just found it. I had to let his hope be enough for both of us.

"I love you, too."

His words made me feel like my heart was soaring even as the rest of me was on the edge of plummeting into the deep unknown.

He kept walking down the path as he rubbed a lazy hand up and down my back. "Everything will be okay. You'll see."

I squeezed him tighter, tucking my hands inside his toasty-warm jacket. "It has to be. You have to be okay. You have to promise me."

"I can't promise anything, but I know I'm going to be fine. You'll see."

Keeping my legs wrapped around him, I leaned back enough to grab his face in my hands. "How?"

"How what?"

"How do you know it'll be okay?" If he had some sort of feeling or knowledge bigger than the terror that was rising inside me, I needed to know.

I looked into his blue eyes and I felt his love and confidence, but it made me desperate. I would do anything to protect him.

"Because I have faith that everything that has happened—that we've fought against—has led us here. To each other. And I won't give up the faith that one day, hopefully soon, we'll get to enjoy a life. That we weren't put here just to suffer. I know that you've suffered a long time before me, but I'm here now. No one is going to take me away from you or you from me. I don't give a shit what I have to do to make that happen."

Oh, God. I wanted that to be true. "You mean it?"

"I mean it." He pulled my hand back against his shoulder. "Rest for a second. I'll carry you."

"I'm not too heavy?"

"I'm a werewolf." He shook with laughter at that. "No. You're not too heavy."

"I don't think anyone's really every carried me, but you seem to do it a lot these days."

"I like carrying you. Relax. It's a bit of a hike. I'll wake you when we get there."

"Okay." I'd been on edge for a while. Never letting my guard down. Never letting go. But with Chris, I knew I could do both.

My eyes were heavy. It'd been a hellish few weeks and I

hadn't slept much, but now Chris was here, and I couldn't help but sink into him. I tucked my face into his neck and felt his hum of approval, and for one moment, I let myself relax. I let myself believe that maybe this dream could be real. I let myself enjoy just being alive for one second. Because it could be ripped from my hands so easily.

So I held on, and as I drifted off to sleep, I prayed that this would last.

CHAPTER FIFTEEN

CHRIS

I LOVED the scent of Cosette. The weight of her in my arms. Her breath on my neck. I didn't mind carrying her. She wasn't heavy, and for once in my life, I prayed that this would last. That this one little bit of happiness was something I could keep.

I'd never felt this happy before, and I didn't want anything to change. I knew it would. There was always something coming. The only way I survived my childhood was learning how to take every day as it came.

This one would pass, and I hoped I'd get another with her.

Tomorrow would pass, and I'd hope for one more.

And one more.

And one more, until we could finally find our happy, safe haven.

I didn't even think I'd ever get this much. So, instead of being afraid of losing everything, I was going to be thankful for what I had.

It'd been a long time since I'd walked this trail, although trail was now a very loose term. I tried to keep the overgrown branches away from Cosette. Her breathing had leveled out and she was asleep.

It was crazy that she'd lived three weeks in time and I'd lived two and had just seen her again yesterday morning. It didn't surprise me that she'd passed out. She was thinner than I remembered and felt too light in my arms.

With each step, the ground gave a barely there crunch, and I let the steady, even pace lull me. As my mind calmed, the memory rose of that night after the fight where we shoved Astaroth back to Hell—two nights ago for me, three weeks ago for Cosette. It was after the fight, after helping the injured and caring for the dead, after the cleanup that always lasted so much longer than the fight itself. I was lying in my bed at St. Ailbe's trying to sleep, but still so wound up, when...

The door to my room creaked as it opened slowly. A sliver of light cut through the darkness. If I'd had any energy, I would've gotten up, but I knew who it was.

Cosette.

I knew she'd eventually come see me tonight. She'd been finding her way into my room more and more. It was funny. I thought the guys in the dorm would say something, but no one had. It helped that the campus was mostly empty these days, but still, it seemed like only Tessa had noticed what was going on between us.

I moved over a little, giving her just enough room but still needing to touch her. Our sides pressed together as we lay flat on our backs.

"When do you leave?" I asked her.

I didn't want to know, but I had to. The battle was over and done. Evil lost. We won. Which meant that Cosette was going home, but I hoped we had at least a few days together. Even if it was a slow, special torture to be around her. To be so close to her and want her so badly, but not be able to do anything about it.

"I'm not sure when I'm going back yet." She let out a soft sigh. "I want my mother to give me some time to see what this new council thing is, but I'm not exactly hopeful. She didn't want me to come back at all, and once she finds out what I did here, I think she might be even angrier at me."

"Why?" She hadn't done anything wrong by helping save the world from a horde of demons. How could her mother be mad?

"Because I already had enough power. If tying ourselves to Eli gives me any more, my life will get...difficult."

There were so many different things 'difficult' could mean. "Are you safe there?" That was the most important thing.

"Probably as safe as you were with your old pack."

Which meant she wasn't safe at all. But she'd been surviving at court much longer than I'd been alive. She was good at taking care of herself, but that didn't mean I felt okay with her going back without me.

Without looking, I found her hand with mine. "If I could go with you—"

"I know."

She rolled onto her side, and I did the same.

That's why we couldn't be together. I could never go with her, and she deserved to have someone that could stay by her side —defend her—no matter where she was. No matter what happened, I would never be that person.

Her gaze darted all over my face. Never steady. I put my hand on her cheek and she finally focused on me.

I could almost feel a question hovering between us. "What?" I needed to know what she was thinking.

I could hear her swallow, and I wondered what she was afraid of.

"Do you really not hold it against me?"

"What?" I had no clue what she was talking about.

"Your pack. You saw me kill a lot of werewolves that night—

when they came back—and I always worried. Even seeing how they'd hurt you, that a part of you..."

Was she honestly still worrying about this? I thought I'd been clear when she asked me weeks ago, but apparently not clear enough. "Like I told you before, no. I wasn't mad then and I'm not mad now about you killing my pack. They needed killing. You saved me." She had. She really had. "So many in my pack were bitten and that made for bloodthirsty wolves."

"Or maybe they were just bad humans that were made worse by the wolf."

"Maybe." She did have a point, but it was theoretical. I didn't know any of those Were before they were turned, and I wasn't sure it mattered. They were monsters and now they were dead.

"There's something else I never told you..." Her foot brushed against mine.

I took it farther and hooked her leg with mine, pulling her closer.

She let out another soft sigh, and her eyes were looking down at our legs. "I don't know why I never told you this, but I feel like I've done something wrong, and by keeping it from you for so long... Just... Please don't be mad."

I ran my fingertip down her cheek, and her gaze darted to mine. "I'm not mad at you. I could never be mad."

"If you are, it's okay. But I should've done more to help you, after."

"You did plenty. You got me healed up and set me on my way. I needed to help myself. If that's what's bothering you, then stop."

"No. It's not that." She bit her lip for a second. "I just... I think you're afraid of your wolf. I'm a princess in the Lunar Court. I can feel the wolves around me. I can see what's under the human side. And I feel you fighting yours all the time. Aren't you exhausted?"

"Yes." I shouldn't have been surprised that she noticed. I

noticed everything about her, so it seemed fair that she was paying attention to me, too. "But I won't give him control."

"Please, hear me now. Please understand something that I should've made clear to you before. You're from a pack of mad, feral humans who turned into worse werewolves. But you—You. Are. Not. Mad. And neither is your wolf."

It was something that I was afraid of for sure, but I didn't know that I'd ever be able to trust my wolf fully. "Are you sure he's not insane?"

"I'm right. I knew it." *Cosette sat up on the bed.* "I knew you were crippling yourself. I'm so mad at you and your wolf and myself for not saying something sooner. We've been battling demons and you haven't let yourself loose and—"

"Shh. There are other werewolves in here, and I'd rather they not know that much about me."

"Sorry."

"It's okay." *I pulled her back down.* "The insanity gene runs in my family. I use art and yoga and whatever I can to keep my wolf in check, but I don't cripple him. I just don't trust him either."

"The question will always be there unless I prove it to you." *She placed a hand on my head.*

I relaxed into the pillows as my wolf rose up, just to the point where I could feel the pain of the change start, but then it hovered there. My breath came in quick gasps. She was in my head, assessing, poking at my wolf, calling it, and sending it away. Calling it and sending it away. Angering it, and calming. Over and over again.

Sweat beaded on my forehead from the strain, but I didn't say anything. I trusted Cosette, and I wanted to know if the wolf was insane. I needed to know if I could trust him.

After a moment, she calmed my wolf, and removed her hand from my head. "He's good. Mad at you for not listening or trusting. I think that's the anger that you're feeling. He's been mad at you for years."

I shook my head. "He can stay mad. I don't care. I'm glad he's not crazy, but that could change."

"I don't understand. I mean I know—I saw—but you can't keep doing this to yourself."

"Yes, I can." I went to my bathroom and grabbed a towel. I needed that moment to calm down.

After the battle was done and the dust had settled, I'd showered and thrown on a pair of gray sweatpants, but now I was sweaty again. I might need another shower, but I wasn't going to sacrifice what might be the little bit of time I had with Cosette on something like that.

I walked back into my bedroom and threw the towel down by the bed. When I lay back down beside her, I was calmer. I ran my hand down her silk robe that probably covered up a too flimsy nightgown. I didn't want to think too hard about any of the other Weres catching sight of her in the hallway.

"Do you believe me? That your wolf is sane?"

God. I didn't want to talk about this. "I do, but what good does it do to let him loose? Why should I take the risk?"

She rose up on one elbow to look at me. "You could be stronger."

I shook my head. "Not like Tessa or Dastien."

"No, but you could be Alpha if you wanted."

I pictured my grandfather. His face partially shifting as he ordered me beaten. The pain of my bones being broken one-by-one.

I shoved the memory down until it was in the past, where it belonged. "I don't want that kind of control over anyone. Being Alpha comes with good things, but so many bad. There's always something to fight, someone trying to test you, and I just want peace. I don't want my wolf. And even if I let him loose, it *wouldn't make a difference with you and me. Having a wolf at all means we can never be together. It doesn't matter how strong he is."*

"But you could be stronger!"

Suddenly, I didn't give a shit who heard us fighting.

"Why do you care? What good will it do?" I got up from the bed. "It doesn't change anything. I'll never be good enough to be with you."

She sat up, rising onto her knees with her fists squeezed tightly at her sides. "You're good enough. It's not about good enough."

"Fine! Then I'll never be strong enough." I turned and started to stomp to the window, but I smelled the salt of her tears. I knew I'd hurt her, but it was the truth.

I stopped with my back to her, my chin to my chest. "Cosette." She was breaking my heart.

"I wish I wasn't from the Lunar Court." Her whispered words were almost too quiet for me to hear.

"I wish I wasn't a werewolf, but wishing won't make this change." I walked back to the bed. "I can't change what I am for you. I would if I could. Believe me. I would give anything for it. Any damned thing. But I can't change this."

"I need you. I need to be with you. Please don't give up."

"This isn't about giving up. It's about who we are. I can't change what I am. Can you?"

She was quiet for a minute. "I'll find a way to leave the court for good. I don't know how, but I can find a way. I'll need time to plan. To make a few bargains. I know I can get away if I just have time to—"

"Cosette." Her words stabbed, and I wished she'd never said it aloud. She'd never said anything about us beyond friendship. Not a single word. I knew how I felt about her, and I was pretty sure I knew she felt the same, but knowing? That was so much

worse. *"Don't torture us with what we can't have. I'm barely hanging in here."* My voice was raspy, and my wolf was pissed at me for turning her down, but I had no other option.

Cosette started to rise from the bed, but she gave the most pitiful whimper. It cut straight through my soul, and I couldn't let her leave. No matter how much it hurt later, I needed the time with her now.

I grabbed her hand before she could reach the door. "Stay. Just for tonight. Please."

She swiped her tears. "Okay. Just for tonight."

I tugged her back, back, back until we were on the bed. Until our limbs were tangled. Until she fell asleep and I watched her, praying for some kind of miracle...

It had been the most wonderful night of my life, but we never crossed the line. Because if even my lips brushed against hers, then I never, ever would've been able to let her go. And I had to. For so many reasons. So many reasons that I wanted to ignore and dismiss and obliterate with my love for her, but I couldn't.

And still, my wolf must've bound us when I eventually fell asleep because by morning, he was frantic for me to claim her. To give her my blood. To bite her. To say the words that would make her my mate.

I'd been pissed at first. Not because I didn't want to be bound to her, but because I didn't want to drag her down. But now she was here, in my arms. Now we'd done more than hold each other. So much had changed in just a couple of days, and I wasn't going to let this pass. I wasn't going to let her go. I'd never loved my wolf, and nothing that Cosette could ever say about him being sane or good or strong was going to change my mind.

Being with Cosette could mean I'd say good-bye to my wolf forever.

And that was more than fine with me.

Fuck my lunar tie. I was trading up. I was getting my fey princess. Nothing was going to stop me.

I kept walking through the trees. We'd be to town soon and then we'd find somewhere to eat, but until then I was going to enjoy holding Cosette.

I pressed my nose to her head and inhaled her sent—memorizing every note—so that if we were ever separated, I'd be able to find her.

She was afraid of what was going to happen and that was okay. It meant she loved me just as much as I loved her. But nothing was going to keep us apart. I wouldn't let it.

CHAPTER SIXTEEN

COSETTE

THE SOUND of a car driving past woke me up. I lifted my head from Chris' shoulder and he stopped walking.

"You feel better?"

"Yes." I dropped my legs to the pavement. I was a little embarrassed about passing out on him, but I'd slept hard. "I'm sorry for making you carry me."

"It was my pleasure." His voice was deep and thick, and I knew by the way he drew out the last word in pleasure-dripped sexiness that it was clearly a joke.

I gave him a shove, but he grabbed my hands and pulled me close. "You said that like you copped a feel, but I know you didn't."

"How do you know? You were asleep." He waggled his eyebrows, but his grin was sweet.

"Because even if you want to flirt, you're too nice to do something like that."

He gave me a mischievous grin. "You sure about that?"

"And even if you had, I wouldn't have minded."

He stopped walking and threw his head back with a loud

groan. "You tell me now?" He started walking toward me, eyes narrowed. "You're right. I *am* too nice."

"I know." He might've been joking, but I wasn't. I took a few quick steps to walk backward in front of him so that I could watch his face. "You help your friends whenever you can. Putting your life at risk against horrible odds. You're giving up everything to be with me—"

He held up his hand. "I'm going to stop you right there. Breaking my lunar tie is purely selfish. Have you seen yourself? You're hot."

I laughed, because I knew that wasn't what this was about between us. He was trying to distract me from giving him a compliment.

Another vehicle drove by—a decades-old pickup truck that rattled so loud even I knew it wasn't going to be running much longer. I turned around in a circle. We were on a small paved road with a faded center line and small one-story buildings gathered together ahead. Trees lined the road on both sides, and I knew we'd probably exited the trees a ways back. But it was a little disorienting waking up in a totally different spot than where I'd fallen asleep.

Chris stepped up beside me. "You okay?"

"Yeah. This is the town?" I hadn't come here when we saved Chris. Van had been in the town, but I'd stayed on the pack's land.

"That's right. You're currently entering Stoney Spring, Texas, known for not much of anything."

I knew he was making a joke, but he was right. The place looked deserted. Aside from a couple of cars, no one had passed us. We were alone on the street.

Chris started walking again, and I matched his pace.

"I used to hate this place. My wolf used to push me to protect them, but I couldn't even protect myself. I got in so much trouble trying to run interference, and... It was a burden." He was quiet for a second. "But when I look at it from this side of things, saving them was how I finally managed to be saved. That hatred was misplaced, and maybe soon I can be in a position to help. It's not looking great..."

I took in the small main street. There was one traffic light off in the distance, but it didn't have power. There were boarded-up shops peppered up and down, left and right, and I wouldn't have been surprised if a tumbleweed appeared, rolling down the street. A few trucks and beat-up sedans were parked around, but even as we got closer to the buildings, the streets were still empty.

There was a squeaking noise, and I turned to see a faded, peeling sign swinging on one rusty chain and advertising a now-closed boutique.

"What's the population?" I looked at him.

"Right now, I don't know. A few years ago, I think around ten thousand—maybe a little more—but that's a guess. It's not like I was in any position to really take a census or anything." He winked at me, and I knew he was making light of his position, but every time he joked about his past—I saw him in that pit.

I smiled at him anyway, because that was what he wanted, and turned back to the town, hoping to hide my sadness and anger from him. It didn't do any good to dwell on it, but I hoped one day we could *both* move past it. "It looks like maybe people moved away."

"Maybe," he said, quietly. Probably lost in his own thoughts just as much as I had been.

"Still, the Main Street area is a decent size. This could be really good. Revitalizing it could be fun." I bet I knew a fey or two that would love to reopen the boutiques.

"You think so?" There was a thread of uncertainty in his

voice that I worried about.

"Yeah. I think it's great to do something with what you've been given. Turn it into something good. I think it could be just what you need to heal the rest of the way."

"What about you? Would you like it?" Chris grabbed my hand.

I loved the feeling of his hand wrapping over mine. I was pretty sure it'd never get old. "I think so. I've never done anything like that before, but I know I'm tired of being my mother's spy. Something new, something good sounds really fun to me." But something was bothering me. "I never thought that you'd want to come back here. It really took me by surprise. What changed?"

"You know, I never wanted to come back here. Never planned on it. I'd pretty much blocked this place from my mind, so I really surprised myself when I told Van to bring us here. Something inside me just...it just popped in and the words came out before I could stop myself. But it felt right. And I think I'm glad we came."

Something popping into his head? Making Chris say something he didn't intend?

No. No. That wasn't right. I knew Chris didn't want to come here, and I hadn't said anything.

This wasn't his idea. It had to have been Eli. I would've felt it if there had been any manipulation from his lunar tie.

But why did Eli want us to come here? What was the point?

I didn't know, and with Eli, I wouldn't until something slapped us in the face. I didn't trust the archon, but I wasn't sure being here was a bad thing. Chris needed to know he was good. Before he gave up everything, I wanted him to know that his wolf wasn't terrible. I couldn't believe I was possibly agreeing with Eli...

The more I thought about his idea for the land, the more I

liked it. "I'm glad we came back. I'm really glad I'm with you."

"Especially since I carried you."

I grinned at him. "It was a nice nap. I guess I do that a lot."

He looked down at me. "What, nap?"

I shook my head. "Sleep in your arms."

"Oh, you don't ever have to worry about that. I don't mind at all. Although, let's keep the poison-induced sleep to a minimum, okay?"

I gave his arm a light slap. "Fine by me."

"This way. Smells like the chicken fried place is still open for business."

That was going to be all meat. Not exactly my speed. "Great. I'll have the mashed potatoes."

"We'll have to get them to make some vegetarian friendly stuff here."

If he was smelling a restaurant that meant that there were people here. It wasn't as abandoned as it looked. "Do you think the people will know who you are?"

"I don't know. Probably not. I don't even know where to start with all of this, but I'll figure it out." He smiled at me. "I'm just glad that this is a possibility."

"What? Having a sanctuary?"

"No!" He put his arm around my shoulders, and pulled me close to his side. "Us. We'll figure out the rest, but I was so worried about you yesterday. Eli told me you were in danger, and now you're here. And while we might've had a little fighting, we're okay. Maybe I'm jinxing us—"

"Yes." I nudged him. "Probably."

He squeezed me tighter. "But I can't help it. I'm with you. I never thought that would be possible, and now we have a shot."

He stopped in front of a brick building. The sign above it was faded and worn, but even my nonwerewolf nose could smell the fried food beyond the doors.

"You ready to do this?" He said it quietly, like we were about to do something scary, but we were actually just going into the restaurant.

"I *am* a little scared, but let's go in there anyway." I pulled the door open, and he shook his head, stepping behind me.

"Princesses first."

I groaned. "Stop it." But I still had that stupid smile on my face.

There was plenty of room in the restaurant, but there were a few groups seated inside, along with an old man tucked in a corner, only his white hair was visible above the newspaper he had open. Plastic-coated red-and-white checkered tablecloths covered the wobbly looking tables. A waitress waved us inside, with a hurried "anywhere you like" as she walked by carrying a tray of food.

Chris was still as he watched the food—nostrils flaring at all the food smells—and his stomach grumbled. Loudly.

One day with no meat and he was ravenous? Gales wouldn't have starved him. There was no way he was really that hungry. "It's only been a day."

"Yeah, but Eli had me walking in those dunes for a full day. I burned a ton of calories, and haven't refueled. I haven't really refueled enough since the fight with Astaroth. I was still eating when Eli showed up." He moved around the tables, to find one against a side window away from everyone else, but only two tables from the old man.

Wait. Did he say yesterday? "God. That feels like forever ago."

The chair moaned under Chris' weight. "Well, it's been weeks for you, but not me."

The waitress skidded to a stop beside our table. She was wearing a pair of worn jeans and a gray T-shirt that had a series of tiny holes at the neck from too many washings.

She cleared her throat and pulled out a pencil and notepad from her apron. "What can I get y'all?"

Chris turned to her. "I'll have four orders of chicken fried steak. Mashed potatoes. Corn. Bread. And water. Lots of ice."

The waitress looked at me for a second, then back to Chris. "Y'all have other people joining you? Because if so, you might want to think about moving tables. This is Texas. Our plates are huge. We're not fancy here, but our portions will fill you up and leave you with extras to take home."

Chris smiled at her, his eyes twinkling just a bit in the sunlight that cut through the windows. "That order is all for me."

The waitress tucked her notepad in her apron. "Look. If this is some kind of joke, you can leave. I'm not going to get stiffed with four steaks when you can't—"

The newspaper crinkled as the old man closed it, folding it neatly on the table, before getting up to stand next to the waitress. He was wearing a plaid button-down shirt tucked into a pair of khaki pants. His white hair was cut short, but still stuck out a little on the sides.

His brown eyes narrowed while he studied Chris for a long moment. "Matthews, right? The boy?"

Chris tensed a little, and I wasn't sure if he was upset or nervous or curious.

"That's right," Chris said.

"Thought you were dead. Lawyers around here say you're still alive, but we hadn't heard from any of you or your family for years. But then there you were on the TV a couple months ago. Your grandfather still around? We haven't seen him in years."

"No." Chris' voice was sharp.

"Anyone else from over there? Land's been abandoned quite a while."

"No. They're all dead." His rasp was getting deeper, more pronounced, and I reached across the table for his hand. He either didn't notice or didn't want it. He was so focused on the old man.

"Good. I'd ask if you were like them, but I saw the news. Helping in that chapel was a good thing. Saving the folks in New Mexico." The old man placed one hand on our table, and leaned close to Chris, gazing directly into his eyes. "You're different from the rest that lived here. What's it called? The pack?"

Chris' eyes started glowing and I knew his wolf was rising up. It was easy to forget that he didn't mind talking about the past—about his pack—with me, but he didn't know this man. And even if the old man remembered the pack living here, he either didn't know or didn't remember that he shouldn't look a werewolf so closely in the eyes.

Time to help this man before something happened. If Chris really wanted to rebuild on the land, then he'd need the town's support. We had to do this right.

"Hi. I'm Cosette. Chris' mate." I grinned at that. It felt nice. And it also got the old man to stand up and turn his focus to me. I didn't care who stared into my eyes or how long they held the look. "Chris is the opposite of his pack, which is why I killed all of them about seven years ago and left him alive."

"Might not want to admit to killing anyone in front of strangers," Chris muttered under his breath, just loud enough for me to hear.

I waved him away. No one here was going to call the cops on me. And if they did, they would regret it.

The waitress dropped her pencil. "I know you." Her face had gone pale and her eyes couldn't have been wider.

"From the TV?" Although I wasn't sure why that would make her so scared. Maybe it was the flaming sword?

"No. From that night. You and the guy with the long hair. You—" She swallowed. "You saved my life. I was just a kid and they had me tied and..."

I saw her now. The child she'd been. I'd wondered what had happened to her, and now I knew.

After we pulled Chris from the pit that night, Van left to go find the pack. But they were already on their way back, and they'd brought humans with them to torture or beat or eat. I wasn't sure what their plan was, and I hadn't asked. I just killed them. All of them. There wasn't much left for Van to do but clean up by the time he came back.

"I remember." That wasn't something I'd ever forget, but I wasn't sure she'd even seen my face. "Then you know we're not here to hurt anyone. We actually came to check on the land. We're thinking of occupying it again, maybe bringing some business to the town."

The old man nodded. "We'd welcome that."

"That makes things easy." I gave him a smile, one that I hoped would convey the message that we were harmless and could be trusted. "Anyway, as you remember, werewolves need a lot of food and we had a couple of crazy days. To start Chris needs four chicken fried steaks, but I'm vegetarian. What do you have for me?"

"*Um... Umm...*" The waitress blinked a few times, then licked her lips. "I..."

The old man patted her shoulder. "This is Lizzie. She's just startled, is all." He patted her again. "Catch your breath, darlin'."

Lizzie took a breath to calm herself, but her hands were still shaking and her pupils were dilated, probably struggling with the memories I was bringing up.

I waited patiently, and finally, she let out another breath, this one steadier. "We have these great big baked potatoes." She held her hands a good eight inches apart. "We can load that up with cheese and butter and chives and *umm*...sour cream. Or cheese sauce and broccoli. Wait. You do eat dairy and stuff, right?"

I nodded. "A life without cheese isn't a life worth living."

She started to smile, but it was just a flash and then gone. "We—We also have garden salads. I can leave off the bacon. The green beans have bacon in them, as do our pintos. *Umm*." She wiped the sweat breaking out across her brow with the back of her hand. "If you're sticking around town, I can talk to Mitch about the menu and—"

"Don't worry." The poor girl was fighting a massive case of nerves or memories, and I didn't need her stressing anymore. "Baked potato is perfect. Loaded up with cheese and chives and sour cream. And a salad would be great, too."

"Dressing?"

"Vinaigrette?"

"We have a balsamic or an Italian."

"Balsamic sounds lovely."

"Drinks? Bread?"

"Chris wants water, but I think we'd both also love tea. Bread is a yes, too."

"We just got sweet for tea."

"That's fine." I hoped that was the last of her questions.

"Okay." She breathed deep. "I'll just be over there." She had a stilted walk at first, almost stumbling before speeding up to rush across the restaurant.

"Folks around here are going to be a little starstruck by you at first. Some might be mean." The old man stepped back a little. "But they'll come around. Took a long while to get over what happened with the pack, and some aren't really over it yet. Others might never be. You really settling down here?"

Chris blinked and his eyes were back to their normal sky

256

blue. My interaction with the waitress was enough to give him time to get his control back. I would've helped him if he needed it, but if we stayed here, he'd have to be able to deal with the town himself.

"That's what I'd like," Chris said. "Might take me a bit before I can clear the land and get a house built and everything else, but it's a long-term goal."

"Good. Town could use some reviving. Things just seemed to get worse after..." The man cleared his throat. "I'm William, by the way. I own the grocery store, and I'm on the town's council. You need anything, you come on and find me. Okay?"

"We will," I said.

When the man was seated back at his table and opened his paper again, I reached for Chris' hand again. "You okay?"

"I think so. I don't know why, but I wasn't expecting anyone to remember me."

He didn't think he was worthy of anyone remembering him, but I hoped one day soon he'd see himself the way that I saw him. Strong and courageous and a survivor. "I knew they would, but I didn't expect anyone to remember *me*."

"I didn't know that people saw you. I didn't ask what happened when they showed up. I felt bad I couldn't get up and help, but I didn't have the strength to—"

"Stop. You were in really bad shape. You needed a week of healing from the fey to recover from what they did to you, and I didn't need your help. So, it's fine." I wasn't sure how much to tell him. He'd already beat himself up enough about all the things he couldn't do to stop them. "Your pack was doing bad things. You knew that already. That's why you sent for me. But I stopped it."

"What was happening? Tell me. I need to know."

I let out a breath. We were here for food, not to dive into this gruesome subject. If he knew what happened here, he would feel responsible, and he wasn't. He'd done everything he could. "It was bad, and not a great topic for the dinner table. Let it be enough to know that this town—these people—have suffered just as bad as you did, and I'm liking your idea more and more. But Van should be here shortly with Elowen. We'll get the chip. Have it out with Ziriel. Deal with my mother. And once all of those impossible things are done, we'll talk about this town, what happened, and how to help it heal. Okay?"

"I don't know that it's okay." He stared at the table, and his eyes seemed to have glazed over with the memories. "I don't know that I can eat and not know."

He wasn't going to be able to eat if I told him, and I needed him to eat. He had to be strong for whatever we faced next. "Innocent people get hurt all the time, and that's never okay. But you have a great idea for how to help not just this town but all kinds of supernaturals. I want to help make that happen, but we have to get through some really tough things first. We can't help anyone until we save ourselves. For right now, let's focus on that, and—"

Van and Elowen fell to the floor beside our table. They were lying there, Elowen half on top of Van, breathing way too hard.

It was the sight of bright red blood dripping down Elowen's face that got me moving. My chair crashed to the floor as I jumped up, gripping a flaming short blade in each hand. "Report!"

"I made sure they couldn't track us. We're safe." Van sat up, slowly moving Elowen to sit, too. His breathing was reedy and there was too much blood on his shirt to have come from the cut on Elowen's brow.

"You're bleeding?"

"Yes. It's been a while since I've been stabbed."

I muttered a quiet thanks to the flaming blades in either hand and sent them away. Out of the corner of my eye, I saw

Chris putting his shirt back on. He'd been ready to shift and fight. His eyes were still glowing, but no fur anywhere. Just smooth, tanned skin.

I knelt beside Van. "Let me see." I pulled up his shirt, and reached for a napkin to wipe off the blood, revealing only pristinely healed skin.

Van gripped my wrist. "I'm fine, Coco. Just need to rest and have food. So, it's lucky we're at a place that can provide both. Although I didn't realize you had left his land. I just thought I'd come to you, but a restaurant? When you knew I was coming back? Really?"

I let out a shaky breath as I rested my forehead on his shoulder. I'd never seen him with a wound this bad. Not ever. "That one could've killed you if they'd used a better blade." But if he was really hurt, he wouldn't be annoyed about traveling into a public place.

"Don't worry. Your mother didn't want me dead. Just hurt."

I jerked away from him. My mother had done this? "What are we going to do?"

"I don't know. She's... It's worse than I thought."

Chris reached a hand down to Van and pulled him up. He looked at our small table, and motioned to the waitress. "Can we move over there?" He pointed to a larger table in the corner, away from any other customers.

Her eyes were wide, her face pale, and I wasn't sure if she was breathing, but she nodded. "Suuuure."

Oh, boy. I'd overreacted a little when I saw the blood, but it was too late to change my actions now. Everyone in the restaurant was quietly staring, no one was moving, and I knew I'd scared the shit out of them, but I didn't care. Van had been *bleeding*. I hadn't seen him hurt in a long time.

Chris pulled out a chair for Van, and Elowen sat next to him. Her clothes were torn and bloody and her long black hair looked stringy, like it hadn't been washed in days. I'd never seen her so rumpled before.

Chris guided me to a chair across from Van, but I was still on alert—checking all the exits, keeping my hands free to summon weapons, analyzing the body language of every person in the restaurant. Still easing back from the killing edge. I couldn't believe that Van had been stabbed and I hadn't been there to help him fight.

When we were all sitting at the new table—two of us on each side—and breathing better, I turned to Elowen. "And you? Are you okay?" There wasn't any other injury that I could see except for the cut on her brow, but fey were fast-healing.

Elowen reached for the napkin holder, dabbing off the blood before vanishing the napkin. A second later, her glamour was in place and she looked perfect. Clothes pressed. Not a hair of her long, dark hair out of place. Her green eyes looked alert. The only way I knew she was hurt or tired was the slight hunch of her shoulders.

"Your mother called me in for questioning," Elowen said after a moment. "She wanted to examine the magic that formed the bond."

Of course she did. It was odd that she hadn't asked me about it at all, but I'd been too busy running around, trying to find information about Chris, to really examine my mother's behavior.

I felt like such an idiot. "I should've known, but I didn't. Your mother turned you in?"

She nodded.

"Kyra? Have you heard anything from her?" Kyra was from Solar, so she shouldn't have a reason to go to Lunar. Her court was arguably just as strong as Lunar, which meant she could fight against my mother's summons. She should be safe, but I would've thought Elowen would've been safe, too.

Elowen shook her head. "She left with Blaze. There was something that came up, and they left together. I went home, and then..." She shrugged. "What I don't get is why you sent Van? How did you know to come get me?"

The waitress approached carrying a tray with four iced teas and four waters. The ice in the glasses were rattling so bad that I hoped the whole thing didn't topple to the ground.

"I, *um...* I brought waters and teas for all y'all? 'Cause I wasn't sure what y'all would want but if you—"

"That's fine." I smiled at her, and then turned to Elowen. "Are you hungry?"

Elowen nodded as did Van.

"They'll have what Chris is having."

"Four servings each?"

Elowen's mouth fell open, but I stopped her before she could say anything. "No. Just one each."

"Oookay. I'll be back with the food. *Um*...Just *um*... If you need anything else, I'll be over there again." She waved toward the kitchen and hustled away.

I'd been so consumed with Van and Elowen that I hadn't realized the rest of the customers were slowly, carefully paying their bills and leaving. I hated that we'd caused such a scene, but I'd have to deal with that later. I had to hope that we'd have plenty of time to earn their trust if—when—we came back.

"What do you need, Cosette?" Elowen said as soon as the waitress was gone. Her tone had a rough edge that I didn't appreciate. "If you didn't know what your mother was doing, then why did you come get me?"

She was mad for a very good reason. And she was right. I did need something, but I also felt like I owed her an apology. "If I'd known what my mother was doing, I would've—"

"Stop. It came out bitchy because I'm tired. Your mother beat me, magically and physically, for the last four days. What your mother's done...well, she'll pay for that. But you only talk to me when you need something. So, what do you need this time?"

Harsh. She was being harsh, but maybe I deserved it. "I hope that one day we can just enjoy each other's company. We were friends—"

"Life will never be that simple for us. We're fey princesses who created a supernatural alliance with an archon as backing. If we were ever going to escape the life-and-death political games we were born into, that hope is gone now."

I wanted to snap something back at her about how it didn't have to be that way. That if she wanted to give up hope, fine. But I was just finding my hope. I had Chris, and we weren't giving up as easily as she was.

But then I remembered that it was only glamour that had her looking so pristine. The image of her greasy hair and torn, bloody clothes killed any anger that was starting to build up. "The bargain that Chris made with the pixie. You have it?"

Elowen grinned and her magic brightened, filling the room with the scent of fresh pine and earth. Leaves fey always smelled fresh.

She turned to Chris. "I wondered when you'd come for it, but I'm not going to let it go easily."

Chris relaxed back in his chair. "What do you need?" He seemed to trust her, but I wasn't sure I did. Not after what she'd said about never escaping political games.

I put my hand on his leg, needing the comfort to get through whatever bargaining we needed to do.

"I don't need anything at the moment." Elowen leaned back in her chair, mimicking Chris' casual posture. "Especially now that Van took me from the Lunar Court. But having this chip means having a direct link to Cosette. It's why I traded the pixie for it. You see, he came to show me that the coin was growing in size. The pixie couldn't figure out why, and he was scared of it—of what it was turning into. But once I knew where it came from, I knew it was going to keep growing." She grinned and there was no happiness in it. I could almost smell the bitterness in the air. "I'm not going to give up my very large, very powerful save-my-life-for-free coin without getting something better in return."

"How very fey of you," I said. It wasn't an admonishment. I didn't blame her for it. I would be doing the same thing.

"Leaves might not have all the laws and rules about bargains as you do. We give some things freely, but I'm not stupid. I'm not going to hand it over with nothing in return. So, shall we make a deal?"

"What do you want?" Chris asked.

"I want a bargain with Cosette."

"No." I didn't want to speak for Elowen, but I was pretty sure that was the last thing she wanted. "A bargain with me is a direct line to my mother."

The scent of pine and fresh air started to overpower the scent of fried food as she sat straight in her chair. "What?"

"You have no idea what making a bargain with me means, but trust me. You don't want it."

Elowen closed her eyes for a moment, and I wondered if it was anger or fear or if she was trying to find her patience.

"Fine," she said when she opened her eyes again. "I've had enough of your mother." Elowen snapped her fingers and a golden coin nearly three inches in diameter appeared in her palm. "Here it is."

Chris moved to grab it, but Elowen closed her fingers around the coin.

"Terms." She said, moving her hand close to her chest. "Should a time arise when I find myself in distress, I want not just you to come to help me, Christopher. I want you and Van and Cosette and Tessa—"

Chris leaned back in his chair, shaking his head. He crossed his arms, and I wasn't sure if it was disappointment or pity on his face. Either way, I didn't like it. For Elowen to bargain the chip away at all was in our favor, but so far, this seemed reasonable. Although, what she meant by distress and the level of risk needed to be negotiated before we came to full terms. But—

"This is what you don't get. What none of you fey get." Chris looked at each of us. "You don't have to make a bargain to get me to do anything. If you were in trouble, all of us would come. Tessa, Dastien, Lucas, Claudia, all of us. All you have to do is let us know that you need help, and we'd be there."

"You would?" Elowen asked.

"Yes." Chris sounded a little outraged that she'd even ask.

Elowen seemed to be as confused as I was. Her mouth kept opening and closing, before she finally spat out some words. "And what about Eli?"

"I can't control the archon. No one can. But I know I, Tessa, Dastien, Lucas, and Claudia would come without any strings. If Meredith and Donovan were able, they'd come, too. I don't know Blaze, Shane, Beth, or River well enough to speak for them, but it's a safe bet that they'd join us if there was a big fight involved. And none of us, not a single one, would want anything in return. No favor or bargain. We wouldn't even need to like you very much. If you're hurting and we can help, we'd come because it's the right thing to do."

A little wrinkle formed between Elowen's brows. "You wouldn't ask anything from me? Hold a debt?"

"No." Chris left no doubt or uncertainty in his tone.

"I..." Elowen blinked and a tear dropped down her cheek.

I wondered why her glamour hadn't hid it from view.

"I..." She started again, but it was like she couldn't form the words.

But she'd never lived outside of her court. She didn't know the treasure of real friendship. "I know." I handed her a napkin. Being at court for the last three weeks made me almost forget how amazing my friends were. "It used to shock me, too, but I've been my mother's spy for too long. The fey are different, and I'm not so sure if we're better anymore."

"I'm not sure we ever were," Van said.

"Is that why?" I asked Van my half-question. It was something we never talked about. How had he gone from being a god to nearly fading into nothingness?

"Yes. That's part of it, and I don't want to talk about the rest." He gave me a look that told me clearer than any words to drop the subject.

That's the most I'd gotten out of him in nearly a century and a half. So, I let it go.

Elowen looked down at the coin. "You'll really help me. If I get taken again? If... Even if it's dangerous? Even if it's in the Lunar Court and you could die trying, or become a slave?"

"Yes." Chris' voice was true and confident. "If you need help, all you have to do is get word to me. I'll come. No matter what. And I'll bring everyone I can."

This was Chris at his best: protective, honest, trusting. It was understandable that Elowen was having trouble trusting this, because it was the opposite of everything that she'd ever known. But I hoped for her sake—and ours—she'd hear the truth in Chris' words.

"Okay." She held out the coin to Chris. "Then take it, and use it well. Because the heart that you and your friends have? It's not everywhere."

Chris took the coin, and placed it in his pocket. "But it could be."

She looked away from Chris then, staring down at the table.

"Maybe, but not in the courts." A shadow seemed to pass over her and she squeezed her eyes shut.

Chris leaned forward, resting his forearms on the table. "Then maybe your courts are broken."

Another tear slipped through her glamour. "Maybe."

The waitress came by with the first tray. "I'll bring the next plate up when you're done with this, Mr. Matthews. I didn't want the food going cold."

"That's perfect. Thank you." Chris gave her a grin that had her tripping over her feet. Poor girl.

Elowen sat straight, eyes wide, hands clasped tightly on the table. "You just—"

"That doesn't mean what it means to us." I gripped her arm for a second, hoping she'd take it as a comfort. "When he says it, it's meant to show gratitude for something, but he isn't bound to her now."

Elowen leaned back in her chair. "I'm so confused."

"It's okay. I was, too, but now I enjoy it."

She looked at me again, her brown eyes flecking with emerald green. "But when someone says those words to you?"

"They still hold power. I'm still fey." I grabbed my fork. "And when we're done, Van will take us to Gales and then he'll take you somewhere safe."

She reached for her glass of water with a shaky hand. "Somewhere that your mother can't find me would be best."

"You'll have to stay with one of us for that," I said, knowing she probably wouldn't like the answer. "I think she's afraid of the new bond we've all formed." I hated that I might have ruined her life. I'd needed help for the spell, and she'd owed me a favor, but now...

"Helen's very afraid, and with very good reason," Van said. "We don't know what it means yet, but your mother's greatest fear is that someone will end up being more powerful than her."

Something about that hit me hard, but Elowen spoke again.

"Back to the school then? That's fine. It was comfortable there."

Comfortable. That was a nice way of saying she felt good being around the Cazadores. They might not have all the powers of the fey, but their strength and skills were undeniable.

"Okay. That's settled, then?" I said, and no one answered, which was enough. "Let's eat."

"Yes. Please." Chris didn't waste any more time before digging in to his food. The mountain of food was nearly gone before I'd eaten more than a couple of bites.

He noticed us watching him. "What? I'm hungry!"

Elowen laughed, softly at first, but when Chris gave her a wink, she laughed harder.

It was nice how he always seemed to know what someone needed in the moment. He was incredibly thoughtful.

He noticed me staring and gave me my own wink. It was silly, but it made me feel safe and loved. Chris was joy. Pure joy. And it pained me when I thought how his family had tried to beat that joy out of him. But then came the pride of knowing someone who could take all that pain, and still be beautiful—inside and out.

I took my first bite and moaned. Food was always better in the mortal realm. I wasn't sure what they did differently, but the potato had just the right amount of cheese and creaminess. I ate slowly and we chatted about the nuances of being fey with Chris. It was interesting and fun and easy, but the whole time I was eating, I watched Elowen very carefully.

She'd been abused for days by my mother and yet here she was. Sitting. Eating. Not smiling though. I didn't know much about her, other than that she'd helped me on one of my trips to her court. Not a lot of fey would do that.

We'd talked a bit years ago, and of all the powers in Leaves, she seemed to be the strongest to me. There was a spark of determination in her that I didn't often see from them. But under it all, I think I must've known deep down that she was as broken as the rest of us.

The wounds she'd shown up with were gone, but for her to have brushed it off as quickly as she did? To shake off days of torture from my mother almost like it was nothing and pull that glamour up so quickly? This was something that she was used to doing. It wasn't the first time she'd been hurt.

And then I started to think of my mother. I'd always thought she was helping me. That underneath it all, she had my best interests at heart. But looking at tortured Elowen and supposed husband-material Van, I wondered if my mother's motivations in every interaction—and her plans for me—were just for her own benefit. Did she send me away to spy to dampen my power? Had I been stunted from growing, the same way Chris was hiding his wolf?

Chris rested his hand on my knee and squeezed. "You okay?"

I blinked a few times, because nodding felt like a lie and I was definitely not okay.

I wasn't sure I'd ever been okay.

And if anything happened to Chris when we cut his lunar tie, I wasn't sure I'd ever be okay.

But I'd live with that fear and not let it control me. For right now, in this moment, I was going to enjoy a simple meal with my friends and loved ones. Because the gnawing premonition was back, and I wasn't sure when I'd get to sit here with Chris and Van again. So, I took a picture in my mind. Something to savor when times got hard, because they would. If I was finally seeing the truth about my mother, then everything was about to get a whole lot worse.

CHAPTER SEVENTEEN

CHRIS

THE LIGHT HAD DARKENED outside as we ate. I'd ordered pie, and nearly finished the whole thing before I called myself good. No one else came into the restaurant while we were there, and on any other day, that would've bummed me out—I didn't want them to be scared of me—but today I was glad that we had the whole place to ourselves. It gave all of us the freedom to really talk about everything—from the workings of the fey courts to bargains to what made the fey so different from anyone else. And the more we talked, the more I realized that I hadn't understood the rules for the different courts at all. Not a fucking bit.

The more we talked, the more I understood why Cosette had been her mother's spy for so long. She maneuvered the conversation like a pro. Any time we hit something that she wasn't allowed to talk about, she'd find a way to circle around to either Van or Elowen or she'd give me enough information that I could figure the answer out on my own.

Elowen warmed up after I agreed to help save her—which felt like the most nonbargain ever—but she ended up being able to tell me more than Van and Cosette put together. It didn't take me long to figure out why Cosette had picked her for the spell. She was smart, strong, cunning, and hated the fey courts and politics as much as Cosette. They were a pair of princesses who had been abused and wanted change. But after we talked, I had information about the courts that I didn't have before and that was going to be vital to my survival.

I'd thought all of the fey told the truth, but that was mostly just a Lunar Court thing. Solar didn't lie, but they didn't kill anyone who told an untruth. Midnight felt that if you were smart enough, you should be able to see the truth hidden inside layers of lies. Gales was just straight-up deceitful and from the sound of it—their morals were garbage.

The more they told me, the more confused I became. Each court seemed to have their own rules, but one thing seemed to be common across all of them: They were deadly. If you didn't know what games they were playing, you'd end up dead—or worse, a slave.

After hearing all of that, I should've been more scared about approaching Ziriel, but I wasn't. I knew what I wanted. With the coin, Ziriel would give it to me. That was going to be that.

And if it wasn't, well, I'd cross that bridge when I got to it.

After dinner, Van took Elowen back to St. Ailbe's. He wanted to be with us at Gales to make sure that Ziriel stayed honest.

I'd paid the waitress with the card I kept under my shoe's insole, more than doubling the total on the tip line because of all the business we'd lost them, and waited for Van to come back.

"Are you okay?" Cosette asked.

"I don't know." I turned my chair so that I could look at her. "I'm a little nervous about what's going to happen when we meet with Ziriel, but I'm trying to stay positive. You?"

She looked everywhere but at me, and I could almost see the

way she wanted to get up and pace. Instead, she was nervously tapping her fingertips on the table.

I covered her hand with mine, stopping the tapping. "It's going to be okay."

Her gaze snapped to mine. "You don't know that."

"I'll make it okay. Just don't give up on me. No matter what happens."

She started to say something, but Van appeared beside us and she closed her mouth, stopping whatever words she was about to say.

"Ready?" Van's words were soft as he glanced from Cosette to me and back again.

I was pretty sure he figured out he'd come back at the wrong moment, but I wasn't sure there was a good moment for him to come back. This was dangerous and scary and there was so much we could lose. But I couldn't think about that. I had to focus on doing one thing. The first step. Getting up from the chair and leaving. Which I would do. I just needed one more look at my mate before we traveled back to Gales.

I gave Cosette a long look, but she shook her head, turning away from me. She was scared. The sickly sweet stench of it filled the air, and I hated it. I wanted to make her less afraid, to be able to say the one perfect thing that would make her okay, but we both had a lot to lose. I wasn't sure I had those words for myself, let alone words that could help her, too.

So, I stood up from my chair. "I'm not ready, but let's do it anyway." I just hoped I didn't lose the food I'd eaten.

I reached for Cosette, and her hand shook in mine as I pulled her up.

"You sure?" Van asked.

Cosette shook her head again, but I pulled her into me.

The scent grew stronger, but I ignored it, holding Cosette against me as I reached toward Van. "Let's go."

The second Van grabbed my wrist, everything went dark.

I couldn't breathe as I tossed and turned. I squeezed my eyes shut and the feeling got worse. I wanted to throw up, but I couldn't even get in any air. Because wherever we were, there wasn't any air.

And then the tossing stopped, and I slammed into the same invisible wall, like last time. I took a gasping breath when Van let go of my wrist, and I fell down. The back of my head slammed into the ground hard enough to rattle my teeth, and I smelled my own blood. If I'd been human, I would've had a massive concussion, but I was a werewolf. I would heal this in a second, but right now, I was pretty sure I hated Van.

"Chris!" Cosette had fallen on top of me, but she scrambled to move. "Are you okay?"

Her cool hand ran across my forehead, and I was sorry I'd worried her.

"Yep. Fine." In a second, I'd pick up my pride, but at least I hadn't puked. "I just need a minute."

She brushed a hand across my head one last time, before standing. "Van is dealing with the guards now, but we need to follow protocol and wait until Ziriel knows we're here and gives them orders about where we can find him."

"Okay." I kept my eyes closed. "Let me know if I need to rally."

She brushed a kiss on my forehead. "Will do."

When I opened my eyes, the room swam for a solid couple of minutes as I got my bearings, but I recovered much quicker than last time. I blinked and watched the ceiling. It looked like we were in a glass dome inside the middle of a raging sandstorm. I sat up slowly, taking in the room. The walls were made of whirling, swirling sand, but the middle of the room had just the slightest sage-scented breeze.

There were torches on the walls and hexagonal tiles on the

ground in a circle, each beautifully painted. It wasn't until I really studied them that I realized the tiles weren't just painted, they were animated. Not video screens, but like living oil paintings.

Magic. Not art.

I made a mental note to ask Cosette about how they were made and if it was a type of magic that I could use to create a piece of art when we weren't in a room surrounded by armed guards.

It took me another minute to get to my feet and walk—somewhat steadily—to where Cosette and Van were talking to the Gales guards. They were in their typical all white, with their golden masks lifted to rest on top of their heads as they spoke.

My wolf wanted me to shift. To attack. They were too close to Cosette. But I ignored him. He might be a territorial asshole, but I wasn't. Plus, I needed to be human to communicate what I wanted.

I closed my eyes, pushing him down-down-down into the depths of my soul, and he fought me. Hard. I was sweating before it was done. Maybe he knew I was about to get rid of him, and I almost felt bad about it... But not really. I couldn't let myself. Not when Cosette's life and happiness were at stake.

Cosette needed to marry for power. Without my lunar tie, we could finally be together, something I never dreamed was possible. Sacrificing my wolf was a price I was willing to pay to be with her. One I'd never, ever regret.

There was a calmness in knowing that, and everything else seemed to not matter.

I took off my jacket and handed it to Van so he could make it disappear. It was way too hot down here for it. "I need to see Ziriel."

The little beast popped in, bouncing in excitement. "You're

back! Back! Are we going to play our game? Do you have a guess?"

I was about to tell the little beast to get lost, but there was slow, *zinging* sound. Van was pulling his sword free.

"I told you three centuries ago that if I ever saw you again, you would die. If I were you, I'd run. And *not come back* until I'm *gone!*"

"You...you wouldn't still be mad. It's been so long! Very long!"

"I am *still mad!*" Van's words were forced through his tight jaw, and he was vibrating with anger.

The air in the room grew colder, thinner, and little zaps of electricity flicked painfully against my skin.

With a squeak, the little beast disappeared, but Van was still shaking as he put his sword away.

I looked at Cosette and she shook her head.

Right. Three centuries was before her time. A former god, but what did it mean? What were his powers?

One of the guards cleared his throat. "This way." He stepped forward, leading us from the room.

With two guards in front of us and two behind, we walked through the sloping tunnels, going deeper underground with every step. I didn't like being sandwiched between them, but I understood their reasoning. Van walked in front of me with a hand on the hilt of his sword and I was looking at him with new respect. Not that I didn't trust him with my life before, but I was suddenly realizing how little I knew about him.

Cosette walked beside me with her hands out, ready to call in whatever flaming weapon she wanted. I was ready to shift if I needed to, but I hoped it didn't come to that. My wolf was on edge, and I didn't trust him. Not today.

I hadn't been to any of the other courts, but I knew I hated this one. I hated the suffocating feeling of being underground.

My wolf was rising up as I struggled to keep my breathing even and my heart at a reasonable pace, but I couldn't stop the sweat that was already beading up on my forehead.

I hated the scent of the sweet smoke, too. My nose burned, and I sneezed a couple of times before I could stop myself.

"The young wolf doesn't like the smell, eh?" the guard in front of me said.

The mocking, slanted smile on his face told me that he was laughing at me.

I really hated these asshole guards. "No. I don't like it."

We passed corridors and rooms. I wasn't sure where we were going—every hallway looked like the last—but I knew we were going down. Down, down, deeper down. Until eventually there was sound. The beats of different types of drums. All driving my heart to race faster and faster until we finally entered what had to be an arena.

Easily, a couple thousand people were cheering around the perimeter of the circular area. The drummers—there had to be at least twenty—were piled nearly on top of each other in the far corner outside the ring. The beats reverberated against the glasslike walls, rattling my bones.

The fighters in the center were moving to the beats of the drums. Fast and swift. Two broadswords each, one in each of their two hands. They were moving so fast—turning to smoke and racing after each other—that it took me a second to realize that the fighters were Ziriel and Rayvien.

The guards led us through the gathered crowd until we were at the edge of the circle, watching the fight unfold.

One sword swung close to Rayvien's face. I was sure she'd gotten cut, but there was no blood. She turned to smoke and reappeared behind Ziriel, but he turned to smoke before Rayvien could swing back.

I leaned down to whisper in Cosette's ear. "Are they sparring or fighting-fighting?" I wanted to assume that this was just some sort of extreme sparring, but it really seemed like Ziriel might kill her.

She stared ahead, frozen—not even blinking—as she watched the fight. "When you step into that ring with another fey, it's always a fight." Her words were so quiet that even with my werewolf ears I could barely hear it. "Whether you decide to kill the loser or let them live, that's up to the winner."

Cosette still had her hands open, as if ready to grip weapons in them, and I wondered if she really meant what she said about Rayvien. About not being friends.

I watched the fight for a second, before leaning down again. "But they're married. He wouldn't kill her, would he?" I'd understood that Rayvien wasn't exactly happily married, but I couldn't imagine killing a spouse would be okay, even for the fey.

"Marriage doesn't matter, but for what it's worth, when Ziriel wins, I think he's going to let her live. He actually cares for her."

He was fighting like that and he cared for her? Not possible.

I jerked back as Rayvien turned to smoke just as one of Ziriel's swords stabbed her. When, she became solid again, a little dot of red expanded across her white shirt.

I knew Cosette couldn't lie, but I didn't agree with her. Ziriel really seemed like he was trying to murder his wife. "And if Rayvien wins?"

When she didn't say anything right away, I turned to her. "And if Rayvien wins?" I asked again.

"She won't. No one beats Ziriel," she said without sparing me a glance.

I went back to watching the fight.

Rayvien moved so quickly, I couldn't track her. Blood flew through the air as Ziriel turned to smoke.

"I was wrong. She's going to do it." Cosette grabbed my arm. Her eyes were still open wide as she watched the fight. "We have to stop her. We need him to cut the tie."

Another swing of the sword. Another spray of Ziriel's blood in the air.

"Shit." Cosette was right. We had to stop her. Ziriel was my best shot—my only shot—at cutting my lunar tie. "What do you want to do?"

"Hold out the bargain."

I pulled the large golden coin from my back pocket. "What now?"

"Yell for Ziriel. Tell him you want to make a deal. Quickly!"

"Ziriel!" I said, holding the glittering disk above my head. "I have a deal to make with you!"

The drumming stopped and Ziriel turned to smoke. His body slowly formed in front of me.

There were beads of sweat coating his brow, his chest was heaving with exertion, and yet I thought I saw a hint of thanks in his eyes. He was fey, and I'd just learned that not giving thanks was one of the only things universal across all the courts. He slowly sheathed one of his swords. The long, curved blade had flecks of Rayvien's blood still dripping from it, but he didn't clean it. Just put it away. Leaving only the carved, twisting golden hilt exposed as it hung from his left hip.

Ziriel stared at me for a long moment before nodding and turning to Cosette. "Back already?"

"Clearly." She sounded bored and she stared off to the side, as if he wasn't worth her time, but I knew by the rigid stance that she was anything but bored.

"And yet, your guards left." Ziriel held his arms out as he looked around the arena.

There had to be at least a couple thousand Gales fey in

277

here, maybe fifty of them in white. Maybe more. I wasn't sure. But the odds against us were terrible.

"You don't have any protection here but Van and this dog."

A growl rose up in me. Being called a dog wasn't something that I would ever—*ever*—tolerate.

Cosette grabbed my arm just as I was about to shift, and shoved her candied moonlight magic into me, pushing down my wolf.

I almost yelped at the feeling, but she was right. I couldn't start a fight. Not right now.

"Are you threatening us?" Cosette's voice was cold and had none of the parts of her I knew or loved in it.

It was her facade, and I knew it, but the sound of her voice becoming something so frozen and hard terrified me.

"Not currently. Just stating a fact so we're all on the same page." The grin on his face was so cocky, I wanted to punch him, but I didn't.

"You want them to attack her?" I asked, but it wasn't really a question. That was his goal.

My wolf was slowly rising despite Cosette's tight grip on my arm. Her sweet lunar magic was still fighting to keep him calm, but I pulled away from her.

For once I didn't give a shit. No one threatened Cosette.

"If they did, they couldn't hurt her." He turned to Cosette. "Could they? You are an archon's daughter. But which one?"

"Does it matter?" Cosette said it like she didn't care about her father, but I knew she did.

"Yes. Yes, it does. To me." He rose two feet up from the ground, and half of his legs disappeared, hidden in a cloud of smoke as he drifted toward us. "I want that piece of information."

"Why?" Her tone was teasing, but still had that thread of ice in it. "Do you want to meet him?"

"Yes. I've only ever met one archon, but if his daughter is here—I will get to meet another. Having more friends in Heaven only helps me." He floated closer. His eyes burned red with greed and power. "Will you introduce us? Will you call him down to us?"

"Absolutely not."

What Ziriel didn't know was that Cosette had never spoken to her father. Never met him, not even once. But she wasn't giving that away. Everything in her posture, attitude, and words gave the impression that she wouldn't do it, not that she couldn't.

They stared at each other for a while, before Ziriel looked at me. "Let's see this bargain you have."

I held it up again.

"It's quite large."

There were so many jokes I could've made with that one sentence, but the way he was looking at me—the way his eyes had turned black with rings of red in them—made nothing seem funny anymore.

Ziriel held out his hand, snapping his fingers when I didn't move fast enough.

I glanced quickly at Cosette, but her facade was so thick, I couldn't even read her.

Well, I guessed this was it. I was placing my bet, I just prayed that it worked out in our favor.

My heart was racing, my wolf was rising, and I knew that in this second, everything about my life was going to change. I wasn't sure what life without a lunar tie was going to be like, if I'd lose everything when it was gone—my strong senses, healing powers, ability to become a wolf—but I would lose Cosette if I didn't try.

Fuck it.

I handed Ziriel the glittering, golden bargain.

"Oh, wow." Ziriel turned to Cosette. "Do you know why this has grown so much?"

"I have a theory." Again with the bored tone, but she stiffened, her back going straight and her chin tilting up. The picture of a prim princess.

"Well, let me tell you what I know." Ziriel stepped back and addressed everyone in the arena. "This is some bargain. Maybe the most valuable one I've ever seen." His voice echoed, bouncing off the smooth, glossy walls. "Not only does it tie to Chris, but because they have a barely there bond that ties them together, it's bound to Cosette. And from Cosette, to her mother."

There were some gasps, but all I could think was that if this coin was that big of a deal, then he was going to have to give me what I wanted.

"But that's not all. From her mother, it ties to her father. The bond there is thick. The princess wouldn't tell me who her father is but one touch of the coin and I know. *I know!*"

There was a chant in the crowd. One voice at first. Then more. And more.

"Tell us! Tell us! Tell us!"

With each chant, my wolf rose closer to the surface, waiting to rip through my skin if anything else happened.

I wasn't even sure if Cosette knew which archon was her father. She didn't show any emotion on her face, but I saw the way she was holding her hands, wiggling her fingers ever so slightly to keep them loose when all she wanted to do was clench them.

"I understand why she wouldn't tell me," Ziriel's voice boomed, and the chanting died. "With the possibility of this much power coming down the lines to her, there is no reason Helen would ever want anyone—even her daughter—to know which archon she fucked."

Cosette sucked in a quick gasp of air, but I couldn't look away from Ziriel. He was floating a foot above the ground, and he started drifting back to us. His feet were smoke and then his eyes...

His eyes...

Oh, fuck no. His eyes.

Red circles surrounded his pupil glowing brighter and brighter with every word he spoke and I couldn't look away. Everything disappeared around me except those glowing red rings.

And then I looked around and everything came into focus. It wasn't one thing, but a bunch of different things that all came together to form one picture, and I finally—*finally*—knew what Cosette couldn't tell me.

Turning to smoke.

Rotten human meat.

Telling fortunes and betting.

Tricksters. Dealing in information.

Eavesdropping in Heaven and Hell.

Even the fucking *containers* in the library.

I knew exactly what he was and what he'd ordered Cosette not to tell me.

Goddamnit. Ziriel was a djinn.

The entire Court of Gales were djinn.

And yet, it didn't change a damned thing. I still had a deal to make. With a fucking djinn.

The fey were known for being incredibly precise with the words they used, especially when bargaining, but djinn? This was their game, and they could *lie*. From what I knew, even the fey didn't like to bargain with a djinn. If he agreed to cut my lunar tie, I wasn't sure what would actually happen. The tie would get cut, but what else?

This was a bad, bad, bad idea, but I didn't have another one. Just this.

Cosette tugged on my arm, pulling me down to whisper in my ear. "When you ask him to cut the tie, tell him exactly to cut the lunar tie and nothing else. Understand?"

I gave her a nod and turned back to Ziriel.

"You want to know who her father is? You want to know?" Ziriel yelled, getting cheers from everyone in the arena.

It was loud, so loud, and I found myself wanting to cheer him on, too. But my wolf rose up, stopping me from letting the magic threaded through Ziriel's voice take hold.

I wasn't sure why Ziriel was getting everyone so riled up to give them information. Why wouldn't he hold it for himself? But it wasn't up to me to understand his motivations. All I needed was for him to cut my lunar tie. That was all I cared about.

Ziriel held up his hand, still clutching the bargain, and the room quieted. "You won't believe that this girl—this golden child—is the daughter of Samael. Poison of God. Archangel of Death."

I didn't know much about archons, other than Eli, but I understood Archangel of Death.

Cosette raised her chin, just a bit. I wanted to comfort her or say something but we were watched.

"Enough with your theatrics." Her voice was proud and confident.

I was there, silently cheering her on and hoping she felt my strength supporting her.

"Are you going to give Christopher Matthews what he wants?"

Ziriel floated over to me. "And what is it that you want in return for this?"

"I want you to cut my lunar tie, but only cut the lunar tie. Nothing else."

He grinned and the heat from the bodies, and the torches and their awful smoke was suddenly gone. "Is that all?" His eyes flared brighter, the red consuming the blacks of his pupils.

This was bad. "Yes."

"Done."

I didn't have time to think, breathe, move. One second he was standing in front of me. The next, pain ripped through my whole body.

At first, I thought it was the severing of the tie—to change something so elemental to me...it had to come at a price—but then Cosette was screaming. The sound coming from her didn't sound human, but full of rage and anger and such sorrow that I couldn't breathe.

I couldn't breathe.

I felt a drip. Hot, wet heat coming from the pain in my chest, and I looked down.

The carved, twisted golden hilt of Ziriel's sword was sticking out of my chest. Dark blood seeped around it. Spreading fast. Too fast.

And even if I pulled out the sword, I knew I wouldn't be able to heal it. The blade was hot inside me. Burning, acidic magic wormed its way through me, and my wolf whimpered and disappeared. He was gone. Gone. Forever.

I was broken. I thought this had been the right call, but as I reached for my wolf and couldn't find him, I knew I'd been wrong.

So fucking wrong.

And this was a magical blade. A supernatural hurt. Something I couldn't come back from.

Suddenly I was looking up at the ceiling. A bright light falling down to surround me.

I blinked and Cosette appeared above me. Her tears rained down, and I reached up to touch her cheek, but I barely touched before my strength faded and my hand slipped down.

She held my hand there. "Please. No. Please. I'll pull the sword and I'll fix this. I can fix this. Just. Just hang on. Van! Van! Help him! Heal him!"

Van pulled the blade from my body. I felt his hands, but they were cold. Way too cold. Frozen.

And everything grew brighter and brighter. I knew I didn't have much time. Just enough to tell her one thing. One little thing.

"Don't let this break you. Find your happy."

"No! Damn you. No! Van! You're a fucking god! Fix him!" She punched Van, and suddenly the pressure from his icy hands was gone.

"I...I can't." Van's words were full of sorrow. "It's not working. The blade is a royal killer."

Cosette looked at the ceiling above me. "Eli! You sick son of a bitch! You get your ass down here and you fix him! Fix him now! *Now! Fix him now, you asshole!*"

But it was too late, because I was gone. The pain was gone and I was floating above her.

I'd let her down. I'd failed. I'd been so sure that I was going to win. I had so much faith in Eli that I didn't think about all the other things that could happen. That did happen.

I felt a tug along the center of my soul, and I was pulled up, up, up.

No. Not yet. I needed to stay, but I wasn't in control anymore and there was nothing I could do.

"I love you." The words were a whisper and I knew she couldn't hear them. Not anymore.

Because I was dead.

CHAPTER EIGHTEEN

COSETTE

I SCREAMED.

And screamed.

And screamed.

And screamed.

Yelling for Van to fix it.

But then he left. To where, I didn't care. Better that he was gone.

I cried for Eli to come and bring Chris back.

For someone—*anyone* -to change what I knew.

Chris was gone—and he hadn't taken me with him.

I screamed until my breath was gone and my throat was raw and the pain inside me was drowned out by the noise I was making, but it wasn't enough. It would never be enough. This pain and sorrow would consume me and I would let it.

I fell, sobbing over Chris' body. His lungs weren't moving and his heart wasn't beating and his soul was gone, but I wanted all of that back. I wanted him back. Oh, God. My heart was shattered. I wanted him back.

There was a gaping, bleeding hole in his chest, but there

was one in mine, too. And I sat up and screamed again as I rocked back and forth, because it hurt—it hurt so badly that I knew that I was never coming back from this.

And then I heard his voice. Not Chris' voice. Ziriel's. I didn't hear the words but his condescending tone.

I'd survived so long by being able to take hurt—mental, physical, emotional—and shove it away. It took a lot to make me truly angry, and it was easily snuffed out or reasoned away. But not today. Anger, like I'd never felt before, rose quick, fast, boiling hot. Smothering the little bits of sanity I had left. Leaving me with only a burning fire to kill.

Die.

Ziriel needed to die.

I would kill him for this.

I stood and my short swords appeared in my hands. Fire ran up them, up my arms, covering my whole body.

Ziriel disappeared, but he'd be back.

"Burn." The voice didn't sound like me—too deep, too dark, too filled with hate and rage—but it was mine.

Drops of fire dripped from the ceiling.

"Burn this place to the ground."

Fire licked up the walls and I didn't care about anything or anyone.

Gales had been infected by djinn demons three centuries ago, and no one had known. This court had always kept to themselves, so no one noticed that they had turned dark and evil. But I'd come for a visit—at Eli's insistence—fifty years ago. I'd almost taken a bite of the flesh they serve here, but I'd seen. I'd known.

I'd tried to rid the court of the demons, but Eli left and I couldn't do it by myself.

This time would be different. This time they'd gone too far. This time they'd killed my mate.

Ziriel poofed in front of me, and he didn't look scared. He was more of an idiot than I'd thought.

He threw Chris' bargain chip at me, and it turned to glittering, golden dust in the air.

The chip was gone. Which meant Chris was gone. He was really gone.

"Van is bringing your mother." He crossed his arms as he floated in front of me as if I was scared of him.

I had nothing left, certainly not fear of him.

"You're going to want to calm down. She won't be happy with you if you start another war."

"I don't give a shit what she thinks. You're dead." The tears were still falling, and I didn't care that he saw them. My words were minced, my jaw was tight, and I was filled with so much rage that I was hot—not from the fire flowing over my skin and clothes—but the fire that was raging inside, starting from the gaping hole where my heart used to live.

Ziriel didn't seem to notice or care about my anger. He watched me with no fear in his red, glowing demon eyes. That was going to change.

"For everything you've done, you deserve a slow death, but I don't care about long or short or how. I want you gone. Gone. Gone from this world. I want you dead. Dead. Dead and burning in Hell!"

A ball of fire grew behind Ziriel.

"Burn him!"

It slammed into Ziriel and he turned to smoke, reappearing ten feet away.

It hadn't hurt him. Not even a little bit. But he'd made a mistake. He was watching me—focused on what I'd do next as I held out my flaming blades—but I was watching Rayvien move behind him.

Her gaze met mine and she gave me a small nod.

And I knew. Knew she would do it. For me or for herself, I didn't care. As long as he was dead.

I stepped toward Ziriel and he grinned, waving me forward when he should've been watching his back.

He didn't see Rayvien pull her sword.

He didn't see her raise it high.

And when the too-sharp blade sliced his head from his body, he didn't have time to react. The same cocky expression was on his face as his severed head bounced on the floor.

There was a loud, angry cry among the fey, and most of them poofed out of the arena. The rest started fighting amongst themselves. And I hoped they killed each other while they warred for a new ruler. Even with Ziriel dead, the anger still burned in me.

The fire felt good and just and better than the searing pain in my heart and the tears that wouldn't stop, so I fed the flames. I surrendered to anger for the first time in my life. I gave in to the rush of power, letting it spew out of me.

"Every single djinn demon will die." I would burn myself out hunting them all until each one of these tricksters died.

I started toward the exit. They might have left this room, but the hunt was on. And when the last of them was dead, I'd let myself burn, too.

"Cosette." The voice seemed like it was far away, but there was the roar of fire and smoke and—

The room went silent and still. The flickering flames froze.

"Cosette."

I spun to face Eli behind me. "You." I built up the power, ready to spit fire at him, but Eli raised his hand.

From one instant to the next, the flames were gone. Doused. Extinguished. Even the fire on my blades was gone as they slipped from my fingers and clattered to the ground. Without the fire, all that left in me was my grief.

I fell to my knees.

The sob that came from me was guttural and loud and sounded like it was coming from somewhere else. I couldn't make it stop. My heart had been ripped from me but why hadn't it killed me? I *needed* it to kill me, too.

I couldn't breathe. Couldn't speak. Couldn't do anything but make a keening, sobbing mess of a noise.

"Peace, Cosette." Eli laid a hand on me.

The keening and sobbing stopped, but that was it. Eli couldn't fix what was broken inside of me. Even if he could do some magic and repair my heart, it was too late. My heart was gone. There was nothing left to repair.

The tears were spilling out of me faster than I could blink them away. The crushing weight in my chest was still heavier than I could bear. The emptiness of my soul was sucking me into a dark, bottomless pit. A place where hope and dreams and love were tortured away until there was nothing good left.

"I'm sorry."

I shook my head at him. "You knew. You got him killed. This is *your fault.*" I sounded mean, evil, full of bitterness, and I didn't give a shit about any of that. I wasn't a princess. Not today.

Today I would burn with justice.

"I didn't know this would happen." Eli knelt beside me, his great gray and white speckled wings spread out behind him. "I was told that Ziriel could break the tie. My orders were to bring Chris here and then stay out of it, but I would've broken my orders if I'd seen this coming. I know I can read minds, but God doesn't let me in on the big picture. I only get pieces and follow His wishes."

He wiped a hand down my cheek and I slapped it away.

"No. You knew. You left me here before and you left him—"

"I didn't leave you here last time. You started killing everyone, and when I tried to stop you—because Gales is very much in the gray area and each life should be weighed—you pushed me out. You locked me out. Something that only your father could do. It was the first time I knew that there was more to you than fey."

"I want him back. I love him. Please." I was choking on sobs, but I was getting the words out. "And he's gone. I can't—I can't —I can't do this without him. I can't breathe. I can't. Breathe. I can't—"

Eli laid his hand on my head. "Peace, child."

Tingles ran from my skull down every inch of my body as his power poured into me.

The grief dulled, but I didn't want it to dull. I didn't want it to go away. I wanted Chris. I needed him back. I couldn't—

"Peace."

The tingles came again, but he wasn't strong enough. Not for this. I blinked up at him through my tears. "I have no peace left." My hair brushed against my face as I shook my head. My peace was with Chris. And then the air was sucked out of me again. "Where's his body? Eli?"

I scrambled up, but I couldn't see it. There was nothing but me and Eli left in the scorched arena.

"Oh, God. Eli! Did I burn it?" My chest was pumping in and out too fast, too hard, but I couldn't stop the panic.

Eli's eyes widened. "I don't know. I don't know, Cosette. But it doesn't matter anymore because—"

"Oh, God. Oh, God. OhGodohGodohGod." I ran around the area, turning in circles, throwing aside the remains of the drums, weapons, bodies of those who had stayed to fight and died. I searched every corner for him, and with every second that passed, my panic grew until it was choking me.

"What did I do? What did I do? What did I do? Did I burn him? Did I burn Chris? Oh, God." I couldn't stop the rambling rant or the tears or the pain that was swallowing me down to a deep dark pit of my own Hell.

Eli flew after me. Reached for me. "Peace."

I shoved his hand away. "There is no such thing as peace, you asshole. I have no peace. I have *nothing left*!"

"And you won't. Not for a while. That's the pain of losing someone you love more than yourself. That love is a gift and in time, you'll feel that it—"

He was wrong. He was so unbelievably wrong. "I can't. I won't ever come back from this. I want to die. Just kill me. Please." I grabbed Eli's warm hands and held on with everything I had left. "Please. I beg you. I have nothing left. Put me to peace. Kill me now." My breaths came in gasping hiccups and I wanted it to end. I wanted to be with Christopher. This was it. This was my answer.

And with that, some of the pain went away.

Yes. I just needed to die. That would fix everything.

He said he would follow me wherever I went, and I would follow him. I would find a way. I would—

Eli's wings were spread wide, covering us in shadows. "It doesn't work that way. I can't kill you."

"You won't!" I shoved him. "You could kill me but you *won't*!" I could feel my face heat with rage.

"You're right. I won't." His face was pale and his eyes were brimming with buckets of pity and he was shaking his head, but all I could see was that he wouldn't do this for me. "There is so much good that you could do—"

Good. I couldn't do any good! "You don't understand. I have nothing left! I'll burn your beloved mortal world to the ground unless you kill me now!"

"I won't do that, Cosette." He took a step toward me, hands out, but I didn't want him to touch me. "I know that you don't understand right now, but I need you to have faith."

I laughed through my sobs. "Fuck that."

"You have to have faith that God has a plan—"

"Tell that to Christopher!" I shoved the archon hard enough to knock him back a few steps. "Where was his plan? Where was God for him? He was tortured his whole life, and still he was good and kind and loving and happy. So happy. All the time. Wherever he went, there was joy. No matter how hard life was to him. And where was his reward?"

"In Heaven."

I took a calming breath. I licked my lips, swallowing down my anger. Okay. I had a new plan. Something I could get Eli to do.

I took one more breath. This would work. "Then send me there." I had to talk calmly to him or he wouldn't do what I asked. "Take me to Heaven. If not to see Chris, then to talk to my father."

His shoulders slouched a bit, and I wasn't sure if it was relief or something else, but it didn't matter. As long as he did what I asked.

"Okay. Okay. That I can do."

"Okay." My father would fix this. I hadn't spoken to him, hadn't asked anything of him, hadn't needed anything from him in one hundred and fifty-two years. But today—today—I would ask something of him.

"Cosette! What have you done, you stupid child." My mother's voice was like ice over my smoldering grief, covering it in frost until I was frozen beneath it.

I looked at what remained of the charred room. Everyone had fled what felt like ages ago but it could've been minutes. Even the fighting fey were gone. It had been just me and Eli. But now Van was back, and he'd brought my mother.

"I did what you asked of me. As I always do." I said the words, but I didn't feel like I was in my own body. Not anymore.

I was floating. "I found my husband." My voice sounded like it was coming from somewhere else. Somewhere so far away.

"You're not as smart as I thought you were if you thought he could ever be your equal. And now your pet is dead." Her eyes narrowed. "Van. Take her home while I clean up another of her messes. I can't even look at her."

My mother's words floated over me like water on the shore. Brushing against me and receding. I was too numb to feel them. Too empty. Too tired.

I'd burned myself out with the fire, and now all that was left was a charred bit of coal where my soul used to be.

I looked to Eli. "Keep your promise." The words were hollow and my soul was gone, but he would do this for me. He said he would.

"I will do as you ask." He reached for me before thinking better of it. "This could not be what was intended. I don't always know the plan, but I would've stopped it if I'd known. Please believe me. I can't fix it, but I will do whatever it takes to make it better."

I looked at the ground. "It doesn't matter." Because nothing mattered. Not anymore. If Chris was gone, then nothing mattered.

I felt Van's arm come around me. The world twisted and tumbled and then I was in my suite at the Lunar Court. I heard him ask if I wanted a bath, but I didn't care about that.

His voice sounded a mile away as he offered me food. Cakes. My favorite treat. But I wasn't hungry.

Water?

No. Where I was, I didn't need water. It was just me and the whooshing sound of my breath in my empty head.

My empty heart.

My empty soul.

I felt him tuck me into bed, but all I could see was a blurry, tear-stained version of the world, and when he turned out the light, even that was gone.

And I was left with nothing.

Nothing but emptiness and pain and heartache that I was sure would kill me. That I hoped would kill me.

When the sobbing started up again, I didn't even try to stop it, because that would've been impossible.

Because Chris was dead. And even if I was still breathing, I was dead, too.

CHAPTER NINETEEN

COSETTE

A LIGHT CAME ON, but I didn't see anything.

A voice in the silence, but I didn't hear.

Questions were asked but I didn't care about the answers. It didn't matter. Didn't they understand that I didn't *care*?

I rolled in my bed, throwing the covers over my head.

"Cosette, please," Van said. "Did you hear anything that I said?"

"No. Go away. Leave me be like you did in Gales. Run off to my mother."

I felt his hand on my shoulder and I shook it off.

He let out a long sigh. "I had to do something before you killed everyone. Chris was already dead, and whether you want to see it or not, there are innocent, good fey in Gales."

"Leave. Me. Now. Or I will burn you, too." And I meant it. He'd fetched my mother, and I wouldn't forget that.

"I'll leave, but your mother has ordered us to get married tomorrow morning."

"Fine." What did it matter?

"Fine?"

The mattress dipped as Van sat, and I scooted to the opposite edge, not wanting to be near him.

"Do you want me to ask for more time?"

"Is the fortnight over?"

"It ended seven days ago. Your mother put the court back on mortal realm time, but time is still moving, and you haven't left your room."

What did it matter how long I'd been in bed? Days, weeks, months. Mother could do whatever she wanted with time, and none of it would bring Chris back.

It didn't matter how long I stayed in bed. I didn't care about anything beyond these walls.

"Please, Cosette." He was begging, and maybe if my heart still existed, I would've answered him.

But it didn't. So I couldn't.

"Talk to me. You're not eating. You're only drinking what I pour down your throat. Please, Coco. I know it's hard, but you have to try to live." He gave me a shake. "Don't fade on me. Not now. You're the only thing keeping me going in this world."

"You'll find someone else." He'd found me. There'd be someone else.

"No. God, Cosette. You're the daughter of my heart and soul. I can't watch you die."

He tried to pull the covers off my face, but I shoved him away. "Then leave." It was only a tiny hint of the anger I'd had back at Gales. Something had happened when Eli doused the fire and I couldn't get it back.

Maybe if I tried it would come back. But I didn't. So it couldn't.

"Never."

I felt him lie down behind me, pulling me close.

"I'm here, Cosette. You have people here who love you. Please, live for us."

"No." Because I couldn't live. Not anymore. Not when Chris was dead.

Not when I'd burned him.

Oh, God. Oh, God. OhGodohGodohGod.

The sobs started again. Each one coming from so deep inside me, my whole body jerked with their weight, and I deserved the pain.

Chris had died because of me.

I deserved this pain.

CHAPTER TWENTY

COSETTE

I FELT like a soulless doll as the servants dressed me in a midnight blue wedding gown, dusted with starlit glitter filled with magic. As I moved, the glitter would flake off and float to the darkened ceiling to become twinkling stars. It was an artistic bit of magic that Christopher would've loved. That was the only reason I hadn't ripped it to shreds.

Van managed to push our wedding a few more days, but I was as empty as I had been since the second Ziriel stabbed his royal-killer sword into Chris' heart.

One of the servants tried to take my locket and replace it with some priceless garbage jewelry. I snarled, so they left it alone—they left me alone—for a while.

But then they were back.

They walked me over to a chair, and started tugging on my hair.

I didn't care. I didn't feel anything. I was empty—heart, mind, soul.

They could do whatever they wanted to my body, but the rest of me was dead. It had burned to ash with Chris.

I was fading. I couldn't keep track of time—it drifted. Sometimes going by slowly. Other times speeding by. My magic was draining away, drip by drip. I'd opened the door inside me and was letting the moonlight inside float out into the air around me. This was the way of the fey when we were done with this world. When the last of my magic was gone, I would be gone, too.

I kept waiting for one of my stupid assassins to come kill me. Get it over with. Especially after the firestorm at Gales. But now that I was broken and weak, I apparently wasn't worth the challenge anymore.

So I was left to wait for the second worst day in my life while my grief swallowed me whole.

Mother stopped by. She made it clear I was pathetic, but her words couldn't hurt me. She reminded me of our bargain. How I was supposed to act. How I was supposed to obey. How I was supposed to give her what she wanted. In return, she would always look after my well-being first and foremost.

I wasn't sure if that last part was a lie. Could my mother lie?

It didn't matter. Nothing mattered.

Maybe I should be upset that Eli hadn't followed through on his promise yet. At the very least he could spare me from today. But he'd come and gone a few days ago. He was trying to find my father, but hadn't had any luck so far. I wasn't sure that mattered. Not anymore.

Van was upset—that we were getting married and that I was giving up—and I would help him if I could. But I couldn't fix either. Not anymore.

He alternated between begging me to live and yelling at me and then bribing, but it didn't work. I couldn't be sure if I even really heard his words, but he'd been alive for millennia. Losing me wouldn't kill him.

But today we'd be married. I stared at my dead eyes in the mirror as the fey ladies tugged on my hair, and I knew I was half-gone anyway. I'd seen someone fade years ago. I held my dear friend's hand as she breathed her last breath. Her baby had died, and she didn't have it in her to live with that piece of her soul gone.

I hadn't understood her choice then, but now...now I did.

The bond between Chris and I had been tiny and barely there, but I'd felt it. The magic grew slowly over time. It wasn't instant like with Tessa and Dastien. Or Claudia and Lucas. Or Meredith and Donovan. For us it grew and grew and grew. From a friendship and understanding and basic caring for each other to this all-consuming love where I didn't think I could breathe without him.

But now I knew I couldn't breathe without him.

So, today didn't matter. Mother wanted me to marry Van, so I'd obey. I'd marry Van, but really, I was just waiting. Waiting for an assassin to come kill me. Waiting for the last of my magic to fade away. Waiting to see if tomorrow would come or if today I'd finally get my wish.

The sound of the air coming into and leaving my body was the only thing I heard. I listened to that whisper of internal wind as the servants came back to put the last finishing glitter in my hair. As they painted my face to make me look less like a ghost. As they dragged me to the moonlight room filled with fey.

If I cared about looking at the room, I'd have noticed the glowing white flowers, the stars that hung below the ceiling, or the music that drifted in the air as I walked. It was the same at each of my siblings' weddings. This one was probably better than the last, since my mother liked to outdo herself with each one. There had been many that I'd been forced to attend as my sibling burned through partners in a quest to become the most powerful. There was some relief to know that I'd only have to do this once because soon, very soon, I would fade away to nothing.

With each step farther down the aisle, the whispers grew.

301

The fey all knew what had happened. They all knew what I was now. Formerly strong. Now shattered by Ziriel. Finally fading.

At least one good thing came from it all—everyone knew Gales was full of djinn demons.

The rest of the fey wouldn't stand for that. Ziriel was dead, but Gales would still pay.

But not today.

Today I was marrying Van.

I didn't see the faces watching me as I walked up the aisle. I didn't hear the music. I didn't smell the flowers. I was walking and breathing and that was it. If I started feeling again, I'd burn the whole court to the ground.

Burn everything until this world was filled with nothing, just like my soul.

I paused when I saw Van standing at the altar waiting for me like a good little god. I think he would've fought my mother over this much harder, but he probably hoped that shifting our relationship would keep me tied to this world. It was a valiant effort, and I loved him in spite of it, but he looked so ill that he nearly seemed ready for his own funeral. His midnight blue suit and glittery tie matched my dress, and apparently his feelings about this sham of a ceremony matched mine, too.

For the first time in days, I smiled. I didn't even realize I'd done it until I saw Van's answering smile.

And then came the guilt.

How could I smile when Chris was dead?

When he'd died trying to save me?

When I burned his body?

I fell to the ground.

The sobbing was back and I couldn't make it stop. And for once, I didn't give a shit about who was watching or that they were seeing the true Cosette. I was done faking it. I was done being my mother's pet daughter. I was over it.

Van ran down the aisle, dropping to his knees in front of me. He called a quick silencing spell, making it so that we were in our own little protected world. "Is marrying me so bad?" He gave me a wink when I looked up at him.

"Yes. It's absolutely awful." I laughed through my tears, but then the sobbing started again. "I'm broken, Van. My heart turned to sand while we were at Gales. All the tiny, charred fragments blew away in the wind, and I can't get them back. I can't do this. I love you, but I can't do this."

"You can." He grabbed my face, pulling it close to his. "You will."

"No. No, I can't. I won't survive it. I'm fading. I choose to fade." I tried to push him away, but he held my face painfully tight.

"Stop! You're not fading. I won't let you. We will do what we've done the last century and a half together. We will survive it. This won't be easy, but we are stronger together. And once everyone is looking the other way, then we will get our revenge." His tone grew so dark that somewhere, deep inside of me, the door leaking all my magic into the world slammed shut.

My flame relit.

"Revenge?"

The burning grew.

I liked the sound of revenge.

His grip lightened. "Yes, Cosette. Your mother forgets what I am, but I have not forgotten. She's pushed me too far. So, I'm playing along with her charade, and once we're married, my plans go into motion." He smiled and let me go.

I leaned away from him. I was seeing a side of Van I'd never seen before. He'd been very careful to keep this side hidden from me. The one that earned him the title God of Destruction.

"I was fading after my wife was murdered—same as you're trying to. I waited until my revenge was done, and was ready to chase her to the next world. But then your mother dangled a beautiful little girl in front of me. One that needed my help. My protection. A father. She didn't realize that she was giving me something very, very dangerous."

"What? Because I'm—"

"She gave me someone to *love*, but she forgot what I am. Vanilor, God of Warfare, Champion of the Powerless, One Who Bathes in Blood. You think I can't take on your irrelevant mother and win? She tried to play me. She tried to hurt the only thing that matters to me in this world. I was too worried about losing you to see it. But now she will remember exactly who I am."

I grabbed his arm. "You promise. You promise you'll help me get revenge? Against Gales? Against my mother? No matter the price."

He gripped my shoulders, bringing his forehead to mine. "Daughter of my soul, I will do whatever it takes to keep you alive. If you wish to drown your enemies in their blood, if that is what keeps you living, then it would be my pleasure."

"The wedding night?" I wasn't sleeping with him. He was the closest thing to a father I had, and the idea of it was beyond sick.

"We fake it."

"But lying—"

"We won't lie." He ran a thumb under my eyes to brush away the last of the drying tears. His eyes were bright blue. Not the same blue as Chris' wolf, but an icier, deadlier, frost blue. The ill look in his face was replaced with deadly hope.

My mother had been an idiot to forget who Van really was. If anyone should rule the fey, it should've been Van. And it made me wonder what had happened to keep him from the throne.

Van rose up on his knees. "Trust me, Cosette. I found a way. I'm taking care of it. I'm taking care of you. Whatever you need to do to stay alive, I will make it happen."

Now, I could look up from where I'd fallen on the floor. I could see the faces looking at me. Watching. Judging.

I looked back at Van. His lips were pressed tight but I could see the determination inside him.

"If this is a manipulation to keep me alive—"

"I've told you the truth. Do I want you to stay alive? Hell, yes, I do." His hushed words were fierce and full of fire. "Would I do anything to give you another reason to live? Yes. And when you're done with your revenge, I'll find another reason for you to live. I will keep doing it until you decide you want to live again for you."

My eyes burned and the tears started again. "I don't deserve you."

"Yes, you do." He cupped my cheek and his shoulders softened a little. "You've never believed it, but you deserve everything. I'm sorry that I didn't see what was coming. I believed as much as you did, but we'll have revenge, and then we'll keep going." He pressed his forehead against mine again. "Okay?"

I wasn't sure if this was a good idea, but the frozen fog in my head was lighter, and I had a purpose. I liked having a purpose. "Okay."

He closed his eyes and bowed his head for a minute before letting out a long breath. "Thank you." He opened his eyes and grabbed my hands. "I know how hard it's going to be to get up right now. To get through today and tomorrow and the next week. But I need you to get up and walk over there. Do this one thing, so that we can move on to the next. Day by day. Minute

305

by minute. I will get you through this. I always have, and I need you to trust me one more time."

I nodded, unable to use my voice as the tears just kept coming. I'd never cried so much. It seemed like it should stop—that I should run out of water or grief—but I didn't.

Van stood, pulled me to my feet, and with one arm wrapped around my shoulders, he walked me up to the altar.

I would do this. I could do this. Because once I did, I would get revenge for Chris. Revenge against Gales. Revenge against my manipulative mother. And then...

And then...

And then I don't know what would happen, but I'd deal with that later.

CHAPTER TWENTY-ONE

CHRIS

THE LIGHT WAS warm and full of love and I wanted to relax, but I couldn't. I needed to go back. Cosette was hurting. I could feel her heart bleeding as it shattered for me down the fragmented bond. I wasn't sure why it was still there, but it was making her pain worse and keeping me grounded. I couldn't move on until it was really gone, but I didn't want to let it go. Maybe that was our problem. Maybe I was the problem.

I was floating in the light, and I wasn't sure which way was up or where I was going or what was happening. But eventually, I started to see some differentiation in the light. Walls appeared. I could only tell because of the slight shadows in the corners. And then I felt myself moving, floating down, and my feet gently touched the floor.

It was also white. I couldn't see a ceiling above me. Just an expanse of white.

I looked around, but I was alone. I couldn't just stand there like an idiot, so I started walking.

"Hello?" I yelled into the white-light void.

I'd thought that someone would be here waiting for me.

That's what they said, although who they were and how the hell they'd know anything was beyond me.

Although, when I thought about dying, I always pictured myself going down the pit. Down, down, down until I was with Astaroth. And there, I'd see my pack.

But this wasn't Hell. Not sure if it was Heaven though. I wasn't sure what it was, but at least it wasn't Hell. No fires or brimstone or sulfur. I was taking that as a win.

I took a breath, and let it out slowly.

Okay. Not Hell. Possibly Heaven or something else?

I needed to talk to someone. I couldn't be here alone forever. "Hello?"

"Christopher Matthews. Mate to Cosette Argent." The bodiless voice seemed to come from all around me.

"Yes."

"What do you have to say for your life?"

My life? That felt pretty vague. What was I supposed to say? "My life was actually mostly shitty. The pack I was born into was evil. They nearly killed me, multiple times, but I survived and they didn't. I eventually found friends. Had about a minute of fun before I started killing vampires and demons. Met my mate, and was ripped from her before we could cement the bond. Actually, I'd really like to go back. If I can. I know...I know that's probably pretty impossible, but I have to ask. I've seen a lot of crazy things in my life, and I can't rule it out." I sighed. "Can I go back? To my mate?"

I waited but the voice didn't come again.

"Hello?"

Damn it.

"I just want to go the fuck home already..." I muttered to myself mostly, but still, whoever was talking to me could probably hear anyway.

Shit.

Cursing at God—if that even was God—was a bad call. I should apologize.

"I don't need an apology." A figure walked toward me, like he'd stepped out of the endless light. He was wearing white pants, a white shirt, and held a flaming spear in his hand.

But it wasn't the spear that caught my attention. It was his wings. I'd thought the room was white, but it wasn't. Not when compared to the brilliant, pure, iridescent white of this angel's wings.

"I'm not God or an angel, but I wanted to meet you."

There was something familiar about him, like I'd seen him somewhere, but I wasn't sure where. "And you are?"

"Samael." He didn't smile or nod or show any kind of emotion at all. He wasn't joking or cocky. He just stared at me, totally stone-faced.

"Okay." The name sounded familiar, but I couldn't quite remember...

"Some people call me the Archangel of Death."

I took a step back. I hadn't been afraid of the flaming spear, but now I was having second thoughts about the guy.

"The thing you might find most important about me is that I am Cosette's father."

And then I remembered what Ziriel had said in the arena. Cosette's archon father was the Archangel of Death. Poison of God. "Right. The archon, Samael."

"Yes."

Well, at least I knew where Cosette's facade came from. No wonder he looked familiar. If it hadn't been the worst day of my life, I would've recognized him right away. I'd filled so many sketchbooks with her face. Their mouths were similar. Lips, too. Hers were fuller, and her eyes were a darker brown than his, but the same shape.

Yep. This was her dad. If he couldn't take me back, then

maybe he'd want to help her. "I can feel Cosette a little, which means that the little bit I'm getting through our bond must actually be a lot worse, and I can't stand it that she's hurting. I really, really want to go back to her, but if that's not possible, if you could help her, I'd really appreciate it. Anything you could do to ease her grief would be good."

"I can't take away her grief without taking away the memories she has of you."

It made sense and it sucked, but that would be better than what she was going through right now. "That's fine. If you could just erase me from her memory, then she'll be okay." I thought for a second.

Damn. This was exactly what she'd done to me at Gales with her lunar magic. But this time one of us was dead. It was game over for me. If forgetting me helped her, then I had to do it. Just like she'd tried to do it for me.

But there was something else. "If you could, I would ask one more thing."

"What?"

"Could you..." This sucked. This totally sucked, but if I couldn't get back to her... "Could you..." I couldn't make myself say the words.

"*Ah.* I know what you're thinking—or what you're trying to think. You want me to put someone good for her in her path. A match?"

Either he had an itch on his cheek, or he'd given me a half-smile for exactly point seven seconds.

"I'm not cupid, but I think I could make an exception, just this once."

I blew out a breath. It sucked, but was best for her. I wanted her to be happy and loved. "Someone really nice and kind, but someone funny. Who can make her laugh. She doesn't do that enough. Also, someone who can see through her facade and not take any of her shit."

"And?"

"A good fighter. Someone strong. Not a werewolf, because apparently there's no such thing as breaking a lunar tie—"

"Oh." He tilted his head just slightly and I thought that was probably the only sign of shock that I'd get from him. "That's not true at all."

Shit. I didn't want to ask, but I had to. "Then I did it wrong? There was an amulet or a spell or something else that I missed."

"No."

I closed my eyes and thanked God my wolf still wasn't anywhere to be found because Cosette's dad was fucking frustrating.

I opened my eyes, hoping to get some answers from him that weren't half-truths. "It's been a very confusing and emotional couple of days. I've never been one to play games, and if I'm dead, then I think that's probably never going to change."

He let go of his flaming spear and it didn't move. It stayed there like Samael was still holding it. "I'm not playing games. Let's have a seat." He waved a hand through the air and a table with two chairs appeared. They were the hammered industrial metal kind that were common at coffee shops and cafes. Utilitarian and sturdy. I guess that's how this archon rolled.

"Okay." I pulled out a chair and sat across from Samael. It wasn't like I had anything better to do.

"Why do you love my daughter?"

I guess we were switching topics away from my lunar tie. It didn't matter anyway. I was dead.

I wasn't sure what good answering the question would do, but he was Cosette's father. So, it made some kind of sense. And maybe it'd help him find someone else for her. "Because she's loving, caring, strong. She's put herself at risk with her family and her people to help us, and never once asked for anything in return." She'd sacrificed her freedom to help us fight those demons, and now was forced to live at court in a life she hated. She'd never once complained. She never even told the rest of our friends what she was going through at home because of what she'd done for us.

"She's always giving too much of herself to everyone around her, and no one sees through the words that she says. No one thinks about the meaning behind them or about what she's purposefully not saying. And she needs that." I thought I could give her that and make her laugh. I saw who she was under it all, and she was good and fun.

"Every time I make her laugh, I feel like a superhero because she needs that laugh. She needs more joy in her life. She can be frustrating and stubborn, but the kindness and self-sacrificing really makes up for all of that. I just... I love her, but I'm here now, so I have to let her go. But, if you could pick someone amazing for her that would be..."

He nodded. "Okay. Yes."

I blew out a breath. My eyes burned, but I wouldn't let any tears fall in front of Mr. Stone-faced Archon. "Okay." Cosette was going to find someone who would make her happy, which meant everything was fine. She'd be okay. So, good. I rubbed the palms of my hands on my jeans, trying to keep all the emotions off my face.

This was a good thing. It hurt, but it had to happen. I couldn't keep her bound to me when she was still living.

A pair of scissors appeared in Samael's hand. The blades were silver, short, and looked pointy and sharp. Almost like a tiny dagger when they were closed. The handles were ornate and golden, and if I wasn't mistaken, they glowed a little.

He reached through me, grabbed something I couldn't see, and then it felt like I was being pulled toward him.

The pull increased until I was leaning over the table. "What's going on?" I gripped the edges of the table to keep myself from sliding across it. I wanted to trust Cosette's father, but I'd just been stabbed by a golden sword, and for something like that, once was really enough.

"Just one second. I have to find the right one. Hold still."

And then he put the scissors way too close to my eye. I whipped my head back as far as I could.

"Watch it with the scissors." I snapped at him.

"Oh, I'm watching." He jabbed the scissors toward me and snipped.

The cut sounded inside my head. It rattled and echoed inside my skull and rippled down through every bone, muscle, molecule of my body, like I was about to shift but couldn't. Yet way worse than that.

I fell back into the chair—nearly toppling backward—breathing hard. "What the fuck was that?"

"What's going on?" Eli appeared at the table. His hair was a tangled mess and his once-white shirt looked rumpled and he had dark circles under his eyes.

He looked like shit.

Eli turned to me and his face was turning tomato red. "Fuck you very much! I've been running around like crazy trying to find you!" He spun to Samael, and I was glad to have his attention away from me.

That was one pissed off archon.

Eli picked up the table and tossed it across the white abyss. "I thought you said he'd be fine!"

"And he *is* fine." Samael motioned toward me slowly.

"But he's dead." Eli stepped toward him.

The flaming spear whooshed into Samael's waiting hand, but he stayed in his chair, watching Eli lose his shit like it was no big deal.

313

As fun as it would've been to watch them beat the shit out of each other, now that Eli was here, I wanted answers. "Why did you send me on such a shit mission? Why take me to Gales when I was just going to die?" I wanted to be mad at him and blame him for everything that went wrong, but it wasn't his fault.

I had to put the blame where it was due.

"That's right. It wasn't my fault." Eli jabbed a finger toward Samael. "It was his fault!"

"This is all going according to plan," Samael said calmly.

Was he insane? How was this part of the plan? Cosette was heartbroken and I was dead.

"You had to die."

I stood from my chair. Finally someone was giving me some answers. "Why?"

"To cut your lunar tie, you have to be dead. Once you're dead, I can snip the little thread that kept you bound to the Lunar Court. No fey will ever be able to turn you into a slave now."

At this point, I was wondering if he had any feelings at all. Or maybe he was stupid because—

"I'm not stupid."

"What are you then? Because it doesn't matter that I can't be a slave anymore. I'm *dead*."

Samael's wings fluttered behind him as he stood. "You had to die so that I could cut your tie, but now, you're going back."

"What do you mean going back?" Eli stepped closer to Samael, and looked ready to kick some ass, and at this point, I was pretty sure I'd enjoy watching.

"He's going back, Elilaios. Calm down."

Eli's hands tightened into fists, and I knew this was about to get ugly. I'd kill for some popcorn right now.

"His body burned, Sam. He can't go back."

Wait. What? "I burned? How?"

"No. His body is just fine." Samael snapped his fingers and the table was back, but bigger, and it had my body lying on top of it.

"Jesus." I stumbled backwards, trying to get away from my dead body.

"Not Jesus. This is you. Christopher Matthews."

Obviously. "I know." My body looked fine. Normal. No stab wound from Ziriel's sword. Even the hole in my clothes and the blood were gone.

Looking at my body was really, really weird. I turned to Eli, just so I didn't have to see it anymore. "Is he always so literal?"

"Yes. It's why he mostly stays up here." Eli sighed. "Well, you had me fooled, Sam. You win this round."

"She's my daughter. I'm looking out for her." He looked at me. "Who do you think gave you that push to go back to your land? To build the sanctuary? You'll both be happy there. She had to wait a long time for you to be born, and now, it's your job to make her happy. Every day. Don't let someone else open the boutique in town. It's one of her dreams, not that she'll ever bring it up. But you will."

I nodded, trying to keep up with Samael. "Okay. Yes. She can do whatever she wants." If I was going back, I'd make that dream come true for her.

"I'll need your word. In writing." A contract fell to the table.

It was thicker than the Bible and the writing was tiny. I couldn't read all of that right now, especially not without a magnifying glass.

"What's it say?" Not that it mattered. If he was sending me back—and without my lunar tie—then I'd sign whatever he wanted.

"That you'll love my daughter. Be good to her. Put all her

315

needs first. Protect. Honor. You don't have to obey, but you have to be respectful of each other. No cheating. Etcetera."

Etcetera? I wasn't sure what that meant, and I wasn't sure I cared. The rest of it was already my goal.

But I didn't need to hand over my soul or do his bidding?

"No. You have free will."

This was a good deal, and I wasn't an idiot. "Where's the pen?"

A golden pen hovered in front of my face, and I snatched it from the air. The pen scratched a bit as I scribbled my signature across the paper. "All right. What's next?"

"Cosette's almost married to Van now." Samael said that so matter-of-factly that it took me a second to process it.

Married to Van? "Wait. What?"

"You better hurry or you'll be too late."

"*What!*"

He waved a hand through the air, and just like that I was falling back to Earth—to life—to make sure my mate didn't marry Van.

Samael couldn't have explained this quicker?

Damn it.

CHAPTER TWENTY-TWO

COSETTE

I TRIED TO STOP CRYING—I really did—but the tears just wouldn't stop. I didn't even try to brush them away. They trickled down my neck, into my dress, and soaked the front of it. I couldn't hear the priestess over my own sobs, not that it mattered. I nodded when I was supposed to. Answered when Van nudged me.

But then everything went quiet. I heard my mother shout my name, but I didn't know why.

I looked up at Van.

"What did she say?"

Van's mouth was open as he stared at something behind me, and I turned to see what he was looking at.

And then I fell. To the ground. Again.

"Oh, God." I hung my head and squeezed my eyes tight. "I'm losing my mind, Van." I turned back to him. "I see Chris over there, but he's dead. So, I'm really losing it now. I need to get out of here. Is it done? Can we leave yet?"

A few nearly silent footsteps, and then they stopped behind me. "Is what done?"

It was his familiar raspy voice, but this could've been an illusion or some form of evil magic or—

A hand ran down my back and I froze. My hands shook, but I forced myself to twist, to look over my shoulder, to see if that was really my Chris.

Chris was squatting with one knee on the ground in front of me. "Hi." He gave me one if his charming grins. "You look terrible."

I started sobbing loud, ugly tears, and I covered my face with my hands.

"Shit. I mean, nice dress, but really, someone needs to get her a makeup wipe. I mean—why didn't someone just magic her makeup. Isn't glamour a thing among you all? Or are you just a bunch of assholes?"

There was a little rustle. "Thanks, Van."

I looked up to see Chris taking a handkerchief from Van. "Come here," he said.

I held still as he wiped my face.

What was happening? I didn't understand. I couldn't...

I turned to Van. "Do you see him, too? Or have I lost my mind?"

Van had tears in his eyes. "Yes, Coco. He's there. He's real."

"Cosette!" My mother yelled again, but I ignored her. For once in my life, I was going to ignore her.

When she yelled my name again, Van moved to block her from me. He spoke to her in a hushed whisper, but I didn't care about anything other than looking at Chris. At his blue eyes.

"Babe." He ran a finger down my cheek, chasing the path of my tears. "I'm okay. I'm here now. Everything is going to be okay."

"I don't understand." I grabbed the stupid cloth, wiping away more tears. He was here now. Why were they still falling? "I saw you die." I swiped at the tears again. "Your body burned."

"No. Your father took it. And then he cut my lunar tie."

I gasped, slapping a hand over my mouth. "Oh, my God. He did? He really did?" I looked at him. Really looked. "Your hair is short. And your beard is gone."

"What?" He ran a hand over his head. "I guess your dad thought I needed cleaning up a bit."

"Cosette." The way my mother drew out my name, I knew she wasn't happy. It was laced with moonlit venom, and I wondered if this was how she always had been. If this was the Queen that everyone talked about, but I never saw. If I was just now seeing all the manipulations.

I'd been stupid to believe and trust her. I knew what she was and what people said. But I thought I knew a different side of her. And I wondered if she kept us all from lying so that she could be free to lie all she wanted.

I could hear Van trying to block her path to me but I was going to have to deal with her in a second.

"Don't you want to introduce me to your pet wolf?" My mother's voice was full of anger like I'd never heard before. I should've been scared or running or defending Chris... But I wasn't. Chris was here. Alive. Breathing. Nothing else mattered.

Nothing except one thing.

I leaned forward to whisper in his ear. "The tie? It's really gone, right?"

"Gone." His lips brushed my ear as he whispered back.

"You're sure?"

"Yes."

"Your wolf?"

"I thought he was gone, but when I came back, he was here. He's fine."

Good. That was so good. "Tell me the rest later." I knew the most important information, and now I had to do the next part.

I stood and my vision grayed a little at the sudden movement, but I was fey. It would take more than an eight-day fast to kill me. "Mother. This is Christopher Matthews. My mate."

"Please, Cosette. Enough with this nonsense." She turned to Chris. "Leave now."

I could feel the warmth of Chris' body standing behind me, and I waited for him to leave because I couldn't really believe that his lunar tie was gone, but—

"No." Chris' voice sounded mildly amused, and I knew if I turned my head, I'd see a small smile on his face.

My mother's eyes widened. "On your knees, wolf!" The power and magic in her sharp command had me staggering back, bumping into Chris.

Chris' arm slid around my waist, holding me steady. "No. I will never kneel before you."

Mother frowned as she stared at him. "What are you?"

"I'm a werewolf, and your daughter is my mate. I might not be the strongest werewolf in the world, but I'm the only one who has severed his lunar tie. So, no. I won't be obeying you or anyone in this court. If you want me to kneel, try making me."

"If it's a fight you want, we've got plenty here for you, dog." Mother was threatening my mate?

No. She couldn't do that. She was violating our bargain.

For the first time since I entered the chapel, I really took in the room. Mother had outdone herself. The night sky illusion was beautifully done. The moon was full and the Milky Way bright in the sky. It hung low, so low that it looked like I could reach up and grab one of the stars to take home with me.

White orchids dusted in glitter covered the pews. So many pews. All filled with Lunar Court fey. A few other, too. But the entire Lunar Court was in attendance.

Nice of them to show up to watch my nightmare of a wedding.

I called in my flaming swords. The dress would get in the

way a little, but I'd fought in a bigger gown. I wasn't about to let that slow me. "I've spent years being your lackey, but I'm done. I'm done running and hiding from court, done taking whatever odd spying job, done doing your dirty work. I. Am. Done. Funny that you came to my room a few days ago to discuss our bargain. You reminded me the reason I agreed to it was my freedom, which you've taken back. You also reminded me that in everything you did, you would put my best interest first."

I looked at Van. "I guess you could say that marrying Van was in my best interest, but only if you didn't know me. Only if you didn't know how Van and I feel about each other." I turned back to her. "Only if you wanted to torture me, break me, and use me as your weapon when you finally lost control of your court."

There were a few gasps in the room, some muttering, but no one was coming to her defense. Or mine for that matter. They were waiting to see what happened before they chose sides. It was how the fey worked.

"Our bargain is finished. Broken," I said. "I'm done with you."

The walls throbbed with light and the night sky above flickered as my mother stepped toward me. "You'll do what I say." Her voice was cold and venomous, and I couldn't help but wonder why I'd never heard that particular thread of evil in her before.

Had I ignored it or was she that good of an actress?

"No. Not anymore. We're done."

The room darkened just a bit and the full moon turned a rich blood-red. "Then you'll die."

Van gave me a slow nod. Mother had put herself and her guards between us. Van was going to try and get to me, but it was tricky to come in and out of space and time while a fight was going on. Usually his magic helped him not land on a person, but in the chaos of a fight, in a room as crowded as this one, it was too dangerous. For him and us.

So we'd fight until we could regroup together.

I looked my mother in the eyes. "Try me."

I felt Chris step back, heard the rustle of his clothes just before he shifted, and when the first fey jumped over the pews, we were ready.

I couldn't think for the first five minutes of fighting. I was moving fast. Injuring when I could, killing those that wouldn't give up. I didn't love it, but I would defend myself. Too many had tried to kill me before.

We needed to leave, but everyone was keeping Van away from me. They knew that the second he got close to me, we were gone. With every fey he struck down, two more stepped between us.

But what I wasn't expecting was Wilken fighting beside Van, along with Gurhan and a few of my other guards. I hadn't even realized they'd be here somewhere with the rest of the Lunar fey.

Blood splattered, but it didn't land on me now. I was too much my father's daughter. Bringer of Death.

I started to hear whispers as the fey stopped their attack, and started to retreat.

It was only then that I caught a shadow over my shoulder. Wings—faint and see-through—had sprouted from my back. They were like ghosts of Eli's wings, but pure white. Each feather glowed with radiant light like the full moon.

And then there was light. More. Everywhere. Blinding.

All sounds stopped.

All movement stopped.

Everyone paused to stare at the light.

The light softened, and a man stood in front of me. His wings were the most pure, iridescent white, and he was holding a flaming spear. The flames gave him away, and I was pretty sure I knew who this was. I had his lips. His eyes. His hair color. He'd finally come to help me.

The truth was, I didn't want to fight with my mother. All I wanted was freedom to live my life. If I never had to come back to court, that would be fine with me.

My father gave me a nod, as if my thoughts confirmed something for him, before turning to my mother. "You will let her go. Leave her be. She's done too much for you over the years, and now she's mine. Your claim to her is revoked."

The glowing walls and the night sky started to flicker and sputter as my mother stared at me and my father. "Sam..."

"You may call me Samael, Archangel of Death, but you no longer have claim to call me Sam. You no longer have claim to our daughter. I've watched as you mistreated her, waiting for her to come into her own, and—" He looked back at me. "Now that she has, I have plans for her."

Plans? I'd been screwed by one archon before, I wasn't sure I wanted to go down that road again, even if he was my father. "What—"

My father's wings flapped open and closed once, twice, by the third time his feet were above my head. He was staring out over the crowd. "Those of you who want sanctuary, may call upon my daughter. She's establishing a safe haven for supernaturals with her mate. Anyone who trespasses with violence or ill will on the sanctuary will answer to the archons."

And as he said the last word, Eli popped in, next to him. And then another archon. And another. Their wings varied in shades of white and gray and black, some were female, others male. But they were all glowing bright. When all seven were there, I could feel their power swirling and gathering until it was ringing in my ears.

"With our blessing, so shall it be!"

They said the words as one, and I felt the magic of their promise bouncing around my head.

Loud. So loud. Until I was on my knees, covering my ears with my hands.

And then it was quiet.

There was a flash of light, and they were gone.

When I looked up, everyone was on the ground, some of them starting to stand. All of them with pale faces or mouths open or shaking as they hung on to a loved one. The fear in their faces was there, but some also had hope.

A few glanced my way, and I wondered if I'd see them in Texas.

But one person hadn't kneeled.

My mother.

She stepped toward me. "Get out. Never come back." The threat in her voice and the way she held her hands tightly made me glad that I was leaving now, and I felt a little sorry for everyone who had to stay.

She turned to Van. "It would be wise if I never saw your face again."

Van didn't seem afraid of my mother's anger at all. "You've forgotten what I am, but I haven't forgotten what you tried to do to your daughter. To me. I'm leaving now, but I'll be back."

"Don't threaten—"

Van grabbed my hand, and I reached for Chris, grabbing a handful of the fur at his neck. As soon as my hand closed on it, we were tumbling in the dark, until we slammed into the ground.

It took me a minute to catch up this time. I hadn't eaten in days and my vision was speckled and gray. The warm sun felt nice on my skin, and I was content to lie here for a while. Especially since my hand was still grasping a fistful of wolf-Chris' fur. He was the only thing I needed.

"You okay?" Van asked.

"Just a little weak."

"We'll get you some food."

Chris was still in wolf form, cuddled against me. I wondered if it was harder or easier to travel with Van in this form, but I'd ask him later.

When I finally sat up, I didn't recognize where we were. I thought we were going to Chris' land, but this wasn't his land. The houses here were all new.

"Van? Where are we?" It felt familiar, but... We were in the country and I... I looked over my shoulder.

"If you don't recognize it, maybe Chris will."

Chris shifted, and Van pulled a pair of jeans from thin air, tossing them at my mate.

"I recognize it." Chris tugged on the pants and looked around.

I still couldn't believe that he was here. Alive. Not even the tiniest scar on his chest from where Ziriel had stabbed him.

"This is my land," Chris said. "But where did all these buildings come from?"

"No." I looked around. It couldn't be.

So many houses. Some small. Some larger. One really big house—with so many windows. A barn. A large Olympic-size swimming pool. And more off in the distance. They weren't here ten days ago. It was too quick for all this to be built. "We were just here. How is this possible?"

"Archons are creators. The visionaries. They helped God do His work. This is easy for them." Van shook his head. "It seems to me that your father has finally decided to participate in your life."

It didn't make sense. "No." I closed my eyes. "Eli!"

"Yes, darling."

I whipped around. "Did my father do this?"

He shoved his hands into the pockets of his jeans. His shirt looked freshly pressed and his hair a perfect wavy mess. The cocky bastard had put me through hell, and he was looking right as rain.

It wasn't fair.

"You'll be fine and looking perfect once you eat." He winked at me. "And we all chipped in on this one."

I wasn't sure how to feel about that. I was dealing with *all* the archons now. Not just Eli. Or my father. But all of them? "Why?"

"Relax, cousin. This is all part of the plan."

"Just because you're an archon and my father's an archon, doesn't make you my cousin!"

"So, I should be your uncle?"

He was really starting to annoy me.

"You know that you're really a pleasure to annoy."

I hung my head, hoping for patience to show up. "What plan? Did you know that Chris was going to die?"

"No. It's hard to know all of the plans. Some I oversee. Some are more your father's thing. We split duties. All I knew was that Chris was supposed to be here, doing this. When he died, I thought something..." He took a breath. "Sometimes it's hard to see what God intends, but apparently Chris had to die for Samael to cut the lunar tie, but he brought Chris back. As only the Archangel of Death could do."

There was one thing that I felt bad about. "Did Ziriel know what would happen? That Chris would come back?" Because if he did, then he'd helped me. And in return, I'd attempted to destroy his court. That wasn't right.

"No. Ziriel only knew that cutting the tie meant death. Not that Chris would come back. He was more djinn than not. Don't let what you did while grieving keep you up at night. I can absolve you of that much."

At least that was something. "Is my father..." I took a breath. "Will he come speak to me?"

Eli shook his head. "He likes to stay up there." He pointed to the sky. "He's not the best conversationalist."

Chris pulled me into his side. "He's really not."

"See, you didn't know how lucky you were to deal with me. I'm the best archon." Eli gave me a big grin and I wanted to hit him.

"What did my father mean about him having plans for me?"

Eli turned his head as if he were listening to something. "*Ah*. Can't talk now. I've got to run, but expect some company over the course of the next few weeks. I decided to give you some time to honeymoon. We've already got Wilken and Gurhan with us. A few others from your court. More are coming in the next couple of days, so get that bond cemented already, you two crazy lovebirds."

And with that, he was gone.

I looked up at Chris. "What just happened?"

"I don't know, but we've got to get you out of that dress." I wasn't sure if Chris meant because it was ugly or if he was thinking sexy thoughts.

He raised an eyebrow at me. *Sexy thoughts.*

"Yes, it's truly terrible, Coco," Van put in.

"Don't call me that," I said. "You know I hate it." But I didn't face him. All I could see was Chris. "Hi."

"Hi. With all these waves of ruffles and sparkles, you look like a starlit ocean."

An hour ago I'd wanted either death or revenge, and now I had everything I ever wanted. It seemed way too good to be true, and I knew it'd be a while before I'd stop worrying about something coming to ruin it.

But for now, I glanced down at myself and laughed. "I guess I do kind of look like a starlit ocean."

He lifted me up, and I tried to wrap my legs around his waist, but the dress was too big.

"Want to check if there's a bed in that massive house?" I asked, before pressing my lips to his.

"We don't need a bed or a house to do what I want to do to you," he said, his lips brushing against mine with his words.

He started to set me down, but I shook my head. "It's too cold for that, Mr. Werewolf who never gets cold."

Van cleared his throat. "I'm leaving before this gets any more awkward, but when I come back, I'll have company with me."

I glanced over my shoulder at him. "Fine. But don't come back for ten days."

"Three."

"Nine."

"Seven! Final offer."

"Fine. Take your week." Van grinned and then he was gone.

And we were alone and safe and free.

Chris lowered me to the ground and we stumble-walked-kissed to the big house. It was warm inside, and we didn't make it much past the doorway.

"Care if I rip it?"

I shook my head. "It's hideous. Do it."

The sound of the silk ripping filled the air, and then his hands were on my skin and my hands were on him. His lips touched mine and there was nothing but us. But our love. But the feel of him inside me.

And when he bit me, I didn't care. And when he offered me his blood and said the words, magic filled every part of my body. Every cell to the point where my teeth were tingling and I felt like I was floating—and then I felt it.

The bond.

It was there and made of light and good and laughter, and it was stronger than any red line of fate I'd ever seen.

And when the world snapped back into view, all I could see were Chris' eyes as his forehead rested on mine.

Hello there, princess. His voice rumbled through the bond and delicious chills ran through my body.

"Whoa," I said, but then my stomach grumbled.

"Do you think your dad stocked the fridge?"

How should I know? "Do you think there's even a fridge? Or clothes? Because I don't think this dress is going to work anymore."

"Only one way to check about the fridge. But I don't think we'll be needing any clothes for a while. Do you?"

The look he gave me made me warm all over. "No, I guess I don't."

My cheeks hurt with how hard I was grinning at Chris, and I felt a little bit like a goof, but I didn't care.

For the first time in my life I was free and happy and I wondered if everything that ever happened had led me here. To this place. With Chris. And if so, then all the regrets that I had weren't really regrets. All the terrible things I'd done—that were done to me and by me for my mother—none of it mattered anymore. I didn't regret a second, even the hardest parts, because now I was here.

"You've got a lot running through that head of yours."

"Can you read my mind?"

"No. Just the emotions." He brushed a soft kiss against my lips. *But I love that you're happy. That I could do this for you.*

I'm more than happy. I'm blissful, and whatever comes next —whoever shows up—I know we can handle it.

Of course we can. Together.

Together.

CHAPTER TWENTY-THREE

CHRIS

SAMAEL and the rest of the archons had fully stocked the main house. Clothes. Food. More furniture and guest rooms than I thought we could ever use.

We had everything we could ever want. The rest of the houses—some with one bedroom, some with three—had only essentials. A mattress. A couch and a table with a couple chairs. That was about it. We figured we'd stock them as we had people, and that it would be months before we got around to that.

It took two weeks before Van showed up again. He gave us a warning though. So we were dressed. But Van hadn't come alone. He had Wilken, Gurhan, and a few other fey—including one of Cosette's cousins.

The next day some Weres showed up.

The day after that, it was Beth—one of the only witches left from the Texas coven—showed up with Elowen.

And then three days later, River—a guy witch in our supernatural alliance who was super into crystals—came with a couple of friends.

After a couple of weeks of nonstop traffic onto the land, I realized that the archons had only gotten us started. We were going to need a lot more houses. Thankfully, my grandfather had been greedy and we had plenty of land and money to grow.

We'd been here a couple of months now. Cosette was setting up a boutique in town. Her cousin was working on getting a crystal shop next door to it. She'd had experience running a similar shop in a mall in Colorado, so she was helping Cosette a lot. Which was pretty great. And Beth was working on getting a cafe started. We'd hired every contractor in the area, but it was going to take time to get everything built.

Still, it was coming together. Piece by piece.

It was crazy how life could change so quickly sometimes. The archons sped it along, but this—this was good. Really good.

And for the first time in my life, I found myself with a pack that I really loved and believed in. Sure, I was okay at St. Ailbe's, but I'd still been working on myself. It was safe to say that I was healed, and with that, we'd breathed new life into the land and the town.

The sun was just peeking over the horizon, and I was sitting in a wooden rocking chair on the massive wraparound porch. I was drawing another sketch of Samael and Cosette. I made the charcoal version of Samael have a grin on his face, and the paper caught fire.

"Really? Again?" I muttered to myself, knowing he'd hear me and didn't care. "She wants one of you smiling with her, damn it. If you won't come down here and talk to her, I think it should be an easy give."

But at least he hadn't burned the whole pad. Just the single sheet of paper.

I started again. This time a picture of just Cosette. The sketch pad in my lap was almost filled—mostly of her.

My mate.

And as if just thinking about her made her appear, there she was, pulling the pad from my hands and setting it on the table beside me before sitting on my lap.

"You're up early," I said.

Her blonde hair was a mess of curl tangles, and I couldn't help but work my fingers through it. She nearly purred when I petted her, squeezing her eyes shut.

"I woke up and you weren't there." Her voice was still thick with sleepiness. "Everything okay?"

"Yeah. I went for a run, and was just enjoying the sun rising."

She leaned forward until she was nearly burrowing into my neck. "It's so weird that you like to wake up early."

I held her close. "I like the quiet before everyone is up."

"Does it bother you that we're not alone here anymore?"

"No." I rubbed my hand down her back. "This is good. Don't you think?"

She nodded. "Really good. I don't think I've ever been this happy."

"Me either."

She stiffened a little and I felt her worry through the bond as if it were my own.

I rubbed my hand up and down her back. "What's wrong?"

"I just...I keep having this nightmare that everything's going to go wrong. Like this is a dream and it'll shatter and—"

"Stop." I pulled her shoulders back, making her sit up so I could see her face. She wouldn't look at me. Her gaze was darting here and there and everywhere but me, so I put my hand against her cheek until her brown eyes met mine.

"I know your father's plans are bothering you, but we don't know what they are yet. And I can't tell you what's going to happen tomorrow or next week or next year, but you know how I know everything's going to be okay?"

"How?" She chewed on her lip.

"Because we have each other. We can get through it. No one is throwing me in a pit again. No one is going to try to assassinate you anymore. Whatever happens next, we'll get through it together."

She smiled. "I think we scared my mother."

"I know we did, and I swear she was going to piss herself when your dad showed up."

That got a chuckle from her and breathed a bit more energy into her eyes.

"The courts are in trouble, and I feel like it's my fault."

"It wasn't your fault. None of this was. As an outsider looking in, your courts look really fucked up, and if *all* of the archons showed up to let them know how horrible they were being, then I think that says a lot."

"Probably." She was quiet for a second. "Do you think Van's going to be okay?"

Things were a little tense between Cosette and Van for a minute. Once we were back together, Cosette's anger at everything that had happened died down. She didn't really need revenge anymore, because I was alive. We just wanted some peace and quiet to be together, but we both knew her mother was going to be a problem.

I didn't think Van was ever going to get over how broken Cosette was—that she'd tried to fade. Seeing her like that changed him. He was on a mission against the Lunar Court and its queen.

"I think Van needs a distraction from his revenge plots. We just need something interesting enough to take his focus off your mother." I watched her and waited for the next question to come. She didn't like using the bond to talk silently when we were alone, but I could feel that she was leaving something unsaid.

"Do you think I'll ever see him again? That he'll come visit or something?"

She didn't have to say who she was talking about. I'd gone over and over my time with her dad. She'd had a lot of questions, but I think the most important thing to her was that he cared about her.

"I don't know if we'll see him again, but I do know that he's watching and that he loves you in his own way."

She rested her head against my shoulder again. "That's good. Right? Even if he has plans, if it involves us, then it'll be okay. Right?"

"Right." I stood, holding her to my chest as I walked inside. "Let's chase the rest of that nightmare away."

She pulled away just enough to look at me. "What did you have in mind, Mr. Matthews?"

I gave her a little eyebrow waggle and she laughed again. "Back to bed with us."

"Good." She kissed my neck and then bit my ear.

"Watch it, Mrs. Matthews."

She hummed. "I like that name so much better than my old one."

We'd gotten the legal paperwork done without the wedding. Cosette said the last one was enough to scare her off of them for a while. That was fine with me.

"Good. I'm glad."

I wasn't sure what was going to happen or what Samael's plans were, but for now, things were quiet and calm and happy and I planned to enjoy every second, minute, hour, day, week that we had like this.

And whatever came next, we had a whole pack to stand with us.

The series continues with ***Alpha Erased***, Book Nine in the
Alpha Girl Series!

Releasing May 19, 2020!
Available for preorder now!

Tessa—part witch, part werewolf, raised human and now
the unofficial leader of a newly minted supernatural alliance—
thinks nothing of her brother, Axel, texting her and Dastien to
meet him. The location pin was in a weird spot, but maybe he'd
found a magical anomaly there. But when Tessa steps into the
darkened warehouse, she doesn't expect to see her brother
laying in a pool of his own blood, smell the sulfuric scent of
black magic, or feel the pain of her mate being shot full of silver.

**Tessa has seconds to make a choice, but there's
only one thing she can do to save the two most
important men in her life—sacrifice herself.**

**The last thing Dastien hears from Tessa was her
plea—*help Axel.*** But then their bond goes silent. He can't
hear her. He can't feel her. And there's no sign of the attackers
who took her.

Dastien does everything he can to save Axel before calling his
friends in a panic. It takes all of them to find Tessa, but when
Dastien's finally reunited with her, there's no sign of recognition
in her eyes.

No magic in her touch.

No wolf beneath the surface.

Everything that made Tessa who she was...has been erased.

Now Available from *USA TODAY* Bestselling Author,
Aileen Erin
Off Planet, Book One of the Aunare Chronicles.

Maité Martinez has always yearned for more than waitressing in a greasy diner, especially when most people have left the polluted ruins of Earth behind for a better life on other planets. It's not just working at the diner that's making life hard for her. Being a half-human, half-alien girl has never been trickier. With the corporate government hunting down the last of her father's alien Aunare race living on Earth, hiding her growing special abilities has become a full-time job on its own.

Every minute Maité stays on Earth is one minute closer to getting caught. The stress is almost more than she can bear, and when a fancy Space Tech officer gets handsy with her at the diner, she reacts without thinking.

Breaking the officer's nose wasn't her smartest move. Now she's faced with three years forced labor on the volcano planet, Abbadon. With the job she's slotted for, it may as well have been a death sentence.

It doesn't take Maité long before she realizes there's more to the mining on Abbadon than Space Tech has let on. As she makes unlikely allies, Maité uncovers Space Tech's plot to nuke the Aunare homeworld. The firepower stored in Abbadon's warehouses is more than enough to do the job ten times over.

As the clock ticks, Maité knows that if she can't find a way to stop Space Tech, there will be an interstellar war big enough to end all life in the universe. There's only one question: **Can she prevent the total annihilation of humanity without getting herself killed in the process?**

TO MY READERS

Thank you so much to all of you who reached out to me asking for a Chris and Cosette book. I absolutely LOVED telling their story and finally giving them their well-earned happily-ever-after. I really hope you enjoyed it as much as I did while writing it.

Up next for the Alpha Girls series is a Dastien and Tessa dual POV novel, *Alpha Erased*. I'm so excited to finally get Dastien's voice on the page!

After that, I'm thinking Van? More Claudia?? But I can always be convinced if there's someone you want to hear about. Just shoot me an email at aerin@inkmonster.net or on Facebook.

Until next time, I'll be posting updates on my books on Instagram (@aileenerin), Facebook (@aelatcham), as well as my blog!

I absolutely love hearing from you. So, please reach out on social media or email me: aerin@inkmonster.net

TO MY READERS

xoxo
    Aileen

ACKNOWLEDGMENTS

This book was so fun to write, y'all. Like *so fun!* It was work, but the best kind of work.

Thank you to Kime Heller-Neal who counseled me through the first draft, telling me to keep going via phone and text numerous times, and then edited the book in the most organized fashion ever. Sorry for the rush to finish this one! You're the bestest!

Thank you to Kelly, Ana, and the entire team at INscribe for all the advice, help, and answering of million tickets. I'm so thankful for everything you do for me and Ink Monster.

Thank you to Margie Lawson. Your knowledge, encouragement, and critiques are taking my writing to the next level, and I'm so grateful for everything you've taught me. I can't wait until January to do it all again!

Thank you to Lola Dodge. You're giving me my sanity back! You're the best Lola around!

Thank you to Sharon Garner for catching my typos, misused words and commas, and all the other million things that would've made for a bumpy read. I so appreciate your keen eye.

Thank you to Jeremy for always being my strongest cheerleader. I literally never would've written a word without your constant prodding, and I'm so incredibly grateful for the love and support. You're my everything.

Thank you to Isabella. I hope one day you know what mommy is doing on her laptop all the time, but you're my inspiration. I love you tons.

Thank you to Nicky for coming in early while I finished this book! I appreciate the gift you give me of being able to work without worrying about the nugget.

Thank you to my family. All of you—from those of you who come help with Isabella while I work or take a class, to the ones who are cheering me on from afar. I appreciate you and am thankful for all the love and support, even if I'm the nerdy weirdo of the bunch! ;)

Aileen Erin is half-Irish, half-Mexican, and 100% nerd—from Star Wars (prequels don't count) to Star Trek (TNG FTW), she geeks out on Tolkien's linguistics, and has a severe fascination with the supernatural. Aileen has a BS in Radio-TV-Film from the University of Texas at Austin, and an MFA in Writing Popular Fiction from Seton Hill University. She lives with her husband and daughter in Los Angeles, and spends her days doing her favorite things: reading books, creating worlds, and kicking ass.

For more information and updates about Aileen and her books, go to: http://inkmonster.net/aerin

Or check her out on:

facebook.com/aelatcham

twitter.com/aileen_erin

instagram.com/aileenerin